D0044974

HESTER

ALSO BY LAURIE LICO ALBANESE

Blue Suburbia

The Miracles of Prato (written with Laura Morowitz)

Lynelle by the Sea

Stolen Beauty

HESTER

A

NOVEL

Laurie Lico Albanese

ST. MARTIN'S PRESS
NEW YORK

This is a work of fiction. All of the characters, organizations, and events portrayed in this novel are either products of the author's imagination or are used fictitiously.

First published in the United States by St. Martin's Press, an imprint of St. Martin's Publishing Group

HESTER. Copyright © 2022 by Laurie Lico Albanese. All rights reserved. Printed in the United States of America. For information, address St. Martin's Publishing Group, 120 Broadway, New York, NY 10271.

Designed by Kelly S. Too

ISBN 9781250278555

For Kirk, Melissa, John, Claudia—
I see the past and the future in your beautiful faces

She had not known the weight until she felt the freedom!

—Nathaniel Hawthorne, *The Scarlet Letter*

A NOTE TO THE READER

Synesthesia is a unique sensory phenomenon that affects less than ten percent of the world's population. A person with synesthesia—or "joined perception"—often experiences multiple sensory responses when only one sense has been stimulated. Many creative people experience this comingling of senses: the painter Kandinsky saw colors when he listened to music, and the musician Billie Eilish reports a wide array of synesthetic experiences that include color, sound, texture, and temperature.

Two types of synesthesia are experienced in Hester. These are grapheme-color synesthesia, in which letters are associated with colors, and chromesthesia, in which sound evokes experiences of color, shape, and texture. Synesthesia was not widely known or researched until the early nineteenth century. Therefore, to the characters in this story, episodes of synesthesia are mystifying and inexplicable.

HESTER

— ONE —

Salem was meant to be a new beginning, a place where the sharp scent of cinnamon and tea perfumed the air with hope; a place where the colors could be safe and alive in me. I was nineteen years old and Nathaniel Hathorne was twenty-four when we met on those bricked streets. His fingers were ink-stained; he was shy but handsome. The year was 1829, and we were each in our own way struggling to be free—he with his notebooks, I with my needle.

Some people will tell you that Nat spent the better part of a decade after Bowdoin College alone in his room learning how to write. But that is a fabrication meant for the ages.

The true story of how he found his scarlet letter—and then made it larger than life—begins when I was a child in Scotland and he was a fatherless boy writing poetry that yearned and mourned.

Sometimes I still picture him in my mind, a lonely nine-year-old boy with a bad limp and a mop of dark hair standing at the edge of the Massachusetts Bay waiting for a ship. He knows that his father has died of yellow fever somewhere in the Pacific Ocean, yet the boy is waiting with pencil at the ready. Something in him knows—I believe this, even after all this time—that although his father will never return, a story just as powerful is coming toward him. It is me, bent into the wind, fleeing home with my colors and my needle and my own set of needs and dreams.

It is me with my red letter secreted away.

LIKE ALL THE women in my family, I was born in a stone cottage in the town of Abington beside the River Clyde. I had red hair and green-blue eyes and was named Isobel for my grandmother, just as my mother was named Margaret for *her* grandmother. "For hundreds of years we've been Isobel, Margaret, Isobel, Margaret—a chain of women going back and back through time," Mam said, and I liked the way it sounded: all of us red-haired girls stitched together like paper dolls.

I lived in a world of magic and color then—my mother's voice a sapphire stream flecked with emeralds, my father's a soft caramel. In summer I ran barefoot through the valleys with my cousins and kin and saw their voices rise up in vibrant wisps of yellow and gold. The wind was sometimes fierce pink, and the sound of the waterfall on rocks glistened silver.

I didn't know my colors were unusual and so I never thought to speak of them, just as I never remarked on the air, or the feel of a blanket at night, or the bark of my father's laugh that I loved so well.

Every year at the summer solstice we burned a bonfire and danced around the maypole, and in winter we hung mistletoe in the cottage. Pap spoke of faeries who lived beneath the May trees, of selkie seals that swam ashore and enchanted the lovelorn, and of brave clansmen who'd died fighting the English.

"A horse with a shining wet mane is a kelpie come to take you away." Pap's voice spooled like caramel as he shook a warning finger at me. "And if you swim in the river and leave your clothes out for the *bean-nighe* she'll steal your soul and that will be the end of you."

"Don't frighten her," Mam scolded, and Pap put up a finger as if to warn me this was our secret.

But when we walked together looking for mushrooms in the spring, he spoke of sprites in white dresses who sat beside the river to wash the clothes of the dead, and of an unlucky lad who'd stumbled upon one and drowned the following day.

Mam grew tight-lipped when Pap spoke of magical creatures and mysteries beyond God, but I knew by the gentle way my mother trimmed his beard, and by the way Pap held her at the waist when they danced round the bonfire, that theirs was a love bond and that it would protect me. Their stories protected me, too.

I WAS MY mother's first child. Five years later my brother, Jamie, came. While she was caring for him, Mam said it was time for my first sampler. She showed me how to make my letters first on a slate with chalk, then with needle and thread.

"One day you'll learn to read." Mam squinted at a line of letters she'd made and the rougher ones I'd traced out beneath them. "I didn't get far, but you, Isobel, will read books."

I'd heard it whispered that one of Mam's aunts had been locked away in a madhouse and never seen again. She'd left behind a rainbow sampler that hung behind my mother's sewing chair. I'd studied it for hints of madness but found none; I looked at it that day and vowed I would make one even more beautiful in my time.

I experimented with a thimble made of seal bone, then settled on a plain tin thimble that fit my small finger. Tongue between my teeth, I worked carefully. When I fumbled and pushed the needle beneath my fingernail, I never cried out. Young though I was, I was full of obedient determination.

I was preparing a green thread for the letter *D* when Mam came up behind me.

"What have you done?" Her angry voice washed over me like soft blueberries and blackberries.

"Is it wrong?" I studied my work. It was neat and straight.

"I gave you black thread to make the letters in black."

"But *A* is red," I said quietly. Like the colors in the wind and the hue of my mother's voice, this had come to me without intention or fanfare. "*B* is blue. *C* is yellow."

"No, they are not." My mother slapped my knuckles with her tambour hook. The blow was hard, and tears stung my eyes. She'd never struck me before.

"Never say that." Her words flashed in blue-black bolts, and I saw the whites of her eyes. She wasn't only angry, she was afraid. "They'll call you crazy or say you're a witch. They'll say the Devil's taken hold of you and they'll want to burn it out of you—do you hear?"

I'd heard whispered stories of witches hanged and burned in the fields, of men and women who did not defend against the Devil and then found themselves full of evil and spite. Witches were spoken of in the past, but evil, insanity, and death were as plausible to me as Pap's selkie seals and deadly kelpie seahorses come to take away the living.

"Isobel—do you understand?"

I nodded wordlessly, but my mother shook me by the shoulders so hard my teeth rattled. She meant for me to be afraid.

"You must defend against it, Isobel; you must pray and be strong—promise me."

"Yes, Mam. I promise."

Mam and I prayed together that night, but she didn't speak of the colors again, nor did I. After that if my mother gave me black thread, I used black. If she asked for red, I used red. One day the sampler that hung behind her sewing chair was gone, replaced by a simple herbal chart my grandmother had stitched long ago. I dared not ask after the great-aunt's work, for I had seen and felt my mother's ire and did not want to see it again.

I told myself there were no colors in voices or letters and I refused my reading lessons, for the letters were not white on black slate but a rainbow of colors that I knew were wrong. Mam seemed to understand and did not push me further.

But even as I kept silent, the colors became more vivid and my dreams wilder. Whether the colors were good or ill, witchcraft or the Devil, I had no power to stop them. I tried praying and wishing them away, and once I left an offering of sugar for the faeries beneath the May trees, but nothing banished them.

Mam and I continued to work our needles together, and the following year when we finished a flowered smock for me to wear on Sundays, she took the red thread and made the letter *A* in the hem, small and neat.

"For Abington, the town where you were born." Her face was smooth and serious as she folded the letter out of sight and began to stitch the hem over it. "And because our women have always hidden away their red letters."

Until that moment it hadn't occurred to me that the colors might run through our family the way our red hair and names cycled through time. If they did, what did it mean? Did my mother have the colors? Were there others like me?

I waited for her to say more, but she did not.

"It is gone now, Mam," I ventured. "Letters have no colors. Words are just words."

She put a hand to my chin and tipped my face to hers.

"You're strong and wise, my sweet Isobel," she said, and I understood that I would have to keep my secret alone, that we would never speak of it again.

MAM'S COUSIN WAS a dressmaker who kept a small shop in the town of Baggar. I was seven years old the year we traveled two hours by wagon cart to visit her.

"To clothe a woman is to hide her failings and frailties," Auntie Aileen told me. "A dressmaker is talented with the needle, but above all she is a secret keeper."

I understood this well, for I was a secret keeper, too.

I showed Aileen a doll's dress I'd sewn of green poplin with colorful flowers strewn across the skirt. Aileen turned the dress inside out to study the seams and the knots I'd made in the backs of the flowers. I held my breath to see if she would remark upon the tiny red *A* folded away, but either she did not know it was there, or she kept silent.

"The work is Isobel's," Mam said. She was proud. "Not one stitch is mine."

"She's well suited for the needle," Aileen said. "When your girl is ready, I'll take her as an apprentice."

I visited Auntie Aileen again when the merchants' wives came to order new winter dresses and sat on a three-legged stool holding her pins and chalks.

"The best dresses offer secrets but no surprises," Aileen said when we were alone. "Little pockets and camouflage for flaws with no hint of what's hidden beneath the flare of a bell sleeve, the bones of a corset, or the inset of a shorting."

She told me she'd disguised a lady's twisted arm beneath a thick bishop sleeve, sewn a hidden pocket into a shirtwaist, and much more. Before long I was able to see the ways that a woman hid herself with a cloak, a cap, or a shoe with a lift to hide a crooked knee. I drew these things in my book, sketches for preserving a lady's dignity.

"You work quietly," my aunt said. "I like that."

Her words didn't generally have hue or shape to them, but I saw these in the thick yellow of an egg yolk.

"Sometimes there's more power in silence than in speech," she added. "Our ancestress knew it and it served her well."

"Ancestress?"

Auntie Aileen tipped her head when she looked at me.

"Isobel Gowdie, Queen of Witches—she's your namesake." Her words were still yellow, which I came to know as the color of truth. "She knew when evil was right there in front of her in the shape of man, and she knew when to be silent and when to raise hell to the heavens."

At this, Aileen climbed onto a stool, raised a broom toward the heavens, and shouted, "'Yea, I am what you say I am—I have lain with the Devil's forked prick inside me, and if you kill me hell will reign on earth.'

"That's what she did when the men came for her," Auntie Aileen explained, catching my shocked expression.

I felt a bolt of fear and excitement.

"And did it?" I asked. "Did hell reign on earth?"

Aileen blinked down at me, climbed off the stool, and straightened her skirts.

"You'll have to ask your mum about it."

WHEN I ASKED my mother, she was angry.

"Aileen is a fool—forget that nonsense and never mention it again."

I fell to my knees as if to pray or beg for an answer, but Mam spun upon me.

"Right here in Lanarkshire County they killed hundreds of witches and more in the Highlands. King James wrote the law and the king could do it again." I saw that fear in the whites of Mam's eyes. "Today, this very hour, law or not, they'd put a woman to death if they thought she had the Devil in her. And if you're not careful, such talk will bring Satan to you."

"Am I bedeviled?" I whispered.

My mother took my wrist and held it hard.

"You must always beware. You must call on God and keep that strange talk out of your mind. Even strong women can fall, Isobel—you must beware of magic and all the things we don't understand."

I worried over my mother's words for months. I didn't want to fall into the Devil's snare. I didn't want to be put in an asylum or hanged from the gallows. I wanted to be a dressmaker, to live in a city and have a shop and embroider dresses with flowers and birds.

I loved the needle and thread, and I feared losing them above all because they let me put my visions into cloth in a way that no one questioned, in a way that brought me praise. They let me keep my secrets in plain sight, where I prayed they would hurt no one, least of all myself.

Scotland, 1662

A strong hand reaches through the dark and drags Isobel Gowdie into the hard autumn light. She staggers into Loch Loy square and blinks at the small crowd of jeering farmers, brewers, and cottars' wives. It's nearly noon—Isobel can tell by the position of the sun as it approaches the familiar kirk steeple. She has not had anything to eat or drink since the tollbooth door slammed shut two days ago, and the air shimmers in waves as the marshal raises a parchment and coughs to loosen his voice.

"Isobel Gowdie, wife of John Gilbert, ye are accused of witchcraft, of using charms, spirit familiars, and maleficence to inflict pain and illness upon the Reverend Harry Forbes and his sons, and of causing the death of five cows and one calf." He levels his narrow gaze at her. "What say ye to these charges?"

Two years ago, Isobel gave Forbes's wife a brew to take away an unwanted child. Last year, the reverend came upon her in the fields at twilight and pressed her into the haystacks, fished his hands up her skirts, and threw her to the ground when she bit him.

Isobel lifts a shaking finger and points it at Forbes. She is frightened and angry now, her mind abuzz with flame and thirst.

"He is not a sacred man," Isobel brays. "He is foul."

"Bring the witch-pricker," the marshal bellows.

The crowd ripples and John Dickson strides toward her wearing a brown cloak stuck with long needles.

"Strip her," Dickson orders. A three-inch needle glitters in his gloved hand.

Isobel's knees are weak, but she does not fall.

She crosses her arms to protect her womb as rough arms seize her from behind to tear away her dress and petticoat. She is six-and-twenty and has never borne a child, but the seed of one has been planted and she means to keep it safe. They bind her hands and shove her up against the stockade, but she will not be harnessed like a cow—she shrieks and swings her head and that is where the first cut is made—her long red braid shorn off with a scythe, then her pubis grazed with a razor that raises blood across her belly and sharp hip bones.

"If she is a witch, she will not feel the blade prick her." Dickson's voice is low, as if coming from the pit where the Devil lies in wait.

Dickson stabs at Isobel Gowdie and she screams.

"She saw you," someone shouts from the crowd. "You have to put it in her arse where she can't see you."

Again and again Dickson jabs at her until she sees it in slow motion, like the day her mother caught a fish with her hand, silver in the blue water, mouth gulping for air, dying without the river.

Isobel's body is streaming with blood when she falls to the ground.

Dickson stands over her and reaches for her ankle, pretends to pull out a needle.

"The barb sank and she did not know it," he proclaims.

It is a lie, but Isobel's voice is drowned out by the shouting crowd, women who once sat beside her in the kirk joining their voices now with Dickson's and the reverend's.

Even Forbes's wife is screaming, the bright words leaving her black maw of a mouth: "A witch, she's a witch!"

"You will stand trial." It is the Laird of Park and Loch Loy, his velvet boots unsoiled even in the mud. "You will stand trial for witchcraft."

The words he speaks bloom like dark roses. Isobel has seen this before—the colors, the words scraping across the air like blood on snow. She closes her eyes. She has not done what they accused her of, but she is surely cursed, for she sees the man's words in the color of evil as if it is Satan himself speaking over her in the square.

— TWO —

The blizzard came when I was eight years old. All day it blew snow sideways across the fields and turned the sky gray. My brother was asleep in a mound of pillows that afternoon when Mam nestled me into the fold of her arms.

"It's time you learned about your namesake," she whispered.

I had a gap in my smile where the last of my milk teeth had fallen out, and I pressed my tongue into that space. Mam was ready to speak of Isobel Gowdie; I didn't ask why, although I understood later that she must have known what was coming.

"A long time ago, in the Highlands near Loc Katrina, your ancestress Isobel Gowdie had the colors like you," Mam said. "People were comfortable with the faerie world then and spoke to God in one breath and the faeries in the next. They believed man lives in the realm between the two."

Mam told me that Isobel Gowdie spoke freely of her colors to the people she loved. As long as the village was prosperous and her salves helped heal the sick and birth babes, the lord of her village was satisfied.

"She didn't think her colors were evil, and she didn't fear the Devil's snare. But when the crops failed one year, and the village cows died, they blamed her," Mam said. "They came to her cottage with torches and pitchforks and called her a witch."

I felt I had heard this story before; there was Isobel Gowdie running for the safety of her cottage, her hair the same coppery red as mine, her gray shift decorated with fanciful flowers that seemed to fall off the cloth and leave a trail behind her.

"Women had been hanged as witches all across Scotland that year and the people feared the Devil was taking hold of her, too." Mam was stitching a row of irises on a tea towel, but she put it aside. "They crowded round her cottage and put fire through the windows and called for her to hang. There was nowhere for her to go but through the chimney and onto her rooftop, where she stood on the burning thatch and screamed—"

Here Mam raised her chin and repeated the same words Aileen had called out: "'Yea, I am what you say I am—I have lain with the Devil's forked prick inside me, and if you kill me hell will reign on earth.'"

I felt terribly afraid, for I thought she would tell me the Queen of Witches had given her soul to the Devil.

"And what happened?" I asked.

"It's said that Isobel Gowdie escaped—that's all I know—and slipped away on a moonless night."

In my mind I saw Isobel's red hair hidden beneath a kerchief as she ran across the countryside from hilltop to valley and on and on through the night. I wanted to ask if she escaped by witchcraft or magic or some special charm, but mostly I needed to know . . .

"Do you see the colors, Mam?"

My mother picked up her work and pulled a blue thread through the cloth before she spoke.

"No."

"Did your mam?" I asked.

She smoothed my hair away from my face and pressed her cheek to mine. Her answer was barely audible.

"She learned to hide what she saw. Just like you, Isobel. But her sister was sent to the madhouse. I don't mean to scare you, child, but you must understand."

"Can you help me?" I was near to tears. "Why do I have them? What do they mean?"

Mam took my chin in her hands and blinked back her own tears, which surprised and frightened me.

"My mother was a good Christian woman. She prayed every morning and every night and she taught me to keep God close so that the Devil couldn't find his way into my soul. You must do the same."

"I've tried, Mam—can't you make them go away?"

She tucked a strand of hair behind my ear.

"I don't have the colors, Isobel, and so I can't help you understand them. You must be careful, for they can lead you to heaven or to hell and I cannot tell you which way is right or wrong. Remember what I'm telling you," she said. "Someday you may need great strength, just as Isobel Gowdie did. One day your time will come."

I was too young to understand all that my mother was trying to say, but she was intent and I was attentive to her.

"When will it be my time? How will I know?"

"I don't know, but when it comes you must be ready."

Mam began to cough and I saw that I had taxed her as my little brother taxed her and the storm was taxing her, and so I made myself quiet and put my head against her bosom and listened to the blue beating of her heart as we fell asleep.

SNOW KEPT COMING that night and through the next. It drifted against the cottage high enough to cover the windows and shutters. We had dry wood for fire and enough hard bread and pickled cabbage to sustain us. It was warm inside with my father and mother. Jamie stood at the window and watched the snow falling until the window was covered, and then he stamped a dance beside the fire that went on all day. By evening my mother had taught my brother to pound flour and snow into dough and mold it into small loaves of bread, and so his love of baking was born.

In the weeks that followed we were busy digging out from the storm, feeding the sheep, emptying the barrels of rainwater, and gathering up the scattered chickens. Mam told us to pay her cough no mind, but by spring there were splatters of scarlet on her bedsheets and sleeping gown.

Pap piled us into a wagon and his brother drove us up to Glasgow. For three weeks we waited in a small room while the doctor treated Mam with camphor and bloodletting. She was pale as the bedsheet— pale as a *bean-nighe*—when she called me to her.

"Pap told you stories of the faerie world." Her voice was a whisper. I nodded fiercely and blinked back tears. "Some people can see it better than others, but remember, it's best to keep those things to yourself. Keep your secret close, Isobel."

Then she was gone, and my colors were gone with her. Letters were simply black, just as she'd taught me. Words were sounds and nothing more. My colors had been my inspiration, and then my curse, and after they left me there was no cure for my sadness.

PAP SENT JAMIE to live with Uncle James and his wife in Abington, but he and I stayed on in Glasgow. He found work in a distant cousin's print shop and let a small room just inside the city walls. There were two pallet beds, a coal stove and a table, and a small window that looked onto the narrow alley.

"White on white," Pap told me as he led me down the street early one morning. I was wearing a plain black work dress covered with a red-and-white ticking smock. It was my first store-bought smock, tied with a bow that rubbed into my back as we walked. "'Tis what your mam said you should do, and so you will do it."

"Why?" My words had become fewer since my mother died.

"'Tis good work, a valuable skill," Pap said. "Scotland makes the finest muslin in the world and our embroidered work is wanted everywhere."

I remembered the day my mother had stitched the small red *A* and folded it away, and the day she told me about Isobel, Queen of the Witches.

But Mam had conscripted me to the tambour shop, a place without color, and I knew it was her way of trying to keep me safe now that she was gone.

Never tell anyone, Mam had said. I had never spoken of the colors, even to Pap. I wondered if he knew but could not fathom how to ask.

He and I entered a stone church through a side door and descended a half staircase into a basement sewing shop. The walls were white, the floors were freshly mopped, and the warming fire on the far side of the room was covered by a tall black grate. There were four tables stretched with white linen; fifteen girls kept their heads down when we entered. Not a single hook or needle faltered.

A tall man led us to a washbasin and told me to scrub my hands.

"The nails, too," the shop master said. His hands were long fingered and pale, as if he soaked them in whiting. His left arm was twisted and folded inside a sleeve.

"Small fingers and no dirt beneath the nails. We'll see if your daughter can stitch as you've said, Mr. Gamble," the shop master said.

I was given a sharp tambour hook and asked to make a running stitch. Mam had taught me how to use the long needle with a hook that pulled thread through and across the fabric. I was quick with the work and my line was true and straight.

"Now a satin stitch," the shop master said. I worked without lifting my hook from the cloth, as my mother had taught me. "And then a string of ivy."

I completed each task without looking up.

"She'll do quite well," the shopkeeper said. "Bring her tomorrow morning and have her bring a white potato or bread for her lunch."

So began my years in Master Dwyer's Tambour Shop, where we decorated, cut, and sewed muslin aprons, caps, collars, petticoats, bridal trousseaux, and infants' robes and gowns. At night Pap told me about his work in the print shop, where he learned how to read and to spell. He bent over the newspaper and sounded out the words and taught me to do the same.

"Your mam wanted you to read," he said, and he made it so.

Without the colors, it was easy. The letters did not worry me anymore, for they were black as they were meant to be. This was the one good thing that came of losing the colors—I could read, and the words dropped away as they were meant to, leaving pictures, people, places, and tales in their stead.

Every girl in the tambour shop was small and clean, each quick with the needle. The shop was a quiet place, for the shop master insisted on it. But the girls whispered to one another while we worked, and I hoped we would be friends.

One day I read a notice before Master Dwyer got to it, and eagerly shared the news.

"An order has come from America," I whispered. The girls looked at me with shifty eyes.

"What did you give him that he'd tell you that?" It was the roughest girl who spoke, and it would take a good number of years before I would understand what she'd meant.

"Told what?" Master Dwyer picked up the note and glared at me. "You can read, eh?"

"Yes, sir."

"See that you don't do it again," he snapped, and the girls tittered. "Reading brings the Devil into a girl's mind too easily."

Master Dwyer's arm had been crushed in the fabric mill and he was generally dour. But that day he called us to join him with cider and biscuits and he was almost jolly.

"An American merchant needs five hundred robes and baptism gowns for women and children in Salem. If they sell, more work will follow. If new orders come, there will be more cider and biscuits, and a bag of oranges for each of you girls."

It wasn't the first time I'd heard America spoken of as a place of riches, but it was the first its good tidings had come my way.

"The New World must be a wonderful place," my new needling partner said as we rolled out the linen. Anne stamped the pattern in blue chalk dust, and we both blew off the excess powder to collect in a small drop sheet. She was the third daughter of a poor coal man. Her lips were chapped and her fingertips calloused.

"I'll go there one day," Anne added. She coughed a tiny splatter of scarlet blood onto the rose vine pattern she was tapping out. It had happened before, and she was quick with a bit of water and baking soda in the tin cup at her feet.

I'd seen my mother cough that way; a month later she was dead. I didn't want Anne to die, but even more, I did not want to catch her sickness and die myself. I told her to sleep with a garlic clove beneath her pillow, as my mother had done, and prayed it would work for her.

That night, while we ate our bread and gravy, I asked Pap if he believed my mother was in heaven watching over us.

"Dunno," he said. "Maybe. Or maybe not."

In Abington we'd spent our Sundays in church and at supper with our whole clan. But in Glasgow, Pap and I stopped going to church. If the weather was pleasant on a Sunday we went walking along the sea, and if it was not, we rested and drank tea in our rooms.

"If Mam is watching and I pray to her, do you think I'll have what I want?"

Pap turned his eyes to me, and I thought I saw a glint of tears.

"What is it that you want?"

"I want to go to America and make beautiful things with my needle."

I didn't say that I was still sad and that I thought this would cure me. I didn't even know how to say such a thing. But I knew that my world had once been full of magic and color and that it wasn't beautiful anymore.

"Muslin white on white is your work, Isobel. Your mam gave it to you before she went to her grave."

My mother had told me that some people could see the enchanted world better than others. I wanted to ask my father to speak of selkies and kelpies and the faeries that lived beneath the May trees as he once had. But he'd stopped telling those stories after my mother died, at about the same time that my colors had left.

"Then I want to be a pattern-maker and a dressmaker." I started to describe a new embroidery pattern to my father, but he raised an ink-stained hand and stopped me.

"Pattern-making is men's work," Pap said. "It is best for a girl not to want anything grand."

My mother had said the same, and all around me I saw it was true. Wanting brought pain, and women who desired and complained the least seemed the most contented. But I wanted the freedom to desire— and to seek after what I desired. I wanted color in all its forms, for I missed the beauty it had brought to my dreams and waking hours.

"I can learn it." I had notebooks full of fledgling designs. I wanted freedom and beauty and the power of the needle.

"No one will hire a girl to be a pattern-maker. Your best hope is to marry well," Pap said. These were words of love, the best my father could offer. "Marry well and you'll never have to work again."

To marry well, I understood, I would have to marry a man with money and means; a man who did not see that I was different or—perhaps even better—a man who saw it and would keep me safe. I was on the lookout for just this kind of husband and knew it would be a very tall task. Meanwhile, I kept to myself and poured everything into my needle.

Scotland, 1662

The marshal nails the parchment onto the kirk door.

"*Hear ye, hear ye—by order of the Laird of Park and Loch Loy under the jurisdictions of our majesty King Charles, Isobel Gowdie shall stand trial for the charges of witchcraft, enchantment, and malfeasances, and all others who have fallen into evil shall be called to confess and repent their coven with the Devil.*"

The villagers look to one another in quiet trepidation, for who among them has not spoken with the wee folk or left an offering for the bean-nighe? And who among them has not called at night through cracks in the shuttered window for spirits who might offer relief for misfortunes, illness, an empty cradle, or a broken heart?

"*As King James has declared and written that all witches shall be forced to confess the names of others in their coven and shall be otherwise punished unto death, so the Laird of Park and Loch Loy decrees before his people and his God that every witch shall be routed out.*"

The crowd cowers as Marshal MacGreggor raises an arm.

"*Go ye, look into your souls and upon your friends and neighbors and do not dither to look into your own hearts and hearth as well, for the Devil can be anywhere—the Devil is clever and may be disguised even as your most beloved.*"

— THREE —

I married well—or so it seemed at first.

Our courtship began in Glasgow on St. Andrew's Day, when Pap's new wife crowded me against the cookstove while I was preparing the roast, and I badly scorched my hand on a hot iron poker. I tried not to blame her, for she was bulky with the coming babe and careless of everyone.

Our regular apothecary being closed for the holiday, I ran to the finest shop at the top of the road and pounded until the door opened. My hand was throbbing, the burn already pulsing into oozing blisters.

"Edward Gamble at your service, my lady."

The apothecary's voice carried a hint of Ireland, and he spoke without a trace of annoyance. He held my wrist longer than seemed necessary, then told me to wait on a wooden bench. After a few moments he returned with a pot of cream that smelled of flax, honey, and something rancid.

"There now." He rubbed the lotion with a gentle touch and the pain began to seep from my hand. "The salve will heal the wound to nothing but a small mark."

His words and voice might have belonged to a mesmerist, so soothing and reassuring were they. When I looked down, the blistering on my hand had faded and the throbbing soothed to the pulse of a tiny timepiece.

"Like magic," I murmured.

I'd been taught to fear anything that hinted at witchcraft, but magic in medicine seemed an admirable and desirable quality, and I told him so.

"Yes." He looked up in surprise and I felt a strange thrill, as if I had found someone who understood me. "That's exactly right, young lady."

Edward charged me only half a farthing and told me to come back in a fortnight so he could see the progress of my healing. I was seventeen and Edward was upward of thirty years old, but he wore a refined waistcoat and vest with a silver pocket watch. Everyone knew the apothecary's wife had died of a terrible cancer he'd failed to cure and that Edward grieved her terribly. I did not think he would romance me, but when I returned as instructed, he gave me a pot of scented lotion and admired the irises embroidered on my bell sleeves.

"The green ribbon is very nice against your red hair," he added.

I asked about the glass jars in his shop and he told me that he'd spent much of his childhood with his father in the hills near Belfast collecting herbs and feathers and things dug from the earth.

"My father was a chemist in search of the secrets to life and death itself," he said. "After my dear wife died, I took up his search."

My eyes roamed about the shop and landed on a carved cross with Jesus Christ nailed to it, mouth open and eyes cast to heaven.

"And what did you find?" I asked.

"Many strange and secret paths lead to life and death's doorway," he said.

I felt a great tenderness toward him. I had lived a long time with my own grief and rarely spoken of it with anyone.

"My mother died when I was girl," I said. "I would like to know the secret to life and death. I would like to see that doorway, if such a thing is possible."

My mother had told me there are people who believe that we live in the realm between the faerie world and the world of God. Edward seemed such a man.

"You seem like a clever, fearless girl," he said. "I am looking for a companion like you."

I didn't know if I was fearless, but I liked that he saw me so.

EACH TIME I visited Edward's shop there was a gift for me: lavender soap wrapped in purple paper from Paris; gold myrrh for my father's rheumatic complaints; fuller's earth and cinnamon; an intricate silver spoon and a small ball for soaking teas or bath salts. Pap's print shop had fallen on hard times and I'd recently begun working with his new wife in the fabric mills in the north of the city. Long days in front of a hungry loom paid little and I was longing for respite and beauty.

In a life where I had little, Edward's gifts were a treasure of indulgence and luxury.

One day he pressed a jeweled canister into my hands. There were sapphires the color of my mother's voice, and pink stones like the sound of the wind when I was a girl.

"Slaves and savages in America have knowledge that leads to the doorway between life and death," Edward said. "Whatever it is, jungle seeds or African potions, a drink or a salve, I'll find it and put it in that very amulet one day—it will make our fortune."

He leaned across the counter and lifted my hair.

"People fear death," he whispered in my ear. This wasn't what I expected of our first intimate exchange, but I did not pull away. "They'll pay dearly for a formula that helps save themselves and their loved ones. You understand this, Isobel. You know what this grief and hope is like."

Then he asked for my hand in marriage.

"I will give you a sewing room of your own, and you will never have to work again."

EDWARD INVITED PAP and me to his home above the apothecary shop and showed us the airy attic that would be my sewing room if we married. On the table by the window was a glorious black lacquer box of drawers, doors, and deep-hinged shelves inlaid with colored glass, shells, and beads.

"An apothecary case from Italy," Edward said. "It's yours to use as a sewing kit."

Edward spoke not of the elixir of life but of his own father and the Rebellion that had propelled his family out of Ireland and back to the Scottish Lowlands they'd left a hundred years before.

"Do you love him, Isobel?" Pap asked as we walked home that afternoon. My father had loved my mother very much and suffered greatly when she died.

"I don't know." I was glad it didn't hurt me to say it.

"Perhaps that's for the best," Pap said. "Gamble is a widower, and he'll be grateful for a young, pretty wife. You can leave the mills before they break you down. It is what your mam wanted for you."

I was approaching my eighteenth year. I'd seen girls become fools for love and knew that kind of passion was dangerous. It was best for a motherless girl to marry a man for other reasons, and I had mine. Pap's new wife was with child and had made it clear the babe would sleep with me and that I would be its caretaker through the night. "Unless you get yourself married," she'd said.

My friend Noreen's husband was a Glasgow printer, newly released from his apprenticeship and established in his own shop. When I went to visit, her girl served us tea on white china plates.

"Marry him," Noreen said. "The sooner the better, while you still have your bloom. A man with his own shop is a good match."

I'd grown up beside a river that tinkled silver when the water hit rocks. I missed that world and had ever longed to return to it. Edward seemed to live in a singular place between fact and fantasy, between science and magic. I thought if he was my husband, I would be free and safe at the same time—that I would not have to sacrifice one for the other. And so I made what we all believed was a wise choice: I married him.

On our wedding night I put on a fresh white muslin nightdress and waited. Edward climbed on top of me and put a hand under my skirt.

"Hold still and it won't hurt," Edward said. It was a lie. It hurt very much. I bit my lip and closed my eyes and felt my tenderness toward him break. But I had my own soft pillow, soft white sheets, and a pearly washbasin. The next night Edward was gentle, and it didn't hurt as much. Noreen had whispered of warm pleasures in her marital bed, but I was happy just to be away from Pap's new wife and to have a good and prosperous husband.

To Edward's home I brought the iris tea towel my mother had embroidered years ago, a basket of prized fabrics, and a romance by Walter Scott that I'd spent years working my way through, page by page. I was proud that I could read, and it pleased my husband. Edward kept his books on a shelf in his shop and often spent the evenings in our parlor reading over chemical formulas or struggling to decipher the alchemy and chemistry books his father had bequeathed to him.

It was understood that we would have a family, for Edward had told me that was what he wanted. I pictured red-haired daughters, proud sons, six of us walking two by two on Sunday mornings. The kitchen maid taught me how to make the stews and fruits my husband craved. Edward was particularly fond of plum-and-apricot compote perfumed with anise. I found the orange star spice in the market and collected it in a glass jar beside the stove. The eight-pointed star seemed a symbol of good luck, and I fashioned that shape into the white work I stitched onto my petticoats and chemise.

Right away I set up my sewing room in the yellow attic and began to design a banner for Edward's shop. Once I'd dreamt of making colorful needlework as magnificent as the grand murals in the Queen's Hall, of hours lost in a rainbow of silk threads that poured like rich oil paint upon the cloth. I'd been discouraged in these ambitions—lack of time and resources, myself being a mere girl, the need to keep my fingers working as fast as I could.

Now I worked with the windows open and the sun shining down on the patchwork of colors and threads. If Edward came upstairs at unexpected hours with red-rimmed eyes and an aching head, I did not pay it much mind. I knew men had different troubles than women and that they managed them in different ways; I had learned long ago in Master Dwyer's shop to dodge a man's moods with a clean swatch of cloth and a neat line of thread.

When the ice cart caught Edward's leg and tore up his ankle three months after we were wed, I nursed my husband tenderly and followed his every instruction. He read the Ripley book and told me to bring him vinegar and silver mercury, a candle, beeswax, and the blood of a tortoise that had been put into a corked glass tube.

"I knew from the start that you would make a fine caretaker," Edward said when I did as he asked. "Someone who doesn't ask too many questions."

He told me he would be better in no time. I believed him and kept at my needle, jumping up to help if I heard him struggling but also keeping a safe distance so that I would not offend his manhood. It seemed to work, and soon he stopped grimacing or crying out in pain.

I PRESENTED MY finished banner to Edward on a sunny afternoon, pleased and proud of the way the cloth and thread had come together.

Edward praised the elegant scrolled border and the red velvet I'd used for the word APOTHECARY. He put the banner on a pole and hung it from the window above the shop that very day, and as we stood in the street to admire it, the shoemaker and his wife asked if I might make one for his shop, too.

In my mind's eye the shoemaker's banner appeared in brown and black with gold trim, men's silver-buckle shoes, a pair of lady's red boots, and the word SHOEMAKER in pinewood-green velvet with a lavender K the soft hue of foxglove.

This startled me. I had come to believe that Mam had taken the colors with her when she died. Now it seemed possible that Mam approved of my union with Edward and that this faint recollection of my youthful visions was her way of telling me so.

It was as if she'd given me back a small vision of my colors again, the same way she'd given me red hair and green-blue eyes.

"I'd like to do it," I said.

The shoemaker smiled, but Edward grimaced.

"Perhaps—" the shoemaker began, but my husband cut him off sharply—"No"—and it was done.

There was something in Edward's expression that cautioned me to be silent. I feared he had seen my secrets, that somehow he knew about the colors, the history of them, perhaps even the tremble of my ancestress as she'd stood on the rooftop and shouted, *I have lain with the Devil's forked prick inside me.*

Until that moment I had imagined I might one day speak of my childhood to him. Now I waved off the shoemaker with an apologetic shrug and followed Edward inside.

That evening and the next he worked straight through supper, servicing customers who'd come to him with croup, dropsy, and fever. At the end of the night he limped upstairs to our parlor. His hand shook as he put a flint to his pipe, but as he drew in the smoke his face relaxed slowly.

I served his favorite plum pudding and asked if I might make the shoemaker's banner "as a neighborly gift."

"*Yurrr* my wife." His rolled *r* sounded slurry. "You won't do anything that gives the appearance that *yurrr* for hire—it would reflect poorly on both of us. I told you from the first."

But I had already drawn out the red boots for the shoemaker's sign, the velvet pinewood-green letters, the lavender *K*. The work had a life of its own; it seemed a gift from someone and somewhere I had not visited in a long time. To let it go felt like letting go of the small bit of my mother and my childhood that had just returned to me. Even if the shoemaker never saw it, I wanted to see what I could create. And so I worked in secret and became accustomed to spending my time at the top of the house in my sewing room while Edward spent his down in the shop.

I DID NOT know my husband was in trouble until a man in a black cloak banged at our door. Edward struggled to get out of his chair and staggered back as the man waved a fist in his face.

"Keep your hands out of the poppy jar and pay us," the man shouted.

Edward scrambled to put something of value into the man's hands and sent him away.

"What does he mean?" I asked.

"The Chinese have made the price of poppy exorbitant." Edward's eyes did not sparkle as they had when we met. "I cannot keep up with the payments."

"Then you must raise your prices," I called after him. *Or let me help with my needle*, I wanted to add.

Edward said something about mercury and vinegar turning to gold, and I thought that his mind had been addled by pain and poppy. I began to cry, and Edward pushed away from the table, angry at my tears. He told me not to worry—"Don't *wurrrry*"—but I took it upon myself to watch more carefully. While he slept I rummaged through his bills and ledgers and soon understood that the compounds, oils, and tinctures with laudanum, mercury, and opium that had made Edward prosperous had also put a terrible craving in my husband that left him helpless against the pain of his torn leg.

He'd managed to keep his habit a secret and paid for what he consumed with a generous margin of profits. But the Chinese troubles had doubled the price of poppies that year, just as Edward's injury had made him hunger for it.

We were on the brink of ruin.

"Is there nothing I can do?" I was on my knees, begging Edward to let me use my needle to help pay his debts, when a pair of strongmen came into the shop carrying clubs and an order from the magistrate.

"Ye are hereby banished to the poorhouse, where ye shall be given as ye need until ye can repent and restore thyself," the constable read.

"It's my leg," Edward pleaded. "Have pity on my pain."

The marshal barged past him. Edward staggered, but my mind went icy clear.

I ran up to our bedroom and put on my finest embroidered dress, then pulled my drab black day dress over it. I turned my red cloak inside out so it would appear worthless, grabbed up a vial of poppy I'd managed to hide away with my mother's wedding gloves, and the sketchbooks I'd kept since childhood. My chatelaine was around my waist where it always remained; I shoved my needle and tambour hook into a hidden cape pocket and rushed back into the parlor where the men were raiding our shelves.

"That is a very old and valuable book," Edward cried out. The men paused, and we all looked at the title before they wrapped up Ripley's *Compound of Alchemy* in a piece of my prized green velvet and threw it into a sack.

WE STUMBLED ALONG Ropework Lane behind the constable, gagging at the stink of the pig fields and slaughterhouse. I held on to Edward's arm, for he was pulling his wounded foot and struggling with the thick apothecary book that he'd managed to carry away. The sky was a cruel, merry blue and the large doors of the poorhouse creaked open like the red-brown maw of a beast.

"Here's your new palace." The warden pointed us to a dark room with straw for a bed.

Edward fell into a heap while I took inventory of what I'd salvaged. I knew there were needleworkers even in the poorhouse, and I'd do whatever I must to work my way free.

"I'm sorry, lass." My husband's eyes were glassy, but he was not beyond shame. "Truly, Isobel, I didn't mean for it to come to this."

Scotland, 1662

The examiner leans over Isobel Gowdie in the dark courthouse.

"What did you do in the kirk of Auldearn? Is that where Satan gave you his commands?" His questions are quick and hard, with breath full of sausage and beer. "How did you kill the cows? Who helped you in your devilish ways?"

Onlookers clutch at their necks and Isobel cannot breathe. She has not had anything to drink for days.

"Water—" she cries into the courthouse. Her fingernails have turned yellow and now she is standing and her arms are raised and her throat is sore.

"Is water the instrument you used to kill the cows?" The examiner's spit flies onto her face, his brown-sausage words sicken her. "With spectral water you smothered the animals to fall and die breathless in the reverend's barn?"

At the smell of yeast and sausage, Isobel recalls Forbes's wife squatting away the unwanted child.

"Spare the child," she moans. "Do not suffer the little children."

The examiner is upon her and Isobel is in a fever.

"Isobel Gowdie, you admit that Satan orders you to hurt the children. Do you admit that you are a witch?"

Frenzied now with thirst and heat and the examiner's spittle on her cheek, she raises her arms and shrieks, "The child—" The words flash and she remembers the reverend's bare legs beneath his cassock and the hands that pushed needles into her flesh. "I have lain with the Devil's forked prick inside me," she moans. The examiner motions for the recorder to take up his quill and begin transcribing the woman's confessions. "And if you kill me hell will reign on earth."

Later, five village women stand in a tight cluster beside the well and shake their heads.

"*Gowdie is no witch,*" *one says.*

"*That ain't what she said.*" *An apron flaps, a fly is swatted. The woman looks over her shoulder to be sure they are alone. "You heard her with your own ears.*"

Another makes the sign of the cross and blinks at the cloudy-eyed crone who stands at the edge of the circle. "The colors, you surely heard her speak of it."

"*I heard her say purple for lavender and yellow for yarrow.*"

"*She said more than that,*" *says the first. "I tell you she woke the faeries, I seen 'em myself.*"

"*Dunna say it again, Mary, or they mayt come after you next.*"

— FOUR —

Rats woke me in the poorhouse, drudging under my skirts. It was our third morning on the cold, hard floor and I was hungry and weak.

"Young and pretty." A man with a twisted spine and keys jangling at his side kicked at my foot with his own. "Get up—let's go."

I rubbed the dirt off my face with the hem of my dress and followed the man down the hall.

In the lord provost's office, I found Pap waiting with his hat still firmly on his head.

"It's done." Pap stood straight. "I sold what I could salvage at Edward's shop, and added some of my own things to make up the difference."

Edward came up behind me.

"Is it enough?" my husband asked.

Pap's face was grim. "Barely."

I was relieved and grateful as we limped out into the cold morning.

"I swear I'll repay you." Edward shook my pap's hand. He was still sick with needing the poppy, but he'd done what he could to pull himself together, and the days off his foot had done it some good.

"Take care with my girl," Pap said. "Get her away from here and away from ruin."

My father pulled me into an embrace.

"Trust the needle, Isobel," he said in a deep, quiet voice. "Anything is possible in the New World. You must believe it and make it so."

He secreted a small coin sack into my palm and kissed me goodbye. I clung to him until I was sobbing and he was weeping, too, but there was no suggestion that I might stay behind in Glasgow. Edward was my husband. To have parted from him then would have been to disgrace myself and Pap, too. I would not have done it, even if I had been given the choice.

I'd set my mind on America, where I would not let Edward tell me how I might use my needle and my talents. My mother had told me my time would come—surely it was now. The poorhouse had set something loose in me, and I would not be put aside again.

ON THE STAGECOACH to Liverpool, Edward kept his head buried in the thick apothecary book murmuring phrases—*the pox, calendula, beeswax, candelilla, cowslip*—as if to prove that he was serious about making a new and prosperous start.

"I thought you had it all committed to memory," I said. I could not help myself.

"It is like the Bible," Edward said. "You can't know all its mysteries even if you've read every word."

He had been good and gentle to me at the beginning, and I wanted to believe in him. But I was also practical, as my years in Glasgow had made necessary. Under the guise of decorating and mending I hid the four gold pieces from Pap in a petticoat hem, each in its own concealed pocket so that they wouldn't clang when I moved. I took care not to let Edward know of them, for Pap had given them to me in secret, and they were all I had to make a new start in a new land where no one had heard of the witches hanged in Scotland.

By the time we reached Liverpool, Edward's eyes were clear and he engaged himself as a ship's medic in exchange for free passage across the Atlantic. The medic's duties involved dispensing oranges for scurvy, echinacea for itchy throats, ginger and licorice or cocaine syrup for nausea or dropsy. The work would be "easy, even uninspiring," Edward said.

I reminded him he didn't have his herbs and remedies.

"All will be well," he said. "The captain provides a medicine box with the ship."

I heard the same assurance in his voice as on the day we met. But I knew there would be poppy in a medicine case and that it would be difficult for him to resist temptation.

"Don't fret," he said, as if reading my mind. "I learned my lesson the hard way. I won't shame you again."

THE *NEW HARMONY* was larger than I anticipated, a schooner with three sails; the captain was a sturdy man with a trim beard and hair bleached by the sun and brilliant blue eyes. He seemed so self-assured that I guessed he must be Edward's age, and yet he moved with a spryness that suggested he was closer to my own.

Captain William Darling admired my red cape and the small bits of white needlework I'd put on the sleeves of my black dress, then put a roughened finger to the tip of his own jacket.

"Seashells and knotted ropes will make a good trim for my cuffs." He spoke with an accent I'd never heard before, neither English nor Scottish.

"I'd be honored to stitch them for you." My sewing box and every color in it had been taken from me the night of our eviction, but I wouldn't let Edward stop me now. "If you don't mind simple cotton thread."

"You won't have to use cotton." The captain smiled. "Somewhere in my hold there are silk threads from China—they'll be yours on our journey."

At that, my fear of being the only woman aboard a merchant ship dimmed.

"You'll have a cabin with a window," Darling added. "And cups and saucers for your tea, Mrs. Gamble."

He told me the ship was loaded with linens, soaps, flax and spices, old paintings bound for galleries in Boston, and cork enough for ten thousand bottles of rum.

"Do they drink so much rum in America?" I asked.

"They do." His smile was kind. I wondered if he had a wife, perhaps children. It seemed that he would be a good family man, smart and dependable. I had a flash of my pap bending over his print trays, inking up the letters, folding me into his arms as he did when I was a girl.

"Cork, cotton, lumber, sugar, rum," the captain added. "'Tis a triangle of fortune for some. The *New Harmony* is one of many schooners that keeps the money flowing. As long as I don't trade in chains and human misery, I'm happy."

I was young and had suffered my own losses. Although I knew about Africans in bondage, this was the first time a picture arose in my mind of men, women, and children taken into chains and torn from one another, and the shadow of it stayed with me as we prepared to depart.

THAT VERY MORNING we sailed onto the sea like skaters on a frozen pond, full of expectation, bent into the wind.

The land quickly faded into the mist behind us, and soon we were wrapped in a shroud of cold and wet. The rain slashed against the sails, the crew shouted into the void, and I became violently ill. Edward gave me dried ginger to chew, but the rolling waves and churning seas were stronger.

For two nights I groaned on my hard pallet, nerves and fears turned to spewing terror, lying in my own sick and wishing that I would die. All that kept me together was the iris tea towel that was once my mother's, the place where she made the tiny red *A* that I pressed against me as I howled.

On the third night of our voyage, we heard the captain groaning for help. Edward pulled on his jacket and boots and soon came back to rifle in the locked box.

"For the captain," he said when I gaped at him. "Something in Darling's side is swollen to the size of a chicken's egg—I'll need a sharp blade."

Somehow, I dragged myself off the pallet and found my tambour hook in the secret pocket of my cloak; we held the sharp end in a candle flame until it glowed red.

The first mate's skin was black as night, his eyes sharp as the North Star. Ingo spoke to the captain in a soothing singsong while I wiped

Darling's brow with a warm cloth. Edward made an incision in his lower left side, then poked in a hollowed length of rye grass. The captain screamed like a wild animal, and with his shrieks came yellow pus that filled the straw and overflowed onto the bunk. Ingo eased a bottle of rum into Captain Darling's mouth, and I used a needle and flax thread to sew him up. Then the captain spit up everything that he'd managed to swallow down.

"Let him rest," Edward said, and we collapsed onto our bunks.

INGO WAS AT our cabin before dawn.

"The captain is fevered." His face was impassive, but I knew by the way he'd ministered to the captain that he cared for him very much. "If he dies, it's bad for your husband. Bad for all of us."

Edward was nowhere to be seen and there was naught to do but attend to the captain myself. I'd had more than enough bad luck; I could not allow it to follow me to America. I recalled all that my mother had taught me about fevers, then soaked rags with cold water and rum and put the cool cloths at the captain's neck, under his limp hot arms, and at the small of his back.

In the morning, whether by my medicine or a small miracle, his fever had broken and the captain was sitting up. There was a pile of maps spread on the tray across his lap, and the color had returned to his cheeks.

"Your husband told me you brought him luck, and it seems now that luck is mine."

"My husband exaggerates," I said. "But I'm glad you're mending."

It was then I noticed the captain's white bed coat and pants decorated with a pattern of white cross- and backstitches unlike any I'd ever seen. There were palm trees and birds with beaks as long as their bodies, flowers bigger than the birds, swirls that looked like the wind itself, all done in white on white. It was crude but expressive work, with knots and welting of different depths giving the cloth the texture of a quilted landscape.

"You must have a woman who loves you." I put a hand to the stitching. "That is lovely work."

"It's my own," Captain Darling said. "I've been stitching sails since I was a lad, and it became habit. When my fingers are moving, my mind is free." He paled and leaned back on his bed. "Sometimes the sea is so bright or mean I need white on white to soothe me."

I spent the day sitting and stitching while he convalesced. From his cabin door I could see the steps that led to the belly of the ship, where I had been told Edward lay curled in his own sick.

"Ingo will see that Edward has everything he needs," the captain said. "You needn't worry."

He ordered his men to bring up a white vest from the stores, and I stitched a new waistcoat for Edward while the captain mended his wardrobe and told me about his childhood in Bermuda.

"A life of filth drove me to the ships," he said. I thought to tell him what I'd seen in the poorhouse, but kept silent. "At seventeen I sailed out with a trade ship that was soon engaged as a privateer in the second British-American war. In 1814 we stopped a Dutch ship carrying Africans in chains from going into port in Baltimore." His eyes hooded. "It was the most wretched thing I've ever seen—Black men, women, and children in despair and agony."

The captain's fingers and needle stopped; it was clear the horror was still vivid in his mind. I fetched him some tea, which he drank in slow sips. Then he patted my hand and closed his eyes and soon drifted off to sleep.

I snuck off to find Edward right then, but Ingo planted himself in front of me on deck.

"He's sick and in no condition to be seen by a lady," Ingo said. I hoped it was the seasickness, but I feared Edward had fallen to the poppy again. I searched Ingo's face, but he revealed nothing.

That very afternoon the wind died and the *New Harmony*'s sails went flat. While the crew kept a restless watch over the horizon, the captain continued his stories and I forced myself not to worry about Edward. Whatever happened, I had to keep myself in good form.

"After the war we went to Sumatra and brought back black pepper," the captain said. "The profit was seven hundred times the price, and I earned almost enough to buy a vessel of my own. I spotted Ingo at a port in Jamaica throwing knots of heavy rope over the side of the ship like they were flower petals. The strongest and most honest man I ever met, white or Black."

The captain's love and admiration for Ingo was clear, just as Ingo's was for him. When I thought of Ingo, I thought of a free man under a starry night and not of Africans in bondage.

That afternoon, when the captain asked what I hoped for in the New World, I told him what I'd never said aloud since my father told me it was impossible.

"I'd like to make a business of my needle in America," I said.

I'd had many days to imagine it, and Pap's gold coins had lit up my mind with possibility. I spoke of embroidery pattern-making and dress-making; of designing ladies' dresses and men's jackets ornamented with brilliant colors and scenes.

"Silks and gold thread," I said, dreaming. "Dyes from India and China, colors I have only seen in windows near the queen's castle or in my imagination. If I could have those materials, I believe I might make a life for myself, Captain Darling."

He gave me a faraway smile, then closed his eyes as if I'd wearied him. This made me feel ashamed to have spoken of myself and my dreams, and I slunk away and curled onto my cot, where I tried to remember the colors of home and wept when I could not conjure the River Clyde, the cottage where I was born, or my mother's face.

THE NEXT MORNING Captain Darling was up directing his men. The wind returned, the sun was strong, and Ingo was shouting instructions as crewmen pulled the sails and tacked with the wind. I found a sheltered place to sit with my needle, and that's where the captain presented me with a long, wrapped package.

I pulled away the brown paper to reveal a rainbow of threads more brilliant than any I'd seen even in the finest shop windows back home— vermilion and India red, indigo and cobalt, the green black of the deepest seas.

"You told me your dreams." Darling's voice shimmered like river water. "This is my thanks to you—silk from China, colors from every corner of Shanghai. I believe you might be an artist if you wish it, Mrs. Gamble."

I choked out my thanks and he touched my arm.

"I owe you my life," he said. I stared up at the words that floated above him like strong blue clouds pillowed against a pearl-white sky.

I OWE YOU MY LIFE

The shoemaker's banner had appeared in my mind's eye as a sewn piece that I might create. But the captain's words were nearly tangible, as if I could hold out an open palm and take them into my hands.

I managed one more word of thanks before the captain was called away and I was alone.

Clutching the threads against me, I slid down onto the floor of the ship. I was dizzy and dazed and feared I was falling ill.

I listened to the crashing waves, the ropes clanging against masts, men calling to one another, and the breeze ripping the sails—everything suddenly full of color. The sea seemed to tilt and I felt as if I were sliding into the faerie world, where mischievous kelpies and lovelorn selkies could steal away your clothes and your memory, your mind or your heart.

Over the years I'd sometimes wondered if I had ever lived in a world where sound was color and voices hung in the air like painted curtains, or if I had merely imagined such things. Now the colors of my youth were even richer than before, sprung from within me as they had not since I was a girl—beautiful, but also terrifying.

I tried to reason with the colors, to keep them at bay so they would not overwhelm me, but they kept coming. The crew's voices were pebbled brown, the ocean's windy roar was the cobalt blue of tumbling sea glass. Every sound around me had its own vivid hue and texture, as bright as it had been in my childhood, the smoky veil of my girlhood grief finally lifted.

After Mam's death I'd learned to accept a more ordinary imagination. In Glasgow, the colorful shop banners had been a joy, but when ruin came so quickly after, it had seemed a warning to stay as far from my colors as I could.

Yet I'd brought about good fortune at sea: I'd helped save the captain's life and nursed him back to strength. I'd made a friend and been given a gift. Waves crashed blue and purple and I laughed aloud, and the sound of my own laughter was a brilliant pink light, something I'd never seen before.

As if I were waking from a long gray dream, old sights from long ago made themselves known and I clutched at my notebook and made my sketches. Stories my mother and father had told me, their tales and colors, returned to me. When I was steady enough to stand, I made my way back to my cabin and drew more. I found the sand-colored linen remnant I'd salvaged from ruin and measured and cut a new lining for my red cape.

By afternoon I was stitching the River Clyde, the cottage where I was born, St. Andrew's grand cathedral in brown and gold, and a red-and-white May tree in bloom. I used a blue running stitch for the river, a brown backstitch for tree trunks, tufted cream for the sheep in our old family pasture, and blue green and brown for the hills in Abington. These were the places and colors of my childhood, the magical world my parents had taught me to both love and fear.

I sewed the caramel of my father's voice into his hair and boots; the sapphire and turquoise of Mam's voice I put into a dress made with jeweled buttons as my mother had never worn in life.

For days I was lost in the work, wishing only for a larger embroidery hoop to make the stitching easier. I'd nearly forgotten about Edward until he staggered onto the deck one afternoon.

"Isobel," he cried in a strangled voice. "Girl, I need your help."

Something in the way he pitched across the ship frightened me, and I pressed myself into a shadow. A passing crewman motioned me belowdecks and opened a trapdoor that I slipped into as Edward collapsed.

"You stay here," the sailor said. "Let Ingo take care of him."

I found myself in a narrow pocket of space just big enough for two empty barrels. A cat and her kittens were nesting in one, and the other was filled with water and bits of trash. For a few moments I was torn between hiding and helping. But when I realized the copper ring on the barrel could be fashioned into a very large embroidery ring, I set my pliers and knife upon it, first prying it off and then filing the edges smooth.

By the time I was back on deck, Edward was nowhere to be seen.

WITH A BARREL-SIZED hoop to hold my cloth tight and secure, I fell fully under the spell of my colors. Suspended between Scotland and the New World, I worked in my cabin or on a bench on deck. At night I sewed by moonlight, and when the sky was dark I lit the lamp in my cabin and picked up my work again.

I finished the scenes of my childhood home and set to work on the selkies and kelpies at the river's edge, the faeries under the May tree, and two Jacobites for the Highlanders' uprising. I stitched my name in emerald green, *Isobel MacAllister Gamble,* and my mother's in magenta, *Margaret Anderson MacAllister.* I stitched my pap's in bold black letters with black thread—*Seamus MacAllister*—and recorded his parting words to me:

Trust the needle, Isobel. Anything is possible in the New World.

In the center I put Isobel Gowdie, Queen of the Witches, with a tiny pentacle on her cape, flying to safety. This was my ancestress—the one who'd seen the colors like me—and I prayed that she might protect and guide me in my new life.

—— FIVE ——

The lookout shouts, "Salem ahead!" and everyone looks east as the shape of the New World begins to piece itself together across the Massachusetts Bay.

"It is a good wind, a lucky wind," Captain Darling says. He smells of limes and the black liquorice he chews while he steers the ship. He points at the flags on passing schooners—"That one's the Union Jack . . . and there's the American Stars and Stripes"—and waves at a black three-rigger heading to sea at a fast clip. "That one's Dutch. And the fleur-de-lis"—I follow his finger to a red flag with a white symbol— "that's the flag of Florence."

Salem appears first as a dark dot, then a blur of ships and rooftops, naked treetops, and a flat land covered with a lace of white snow. At the harbor's embrace, the wind dies and the sharp scent of pepper, sweet cinnamon, and tea perfumes the air. Every hand is on deck pulling ropes, climbing, shouting, tossing, tugging, catching, and cursing, all of it yielding a clamor of colors that I pray will settle down, and soon, thank God, they do.

I smell burning fires and food cooking in the town hearths, see men bustling along the wharves, and hear the sounds of hammers and dogs as the land comes quickly at us. Shouts go up like a spark of flame against the cool sea. The hard knock of wood on wood startles me as we bump up to the wharf and the ship comes to a stop.

It is the third of March. We've been at sea for thirty-three days.

I wrap the red cape around myself with its newly stitched memories pressed against me and hidden from sight. Before we step off the *New Harmony*, Captain Darling takes Edward by the elbow and shakes his hand. Edward has cleaned up. He wears the new white vest beneath his waistcoat and is freshly shaved for our arrival. He's thinner than he was at the start of our journey and more leathered.

"Dr. Gamble, I'm alive thanks to you," the captain says. "I hope you'll sail with me again for luck and profit."

I don't know why the captain is excusing Edward's seasickness and weakness with the poppy, but then I realize that America is indeed a land of new opportunity and the captain is forgiving, even generous. Edward left home a ruined apothecary and arrived in America a doctor. If I work hard and am clever, then perhaps I will make something new of myself as well.

SALEM—*SALAAM*—MEANS "PEACE" IN Arabic, the captain tells us, but the docks are anything but peaceful. The city greets me in the tongues of a hundred lands, the music of a thousand voices, monkeys and birds in small cages cawing and clucking—a cacophony of everything loud, bright, and new.

There are sailors of every color, Chinese men and Indians, short men with dark skin and gray teeth pushing carts and hauling crates, exotic women wrapped in cloth the color of spices, wine, tangerines, saffron, and more.

I'm a small bit of dust in this great swirl of color and sound until a stout old woman with cheeks pink from age or drink pushes right up to me and catches my wrist.

"You." Something in her is familiar, and for an instant I think she knows me. "You've come from the low country." I try to pull away, but her grip is strong. "There's a blade in your pocket—hold it tight."

My fingers twitch for the hook tucked inside my cape, and then Captain Darling is upon us, waving a flat hand in her face.

"Get away, Sally, you're scaring the girl."

"Beware the devil in the forest," Sally says. Her eyes roll back in her head and she looks for a moment as if she might faint. Then she jerks once, her arms fly up, and she falls to the ground.

"A fit," Edward says with a great thrust of authority. "She's fallen into a fit."

A slender, brown-skinned young lady wearing a striped baker's smock runs up and takes the woman's shoulders.

"Widow Higgins has the spells," she says. She looks to Edward, who kneels to help as a small crowd gathers.

"Back away, give the widow room to breathe," the young lady says.

The captain spreads his arms to help break up the onlookers. Edward cradles the woman's head. Folks step back and my neck tingles, then something tugs at a corner of my sight like a pulled thread.

When I turn, three boys are raising up a cry as they run around a man on the wharf. The boys are heading our way, but it's a man reading a book while he walks slowly down the pier who draws my gaze.

He's tall, with a long black cloak, and thick, wavy hair. His gait tips slightly to one side and he seems not to notice as the wharf runners and errand boys scamper around him. In Glasgow, men of books were of another world, one where even Pap could not go, though he had ink on his hands. But this man is right here among the riffraff and scurry of the wharf, a dramatic figure whose cape waves as the boys in breeches fly toward us, breaking through the circle and skidding to a stop.

"Did the witch prick you?" The tallest boy points at me as if he knows my secrets. "You'll have warts and frogs in your aprons."

Now the captain is angry—he swings at one of the boys, then the others. They scatter like beetles, each in a different direction.

The Widow Higgins regains herself and sits up.

"She'll be fine now," the young woman says.

Edward nods and rises from the rough boards. A hard wind blows, and when I look again, the tall man with the book is staring at me from the same distance of some thirty or forty meters. My red cape is flapping open in the breeze and his gaze seems fixed on the figures I've sewn there.

I tug the cape closed—the stories from home are meant for me alone—and lock my eyes upon his. Edward once said I was fearless, and I believe he made me so. If this man thinks I will shy under the power of his stare, he is wrong. I don't look away until the captain takes my arm and breaks the spell.

"Now we eat and secure lodging," Darling says. "I'm sorry that was your welcome, we'll have to do better, lass."

When I look again, the caped man is gone.

EDWARD SLAPS CAPTAIN Darling on the back and we make our way through the throngs on the wharf street.

We're in a marketplace filled with carts, sailcloth awnings, and wagons from which men and women hawk vegetables—some I recognize, but many I do not—fruits and nuts, silver fish, black iron pots, shoes with buckles and shoes with hooks, ladies' silk slippers, clay plates and jugs laid out upon a fat open ladder. A brown-skinned woman, wrapped in a colorful cocoon of cloth, squats on a blanket beside burlap sacks filled with fragrant spices and calls out, "Tasty, tasty," her words thick with another language.

A dark-skinned woman with a white turban covering her hair stands behind a bench spread with sashes and belts and small piles of brown eggs. Her sashes are embellished with flowers, her belts embroidered with berries, lanterns, ships, horses, and trees that seem to dance or move with the light.

In the twining ivy stitched in shades of green upon one of her shawls, I see strange letters folded together, as if the letter *S*—lilac to my eye—has been crossed with the orange letter *F* over and again, almost like men running. A shift of my gaze and there is the word *SAFE* rising and falling inside the shape of a lantern. The threads are all one color, but what I see is a lilac *S*, red *A*, pumpkin-orange *F*, and green *E*.

I run my tongue along my teeth, trying to decide if the woman has done this bit with her threads intentionally—and quickly determine it must be my imagination, a trick of light playing upon my colors. I have been too long at my needle and too long at sea. I must be careful lest what's real and what's only my imagination become so tangled that I betray myself in word or deed.

"Captain." The Black woman nods, and Darling returns the greeting.

"Come along." Edward tugs at me and I stumble. Darling catches and steadies me in one motion.

"It'll take a while to lose your sea legs," Darling says, as if he hasn't noticed Edward's roughness. He keeps me steady at his side as he greets friends and points out several shops. Despite his limp Edward stays a few steps ahead, marching with the determination of a thirsty man toward a tavern.

"And there's the East India Marine Society Hall." Captain Darling indicates a tall building with high glass windows overlooking the harbor. "You must see what's inside, Mrs. Gamble—I'll give you a letter of introduction, it's a house of wonders."

We've just turned onto a cobbled street with our backs to the sea when the tall man in the long black cape lopes toward us. His hands are empty now and there's a lump beneath his cape where he's slung a leather bag across one shoulder.

"Welcome back to Salem, Captain Darling." The man's words are pale red trimmed with gold, like a prince's old, furred vestment.

"Hail to you, Mr. Hathorne," the captain answers without slowing. "I've brought new books from London—they should be at Mrs. Batchelder's shop by Thursday."

Hathorne's face lights up, but just as quickly he seems to tuck away his delight. I see he's younger and more robust than his gait suggested before, perhaps not more than five-and-twenty. His features are strong and pleasing, but his voice is gentle.

"I hope I'll have coin enough for one," Hathorne says. His eye catches mine and when he sees me startle, a small smile teases at his lips. "Especially if there's something exciting in the lot."

The book at his nose, the tender hitch to his step, the lament of coin, and the colors of his voice all suggest a faded prince of Salem. A caped man with longings and dreams.

"I'm sure you'll find something." Captain Darling doesn't linger long enough to make an introduction, and in a few more paces Mr. Hathorne has left my sight and the captain is leading us up a step into the Charter Ale House.

∞

THE ALEHOUSE IS dark and warm with polished walnut booths and the cheerful clang of pots and spoons. Darling leads us to a booth tucked in the back, and no sooner are we seated than two American seamen step up to greet him. The captain gives them details of our crossing, then lifts his shirtwaist to show the fresh scar on his belly.

"Dr. Edward Gamble and his wife saved my life," he says. "I'll be damned if she didn't stitch me up with Scottish muslin."

"You've come from Glasgow?" one of the Americans asks.

"That's right," Edward says.

Darling lifts a candle to better show off his scar. I see my stitches running across his skin like a neat row of small black ants. I cannot shake the feel of the boy's fingers on my wrist or the way he called the widow a witch.

"Then you're a Scot?" the other man asks Edward.

Edward hooks a thumb into the watch pocket of his vest where I have stitched his name.

"Aye, that's right." He thickens his brogue like a showman. "And we've brought the captain good luck."

"That may be," the first man says. "But we had better luck handling the English than your countrymen did." His tone is jocular, but his expression is not. I think he doesn't like that we are Scots.

"I left home to find a better life," says Edward.

"And how will you earn your living?"

"I'm a doctor—trained in healing, pharmacy, and surgery."

He doesn't look at me. I feel the small blade in my pocket, the very instrument Edward used for his first "surgery."

"Will you be taking lodging here?" the man asks Edward.

"Yes, and I'll establish a practice as well."

"After you've come with me to Bermuda," the captain says to Edward. His shirt is tucked and buttoned back up. He puts an arm around my husband's shoulder. "We'll see your good wife installed in a cottage, and then you'll sail again with me."

This is the first I'm hearing of such a plan. I see Edward hesitate, but I don't believe it is on my account.

"I'll commit one percent of my profits to you," the captain says.

"Three," Edward says.

"Too much," the captain says. "My investors put up a small fortune and take five percent each. At one percent you might get as much as two thousand dollars."

"Then one and a half percent, and we are agreed," Edward replies.

The captain thinks for a moment, then grins. The men shake hands, light their pipes, and begin to drink whiskey. They order warm oysters and creamy potato stew, and neither says a word to me.

I'm gloomy now. Much as he has disappointed and troubled me, Edward is my husband. I know no one in Salem who will vouch for me, no one to walk or sup with. I've never been alone before, and I'm of two minds about it—just as I have been of two minds about so much since we ran from ruin.

"If you don't mind, gentlemen, I will say good night," I finally say.

The men barely give me a nod, then call for more whiskey.

IN OUR ROOM I take off my clothes and re-count the four gold pieces sewn into my petticoat, then hang the dress on a hook beside the bed. It's been a long time since I undressed at my leisure, heard the clop of horses' hooves and the sounds of a city, or felt solid ground beneath my feet.

I open the trunk and take out the dress that I concealed the day of our eviction. It's embroidered with the same yellow-and-purple irises as my mother's tea towel; I run my palm across them to soak in their strength and wisdom.

The chamber is cozy and quiet, and when I pull the blanket to my chin and close my eyes, I feel the sea rolling away. I recall the smells of Salem as we drew closer, the crowded market on the wharf. I think of the widow's warning and the way the boys called her a witch. And I remember Mr. Hathorne's eyes, the way he held my gaze and almost smiled.

This is the New World, and if I take good care then anything is possible—my needle, a new start, and even a man with a red-and-gold voice who spins around corners with his cloak flapping, just to steal another look at me.

Salem, 1656

The smattering of cottages along the narrow dirt lanes are modest, and the three ships in the harbor huddle together like dark birds sleeping in the tides. In the largest clapboard house in the new settlement, Goodwife Hathorne climbs into bed beside her daughters and bundles them under a stack of quilts.

Soothed at last by the brandy he dreamt of during battle, Major William Hathorne calls his oldest living son into his tiny study and hands him a well-worn book. John is fifteen years old—not as tall as his father but full of the same vigor. It is their first moment alone since the elder returned exhausted and shaken from the Indian wars in the northern woods.

"This is the book they use in England and Scotland to rout out witches and other bedevilment," the major says. "We must rely on it to keep our people and plantations safe."

John runs a reverent palm across the soft leather cover: A Discourse of the Damned Art of Witchcraft *by William Perkins.*

"Men of our station and property are God's messengers charged with driving the Devil's rule out of this heathen land," his father goes on. "We must prepare to stand between Satan and the innocents."

Long into the night young John Hathorne reads about the Devil and his minions: weak women easily led because they are alone or greedy; unbaptized savages seduced by Satan because they are ignorant of the Evil One's wiles.

He sits at the edge of his narrow bed and makes careful notes in a marbled notebook. One day he may be called to do his father's work driving Quakers and other demons out of Salem by lash, proclamation, and the strength of God.

And he will be ready.

— SIX —

Edward's snoring wakes me our first morning in Salem. He's on the floor beside the bed, boots sticking straight up where he landed, coat stuffed under his head for a pillow. His face is red from drink and there is a cup of ale spilled across the floorboards. The copper clang of pots and trays below mix with sounds of land and home that I have missed: carts rolling over cobblestones, women's pastel voices calling to one another, the smell of fresh baking bread.

The morning sun shining through the white curtains makes a delicate scrim of lace flowers on the moss-painted wall, and soon a man's deep voice rises up to my window as if he's standing directly beneath it.

"The type is being set this morning—you'd best get your advert to the office straightaway. And I'm sorry, Nat—your story won't run this week. Maybe I'll get it in for next week."

I peer over the window ledge and spy Mr. Hathorne—now I know his name is Nat—with hands jammed in his pockets, head bent. I watch as the two men walk down the street and turn the corner out of sight. My legs wobble as I step over my husband to pull on my iris-stitched dress, but the room steadies as I lace up my boots, grab my cape, and latch the door behind me.

The alehouse is still closed as I slip into the street, but the city is awake with horses, carriages, and shop owners readying for the day. The air smells of the sea, and gulls caw overhead. The townsmen are dressed in plain brown and black day clothes, the women in simple skirting and dull cloaks. Their clothing matches the gray sky, the beige landscape, the sand-and-pebble walkways, and the alleys where chamber-pot slop and horse dung are washed away. It is a small town compared to Glasgow, and I feel the peace of the place as a welcome respite.

I'm not looking for Mr. Hathorne, not in any direct sort of way, but I keep my eyes alert for a tall man in a long cape who leans just slightly to one side as he walks with a steady lope. I haven't gone far when I see Mrs. Batchelder's shop—the very shop Captain Darling said would sell the books from London. A display of leather-bound notebooks and a packet of colored pencils in the window catches my eye, an envious spectrum of hues I could put to great use for my sketches.

I'm imagining how I will design my first gown when a woman's voice startles me.

"The pencils are beautiful."

"Widow Higgins." I turn and greet the woman from the wharf. "Good morning to you."

She stands so close that I can feel the brush of her skirts on mine.

"I'm afraid I gave you a scare yesterday, Miss . . ."

"*Mrs.* Edward Gamble." I take a step back. "And there is no need to apologize—it takes more than a fainting spell to frighten me."

With a nod to the colorful irises that decorate the bottom of my skirt, she compliments the work and asks if it's mine. I tell her it is.

"And may I ask—where did you learn?"

I take in her plain black dress and the sharp glint in her eye. I do not like her so close, as if she sees something I want to keep hidden.

"My mam taught me. Home in Scotland."

"Scotland, is it? Not Ireland?" She doesn't wait for an answer. "'Tis a pity, for you sound like an Irish lass."

"Where's the pity, Widow Higgins?"

"I suppose it matters little." She shrugs. "New Irish aren't liked in Salem—drinkers without enough sense to control their urges. New Scots are a rough lot, too," she adds.

Has she seen some weakness in Edward, some worry in me?

"I assure you, my mother raised me well."

"Did your mother make her money with the needle?"

"No," I say. "But I worked in a tambour shop. White on white, for almost ten years."

She touches my sleeve. I feel that she's sought and found me for a purpose. But what purpose?

"We have many fine embroiderers here," she says. "The Peabody sisters teach needlework in their school for young ladies. But your work is quite special. Will you be taking assignments?"

"Assignments?"

A sallow man in a black hat trudges down the road pulling a cart behind him, and when he passes, I see the bodies of the dead wrapped in burlap and gray cloth. He looks at me, but I look quickly away, for it's bad luck when the undertaker looks you in the eye.

"Will you work for hire?"

"I would like that very much," I admit.

"And what meeting will you attend in Salem?" she asks.

I search for something in her eyes, something in her words, but there are no hints.

"I beg your pardon?"

"Church, Mrs. Gamble. What is your church? I pray you're not a Catholic."

"No, I am not." I do not add that Edward is a Catholic or that I believe in God the Father and Jesus Christ but I also believe in our stories and myths, selkies and elves and changelings that come when the wind rises and birds fly across the sun. "Where do *you* worship, Widow Higgins?"

"I go to East Meeting House," she says after a moment's hesitation. She drops her voice, as if to share a confidence. "If you live here you must take meeting every Sunday and be sure you're seen doing it."

Her words have softened.

"I appreciate knowing it."

"Now." She claps her hands as if she is about to deliver news, and her face livens. "Your husband is going to sea, and the captain has asked if I'll let you my cottage. There's a good well and a garden that only needs to be hoed and planted. You'll be snug there—you may see it and decide if it's to your liking."

I can't imagine when this exchange happened or if she's even telling the truth.

"You're very kind," I say. "I'm sure if Captain Darling suggested it, my husband will view it favorably."

I make an effort to get on with my walk. The woman makes me uncomfortable, it is undeniable. A secret, I think. The woman has a secret, or she is seeking to know mine. And the boy called her a witch. I do not wish to be anywhere near her.

"There's a dressmaker in town who needs a stitcher." Widow Higgins steps back at last and brushes the front of her white apron. "Ask at Felicity Adams's piece goods shop and tell her I sent you."

"Perhaps I will," I say. But my plan doesn't include working as anyone's apprentice. I've had enough of putting my hand to work for someone else's gain.

BACK AT THE inn, Edward is on the chamber pot. He grunts and puts a hand in front of his face when I enter our room, as if that might shield me from the unpleasant sight and smells. I shut the door and wait in the narrow hallway, where I overhear the men below talking about two barrels of oysters, a new batch of cider, and twelve loaves of bread.

Edward opens the door when he is decent.

"You found us a cottage?"

"Yes, and the price is very good." He tugs down his coat sleeves and pulls the lapels together for his necktie. I smooth the paisley neck cloth for him. It's my favorite blue, the color of a robin's egg.

"It's past the wharves, on the other side of the pond," he says. "The captain said there's a garden, a brick hearth large enough to stand in, and a sunny place for your sewing."

So, the widow spoke the truth.

I hand him the necktie and he threads it beneath his shirt collar.

"The cottage belongs to the woman who has spells," I say. "You didn't ask if I'd like to live there."

"I thought you'd prefer to be a mistress and not a boarder in someone else's home." His voice is sharp. "It's as far from pig fields and the alms-house as you please."

"I might have seen it, Edward."

"You'll see it this morning." He gives me a stern look, and I know further protest is futile. "I've ordered up a wharf runner. He'll be here shortly."

THE WHARF RUNNER is a dark-skinned man with a scar across his cheek.

"Zeke," he says with a nod. His eyes are friendly.

Zeke loads our single trunk into the back of a blue farm wagon, and Edward helps me climb onto a horse-blanket seat. I'm barely settled when Zeke flicks the reins and launches into his own tale.

"Been here since I was a boy." Zeke's words are liquid like tea and slippery like elm. Once again, someone new is speaking in colors and I am so distracted that I lose track of what he's saying.

". . . live out by the widow's cottage with my cousin Mercy, her chil-dren, and the chickens. Mercy's good with the needle like you"—Zeke nods at my cape, where the interior has fallen open to reveal the fanciful creatures I stitched beside the captain—"takes her wares down to the docks on market days."

I remember the Black woman with the white turban and high cheek-bones.

"I think I saw her yesterday." I hesitate and then come out with it. "Her work was unusual"—the S and the F, crossed like running figures—"almost magical."

He gives me a sidelong glance. "Could be her." His words get smaller so that they are tiny as ants. "But I don't know about any magic."

The bay is out of sight when Zeke turns his cart into a broad road lined with cottages and sail shops and shrubs that put me in mind of a hedgerow back home. The Salem air smells of pine and the briny sea, and shadows play upon our faces as we ride out of town and into the scrub. It is silent here but for the rattle of the wagon wheels.

"That's Mill Pond to the left," Zeke tells Edward. He waves away from the water, and my husband looks into the distance. "Up there is the old tar works and way beyond is Gallows Hill. Folks say sometimes you hear spirits moaning when the winds blow through the Witch Woods."

"Witch Woods?" I ask.

Zeke flicks his eyes onto me.

"Right—'course you don't know anything about that."

Although I struggle not to show any reaction, something must change in my face, for Zeke tips a hand to his cap and says, "Don't you worry about it, Mrs. Gamble. It's a thing done and gone."

I stay silent and keep myself focused on what is right here: the trees, my husband who has decided to go to sea, the color of the wind through the trees that hums in a faint melon orange.

THE WIDOW'S COTTAGE sits at the edge of a wooded grove and fronts a narrow yard surrounded by a crumbling timber fence. The house is whitewashed stone, with two windows and a Dutch door painted green.

The single-room cottage has the mustiness of a cupboard sealed shut for a long time. My husband inspects the large hearth while I pry open the shutters. Cobwebs stick to my hands and dust fills the air. The smell of earth and wet rocks enters with the wind when the first window pops open.

"It'll have to suit you," Edward says.

It does.

The isolation at the edge of the woods puts me in mind of the cottage where I was born. The silver silence is a kindly one, smoothed by the sky and the soft purr of insects and the quiet forest life. I feel at ease but for the thought of the Witch Woods and the moans of the dead in the wind. But Zeke said those things are done and gone, and I've made up my mind to ignore that talk.

Edward and Zeke pace off the perimeter of the cottage clearing while I unpack the trunk and wipe down our new hearth. I'm stacking books on a small table when Edward comes inside with the Black woman from the docks, and two children close behind. I guess the girl to be about five, the boy about nine years old.

"This is Mercy." Edward says. "The children are Ivy and Abraham."

Mercy's eyes are on the ground, but the two children peer up expectantly. I can see by the way the small ones look at Edward that he has been kind to them, and I am glad.

"They live up the rise, through those trees out back," he adds.

Mercy is wearing a colorful turban and a plain dress belted with a length of felt that is embroidered with a bright chain of flowers. The children stand just behind their mother, Ivy holding up the ends of her apron and Abraham leaning to one side holding a large bucket covered with burlap. His curly hair is tinged with a reddish hue and his face is freckled—the freckles don't seem right on Mercy's child, but there they are. A light line of freckles dots the girl's cheeks, too.

"I saw you in the market yesterday," I tell Mercy. Her cheekbones are wide, her lips full, and she holds herself like a rod, straight and narrow and strong. I'm happy for a neighbor who might be a friend, and right away I want to ask if she meant to stitch the words I saw in her work, but I restrain myself.

"Likely did." She still doesn't look at me. "I sell my pieces to have a little extra for the children."

"Mercy uses water from our well," Edward says. "She sends the children to fetch it, and in exchange they bring eggs and things from the garden."

With a tiny nod from her mother, Ivy steps forward and opens her apron. Inside are four brown-and-cream-colored eggs. I take one; it's still warm. Abraham takes a few steps in my direction and puts down the bucket. He tries to suppress a grin, but when I smile, he lets the grin light his face. I can tell that the children are happy and loved, and this warms me to Mercy.

"Goat's milk." There's pride in Mercy's voice. "Fresh this morning."

Behind her in the doorway, Zeke has taken off his hat and is holding it in his hands. He seems to be watching over Mercy and the children, and I wonder if he's also the children's father, for a cousin can also be a mate and there's affection in his eyes.

"I've never had goat's milk," I say.

"Same as sheep or cow." Mercy nods. "Boil it for curds or put it with oats or bread for supper."

I'm touched by this welcome, yet the woman still hasn't looked at me.

"The water is there for the taking," I tell her. "There's no need for you to bring me eggs and food." I mean this to be a gesture of friendship, but Mercy seems not to take it so.

"Then you don't agree?"

"Oh, but I agree very much—I mean to say that you can take all the water you need, and you need not give me anything in return."

"I do what's fair."

I have the feeling she could stand for hours in the wind and never falter, never bend.

"I'm grateful." I try again to show that I mean to be a friend. "I'm glad to have you as my neighbors."

Mercy puts a protective hand on the girl and blinks up at me at last.

"We won't be bothering you," she says, and I can see she intends to keep her distance. "The children come in the morning, fast and quiet as you please. The chickens and goats can't keep themselves."

As she gathers her brood, she sees my mother's gloves on top of our trunk.

"Pretty." She bends to look more closely at the beadwork and letters entwined with angels. "Beautiful work."

Her words shimmer when she says this. Perhaps it is not natural for a Scottish woman and a Black woman to become friends, but I'd like it to be so.

"My mother made them. She wore them on her wedding day, and I wore them on mine."

"The Silas girl's getting married this summer, you might show them to her mama," Mercy says. "They're special."

Her words are a kindness, and I reach toward them.

"Wouldn't you want the job for yourself? Your stitches are very fine, and your work is wonderfully intricate."

I want to say more, but she doesn't give me a chance.

"Got enough to keep me busy right here without it." At that she turns and walks up the hill with her children, who leave as quietly as they came. Zeke lingers a moment longer.

"We're up through those trees, on the other side of the low rise." He points to where the trees thicken. "In case you need anything."

WE SLEEP ON the floor that night, and the next day Edward purchases a slat bed and a large table. He hires Zeke, who helps carry the items into the house, talking all the while.

"You got a fine garden out back, Mrs. Gamble, just needs hoeing, weeding, and planting." Zeke wears a straw hat with a neat blue band around it and tips it back when he looks at me. "Wild blackberries in spring, orange squash in October. You plant a rainbow out here, you'll eat all year long."

"A rainbow?"

If he notices the word startles me, he gives no hint of it.

"Berries and plants in every color is the best way to grow a garden that makes you strong against sickness and bad spirits."

I follow him out back as he ticks off a long list of foods—yellow and green peppers, red rhubarb, purple potatoes—then roots out a rotted squash and pulls a few seeds from the soft flesh.

"Dry the seeds before you put them in the ground." He points to an old shed in the back of the lot. "Might be some tools in there," he adds before he and Edward head into town for supplies.

In the shed I unearth a hoe, a large old bucket, a rake and an ax, and a large cupboard littered with animal droppings. Mice rustle underfoot as I drag and push the heavy cupboard outside, where a finger through the crusted top reveals it's made of blond wood with a backboard of white- and blue-painted tiles. By the time Edward comes home I have cleaned up the piece and we lug it inside together, where it makes a fine centerpiece beside our hearth.

At last, we stoke the fire and eat our bread and beans as evening falls. In my mind I see Zeke's words in patterns of color—whether the colors are a curse or a gift I still can't say, but soon I'll be a woman alone and I must make use of what's mine.

When Edward begins to snore, I sketch out a design for a pillow with Zeke's very words—*Plant a rainbow*—and stitch it as the night bleeds dark outside my window. I make the letter *P* spring-grass green, *R* a deep orange, and the *W* a bright royal blue. This is how the letters appeared to me when I was a girl and how they appear again now—a rainbow across an ocean of time and space.

Scotland, 1662

A rope hangs from the gallows and a torch burns at the guard post. In the morning they will come for her.

At the sound of footsteps outside the prison door, Isobel Gowdie lifts her head from the straw. Her shaved hair has begun to grow in a jagged red halo around her scalp.

"Stop and say your name," the guard calls.

"'Tis John Gilbert."

Isobel stands on shaking legs. Her husband has come—she can scarce believe it. John is a good and sturdy man, but neither rich nor clever enough to bribe the guard and set her free. "You'll surely let a man say goodbye to his wife," he says loudly.

Isobel hears the sound like coin on metal—not at the front of the cell but at the rear. Her husband's voice drones on as a hand slips through the barred window at the back of the jail and hacks apart the wooden bars. The reverend's wife's face appears through a slot no larger than a small cupboard; an eye, a nose, a hand that waves for her through the dark.

Isobel hesitates. She knows Satan can take the shape of a cat or dog or even a man. But Forbes's wife is insistent, flapping her hand and hissing, "You don't have much time."

From the front of the jail she hears the guard shouting at her husband to "move on, you cannot be admitted." Gowdie is so thin she nearly melts through the space Margret Forbes has made for her.

"Run toward the full moon," Margret says as she presses a small bundle of food into Isobel's hands.

But Isobel knows better. She runs into the deep forest glens; she runs along the river and never looks back.

—— SEVEN ——

New Harmony
Now accepting cargo and investment
Sails **March 16, 1829**
to **BERMUDA** and **LIVERPOOL**
with stops in Ports of Baltimore and Charleston
Captain William Darling taking appointments at
Charter Ale House
noon on Mondays, Wednesdays, and Thursdays

It takes twelve days for the *New Harmony* cargo to be weighed, recorded, sold, and delivered. An advertisement is posted in the *Salem Gazette* and the captain and his first mate take meetings in the Charter Ale House with investors, traders, and manufacturers. Edward buys himself a new coat and a day dress for me, and each night he tells me about the goods the captain has added to the ledgers: English and Scottish linens, shoes made in Lynn, pottery and metal barrel staves manufactured in Marblehead and elsewhere in the Commonwealth of Massachusetts.

"Shoes are best." Edward leans back as I put a steaming plate of potatoes with goat's milk in front of him. "Light for their value and the space they use."

All week Edward tromps the Salem streets and calls on apothecaries, druggists, and doctors to raise capital for his own ventures. He speaks with new confidence about wooing investors and bargaining with merchants.

"They want cola leaf from Peru and cocaine from Mexico," he reports. "Americans are looking for medicines to protect them from the pox and other calamities, and I'll charm it from the slaves and savages."

Robust after a week on land, Captain Darling and Ingo spend two evenings at our table charting out their journey. The course will take them to Baltimore, then south to Virginia and on to Bermuda, across the Atlantic to Liverpool, and then back home to Salem.

"If all goes as planned, the *New Harmony* will return in July with a full hold and a good profit," Captain Darling says.

I consider warning him of what befell us at home but decide it's best for my husband to have this new opportunity. Captain Darling has sailed his ship to China and back more than once. Surely he's an excellent judge of character. It's my hope that he will bring out Edward's strength and set our lives on a true and right course.

Edward must see emotion in my face, for he takes my hand and touches his lips to my scar, all that's left of our first meeting.

"We'll have wealth and prosperity again," he says. The captain busies himself polishing his pocket watch. Ingo is quiet as always, his eyes watching.

"I hear of great tropical herbs and medicines in the islands," Edward goes on. "I'll bring back plants that are new and rare—riches for you and for our child."

The captain doesn't look in my direction and I'm thankful, for I've flushed to my scalp at the allusion to the pastime Edward enjoys each evening, while I lie back, staring over his shoulder, thinking of new uses for my needle and thread, and hoping for a child to take hold in me.

WHILE THE MEN draw up agreements and crews load the hold, I make our cottage snug with new yellow curtains, freshly whitewashed walls, and waxed floorboards. I, too, am making plans for myself in this new city. I've listened to the captain and learned some of the words and phrases of business: margin, profit, percentage. *What percentage will you give me? What margin will I ask, and what agreement can we strike that profits us both?*

The path to town is a little more than thirty minutes on foot, past the Mill Pond and hedgerow to the small bridge beyond Broad Street. I go whenever I'm able, for there's always some new notion to find, some new street to discover.

Salem is home to ten thousand people and is nothing like the teeming city of Glasgow. Glasgow was full of gray and brown stone buildings, brick factories, towering cathedrals, and a large park green that was often filled with workers protesting their pay or some other civic matter I had not heeded.

Here the people are quiet, and I do not see evidence of political agitation or the public drunkenness that could be found in the alleys back home even on a Sunday morning.

Along Derby Wharf, victual sellers and fishmongers ring their bells and shout out the day's offerings. A farmer pushes a cart piled with carrots, potatoes, and radishes—items I will grow in my small garden if I tend it right. Derby Street runs along the waterfront, and it is a place of wonder, with storehouses filled with pepper, coffee, cinnamon, cloves, nutmeg, ivory, dates, figs, and raisins sold from upturned kegs and barrels.

Even the heaps of trash and rotted vegetables, the fish innards pounced upon by wharf cats, and the mounds of horse manure mixed with hay at the edges of the brick road do not ruin the sense that the Americans are orderly and kind.

Twelve noon is the fashionable hour for calling in Salem—I deduce it by the ladies leisurely walking along Chestnut Street with intricate beaded and fringed camel-hair shawls draped over their shoulders. Some ladies sport fabulous leghorn bonnets decorated with plumes and flowers; a few wear black or white embroidered lace veils draped over their faces. In a milliner's shop on Essex Street, the window and cases are filled with handsome ribbons and veils that can be embroidered with delicate flowers on the scalloped edges; across the road is a genteel men's shop with a broad-coat and a waistcoat displayed upon a mannequin placed in the doorway.

To make up for my lack of training in dress- or pattern-making, I let the streets become my teacher. Servants' dresses are simple and crisp, while wealthy ladies' walking dresses are made of rich black silk.

Like women everywhere, the wealthy are dressing for one another. Their calling outfits are printed muslin and chintz, pink- and mauve-striped silks, and other dear fabrics that are sewn so that the wearer seems to float above the wooden sidewalks and glide effortlessly from carriage to parlor door. Against their simple dresses, some of the ladies wear shawls ornamented with fringes, beads, and flowered embroidery, each more elaborate than the next. Three ladies in dresses the color of tulips, with veils that match, turn a corner at the top of the street and enter a house where the doors seem to open magically for them.

Widow Higgins doesn't sneak up on me during any of my walks through town, and I am glad. And when I find myself looking about for Mr. Hathorne, I try to push him out of my mind as well. A handsome man who makes my tongue flatten against the roof of my mouth will not help me in my efforts. I must find inspiration, not flirtation. Yet I cannot deny that all of it—the colors, the designs I make in my sketchbook, the wind off the sea in Salem, the hope for another glance at Mr. Hathorne's smothered smile—intoxicates me. The promise of the New World feels within my grasp.

In a dry goods shop, I find a new ladies' magazine that features an illustration of two Boston women in fashionable walking costumes. Each wears a high skirt and a trim belted jacket, each carries a parasol and sports a wide-brimmed hat. Their skirts are narrow, their waistcoats made with intricate detail.

I haven't seen this narrow skirt fashion in Salem and decide that I will make one ball gown and model a second dress upon this fashion. I will use my gold to buy striped silk, muslin, chintz, lace, and brocade cotton. When I'm finished, I'll present a shop owner with a beautiful dress embroidered with orchids on the hem—orchids, the exotic flower that is traded for riches—and my finest decorative work on the sleeves, collar, and waistband. I'll ask him to display it in his shop, and then I'll do as the Widow Higgins suggested: take assignments. In time, I'll save up enough to open a shop of my own. The colors and pictures I've drawn and dreamt of since childhood will be embroidered upon my work. And what I learned from Auntie Aileen—hidden pockets, tricks to hide a limp or a lump, the dropped waist for a stout woman, and long buttons for a tall, skinny one—will one day be part of my trade.

There's a night when I think to tell all of this to Edward—I do not intend to ask his permission—but he's brought home a cask of rum and is sipping from a tin cup as he turns the pages of his thick reference book, murmuring to himself. *Clink*—I hear the cask against the cup. *Clink*. I know there is a point at which Edward will become drunk, but he will want more, and still more.

"Edward, I'll make you a cup of tea and we'll go to bed."

I let my dress drop, for having him hover above me with his rum breath is better than watching him empty the cask and keep me up through the night.

He pushes away his book and looks at me with a strange expression. I've never presented myself to him in this way and am afraid of what he'll say.

But he says nothing. He drains his cup, extinguishes the candle, and takes me to our bed. In the morning when he's left for town, I pull the cork from his rum and pour what remains into the ground.

THE THIRTEENTH OF March is a crisp and sunny Friday, just three days before the *New Harmony*'s scheduled departure. With basket and notebook in hand, chatelaine at my waist, and a gold piece in the pocket beneath my skirt, I walk into town with the happy task of assembling materials for a new dress.

The proprietor nods when I enter Blackwell's Store House on Essex Street, where two ladies are inquiring about velvet piping and trim to update a Sunday dress. The storehouse is brimming with trunks and crates stacked with fabrics and trays upon trays of buttons in every shape, size, and color. As I make my way toward a blue-gray cotton at the rear of the shop, I spy a man seated on a barrel tucked into a corner. He's writing in a notebook open in his lap, and he doesn't look up.

It is Nat Hathorne.

I step back to take my measure of him: dark hair combed rakishly behind his ears; long body folded at a strange angle so that he can bend over the page and write. Hunched in this way, he seems more vulnerable than he first appeared—vulnerable, yet still impenetrable. A man of letters and books, but also of yearning and mystery.

"Mrs. and Miss Hathorne, I'm sure we can find a suitable price," the proprietor says to the ladies.

Hathorne keeps his head bent, pencil moving. I run my hand over a pile of soft cloth and envy the haze of his concentration, the singularity of it. I think he must be a poet, for only a poet could be so lost in words on a page. As for the soft violet haze that seems to surround him, I've only seen such a haze once before, when Mam was working on a memorial sampler for her parents. Like Mam on that day, it seems the man is deep in his own enchanted world. I'd like to step into the enchantment with him, to be held in the flicker of light and shadow in his face.

When Blackwell says something to make the ladies laugh, Hathorne's pencil stops and he looks off to the right. My heart jolts and I fade to the back of the store, keeping out of his sight as the women pay for their goods and have them wrapped.

Only after the doorbell rings behind them do I let out a sigh and pull open a drawer full of buttons.

"Ladies do like their buttons."

It's him, his words a royal parade of faded red and gold. The room with its rich piles of colored cloth seems to spin slowly as my hand flutters over a tray of exotic buttons.

He's so close I can smell horses and fire on him. His clothes are those of a gentleman, worn but well cut. He's slung his long cape over his shoulders and it is too long and rich for the rest of his garb. I don't know if he's wearing the cape with some irony—knowing it's too grand—or if he thinks it suits him. Perhaps a bit of both, I think, for he has the bearing of a man who is aware of the dramatic figure he cuts.

He reaches for a scrimshaw ivory button carved with a delicate hibiscus flower.

"This one is exquisite." He holds out his hand, and I put out my open palm. His fingers are stained with black ink like my father's.

"I have an eye for beauty," he says. I keep my eyes on the button, and when he pours it from his hand into mine, I feel a current between us. "Though I don't often see it in such fine and exquisite form," he adds.

My throat is tight. I see hair on the backs of his knuckles, the worn cuff of his cotton coat.

"Where do you suppose it was made?" I ask.

"Ireland?"

Confused, I look up at last. His face is very pleasing, with a high forehead and deep-set eyes. There's nothing of the fire in them today. They're cool and penetrating, and behind that is something timid, I am sure of it. Yet he stands close. How much time passes as we look at one another I cannot say—perhaps it's the snap of two fingers. Perhaps it's a full stanza of poetry.

"I saw you get off the ship with your father," he says. "With your red hair and brogue, I guessed you must be an Irish girl."

He's mistaken me for a maiden without a husband. I have a choice, and I do not correct him.

"Scotland," I say. "Scottish, not Irish."

"Ah." He tips his head and indicates the trio of buttons. "If you admire exotic and enchanting things, you should visit the East India Marine Society Hall. Our ship captains collect treasures from around the world and bring them home to Salem—carved figurines, voodoo dolls, ornaments and costumes made of shells and coral."

Just then the store bell rings and one of his companions pokes her head through the doorway.

"Come along, Nat—Mother's waiting."

"Pardon my sister." He makes a funny little bow, and I can't see the expression on his face. "I hope you use the buttons for something splendid."

I find my voice as he spins away.

"And I hope you found a book at Mrs. Batchelder's shop," I call after him.

I'm still holding the scrimshaw hibiscus in my palm when the proprietor approaches. Although the price is dear, I buy all three buttons—one carved with a flower, one with a bird, and one with a boat. My first purchase for the dress I'm imagining.

I ARRIVE HOME to find Edward pacing the yard. Our garden plot is still thick with weeds and old dried leaves blown into piles through the winter. Edward hasn't bothered to pick up a hoe or a rake, although I lined them along the shed for just that purpose.

"It seems they don't trust foreigners here!" he shouts, as if he's been preparing all morning just to tell me this. "But I won't give up—I only need to interest one or two more investors to come back a rich man."

The button carved with a hibiscus flower still burns in my palm. It's proof of the words I spoke with Mr. Hathorne, the nearness of him, and I pocket it away quickly. Inside the cottage I wrap up my silver with the three remaining gold pieces and hide them beneath a stack of table linens in the deep back of my cupboard.

"I have a new idea for the elixir—" Edward bursts through the door. "I heard Ingo speaking of nests and branches, and I believe the brew he fed the captain was full of spiderwebs and herbs from the savages."

Long into the night Edward sits over his book, imagining new formulas made of plants that are found only in the tropics or the jungle islands. But all I can think of is Mr. Hathorne, the rustle of his cape, the purple haze that hung around him, the regal red and gold of his voice.

He assumed me a maiden, and I didn't correct him. Here in Salem I, too, can be someone new. I feel a possibility that brings the fast-beating excitement of colored voices, the pink wind, the hum of faeries beneath the May trees. Though the colors still frighten me, they have also begun to inspire.

CAPTAIN DARLING IS waiting beside the ship when Edward and I reach the dock on the morning of their departure. The captain's royal-blue jacket has been decorated with new brass buttons and yellow tassels on his epaulets. With his gaze upon me, I feel the sturdiness of his strength, the diligence of his guard.

"Don't tell me you repaired the jacket yourself?"

"Once it had your fine work on the cuffs, the jacket needed new trimming." Captain Darling winks, and I feel the familiar warmth of his presence. "I put on new velvet piping as well."

The captain takes my hands in his. This gesture is accompanied by the boom of a nearby sail catching the wind, and I see turquoise blue rimming the greens and browns of the landscape. I'm momentarily one with the colors of the earth until he releases my hands.

He's given me an envelope.

"A letter with my insignia and seal," Darling says. "Present it at the East India Marine Society Hall, where you'll find much to inspire your artistry. And if you're ever in trouble you can turn to Mr. Saul, who is custodian of the Hall," the captain says. "He's in my debt, and I am in yours, Mrs. Gamble."

"I won't forget." His kindness, his generosity, his goodness—all have saved me as much as I might have helped save him.

Edward puts his hands on my shoulders, and I look in his eyes for something to keep me resolute while he is gone.

"I'll return to you before summer ends, and we'll begin our new life together."

"Write to me of news and your safety," I say as the men climb the gangway.

I feel tears, but they're more for the captain than for my husband. Edward has pledged to return to me enriched, but Captain Darling found the cottage, he sent Mercy and her children with eggs and milk, and it's he who has given me his name and letter for protection.

The *New Harmony* stands alone in the locks for a good thirty minutes awaiting the captain's signal for release. A father in short breeches stops with his son to watch the launch, and I listen as he tells his son of a voyage he took long ago with his own father.

At last the captain shouts his command, the supports are knocked away one by one with a loud boom and splash, and for each there is a cheering from the little boy and a handful of others who've come to wave small American flags. Two brown-skinned girls in baker's smocks race to the waterfront at the last minute, pull off their aprons, and wave them toward the ship.

The boy's father greets the girls, and one reaches into an apron pocket and gives the little boy a large cookie.

"Thank Miss Remond," the father says as we watch the ropes tossed up and sails reeled out, and the boy does.

We all stand riveted as the *New Harmony* rises on the tide and then seems to drop a foot or more into the open water before it is swept into the winds. I watch the gray-and-white sea until the ship fades into the horizon. It is a strange feeling watching my husband sail away from me, for there is much to be wary of, alone in a new city. And yet if I am honest, I am not sorry to see him go. I pray that he will return a stronger and better man.

This very afternoon I write a letter to my pap. I tell him I've arrived safely in Salem, that his new wife and her babe are in my thoughts and prayers. I ask after my brother, Jamie, and say that Edward is well. I omit that I'm alone now. I say nothing about my ambitions, for they are my own and Pap is far away. I'll use his gold to make something of myself, and then I will tell him.

Salem is a wonderful, colorful city full of promise. I am grateful for all that you taught me and all that you gave me, Pap. Every night I pray for your health and happiness.

Your devoted daughter, Isobel

Salem, 1689

The Reverend Samuel Parris arrives from Boston with a Bible in one arm and a musket in the other, eager to take on his role as minister of Salem Village. The new meetinghouse with its smell of cut pine cheers Parris, but the refreshment of a new beginning fades as Major William Hathorne strides across sand and shale and welcomes him with grim pronouncements.

"Our Salem Village is under siege," Hathorne says. "We are fighting battles on two fronts—here, between neighbors, and in the northern territories where our families suffer horrors at the Indians' cruel hands."

Parris clutches his Bible as the major warns of savage Indians that perform black magic and voodoo to render the colonists' gunpowder and muskets impotent.

"My family has just become possessed of six thousand acres of Maine wilderness that the savages refuse to yield," Hathorne goes on. "We must seize what we've claimed and make our village a refuge for those brave families who return in need of respite."

Tituba, the Sea Island woman whom Parris brought north from Barbados, stands behind the men and listens with her eyes cast down. She hears authority and a tendency toward cruelty in Hathorne's voice, and she does not look up until a man comes to stand behind the major. This man has strong bare feet in leather sandals, fringed knee breeches made of animal skins. A torso that is naked and strong.

When Tituba looks up, John Indian is staring right at her, his slave sorrow and desire as plain as her own.

—— EIGHT ——

At the East India Marine Society Hall on Essex Street, life-size figures of a Chinese man and two foreign merchants greet me inside the entrance. The Chinese man wears a blue gown embroidered with a rich pattern of symbols and flowers, the first merchant wears a camel-hair scarf with fringes the length of a man's arm, and the second is dressed in a two-button smock and a queer little cap with a green tassel.

The colors are enchanting, the figures inviting. I've come in search of exotic inspiration, and it seems I have come to the right place. But then a voice booms, "Members and their guests only, I'm afraid," and a short man in knee breeches and brass-buckle shoes steps from between the life-size figures, breaking the spell.

"Are you Mr. Saul?"

"I am indeed." He is friendly, and when I hand him the note Captain Darling gave me only yesterday, he nearly whoops his welcome as he opens a large guest book for me to sign.

"You are in for a great adventure today, Mrs. Gamble," Mr. Saul says. "We have wonders, artifacts, souvenirs, memorabilia, and relics from around the world. You have the hall to yourself this morning," he adds, and directs me to a set of stairs.

I climb into a light-filled atrium of soaring windows and rows of glass display cases. The windows face sea and sky, and the air is per-fumed like the inside of one of Edward's most precious apothecary jars: musty, exotic, full of promise and something mysterious waiting to be discovered. It's been only a day since my husband left, but already I feel the freedom that my gold coins, my scrimshaw buttons, and my needle might bring if I'm careful and clever.

Soon I'm studying an African queen ant as big as a man's shoe, hu-man skulls decorated with colorful wooden beads, nose bones from the deep Congo, a healer's mask and a medicine rattle carved with what seem to be erotic symbols.

Each item is displayed with a hand-lettered card that identifies the captain or shipman who delivered it to the collection, along with the date. I find magenta silk lanterns from Shanghai brought by Captain Darling in 1826, a Japanese kimono brought by Captain Henry Silas aboard *Cleopatra's Barge* in 1820, and a packet of oversize seeds brought from the West Indies by one Captain Nathaniel Hathorne in 1803, when Hathorne would have been either a mere babe or just a twinkle in his mother's eye.

It strikes me that both Mr. Hathorne and Captain Darling thought I would like it here among the strange curiosities. They saw something in me—something odd, I suppose, but also something true. Something that longs for unusual and exotic enchantments.

The sun blasts through the windows, and it grows hot inside the hall. Since I'm alone, I take off my cape and drape it over a chair in a corner, loosen my bonnet, and remove my gloves. When that isn't enough, I open the knot at the top of my shirtwaist so that I might feel the cool air at the base of my throat.

I'm feeling refreshed when I come upon a beautiful canvas from Polynesia embroidered with beads and rope work, patched with bits of unfamiliar cloth in many patterns. A spotted leopard pads across the front of the canvas, large and ominous. In the water is the head of a giant eel—it seems to be poking out from the back edge of the canvas.

I feel the whole scene alive with the sounds of a crashing sea, rolling drums, women and children shouting on the shore, and the purr of the leopard like a song of danger.

The captain told me that banner weavers and embroiderers often design their work to be flown as flags or hung in windows where they're seen from all sides. This means the work has no secret stitches, not even one place for a mistake to be folded away. I must see for myself if the artist has made the leopard's body on the back of the canvas as it is on the front, as lifelike as a specimen found in a jungle paradise.

"Polynesia," I recall Captain Darling telling me, "rhymes with amnesia, because they say that when you visit that island, you forget everything else you ever loved."

Blinding sunlight floods through the windows. I peer over the staircase and see Mr. Saul bent over his ledger. I'm alone. I slip the tambour hook from my cape and use the sharp tip to pick open the locked cabinet door. It springs easily, and I'm able to slip my hand inside the case. The canvas hangs from a large metal pole. I hear only the pounding of my own heartbeat as I begin to lift up a corner of the piece. The canvas moves slowly. Only a few more inches and I'll be able to see the back and learn the secrets of stitching and design that were used in its creation.

There's a step behind me, and I freeze.

"I've always wanted to see the back of this piece."

It is Nat Hathorne. Again.

Has he followed me? I'm exhilarated and embarrassed to think he's been watching me among the display cases.

"You must be quiet," I whisper. Below, I hear the custodian cough and his keys jingle. "Please."

Hathorne nods. He's close beside me, all warmth and heat. I raise the tapestry high enough to see that the back stitches are the mirror inverse of the front, equally bold and vivid, alive in the canvas itself. Satisfied, I let the tapestry return to its place and hold my breath as the latch clicks shut. Then I quickly tie the knot in my shirtwaist and grab for my cape.

When I return the tambour hook to the hidden pocket, Mr. Hathorne's eyes dart to the colors and scenes in my cloak, the blue water and white-and-gray rocks, the red comet streaking across the Scottish skies.

"Halloo?" the custodian calls from the bottom of the stairway. "Mrs. Gamble? Mr. Hathorne?" His voice comes closer as he climbs the open staircase. "It is almost one o'clock, I'll be closing up shortly for the dinner hour."

Instinctively we move away from one another. When Mr. Saul reaches the landing, his face is flush.

"There you are," he says. "You're quiet as two church mice."

"Except no one is stealing the cheese." Hathorne's mouth twitches and I'm afraid that he'll laugh—or, worse, betray me.

"We'll have no stealing here," the custodian says without a hint of ill will. "Although we do have a good number of mice, I'm afraid. Got to be careful they're not nibbling at the treasures."

The custodian looks behind me in the general direction of the leopard tapestry.

"Is that your bonnet, Mrs. Gamble?"

I'm terrified that I've left behind some sign of my indiscretion, but when he smiles it's clear there's nothing amiss, and I snatch up my gloves and hurry down the stairs so I'm first out the door.

I'm RUSHING AWAY from the waterfront when Mr. Hathorne catches up with me. He's a good deal taller than I am, and easily matches my pace.

"Please wait." His voice is more pleading than commanding. I notice his worn boots, mud-splattered and old.

"Why are you following me?" I'm addled and embarrassed. I broke the rules, and he witnessed it.

"I believe it's I who should be questioning you," he says. "What did you intend to do with the tapestry?"

"I only wanted to see what was on the back of the material, to see how the work was done." My words are defensive, my fingers already tracing out the leopard and palm trees.

"Why?" He sounds more curious than angry.

"I'm a needlewoman and a dressmaker." If Edward is a doctor, then I'm a dressmaker.

"Then the scenes in the cape are your work?"

Once again, I've forgotten what my cape reveals. I try to hold it close, but I'm walking fast and it flaps open and shut, open and shut.

"Yes, they are."

"You wave your cape the way a lady at a party waves her fan—"

"I don't go to parties where ladies wave fans."

"Good Lord, nor do I." His exclamation is loud, almost funny. "Parlors and gatherings with cocktail napkins are enough to put me into a faint."

This makes me smile, and at the curve of my lips he leaps ahead of me. "Please slow down."

"We haven't been properly introduced," I say, but he puts an arm behind his waist and offers that charming gesture of a bow.

"Nathaniel Hathorne. Of the Salem Hathorne and Manning families."

His eyes from this angle are the color of honey in a glass jar.

"Why are you following me, Mr. Hathorne?"

"I'm the one who told you to visit the Marine Society," he says. "I go almost every day—I didn't follow you there—after all, it's a private place, how did you even get inside?"

"Captain Darling gave me a letter of introduction, but that's no matter. You're following me now." We lock eyes; he will not deny it. There is something in this exchange, some brightness that makes me feel buoyant. "And you stared at me on the wharf the day we arrived."

"You're a bold woman, Mrs. Gamble." He says it with some admiration, as if he assumes I've always been a woman who unlocks display cases with my sewing tool and speaks freely to handsome young men. "Especially bold for a newcomer whose husband has just gone off to sea."

I lose the rhythm of my step, for he has laid it clearly between us: I am a married woman and Edward is my husband, not my father. Mr. Hathorne doesn't say outright that I failed to correct him that day in Blackwell's shop. But I didn't, and he knows it.

"It's hard to keep secrets in Salem," he says, as if reading my thoughts. I cannot tell if he speaks with sympathy or if there is more to it. Either way, I understand that someone has been gossiping about me. I imagine Widow Higgins clucking at him on the street, and I tear at my fingernail, shredding off a good chunk of the cuticle.

A sharp pain yelps through me and I pop the bloody finger into my mouth.

"You're hurt." Something wolfish crosses his face as he produces a clean white handkerchief, tugs my finger gently from my mouth, and wraps the cloth around it.

I cannot bring myself to look at him. A bit of blood seeps through the cotton and we both watch the crimson spread.

"I've soiled your handkerchief."

"Don't worry, our house girl will clean it."

"No." I pull away my hand. "I'll do it myself."

He seems to consider my hair, my costume, even my shoes, which have just splashed through a muddy puddle.

"Despite your boldness and your temper, you're quite charming, Mrs. Gamble."

One expression of impatience and he says I have a temper! Why is it that men are not subject to the same quick judgments as women?

"If I have a temper, it's because you've drawn it out of me with your"—I struggle for the proper words—"your close observations—too close, sir, I might add."

I match his gaze with an intensity of my own.

"I suppose I owe you an explanation." He nods as if he has just decided something. "You see, Mrs. Gamble, with your red hair and sharp eyes, you are just like a girl I've been inventing."

"What do you mean by that?"

He peers at me with almost affectionate familiarity. I can still feel the warmth of his hand on mine, a trace of his breath on my neck.

"I write stories." A shrug tells me he is both proud and wary of his writing, as I am with my colors and needle. "I invent them, sometimes from history, sometimes from my dreams. I must invent the people in them, too."

"You're a writer."

"I try," he says. "I've been writing a story about a red-haired girl during the witchcraft delusion."

Again, the word *witch* startles me.

"What is the witchcraft delusion?"

We've come to a narrow alley lined with distilleries and coxswain shops. The bright sun has disappeared and there is a fog at the end of the street, rolling in from the sea. He looks around as if he doesn't want to be overheard. But there's no one within hearing distance.

"Some hundred and fifty years ago in this very city, fourteen women were hanged as witches."

In a few halting sentences he explains that schoolgirls came together to accuse old widows, new mothers, ministers, and even a young girl of witchcraft.

"The women were killed on the false accusations of a few hysterical girls and one Indian slave woman," he says.

"And what happens to the girl in your story?"

"I imagine her on Gallows Hill with the others."

My hand goes to my throat. I thought I'd left these tales of horror behind in Scotland.

"Did they hang a *child* here?"

A pair of men brush by us and pass into the alley. We step apart, our intimacy broken.

"Little Dorcas Good was arrested and charged with witchcraft. I've spent months reading through dusty courthouse records, but that's all I know of the child." He shakes his head and looks at the bloodied handkerchief still wrapped around my finger. "I can see I've upset you, Mrs. Gamble. I've spoken too freely and I'm sorry for it."

Before I can reply, he's bidden me a sudden good day and spun away down the street, his too-large cloak flapping like the wings of a bird.

ALL THE WAY home the skies threaten rain and my mind writhes with talk of the little red-haired girl, the witchcraft delusion, and the tapestry in the Marine Society Hall.

Rainclouds open as I near the cottage, and I run to my door. Inside, I go straight for pencil and paper so that I can record the leopard and the palm trees and everything else I can remember from the tapestry. Soon I have sketched a sea-colored dress decorated with red and gold. On the dress a leopard walks through a tropical thicket. The scene is one of powerful enchantment, equally frightful and mesmerizing, much like Mr. Hathorne himself.

Rain pounds outside as I draw the dress on a girl, then on a woman. The sketches are rough at first, but soon it's just as it happened on the ship, a cascade of colors and pictures pour out of me at once.

As evening falls, I calculate what it will cost to buy materials: four dollars for rich gray silk, two for trims, threads, and brocades. The scrimshaw buttons will be the finishing touch, one at each wrist and one at the neck.

I imagine Nat Hathorne admiring the dress on me. Admiring its boldness and the colors that match his voice. Putting a finger to a button at my wrist and then to one at my throat.

Scotland, 1663

Asleep beside a cold stream, Isobel Gowdie wakes to the sound of voices in the river rocks. Her aching hands are covered in mud and blood, and she remembers her tiny child coming as if in a dream, perfect and unmoving. She looks around for the watery grave but sees the white lights moving along the rocks and knows the wee faeries have come.

She stands and follows them, as she knows she must.

Dawn turns to day and to night, and for one full cycle of the moon she leaps from rock to rock, following the trill of faerie lights until at last, hungry and exhausted, she falls at the mouth of a wood hut and wakes at the feet of a crone.

The old woman's face is like the bark of an old tree. She patches Isobel's hands and coats her pinprick wounds in a thick ointment that smells of sap and ash. The crone feeds her bits of bird eggs in blue shells, broth made of turtle and frogs, and little by little Isobel grows stronger.

"Let me stay," Isobel says when she is healed. "I will do anything for you."

She has a new brown cloak on her shoulders and there is a ring of flowers around her forehead like a halo.

The old crone shakes her head. "You belong in the world of men," she says.

Isobel stands beside the tree that was her home and refuge for many months. She does not want to leave it.

"The world of men doesn't want me."

The crone puts a hand upon Isobel's crowned head.

"You will give birth to a line of strong women who will carry your seed across the oceans and join with others who live for freedom."

"It cannot be." Isobel bows her head and clasps her womb.

"And yet I have already seen it," the crone tells her with a soft smile. "You must fly from the nest, little faerie child."

— NINE —

By morning the rain has stopped. I prepare a basket, review my list, decide where I will go and how I will bargain for silk and threads. One of Pap's gold pieces should bring me eight or nine dollars—more than enough to buy what I need.

I'm distracted and excited and cannot readily put my fingers on the coins. I kneel down and reach farther into the back of the yellow cupboard, where I find the welt of wool in which I hid them.

The wool is folded upon nothing but itself.

I pull everything out of the cupboard.

I search the wax cloth, the tarp pieces, the lace from home.

Perhaps I'm going mad. I think back over my steps the week prior: buying the buttons, bringing them home, hiding my money in a bit of cloth. I put the silver and gold together and stored them away in the cupboard. A few minutes later, Edward came into the cottage.

He was frustrated when he went out to meet Salem's apothecaries and druggists. He complained that they didn't understand his ambitions and didn't like foreigners. But later that very day he stopped complaining.

All of my money—the silver change from the buttons, the gold pieces from my father—was wrapped in the same bit of cloth I hid away in the cupboard. I remember it clearly.

Now it's all gone. And there's only one reasonable explanation.

∞

I WASN'T ANGRY when Mam told me to hide my colors or when Pap put me to work. I wasn't angry when Edward forbade me to make a banner for the shoemaker. Even when he lost the shop and we were sent to the poorhouse, I was more despairing than angry.

Now my rage is fuel and fire.

I pull everything from the shelves, spill out Edward's formulas and papers, kick away his old Sunday coat—the filthy coat of a thief, I would never reuse a single thread—and throw it all into the hearth, strike a match, and watch it burn.

When everything's reduced to ash, I wash my hands and face and take stock of what I have. Silk thread. Scrimshaw buttons. My sketches. Needle and sewing tools. Three embroidery hoops. Edward's fat apothecary book that might still be of use. A sharp stiletto, a thick, long canvas needle from the captain. Scissors. My dress embroidered with flowers. The red cape. My mother's gloves.

Well water. A yard for a garden.

"Plant a rainbow," Zeke said.

IT'S ONLY A short way up the rise to Zeke and Mercy's place, and I stomp and slide through the mud in my haste. My hands are still shaking and I am splattered with dirt when I enter the yard. Chickens are clucking and goats bleating. Zeke's cart is on the gravel. There's no sign of the children.

The plot is less a farm than a small clearing with three low huts tilted against a central brick chimney. The yard is filled with chickens—white, brown, orange tailed, perhaps thirty of them pecking and fussing. Trees overhang the dirt, branches greening with leaves and buds. Behind the huts are two rows of chicken coops cobbled out of wire and old crates. They lean together in a maze of straw and wood. Mint and what looks like pennyroyal are sprouting at the edge of the dirt, glistening with last night's rain.

Mercy steps into the yard, wiping her hands on an apron. She's in a gray work smock and her arms are bare. The chickens peck and chatter at her feet, and I remember the rats rummaging under my skirts at the poorhouse.

"What do you want?" She makes no attempt at niceties.

I nearly tell her that Edward has stolen my gold, but at the last moment I bite my tongue. Secrets aren't easily kept in Salem, and I don't want the whole town knowing my husband is a thief.

"I've been robbed, and—"

"Nobody here robbed you." She raises her chin.

"I don't suspect you—it's just that I hid my gold and it's been taken."

Mercy's eyes are hard on mine. She means for me to know that no one in her family is a thief.

"Your husband went around looking for investors. Talking about an elixir of life and other notions that drive men to greed. I put the blame on him if I have to guess." I don't confirm her suspicion, nor do I deny it.

"All I know is that I must have a way to eat and earn my keep. I have no family here, and now I have no money."

I stop at the sound of a footfall on the path. It's Zeke. He's carrying a heavy feed sack on his shoulder as easily as I might carry a bit of cloth.

"We don't get many visitors this way." He looks at me from head to toe. He doesn't seem happy to see me either.

Mercy juts her chin at me. "I got squash and melon seeds for planting. Still early enough for pole beans. You plant them on your land where the light is good and you can have half of what you grow."

"Half?"

"You got money for seeds?"

"No." I can smell the singe of Edward's burning papers in the air.

"Then you'll pay me back in food or coin, whichever you choose is no matter to me."

It is a start, and more than she owes me. I agree.

"Is that pennyroyal in your yard?" I ask.

She crosses her arms. "What do you know of it?"

"My husband is an apothecary. I have his reference book in my cottage. I think it's used to make salves for cuts, burns, and rashes."

I don't say I've noticed the cuts and scratches on her arms from farmwork and chickens, but I know the salve will be useful to her.

She nods. "You take some and make an ointment for me, that's fine."

I HAVEN'T WORKED in the dirt since I was a girl. At first it's hard lifting the soil and laying in seed, but when Zeke comes with his hoe the work goes more easily.

"The soil's hungry," Zeke says.

"For what?"

"Chicken scat. Ash. Eggshells. You work them into the dirt—I got plenty in my coops."

He trudges up to his clearing and carries back a foul-smelling bucket, which he dumps and works into the wet ground.

By afternoon we've planted two rows of squash and pole beans and I am covered in mud. The one o'clock dinner bell in the distance reminds me I haven't eaten since yesterday morning, but then sweet Ivy comes down the rise carrying half a stewed chicken for our dinner. She holds the pot on her shoulder the way Zeke carried the feedbag, and despite the mud, her dress is clean.

"Mama says you're hungry." The color of Ivy's words are soft melon—round and almost fragrant, stoked with deep green.

She dips bread into the gravy and gives it to Zeke. We eat standing, without talking, and I realize it's the first meal I've shared with anyone since Edward left.

When we finish, I send the two of them back to Mercy with my thanks, and vow that I'll make something pretty for Ivy. I stir the ashes of Edward's burnt clothes in the hearth and pour them into the garden soil. Ashes to ashes, they will feed the seeds. It feels like witchcraft, but I don't regret what I've done. And when my bleeding comes later, so that I know I do not carry Edward's child, I do not terribly regret that, either.

IN THE MORNING I put on my iris dress and go directly into town. It's too cold to wear anything but my red cape; I tie it about my shoulders, fasten the hook across the bosom, and tuck my mother's wedding gloves into my basket. If there's no gold to buy yards of fabric and embellishments for fancy dresses, then my plan must be to decorate something smaller and much more affordable.

I pass the stagecoach office and stables, and a print shop and storefront for the *Salem Gazette*. The stagecoach offices are empty, but the *Gazette* is lively. Shoeless boys wait on the boardwalk out front, and a man comes out with a stack of newspapers piled in his arms.

I fish two precious pennies from my basket and trade them for a copy of the warm paper.

On the front is a poem by Percy Shelley and below it a silly poem about a girl named Charline and her beau, Tom. Inside are half a dozen pages of advertisements for everything from French muslin capes and collars to British ginghams, leghorn bonnets, broadcloths, cashmeres, buttons, handkerchiefs, cravats, black Italian crepe fabric, and more.

I note three shops that advertise fine clothes of silk and wool and another two that have just gotten in a shipment of gloves. Then I set off.

At the door marked *Mr. Isaac Newhall, Importer and Proprietor*, I climb a narrow set of stairs into a room filled with piles of fabric, crates of books, paper, kitchen supplies, tools, and many unusual knickknacks I've never seen or imagined. A tall, ghostly man in steel spectacles is writing in his ledger book.

"Good day. Would you be Mr. Isaac Newhall?"

He seems to stretch himself two inches taller before he speaks.

"Who is asking?"

I rush to answer before I lose my nerve.

"My name is Isobel Gamble, and I wish to embroider two pair of gloves for your shop. My work is exceptionally fine, sir. You may see it and decide for yourself."

Newhall is scowling.

"Women in Salem do their own needlework," he nearly shouts, his pale face coloring. "The days of foreign opportunists in Salem have been gone since the embargo."

He lifts an arm as if to sweep me out of his store, and I cower away.

"If you need work, look to the fabric mills in Lowell," Newell yells as I reach the bottom of the stairs. "They take plenty of your kind."

In a flash I smell the dust of the Glasgow factory, feel the dark of the long hall where girls as small as Ivy trudge between the machines to change and reel the bobbins. Nat's warning about judgment in Salem echoes as I go.

Across the way at Chaise & Harness, a fair and pretty woman tells me she has no use for my skills or services. She has a child in a cradle beside the hearth and milk stains on her shirtwaist. The young mother—or perhaps she is a wet nurse, I cannot be sure—has enough goodwill to suggest I call on the Cranford sisters, who work up past High Street in the direction of Marblehead.

"They often supply gentlemen with gloves for fine occasions," she says. "And you might try Mr. Remond at Hamilton Hall—sometimes he takes a chance with outsiders like yourself."

The Cranford shop is in a house with two large windows, one displaying a handsome black day dress, the other a gown made with cabbage-rose damask and a sweetheart neckline. The shop smells of newly cut cloth and a steaming iron press. The interior is clean and fine, with a form for fitting in one corner and a millinery selection of bonnets and caps with feathers, flowers, and colorful netting.

A servant girl is sitting on a stool working a bit of white cloth in an embroidery hoop. Her thick yellow curls are pinned into a white maid's cap, and she smiles when I enter.

"The ladies are busy, but you may wait." She has a strong Irish lilt, and her words are green as the great meadows. "I'm with Mrs. Silas," she adds. "I'm her lady's maid."

I take a seat opposite her on a small tufted bench.

"I'm in no hurry," I say.

The girl's face lights.

"You're a Scot! Where are you from? What's your name?" Before I can answer, she rushes on. "I'm Nell—come from Cork County in Ireland with my aunt and cousin six years ago. They've gone to Philadelphia, but I'm happy with the Silas family and I've got a beau—a dairyman. Stephen's the reason I stayed."

When she finally stops to breathe, I tell her my name and that I'm new to Salem.

"I'm living at the Widow Higgins's cottage. I have a husband and he is already at sea."

"There are lots of sailor's widows in Salem," Nell says. "The wives who get along best are busy with home and children—then there's no lonely time."

From the neighboring room, the imperious voice of the shop mistress rises. She's directing an assistant to pin, crimp, measure, and record. I imagine the silent girl on her knees with pins in her mouth.

"Would your Mrs. Silas be the wife of Captain Henry Silas?" I ask. I've heard Silas is one of the wealthiest men in Salem.

"The very one." Nell seems proud. "You don't need to be long in town before you hear the Silas name and remember it if you're clever."

She picks up a needle and hoop and shows me where she's working the letters *HH* in a blue thread that fades from dark to light.

"Mrs. Silas lets me make napkins for Mr. Remond at Hamilton Hall," she says. "He's in need of two hundred napkins and table coverings for the Light Infantry banquet in October. 'Tis a good way to make extra coin if you're of a mind."

There's a bustle of activity behind the curtain door, and the dressmaker speaks in a strained voice.

"A Sunday dress without a corset isn't advised."

"Then I'll order one to fit with a corset and one without." Mrs. Silas's tone is sharp. "And a third for my daughter's trousseau. Charlotte's measurements are quite as mine, you know."

"Very well," the proprietress says. There's something coy about her words that I don't like. "And how is Miss Charlotte enjoying the Middle West?"

"She's faring well," Mrs. Silas answers. "They've extended the trip by another month to see Indians bring out their kayaks in the spring."

Talk behind the curtain gives way to the rustle of fabric, and Nell turns to me.

"Are you here to have a dress made?"

"Goodness, no. I'm here with an inquiry for the mistress of the shop."

I take my mother's gloves from my basket, and Nell admires the work.

"The details are wonderful," she says. It's the first time I've spoken to a friendly woman my own age since I left home, and I feel trustful enough to open up my cloak.

"This is all done by my hand." I make sure that only the cottage and the woodlands and the journey across the sea are on display for her. As Nell exclaims over the swirl of water and the shape of the ship, a handsome lady with steel-gray hair and milky skin sweeps through the curtain.

"I am Miss Cranford. Let me see your work."

I jump up and hold out the cloak. She runs her hands across the stitching before she even looks at it. This is a woman who knows the feel of a seam as it should be, the proper tightness in a stitch, and how to tell a straight and square piece of work simply by holding it.

When she looks at the figures I've sewn, a silence descends. She opens the cape fully and studies Isobel Gowdie and the red star streaking across the sky.

"Where did you come from?" Miss Cranford demands.

"Scotland. I arrived two weeks ago on the *New Harmony* with Captain William Darling. My husband is an apothecary—a doctor."

She shoves the cape into my hands, steps to the door, and opens it.

"Good day to you," she says. All eyes are on me. "Be on your way now," she adds.

I leave in a jumble of confusion and shame and firmly vow to keep my cloak and my secrets at home from now on, where they cannot be judged.

I am only a few steps away when Nell calls after me.

"Wait!"

She has run from the shop, yellow curls bouncing free of the pinned white cap.

"Not everyone is so wicked to us," she says, bounding up to me.

"Us?"

"Lasses from Ireland and Scotland. Newcomers. Outsiders."

"But this is the New World—isn't everyone new here?"

"Not if your family has been here for generations. Salem is an old, odd place, not welcoming to outsiders." She tries to tuck her wild curls back into place. "But I'm very glad you're here. Come see me at the Silas house—knock at the kitchen door and ask for Nell."

∞

FELICITY ADAMS'S PIECE goods shop is located in a ten-by-ten hut that's been expanded into an alley off Essex Street. There's a bolt of black silk in the window, and the woman who looks up when I enter has a round, smooth face that reminds me of the moon.

"Good morning to you," she says. "How may I help?"

"I'm told you are in need of a stitcher." I try to take the thick brogue out of my tongue and curtsy. "And I'd like to apply for the position."

I see the woman hesitate and quickly say what I preferred to avoid.

"The Widow Higgins sent me. She said I am skilled."

Mrs. Adams is neither friendly nor hostile, merely all business.

"Show me these skills."

I turn my back as I remove my cape and fold it onto the bench, then stand to show her the details on my dress and the stitching in the hem and petticoats. I talk about my aunt's shop in Baggar as if I were there only a few short months ago—it's not entirely honest, but I must do what I can to find a foothold in Salem.

"Ladies come from as far as Boston for my dresses," Mrs. Adams says. "Discretion is just as important as careful tailoring."

"It's what I taught myself above all," I tell her. "Discretion and the ability to conceal a woman's imperfections."

Soon we've agreed that I'll be a stitcher and a pinner, and if she's in great need I may also serve as a cutter. For my labor I will be paid a modest wage of ten pence for an afternoon, twenty for a day.

"One more thing, if I may."

I show her my mother's gloves and the lady listens to my proposal. Then she gives me three pair of unadorned gloves.

"You're correct, Mrs. Gamble, men and ladies will want new decorative gloves for the Light Infantry banquet. They won't think of it until the heat breaks, but we must have a longer plan."

I'm pleased that I've already begun to think as the proprietress of a shop might.

"I'll bring them to you when I've finished all three pair," I say.

"I'd like them by April first." Her sharp tone takes me by surprise.

"I'll need a little more time," I stammer.

"April third and no later," she says. "Bring me a selection then."

"Yes, ma'am. You may decide for yourself which are worthy."

"There is no question—I will take only the best."

As I AMBLE along Essex Street, my burden feels lighter and it seems the sun is shining for the first time in days. I've walked only a short way when I pass the Manning stagecoach offices and then Nat Hathorne himself is in front of me, hands shoved into his pockets.

"What brings you this way, Mrs. Gamble?" He's shy but cheerful. Whatever sent him reeling away when we last parted is gone now.

"I've just taken a position at Felicity Adams's shop," I tell him, but what I really want to say is that my husband is a wretch; he stole my gold and forced me to take up labor for pennies.

"That is a good bit of news." He points a thumb behind him toward the office and stables, from which there is the distinct odor of manure. "I help here with the books and horses."

The stagecoach belongs to his uncles, Nat says. "My mother's brothers, a funny lot of fellows," he adds with good humor—and I tell him I'm to be a stitcher for Mrs. Adams.

"But you're a dressmaker." He remembers. "Has she seen what you can do?"

"I'll decorate gloves for her, too." I rush to say it, for I don't want him to pity me. I don't want folks knowing I'm in a precarious situation. "I hope to do much more one day. But the gloves are a quiet agreement— you mustn't speak of it, even if it is hard to keep a secret here."

He tips his head in that way he does, as if studying something that only he can see.

"I can keep secrets," he says.

I stare back until he gives the slightest squirm. His hands, I notice, are splattered with blue ink today.

"And what about your writing—have you finished your story about the poor red-haired girl? I hope you've decided to let her live."

He gives a glance toward the stagecoach office and begins to walk alongside me.

"I've put it aside and finished a strange little tale of an old married couple instead." He leans closer as we thread through the street. "I've sent it to an editor in New York who's reading two other stories of mine this week."

His eyes are shining now, a moonlight glow to match the red and gold of his words. "And Mrs. Gamble, I'll ask you to please keep my confidence as well."

"But when the stories are published, your secret will be out."

"No." He shakes his head. "I publish anonymously—no one knows they're mine."

"Ah, like Walter Scott."

"You've read Scott?" I'm pleased by the expression on Hathorne's face—as if I'm a prize student and he's just discovered that I can do sums in my head.

"I spent many evenings with his stories back home, long before we knew he'd written them."

"And who's your favorite of his heroes?"

He's testing me, but I don't mind. I'm more grateful than ever for the hours Pap spent teaching me to read.

"I always loved Rebecca," I say. Rebecca is a healer who's tried for witchcraft in *Ivanhoe*; I dare to say her name and put the subject of witchcraft squarely between us again. "But Ivanhoe saves her, and so he's my favorite hero."

Nat gazes at me as if I'm a puzzle he wants to understand. And he is the same: puzzle and intrigue. Handsome, too. There's a small chip on his front tooth I never noticed before, and he flicks his tongue upon it.

"Ivanhoe is grand and brave," he agrees. "If I could write a book about a noble knight, I'd do it. But my stories are dark and sometimes tragic." He pauses, considering me. "Bloody, even."

He glances at my hands and I'm thankful for the gloves covering my torn cuticle.

"Your handkerchief is clean," I tell him. "I'll bring it to you now that I know where you are."

We turn onto the wharf street and he bends again so that only I can hear.

"Would it be an imposition to ask you to stitch some decoration on the handkerchief for me? My sisters don't take to needlework, and I have no one else."

I've read enough of Scott's romances to know that a knight who asks a lady for a token of herself—a lock of hair, a snippet of her lace, a sample of her needle—is wooing her. I know I should put him off. Yet I've been lonely here, and no man has ever spoken to me with such intelligence and curiosity. There is something of a fallen nobleman in him, some yearning that strikes a tender chord in me.

"Perhaps a monogram of your initials?" I offer.

His face lights.

"And a sprig of hawthorn blossoms?"

I laugh at his invention. "There's no flower with a name so close to your own!"

He pushes his hair behind his ears and describes a low, wide tree with curled, gnarled branches. "In England I believe they call it the May tree—"

"We have the May tree in Scotland," I blurt out. "It's where they say the faeries live."

"Here we call it the hawthorn tree." He pauses and waves his fingers across his eyes, then recites from memory: "'How sweetly bloom'd the gay, green birk, / How rich the hawthorn's blossom.'" He gives a funny wave. "Your own Robert Burns wrote about it in the poem he calls 'Highland Mary.'"

"My pap said the May tree is magical—if you fall asleep beside it you might wake in the world of enchantment and never get back to your life," I offer.

"There's a tale like that about our May trees in Salem—they say if you wander off the path beside them you can be lost for days in a world of enchantments." He seems to lose himself, but then he blinks and his face clears. "You know, that's what I strive after. To live only in my imagination, only in a magical world."

We've reached Water Street, and the wind blows salty tears into my eyes.

"But the faerie world isn't for men." I remember my pap's warnings. "Faeries and demons are jealous creatures. One can become dangerously lost in their enchantments."

"Perhaps," he says. "And yet I'm ever trying to get there and stay as long as I can."

We stop at a little bridge near the top of Mill Pond.

"I daresay the Scottish wish for enchantments, too, Mrs. Gamble. Isn't that why you weave magical creatures into your clothing and make little amulets to carry in your pockets?"

"Not I." I am quick to deny it, although I have ever been drawn to the world of enchantments. "I carry a needle in my pocket. My imagination is practical."

"Well then, will you put your practical imagination to my cause? Will you stitch my initials?" He smiles, and I can't help but smile back. "And the hawthorn blossoms, too?"

There is so much I want to ask about the magical world he seeks and the things that happened here in Salem. And about him. There is much I want to know about him.

I tip my head, not trusting myself to speak.

"Then it's agreed." He points off toward a ring of gray rocks that stand near the sea like sentinels. "Sometimes I sit there with my notebook. Maybe I'll see you here one day with your needle?"

The prince has invited me to sit with him beside the sea. I imagine a trident, a gold crown, the faded vestment of his cloak around me. All of it enchanted and enchanting.

AT HOME I search through Edward's book of medicine and plants and find, at last, a reference to the May tree, also called the hawthorn flower, also called the thornbush, belonging to the same Latin family as the traditional rosebush.

I run my finger along the thin tissue page and hold a candle to light the words.

A tincture of hawthorn may be useful in healing a broken heart.

What magical beings brought this man to me the very same week I learned that Edward stole my gold? I was never a woman with a temper until now, and somehow that rage and anger has brought me from that moment to this one; from Edward's betrayal to Nat's invitation.

I prop open the book to the hawthorn illustration and sketch it into my notebook beside his initials. *N*, a red letter. *H*, a copper yellow. I bind his handkerchief in my embroidery hoop and begin with white and pale greens for the hawthorn flower.

My colors are blossoming, and with them I've found a new power in my needle. Is it witchcraft? A mere trick of light? A strange dream that stays even when I'm awake?

I can no more vanquish the colors than summon them. Sometimes they're bold and light, as the captain's words that hung upon the sea like white and blue clouds; other times they're dense like the faded robe and crown of Nat Hathorne's words. Some voices are subtle, the soft and slippery melon pink and green—Ivy—or rich, like plump elderberry and plum fruit—Mercy.

They aren't solid and hung in the air overhead like a rainbow, yet they're more tangible than a fleeting thought or memory. Here in Salem, my colors help me to see what I might otherwise miss: the delight of yellow and red flowers beside a patch of lavender, the power of a leopard marching across a gray silk dress. The heart-healing hawthorn flower stitched upon a white handkerchief with a tiny red *A*, for Abington. The intrigue of Nat Hathorne's words lined up like a row of crowns.

It's LONG PAST midnight when I finish my work. The branch of flowers is curled around Nat's monogram like two hands holding a heart. Perhaps it's too much, yet it's exactly as I intended.

As I take the pins out of my hair, I think about Nat's story of the red-haired girl, about the May trees and the Witch Woods where Zeke said the winds howl with long-ago cries. Holding a spoon to catch the light, I study small pieces of my reflection—an eye, my lips, the hair that curls along my cheek.

I am changing. I'm alone here, but my colors are everywhere now and they have become a new and strange kind of company. Until today it never occurred to me that a person might want to be lost in an enchantment. It never occurred to me that I need not hide from the visions that feel beyond my control—that instead, I might surrender to them.

Perhaps I will dare to go with Nat into the world where stories offer an escape. Perhaps I may even offer my own enchantments in return.

Scotland, 1673

Isobel's new husband is a cottar who pays in eggs and potatoes for what he needs. Their three sons are born easily, but this fourth birth is full of blood and screaming, and Gille is so frightened, and the boys so atremble, that he sends for help.

Night is creeping toward dawn when the midwife holds a lamp between Isobel's legs and sees wet and struggle—and the marks made by the witch-pricker years ago. Isobel has told Gille they are scars from the pox, but the midwife has heard of the Highland red-haired woman who endured the witch-pricker and then escaped, and she knows what she sees.

Using strong hands, a fat wooden spoon, and a pot of lotion, the midwife coaxes the child into the world, cleans the blood, and hands the swaddled bundle to Isobel. There is a flash at the window and Isobel sees the bright tail of a shooting star. She hears the whistle of wet wood in the hearth like a scream.

"The girl has flaming red hair," the midwife whispers, her words like silver mercury in a glass. "Like yourns. Whatever you done before, you must be sure nigh you or the child do it again."

All year, and the next, and the one after that, Isobel keeps the girl at her bosom. Twice as long as the boys. For she knows the price of enchantment and salvation must be paid again and again, and she knows the sprites who saved her wanted nothing less than her first sweet girl-child. She has seen it all, the cruel greed of men and faeries, and she wants only to live in her cottage and keep the lamplight on and hold her family close.

—— TEN ——

My first days at the shop are full of measuring, pinning, kneeling, and sweeping the hearth beside Abigail, the shop cutter. Mrs. Adams is curt with us and charming with her customers even when they splatter spring mud on her floors, and I learn to anticipate her abrupt mood changes when one of the city's wealthier wives enters.

To avoid unfriendly questions about my brogue, I speak as little as possible and listen as Salem ladies talk of society and imported fabrics, London fashions, and the British embargo that stifled the city's prosperity in the second war with the English. Two sisters trade ugly whispers about a Quaker girl their brother fancies, another bemoans that Mrs. Spencer has raised the price of her Gibraltar candies two pennies, and mothers and daughters argue over the cost of their new costumes for the Salem Light Infantry banquet to be held at Hamilton Hall at the end of October.

"Whigs and Democrats had best get along at the banquet his year," Mrs. Adams announces one afternoon when the shop is empty. "For no matter a father's politics, daughters are in need of husbands."

While gossip and fashion make up most of what I hear at the shop, there is universal delight for the fine foods Mr. Remond—a Colored caterer from the islands, they call him, who is also a skilled oysterman, a food importer, and a cook known for outstanding turtle soup—will serve for the banquet. Mr. Remond is a very successful man, unusual for someone of his race, I've gathered, and I am alert to his name whenever it is mentioned.

"Don't forget Mrs. Remond's cakes," Mrs. Adams reminds a customer. "You'll have to leave room for her rich desserts at the end of the night."

I listen closely, but the gossiping ladies say nothing about Nat Hathorne or his family, though I do learn that Nat's uncle Robert Manning has planted ten more prize-winning stone fruit trees in his garden.

"Manning's prices are outrageous," plump Mrs. Williams says as she stands before the looking glass and admires herself in a new blue day dress. "But I like a freshly picked juicy plum and my husband is not so clever to plant a tree himself."

I AM NOT lonely without Edward, as I once feared I might be. Whether there is bitter March rain or weak sun, I wake each morning thinking of Nat—and each day I put his finished handkerchief in my basket and tromp through wet streets hoping to see him again.

More than a week has passed before he finally steps onto Derby Square as I enter from the south. His attention is elsewhere, and I reach his side without his notice.

"Good morning, sir. What occupies your thoughts so deeply?"

I hope that he'll turn to me in delight. Instead, he is ghost-eyed and his face looks bruised with lack of sleep.

"Ah, Mrs. Gamble." We fall into step together. "I'm afraid you've caught me brooding."

"Is it your writing?" I'm relieved when he nods, for the moment I asked, I realized he might be troubled by a romance in town that would make my beguilement ridiculous.

"The publisher turned down those first two stories—said he wants something truly American." Nat keeps his voice low as we turn off the square toward the South Bridge. There are more people here, but they're shipmen and crew, strangers who take no notice of us.

"And what is truly American?" I wonder aloud. Before we arrived, I thought the New World was made by and for new people. But here in Salem it seems there is a long requisite of what a person must do, say, and be, in order to be *truly* American.

"The struggle for democracy is what he's looking for," Nat says. "He says everything I need to tell about America's triumph over tyranny is right here in New England. I've got a new idea—stories within a story, a lost manuscript, and something told in a grandfather's chair—tales that have both the ring of truth and the spirit of magic, if I can do it."

"Truth and triumph seem easy enough." I mean to encourage him. "And easier than the witch trials or magic, I'd guess."

He stops at the top of Fish Street, where men are already laying out nets with the morning's silvery catches.

"But truth and triumph aren't what I'm after," Nat says. "What's true is often hidden from sight—religious fervor disguises cruelty, dark desires hide behind a mask of conformity."

Yes, I want to say, I'm very aware that the truth is too often concealed by good manners and a masked face.

"Why not write of goodness?" I ask. "Surely there's also true goodness in Salem, and I imagine it's far easier to write than darkness."

He scowls.

"Goodness doesn't make exciting stories. It's not like needlework, where pleasantry is the goal."

His words sting.

"There's more to dressmaking and needlework than pleasantry." My voice is sharper than I intend. "Every woman has secrets, and it's the dressmaker's job to keep them—to use her skills to make an unattractive woman beautiful or a plump woman appear neat and trim. To hide what might otherwise bring mockery or shame."

That familiar half-smile tugs at his mouth, nearly lifting away the furrow in his brow.

"You always intrigue me, Mrs. Gamble."

His words unnerve me further.

"I only mean for you to see that the needle is artistry, too," I say. "There's struggle in my work as well."

"I'll admit the domestic arts have merit," he says. "But what secret struggles women have, I can only guess at."

I reach into my basket for his folded handkerchief and press it into his hand.

"I've done as you asked and stitched your initials and the flowers on your handkerchief. I hope you find them pleasant," I say. He looks at me as if he knows I have secrets—but if he thinks I'm going to share more with him now, he's wrong. "And now, sir, I'm off to the shop."

"Wait," he calls, but I toggle around a woman with a cart and walk away just as abruptly as he left me on the distillery alley, for he has stung me more than I care for him to know. Then again, there's his smile, his expression. *You intrigue me.* No man has ever paid me a more compelling compliment or gazed at me with so much wonder.

"I saw you this morning with Nathaniel Hathorne," Abigail says after Mrs. Adams has left for the day. "There's something odd about him, don't you agree?"

I'm on my knees helping her assemble a chambray day dress. There are pins between my lips, and I cannot reply.

"He's a cardplayer and a bit of a recluse," Abigail continues.

What can she have seen? We exchanged only a few words; I gave him his handkerchief and quickly parted. I was ruffled; perhaps she noticed?

"Awkward and silent in company, too." Abigail rotates the dress form and cinches the waist for a pleated skirt, then snaps her fingers for more pins.

She's perhaps a year older than me, the youngest daughter of a butcher in Marblehead. Her face is pink from the beef scrapple she brings to eat each day, but she's not a stupid girl.

"He writes stories, they say. I've seen him waiting for the postmaster, holding his package to his chest as if he can't bear to let it go," Abigail goes on. "The older sister got her heart broke by a violin player and stopped taking callers. It's a strange family."

I spit the pins into my palm and wipe the back of my hand across my mouth.

"Mr. Hathorne is handsome." I mean to tease more out of her and so I say it plainly. "You must have noticed."

She blushes.

"You've noticed—of course you Have." Abigail isn't betrothed, nor do I think she has a beau. "I'm a married woman, Abigail. You may have Mr. Hathorne for yourself—there's no need to scare me off with talk of his strangeness."

Her blush raises up a line of freckles across her nose.

"He'll never court a butcher's daughter," she says. "The Hathornes are one of Salem's oldest families, and that matters here."

"Don't be certain," I say, although I'm fairly confident he won't court Abigail. "I think a young lady with a fine imagination and a tasteful wardrobe will suit him best."

"A young lady with a tasteful wardrobe *and* a large dowry," she says. "The Hathornes have come down in the world—the name alone won't keep them from poverty. It's all on Nathaniel."

"I believe his uncles run a coach line?"

"But they're not generous. Nathaniel and his sisters are poor—people say it's the curse."

"The curse?" The chambray is pinned, and I stand to brush out my skirts. I've worked at the shop less than a week, but I already know that Abigail is a girl with many silly superstitions.

"Haven't you heard about the ladies hanged in Salem?" she asks.

Is it better to admit knowledge or pretend ignorance? It's no matter, for Abigail keeps talking without waiting for my reply.

"My granny told me the story when I was a girl—said folks in Salem lost their minds and blamed witchcraft and Devil worship on innocent souls. It was madness and greed, Granny said. They killed more than a dozen women, took their property, too."

"What has that to do with Mr. Hathorne?"

She looks up from the work, and her eyes are very clear.

"Hathorne's great-great-grandsire was a judge at the witch trials, Isobel. Condemned innocent women to their deaths and watched them hang with no regrets. One of them screamed from the gallows: 'A curse on you and your children and your children's children—you'll all die with blood in your throats.'"

I shiver. Nat spoke of the women who were hanged, but he said nothing of his ancestor's part in it.

"The family suffers for it," Abigail adds. "You can see it on him, I think that's what makes him queer—his cursed bloodline."

Is it true? Is this what drives Nat to darkness?

"But if the women weren't witches, then how could the bloodline be cursed?" I ask. I fear being found out for my own colors and ancestry. "And even if it *is* true, the curse is no fault of his." I'm busy wrapping up the salvage cloth and try not to sound too keen about her gossip.

"I suppose not," she says.

"And you *do* think he's handsome, don't you?"

She blushes.

"I imagine he'll be attending the Light Infantry celebrations," I venture. "Perhaps he'd escort you."

Abigail laughs, and I believe I've hidden my strain.

"I hope I'll have an escort, but it won't be Mr. Hathorne."

She describes the new gown she's planning for the banquet: magenta silk and ivory taffeta with a cinched waist, and a new hat with flowers to match.

"And gloves," she says. "I'd like a special pair of gloves. Maybe I can buy yours."

"Felicity's price is very dear, I fear."

"Then will you teach me?"

"If there is time," I say. "And if we can hide it from Mrs. Adams."

I don't tell her that I'm still teaching myself how to embroider on gloves. Or that the rose petals I tried were small and clumsy, the hibiscus blossom too sprawling. I'll have to do better, and soon.

Pleasantry, as Nat said, won't make my name in Salem.

AT HOME I sharpen my charcoal stick and draw the first black lines for the leopard to fit a man's glove. Lamplight flickers across the table where I've pinned the gloves upon a piece of cork, and I feel the power of the animal as I sketch across the expanse of two gloves.

I imagine Nat watching me as I work, appraising me, looking at me with that sly smile. Whatever is between us is a secret that neither has yet to say aloud. A brightness with buoyancy and, beneath it, something more . . . the enchantment that we share—he with words, I with color.

Abigail says there is a curse on Nat's family, and I know how difficult it is to live with the weight of family shame and secrecy. I imagine saying all this to him, watching his face turn from curiosity to wonder as I reveal my own secret histories—the way Isobel Gowdie stood up to the men who accused her, my mother's warning, even the enchantments of the colors themselves.

I've given him a token of May tree flowers stitched upon his handkerchief, one with a tiny red *A* concealed in the middle of the flower where the pollen pools.

Perhaps that *is* witchcraft? But I cannot fathom it, for they say witches have covens and know how to conjure spells, and I would never dare to do such things.

And yet I'm certain that my needlework is more than pleasantry and ornament.

A needle can adorn a bridal cap with silk roses, decorate a child's dress with bluebells, prepare a gentleman's gloves for ceremony, and cheer a home with yellow flowers splashed across fresh white sheers. But that's not all.

My needle saved the captain's life. A needle can lance a wound. It can keep a babe from falling out of the womb. It can stanch bleeding and hide coins in the hem of a bodice, and it can sew together a thief's fingers—as I witnessed when an old man was caught too many times with his hands in the till at Marlin's Tavern.

I was perhaps ten years old and stood in the shadows and watched the barkeep hold down the thief until the dark-clad shroud-maker arrived. They shoved a whiskey bottle into the thief's mouth and splayed the man's hand flat on a table. The shroud-maker was calm as he took out a needle laced with horsehair and stuck it through the meat of the man's thumb.

The thief was screaming when a hand on my shoulder tugged me away.

"Isobel, that's not for your eyes," Pap said. But I'd already witnessed the purple back of the thief's throat and the grim set of the shroud-maker's jaw. I'd seen there was dark power in a needle, too, more power than my mother had ever revealed.

Now that I think of it, I would like to see someone sew my husband's fingers together. I would not have to be a witch to do it, either.

— ELEVEN —

All of Friday and Saturday evening I sew the leopard, using gold and copper silk threads to make the spots. I think of the letters I spied in Mercy's work and begin to play with the contoured stitches. I zig them, then zag them: I curve bits of letters to spell out *S-T-R-E-N-G-T-H* in the length of the leopard's spine, then fill the space around the letters with the same brown thread.

STRENGTH. The word is there, and it is not there. If I look carefully, I can see it; if I blink, it's gone. I imagine Mercy stitching the word *SAFE* into the shawl so that the woman who wears it might feel protected when she leaves her home. I want the man who wears these gloves to feel their strength as a deep mystery: present, but invisible.

It takes most of Sunday to sew the rear half of the leopard's body on the left-hand glove, with a tail curving around the pinky edge and into the palm. When I'm finished, I turn the gloves inside out and snip off all of the thread ends. This is the moment that excites me most, when I slip my creation upon my own body to see how the stitches lie and how the fabric and ornament move when they are worn.

But when I put the glove onto my own hand, the leopard's legs twist the wrong way and the tail is a slippery snake that slithers across the palm. The work has failed—there's no magic in it, certainly no witch-craft. I'm a fool to think I have any power beyond what's modest and mortal. I rip out the stitches and begin again, and by dawn the gloves are so full of holes and charcoal marks that I've rendered them useless. I shove them aside, then bend over my table and weep. I'm tired, hungry, and sick with despair. I've promised Felicity three magnificent pair of gloves by the end of the week, and that day is fast approaching.

IT HURTS ME to use the very last of my coins to replace the ruined gloves, and for caution's sake I go back to the Marine Society Hall with my sketchbook and draw out the leopard again. I make careful note of the scale of legs to body, body to ears, and so on. I won't make the same mistakes again.

When the sketch is finished, I study a case filled with shells and primitive ornaments from Polynesia, and note a shark's jawbone brought from the Pacific Ocean by one Capt. N. Hathorne aboard the *Nabby* in 1803. I discover a showcase of needles, some as tiny as an eyelash, two as long as a man's arm, in a case labeled *Witches' Needles, Salem 1692.* Beside them is a small row of cornhusk dolls labeled *Poppets,* from the same period in Salem. All of it seems not a repudiation of the witch trials but a further cataloging of them—proof, tucked into a corner of a small hall, that the city still believes witches once lived in Salem.

As the sun beats down through the domed glass ceiling, I can't help but wonder which of those needles were taken from the poor souls condemned to death by John Hathorne's judgment.

On my way home with the new gloves and sketches, I go out of my way to pass by Hamilton Hall. The doors are shut, but the windows and curtains are open to the April breeze and the sound of merry, industrious voices pours into the street in a collection of bright colors. Through the windows I see men waxing tables and cleaning chairs, women and children polishing candelabras, and a circle of women sewing and ironing. All are dark-skinned like Mercy and Zeke, and soon I have spied my neighbor sitting with a group of women, her needle moving swiftly through a long sash, her face soft with companionship.

Beside a platform stage, a Black man stands with his booted foot upon a low stool, giving directions and encouragement. He holds himself with a noble air and seems to have something kind or friendly to say to everyone. This must be Mr. John Remond, whom the town speaks of with such great respect. As he bends over a child sweeping out a wooden bin, I sense in an instant that Mr. Remond is reliable, capable, and powerfully good. I understand why he is spoken of with such affectionate admiration.

The singsong island voices of the men and ladies stay with me as I reach the corner of Higginson Square and come upon a large, lantern-shaped sign announcing *Remond's Foods & Fancy Cakes.*

> *Fresh cookies and candies: 5¢*
> *Oysters: 2¢ pound 4¢ bushel*
> *Pheasants: 1¢ each $10 dozen*
> *Turtle Soup: order 2 weeks ahead,*
> *price on request*
> *Cakes: fancy and plain, $1 and up,*
> *2 days' advance order*

The glass window is piled high with fancy cookies; inside I see a pretty Black lady polishing a cake. She uses her spatula to smooth the frosting and a small sculpting tool to make meringue scallops. Behind her two girls are mixing batter, and there's a boy churning butter.

The older girl wraps a trefoil-shaped cookie in parchment and waves for me to have it. A bell rings when I enter, and the air inside the shop is sweet and warm, reminding me of the years when my brother was learning to bake.

"I'm afraid I don't have an extra penny today," I tell the girl.

When she looks up, I recognize the young woman who helped Widow Higgins on the day of our arrival.

"That's all right," she says. "It's our way of welcoming you to town. You live out near Zeke's place?" she asks as I nibble at the cookie.

I'm no longer surprised when folks seem to know me.

"Yes," I say. "I'm Mrs. Isobel Gamble."

"I saw you at the sailing of the *New Harmony*," she says with a smile, and I realize she is one of Mr. Remond's daughters. She's pretty and sharp, approaching the first bloom of young womanhood. Her words are gold, pure as a coin. "I heard it was your needle that saved the captain's life on the crossing. We're very grateful to you."

I don't know what she means by "we," but she continues before I can inquire.

"I hear Dr. Gamble is traveling with Captain Darling now. You have nothing to fear with them together; the captain does not miss his mark."

I am forced to say a few kind words about Edward lest I seem a bitter wife; I even ask about the sugar that Captain Darling will be bringing north.

A cloud crosses the girl's face.

"We don't like getting our sugar from the islands, but Papa says we have no choice."

"And why is that?" I ask.

She cocks her head as if she has just remembered I have come from afar. Or perhaps she is taking her measure of me and deciding if I am dull-witted.

"Sugar plantations in the West Indies are the meanest place in the world, ma'am," she says. "Papa saw for himself the way they work their slaves to a brutal death."

Mrs. Remond comes from behind the counter and puts a hand on her daughter's shoulder.

"Don't let my Nancy be bothering you," Mrs. Remond says. "You enjoy your cookie now and the rest of your blessed day."

As I open the door, I remember I have seen these same lantern and trefoil shapes woven into the sashes and belts Mercy sells on the wharf. I suspect it's more than a coincidence, but what does it mean? My mind goes to the ships, slaves, and sugar plantations Nancy spoke of just a moment ago, and I feel there's something important hidden here, if only I knew how to look and what to seek.

∞

ON MARKET DAY the square is filled with farmers selling crates of potatoes, onions, wheat, and rye. The sausage man is calling out his price;
there's a bald dentist pulling teeth and dropping them into a bloody
bucket, a doctor with his pharmacy displayed beneath a canopy, and a
woman selling baskets of muddy black mussels.

I find Mercy in the same spot on the wharf where I first spied her,
wearing the same white turban. To her collection of sashes and belts
she's added a gold shawl trimmed with black whipstitch and tassels, a
belt with a line of working farm men lined upon it, and a pair of ladies' slippers decorated with crisp blue boats. I notice there are no pieces
made with lanterns and trefoils today, but there is an abundance of those
made with trees and fishes.

"Where do you find time to do such beautiful work?" I ask, even as
I'm studying the stitching to learn something of her technique so that I
can borrow it for my own. Mrs. Adams expects her gloves and I cannot
afford to make another mistake.

"I do what I have to." Mercy is cool, and I'm glad I didn't bother her
at home.

Ivy is crouched behind her mother, playing with two rag dolls. Her
light freckles and blue-brown eyes set her apart from the darker children
in Remond's cake shop, and I wonder how it is that Mercy's child has
such unusual coloring.

"You're very skilled," I try again.

Mercy shrugs and looks over my shoulder toward the pier.

I see no words or letters rise up from her work this time, but perhaps
I'm too tired to catch them. Perhaps the month at sea wrecked my eyes
when I first landed. Or perhaps there are no secrets, no words, no meaning in the shapes and colors she's worked with her needle. Perhaps it's
just as I fear: the colors are some crack in my sanity, some indication of
bad witchery or madness.

"You planning to steal my designs?" Her words startle me.

"Of course not," I fib, though it is nearly what I am hoping to do. "I
need your help and I have something to give in exchange." Yes, everyone wants an exchange, just as I saw with the captain and Edward. "The
pennyroyal has taken root in my yard and I'll be making the ointments
when I can buy the beeswax."

Mercy nods.

"Good. I can sell that here, too. Sailors got lots of cuts and bug bites and sun blisters that need curing, if that ointment is all that you say it is."

I pick up a small purse that she's stitched with a scene of two boys fishing.

"I'd like to learn how to make scenes in miniature," I say. "For a pair of gloves, for example."

She takes the purse from my hands before I can examine it further.

"You're keeping my customers away," she says sharply. She is taller than me, strong and wiry in the open air.

"Mercy, I am in a bind." I hate to admit weakness again, but it seems I have no choice. "I've promised something I haven't yet mastered."

She sucks her teeth. Her glance bounces off me.

"What do you need?"

"To make a pair of gloves."

"Why gloves?" she asks.

"Gloves are small and I thought they would be fast and simple, but they're not."

"You got a glove form?"

"I don't. Is it necessary?"

"I can show you." She looks across the wharf to the place where the ships are coming and going. Several seamen are heading our way, and some ladies are walking behind Zeke and a few others carrying travel trunks. Last month I was the one arriving full of hope for good fortune in the New World. I was innocent of what troubles lay ahead, still ignorant of the fading prince of Salem who would see me as a girl who'd stepped from one of his stories. Still ignorant about the depths of Edward's depravity.

"Don't crowd around me now," Mercy says, waving me away. I see two men stagger under the weight of a lady's heavy trunk. Zeke tips his head toward me, but nothing more. "Go on home—I'll help you later."

I do as she says and head back home. On the way I pass by the Manning stagecoach offices, but there is no sight of Nat, only the thumping of two drummers and a row of old fellows in uniforms practicing a marching tune near the Common.

∽

IT'S LATE AFTERNOON when Mercy comes to my cottage. Behind her in the yard is a tabby cat I've never seen before. The cat is black and gold, the colors of the leopard haunting my thoughts.

"Did she follow you?" It seems strange that a cat with leopard markings would appear on just this day.

"Hope not," Mercy says. "Cats and chickens don't mix. Give it some scraps so she don't follow me home."

I do as she instructs and lead Mercy into the cottage, where she casts an arched eye at my failed gloves.

"Why you making something so grand as a leopard?"

"The gloves have to be special," I say. "I have to make a fair and good wage to make up for what was stolen."

"Got to be what folks want," she says. "First lesson."

From a black sack she takes a hollow form made of wicker and straw. The form has five fingers so that a glove can be slipped upon it and a needle passed beneath and inside.

"Zeke made it," Mercy says. "You can use it now, but you got to get your own."

I slide a fresh glove over the form and see that it makes a generous space at the wrist so that the work will go more easily, and it even allows for repairs and whipstitches along the fingers.

Mercy turns the pages of my open sketchbook.

"This here." She points to an iris my mother drew a long time ago. It is long and elegant, set in a swirl of lovely green leaves. "Salem folk will like it. Iris flower means courage and protection."

I use my charcoal to draw an iris up the length of a glove and the long leaves as trim along the edges. Filling the space with the flower seems something new and different.

"What do you think of it?" I ask Mercy.

She gives a nod, and it is enough.

I expect she'll be on her way once my stitching goes well. But she takes out a sash and picks up her own needle. Side by side with her, I feel a ghost of the camaraderie I had once with my mother. She looks at my thread and I look at her needle.

"You got a quick hand," she tells me. "Quick is good. Just as important as pretty, if you want to make a living on it."

She has put a trim of lavender flowers along the edge of her sash.

"Why don't you sell your wares at a dry goods shop or a dressmaker?" I ask.

"White folks don't much like to buy from Black folks," she says. "Anyway, I like the wharves. Men looking for something to bring a lady or a son, and my price is right. I see new things there," she adds. "Arabs and Spaniards come with fringes and colors like we never dare. Gives me ideas."

I think she's around thirty-five years old, but I cannot be sure. Her skin is smooth, but her hands are not. Her eyes are clear, but she's missing two teeth in the side of her mouth.

"I like to work at my leisure and stitch what I want," she adds.

"I'm making what I want," I say.

"Are you?" Her eyes are flecked with tiny spots of amber. "The lady didn't tell you what she wants?"

"She said flowers," I admit. "But when I've mastered the form, I'll sew the leopard and I know it will impress her. If not, then I'll take it elsewhere."

Mercy studies the animal as I've drawn it, then looks to the gloves where I tore out the stitches. She squints as if she sees something there in the ghost of the stitches, and I wonder if she can tell I've tried to imitate her work by hiding words in the threads.

"Leopard's got strength," she says, as if she truly can see the word I hid and then erased. "A hunter but always alone. Some say the leopard is death." The colors of her words change as she speaks, darkening from elderberry to midnight. "My mama taught me about animals. Owls are wise. A hawk is a message from the dead. Foxes are wily."

"What animal is courage and power?" I ask, for that is what I want to stitch.

Mercy thinks on it.

"Bear," she says. "Big black bear."

I look at the gloves, and at my sketches.

"A black bear will look terrible on a pair of gloves," I say.

Mercy's laugh surprises me; the sound is rusty and hard, like the bark of my dear pap's laughter.

"Sure would." She puts her hands in the air as if they are bear claws, and I do the same.

Soon we're both laughing. I feel warm in a way I haven't since coming to America. Mercy's face is open, her smile as wide as her cheekbones.

"If the lady asks for flowers, you best do what she wants." Mercy wipes the back of her hand across her eyes. "It's fine what you have there, elegant and new so that Mrs. Adams will want them in her window."

"I can't thank you enough." Now that there's a thaw between us, I want to keep it that way. I take the pillow with Zeke's words done in my colors and thrust it into her hands.

"For Zeke," I say.

She scowls as she looks at the letters, but I misunderstand her expression.

"It says *Plant a Rainbow*—"

"I know what it says," she snaps. "I learned my letters, but he can't read."

She thrusts the pillow back at me. "You keep it here; don't make him feel less."

I fear I've insulted her and her cousin at the same time—by assuming he could read and by assuming she couldn't—and put the pillow away just as quickly as I can.

"I'll pay Zeke to make me a form for the gloves as soon as I have the money," I say.

"That's better," she replies. "My cousin's always looking for money to put something new into the yard or a pretty ribbon in Ivy's hair. You do that, he'll be happy." She lifts her chin and narrows her eyes. "Just don't be bothering me at market day."

FELICITY TURNS THE gloves inside out and inspects the cuff lining. After two long nights working by lamplight, I've delivered her gloves as promised. Two are elbow length with yellow-and-purple irises, the third sports a boat rendered in navy blue above a pea-green sea. A fish is freedom, Mercy told me. An iris is courage with a secret at its heart. I've hidden these words in bits of curved stitches so tiny only I can see them. But they are there. *FREEDOM*, a secret kept.

"They'll do nicely," Felicity says.

I wait for her to spot the tiny *A* tucked inside a fold of the seam, or for her fingers to run across the stitches and find the hidden letters, but they are all too small to notice.

In the shop window, we pair the flowered gloves with an open-brim yellow hat and put the gloves with the boat scenes beside a lace shoulder cape and matching veil. I'm satisfied with the sixty cents Felicity counts out as payment, until I see the price she's marked on a white tag and attached to the gloves with a bit of string.

"Do you think a lady will pay two dollars?" This is ten times what she's paid for my labor.

"If one lady pays it, others will follow." Felicity's words have color for the first time, brown with pink and burnt amber.

"Two dollars seems a very dear price," I say.

There's shrewdness in Felicity's narrowed eyes.

"These are novelty and fancy." Her voice seems to move like cloth, stretching as if to shred apart the stitches of her words. "We'll know in a week if the price is too high. If necessary, I'll lower it—else take them out of the window and admit that there is no desire for such impractical gloves."

There's a threat in what she says, and I don't miss it.

"Someone will want them," I say, for it must be so.

"And when someone does, they'll buy them from me." Felicity advances toward me, and although I do not mean to, I shrink away. "The commissions must come through this shop, that's our agreement. You *must* refer the customer to me directly, and never tell them you are the stitcher. Otherwise, they'll try to undercut me. And that can't happen. Remember, Mrs. Gamble, I took a chance on you, and you must never take work behind my back."

When Felicity has gone for the day, Abigail says, "Don't test her, Isobel. Mrs. Adams's family's been here a long time—she can be a vengeful sort if she thinks she's been wronged."

Salem, 1691

Winter is coming, and the squabbling village has failed to pay the Reverend Samuel Parris the monthly stipend for his ministry duties.

Leaving Sunday meeting pale and exhausted after hours in the pulpit, the reverend finds twelve-year-old Ann Putnam standing separate from her parents and siblings, her eyes glazed and blazing. It is well-known that the child's father is engaged in a bitter battle with John Proctor over a disputed patch of timberlands, but Putnam is an ally in favor of paying Parris what he's owed, and so Parris kneels and puts a hand on the girl's damp forehead.

"You're safe here," Reverend Parris says. "The word of God defends us against savages, neighbors, witches, spells, hunger, and strife."

Bedraggled and shivering, the too-thin girl looks behind Parris to where Tituba and her husband, John Indian, are waiting. For a frightful second Ann's eyes roll to the back of her head, and just as quickly she is righted.

Parris doesn't know that Ann has already spoken of witches tormenting her father in Maine. That she pointed a shaking finger at a trio of Indians and cried out for the Lord to protect them all from Satan's evil. But soon enough he will see it for himself—first his own daughter and niece, then Ann and her cousin, will cry out in anguish at the sight of Tituba.

— TWELVE —

On the first warm day of April I walk through town to a crooked path lined with hawthorn trees that form a long hedgerow along the woods. The blossoms are coming in hard new buds, the branches as yearning and twisted as I feel.

I've suffered theft and secrets, lies and threats, since coming to Salem. There's been abuse of my skills and suspicion at the way I speak. My only pleasures have been roaming the Marine Society Hall among the treasures, my time at work with Mercy or on the gloves, and the hour—for in truth it has amounted to little more—I have spent with Nat.

Yet it's Nat who looms largest in my mind and Nat to whom I wish to speak of all that perplexes me here. And because I dare not ask for him at the coach offices, I must linger where I might spy him in the open.

WEARING A FRESHLY aired dress, I make my way to the Charter Ale House where the shipping news is posted on a board each day, and pretend to study the announcements.

I read and reread bulletins about the *Grand Turk,* the *Quest,* the *Friendship,* and the *Rising Sun* while keeping one eye on the passersby and hoping Nat will be coming from the postal window as he usually does on a Monday morning. Men and women come alone and in pairs to read that the *Pallas* has just come from Virginia, and the *Kahawa Freeman* is selling lots of silk and painted china from the port of Cantos. Seamen check to see how much longer they have in port, and shop owners and investors anxiously scan for updated news of their awaited cargoes. Some give a little clap or cheer when they find what they are hoping for; others sigh in disappointment.

After what seems like hours, Nat finally comes into the square carrying a book under each arm. I'm proper, even demure, as he makes his way to me.

"I haven't seen you in many days," he says. "How goes your time at the shop?"

I'd like to blurt out my complaints about Felicity, but decorum ties my tongue. "All is well."

"And your work—have you finished your . . . ?"

I'm delighted by how naturally we fall into step together, and by the way he asks about the gloves without naming them.

"They're in the shop window."

"But you're not pleased?"

I don't think my expressions are transparent, yet he easily reads my face.

"Her price is extravagant," I admit. "And what she pays me is pure thievery."

We've walked out of the square and are headed north, where the streets thin quickly and the legal and accounting offices are replaced by storehouses and barrel makers' workshops. A boy with a hoop runs toward us, and Nat gives a little shout to direct the boy out of our path.

"Felicity Adams is a shrewd woman," he says.

"I'm learning from her."

"Are you?" There's his familiar half smile. "What are you learning?"

"The price of goods and services," I say. "And what might be popular among the fashionable ladies. Also, it seems I'm learning that needlework is meant to be a pleasantry."

We stop near a candlemaker's shop, where the air smells of tallow and fire.

"I'm sorry you took that badly," he says. He puts a finger to my basket, just as I once imagined him touching the button on a dress I never made.

"The hawthorn flowers you stitched are quite lifelike," he says quietly. "I never properly thanked you."

A pair of ladies brushes past us, and I take note of bright red cherries embroidered on a white shawl.

"Salem ladies are wild for fruit on shawls and sleeves this year," he says, following my gaze.

"How would you know that?" I'm surprised, but pleased.

"My sisters sometimes speak of fashion."

"Do you know which flowers and fruits are most fashionable? Surely not the May flower," I joke. "Is it cherries and grapes, or apples, or perhaps peaches—"

He laughs and shifts the books under one arm.

"I'll ask Louise if I see her at supper this evening. But we don't often dine together," he says. "I prefer to dine alone."

"I'd never dine alone if I didn't have to." I'm sorry as soon as the words leave my mouth, because it sounds as if I am lonely.

"I'm a solitary man," he says. "Does that surprise you?"

There it is, lament and desire, retreat and appeal.

"More solemn than solitary, I think. And more solemn than you need be."

The look on his face, as if I have laid bare a secret, thrills me.

"Perhaps I see myself in you, and you in me," I add more gently. "We're both solitary in our work. But solitude isn't necessarily our finest state."

He looks at me over the edge of his nose.

"There you go again, Mrs. Gamble." His words are hammered gold, and for a moment I am blinded. "Intriguing me as you do."

If I ask him to say more, I believe he will.

"I've changed the end of my story because of you." He steps closer. "It was meant to be a ghastly story about cruel death meted out against a child, but I can't do it. Not now that I've met you in the flesh."

"I'm not the girl in your story." I try to sound easy, but there's a tremor in my voice and I hear it, and so must he.

"But to me, you and she are the same." He tilts his head and looks at me closely. "From the first time I saw you on the wharf, I felt I'd summoned you with my own mind."

I step away from him. "Imagination can't conjure a true and living person."

"And yet here you are, with magic of your own and witch marks sewn into your red cape."

My throat goes dry. I am glad I left the cape at home.

"You can't deny it. There's something in your needlecraft I've never seen before."

"You make too much of it."

"I insulted you when we spoke last, and I'm sorry for it." He drops his voice. "Let me help you, Mrs. Gamble."

"Help how?"

My emotions with him skitter and scatter. First I'm nervous, then I'm frightened, and now I'm flooded with gratitude as he talks about what I might stitch and where I might have my work seen.

"The Light Infantry banquet is the most important event of the fall season, as you've surely heard," he says. "You must embroider a stunning camel hair shawl and wear it that night. I'll do what I can to make sure your work is noticed without giving myself away. And that's not something I promise lightly, for I hate going out to such things."

"My husband will be back by then," I murmur.

"That won't change your work," he says, hardly blinking at the mention of Edward. "Besides, I know about Salem seamen: they come and go and the women are left to make their way. My mother was one of those women, and she did not fare well. I would not like to see the same happen to you, not with so much skill as you have."

We stand for several moments together, and I recall what my father told me: enchanted beings live beside the sea. They rise and look beautiful, but they keep their powers hidden from sight, much as the placid sea is always brewing a storm somewhere unseen.

"I will make something glorious," I tell him. "It will be our secret until then."

Salem, 1692

A raging blizzard blocks the roads to Salem Village, keeping horses and carts and even the most determined worshippers at home on Sunday morning.

In the nearly empty meetinghouse, the Reverend Samuel Parris pounds at the pulpit. It has now been four months since the congregation paid his salary.

"I warn you there is terror and destruction coming," he shouts.

Days later his daughter and niece collapse onto their pallets, twisting and shrieking and slapping at invisible demons.

"Make it stop, Papa, make it stop," nine-year-old Betty cries.

For three cold, frightful days and nights the girls shiver and scream and show him scratches, marks, and bites that neither Parris nor the good Dr. Griggs can explain but for the most diabolical reasons.

"I fear the girls are under an Evil Hand," Dr. Griggs pronounces.

Parris falls to his knees and calls upon the Lord, for what he fears has come to pass. He fasts and his household does the same: wife, daughters, and niece—even the slaves Tituba and John Indian—go without food. But the girls keep screaming.

"You must send for help," Elizabeth Parris begs her husband. "Please, Samuel, I fear the worst."

Reverend John Hale and John Hathorne arrive at the parsonage in a flourish of heavy robes, spouting Testament and passages from William Perkins's book on witchcraft. With fingers blue from cold, they point at writhing, moaning Betty Parris and her cousin and they shout, "Out, Satan, be gone before the Lord."

Then they, too, fall on their knees to pray and fast.

Yet the girls' agonies go on. Terror and gossip overtake Salem Village. Neighbors stay in their homes keeping close watch upon their own daughters and wives for signs of demonic possession. The souls and bodies of every villager are in danger when Goodwife Mary Sibley decides that she must help.

Just before dawn on the morning of February 21, Mary Sibley slips across the frozen ground to the Reverend Samuel Parris's kitchen door and whispers to Tituba.

"You must make a witch cake."

Tituba has heard of such things in the Georgia Sea Islands, and she hates to see the girls suffer. She does as instructed and mixes the girls' urine with rye meal, shapes it into a cake, and cooks it in the fire ash.

"Now you feed it to the dog." Goodwife Sibley points at the brindled mutt that lurks about the Parris cottage. "This will reveal the true witch in our village."

— THIRTEEN —

The camel-hair shawl Nat suggested for the ball is far more costly than I can afford, and no amount of bargaining at Blackwell's lowers the price enough.

As I count out the last of my coins and watch the clerk wrap up a plain cotton shawl with a small fringe, I silently seethe at Edward. More than ever my husband seems weak and cruel in comparison to Nat's goodwill and intelligence; more than ever I wish to be free to make my name and have my dreams and a dress shop—and money—of my own. I will be bold and fearless, just as Nat once said I am.

I'M HEADING TOWARD the Common to study the ladies' Saturday morning calling costumes when I hear a sharp peal of laughter that spins my head. Across the lawn a girl and her beau are leaning beside a wide sycamore. I cannot see their faces, but there's a gentle curve of their figures as they lean toward one another. She laughs, and he laughs.

Their hands touch and the man pulls the girl's hand to his lips. He does it slowly, and I am lost in a shock of desire: I want Nat to put my hand to his lips just like that.

When her hand reaches his face, the church bells ring twelve. A dog barks behind me, and a man shouts a name. The enchantment is broken. The beau drops the girl's hand and hurries away. The girl jumps up, grabs at her basket, and rushes across the pebbled walk. Her feet churn like butter paddles; stones skid from the bottoms of her shoes as she runs.

At the edge of the Common, she jigs to cross the street. A bundle falls from her basket, but she does not realize.

"You dropped something," I call, but a carriage in the road drowns out my voice.

I retrieve the bundle and cross the street just as she enters a black iron gate at the rear of a great house. When she pulls down her hood, I recognize the yellow curls of the Irish servant girl I met at the Cranford shop.

"Nell!" She turns when I call her name. I wave the package.

"Isobel," she cries. "I'm so very happy to see you again. I've wanted you to call on me—why haven't you come?"

"You dropped this on the green."

She takes the package and gives a startled cry.

"This was made special for the captain." She shows me a razor and strop, a mother-of-pearl brush for shaving powder, and a copper shave bowl inside the velvet sack. "They're very dear—it would have cost me more than two months' wages to replace them. I can't thank you enough."

I've noticed the Silas house on my walks: handsome brick with a painted yellow door and a freshly hoed garden, a carriage house, and two horses in the yard. I hear a goat, and voices coming from open kitchen windows. A door opens at the back of the house, and someone waves a cloth over the rail.

"You're an honest and kind friend." Nell's words are the same earnest, cheerful green as on our first meeting. "And your work is very fine."

I'm wearing the dress trimmed with irises at the sleeves and hem. Nell runs a hand over the stitches. "Mrs. Silas needs someone who can keep her tongue and do good work for her—someone who can keep a confidence. Someone we can trust."

She's so openhearted, I want to take her face in my hands and kiss her cheeks.

"I owe you a true and proper thanks," she says, and then, as if she has decided something, adds, "Wait here."

∞

It's NOT LONG before the kitchen door swings open and Nell latches on to my arm.

"If Mrs. Silas agrees you're suitable, you'll be asked to work on a dress for Miss Charlotte."

"The Silas daughter?"

"Hush, no questions. You must meet the mistress first."

Nell leads me through a large kitchen to a narrow staircase at the back of the house, then up a flight of stairs. It's my first time inside a grand Salem home, but the rooms go by so quickly I barely see the papered walls or rich window trims.

"Mrs. Silas will ask you questions, and you must answer honestly," Nell tells me as we climb a second, narrower set of stairs. "If you don't say the truth, she'll know it. I don't know how, but she does."

We reach a small landing beneath the slanted peaks of the rooftop. It's very warm, and the air is stale, but a tiny window reveals a view of the bright blue sky and a slice of the ocean beyond.

"Remember, Mrs. Silas is an important lady in Salem," Nell says.

She goes through a single open door and closes it behind her. I hear muffled voices, and when the door opens, it is Mrs. Silas.

The lady's back is stiff, and she walks as if she has been sitting for a long time. She's wearing a simple day dress and a white apron, as if she's a cook and not the mistress of a great house.

She leads me to two narrow chairs where we sit knee to knee.

"You've just come from Scotland," Mrs. Silas says. It's not a question.

"Yes."

"Do you know why Sarabeth Cranford chased you out of her shop that day?"

I shake my head.

"She said the symbols and signs in your cape hinted at witchcraft. I don't believe in such nonsense, but you ran off without looking back. I know that you have secrets, Mrs. Gamble."

Nell said the Cranford sisters sent me away because I'm Scottish. But Mrs. Silas is saying something very different.

"You must tell me what trouble you're hiding if you wish to work here," she says.

I need money, and there is wealth and opportunity here. I understand the lady means to have a secret of mine before she will trust me.

"In my red cape I stitched a story from Scotland, a legend of Isobel Gowdie, who was accused of witchcraft."

"And why would you choose that story for your own?"

I have but a moment to decide. Her words have no color and reveal nothing in hue or shape. Yet somehow, I know that the truth about Isobel Gowdie will be far less dangerous for me than her secret is for her.

"She escaped and lived. She had children, and I'm descended from one of them."

Mrs. Silas contemplates me for a long while—long enough for me to see into her eyes and know that beneath her wealth and strength, she is afraid.

"Nell trusts you, and so will I," she says at last. "I will pay you well for your work and your strictest confidence. This isn't to be taken lightly. If you betray me, I'll see that your husband's reputation is destroyed. And yours as well."

I'm unsure of what to say—thank you? I understand? I do not like it, but I have to work, and I know how to keep secrets. If this is the price, then I will pay it.

I do not let an instant pass before I nod.

"You will make the necessary alterations on my daughter's gown," she says.

Nell brings out a sumptuous gown of shimmering pink silk and organza decorated with deep pink and yellow roses. The roses appear to be velvet appliqué, but on closer inspection are embroidered with French chenille thread. Each bud and blossom is a tiny masterpiece.

As I follow Nell down the stairs with the dress, I hear a sweet, peachy voice say, "Mother, I would like to meet her," and Mrs. Silas's gruff "Not now."

"Is she ill?" I ask Nell when we have reached the small sewing room on the second floor. "Why is she in the attic? Is she being punished? What has she done?"

"Charlotte's with child," Nell whispers. "Her mother's kept her in the house since winter. She won't leave until her wedding day."

Nell tells me the wedding dress was made in Philadelphia, where the groom's family lives and where the bride will live after the wedding. The gown must be worn, and there must be a public ceremony.

"His mother doesn't know Charlotte's expecting," Nell says as I study the flowers that cover the dress. "Mrs. Silas feared she'd break off the wedding even though the child—Charlotte swears it—is his. It was all done through the groom and his father; they've been promised a new printing press to go with their news businesses." Nell shrugs. "I suppose it's payment for an expectant bride—spoiled goods, even though he's the one who did the spoiling."

"When is the wedding?" I ask.

"The ninth of July."

"The bride will be well along by then. Why are they waiting so long?"

Nell leans close.

"This is how it has to be," she says. "Poor Charlotte was sick with heartbreak, and it took longer than they hoped to settle things. I cannot tell you what I've seen in this house—you must understand that the Silas family is known everywhere, by everyone. We need someone who won't gossip, Isobel. Even if the town suspects, they cannot know. I'm loyal to Mrs. Silas, and you must be, too."

CHARLOTTE SILAS IS pale and delicate, brown-haired and clear-eyed. She's younger than me by a year or two, the only daughter and the youngest of four Silas children—her brothers all married, at sea, or both, as Nell has told me.

"Your dress is very pretty." Charlotte eyes my iris needlework. "I wonder what the ladies in Salem think of something so exotic and new."

"I couldn't say," I tell her.

I fear her legs beneath the bedclothes have grown weak, but when I ask her to try on the dress she stands quickly and puts up her arms like a child. Charlotte is slender, which makes her condition more obvious than if she were plump. Thanks to the time in my aunt's shop and the dresses I made for myself before I left my father's home, I see right away what must be done to conceal the child.

"The extra fabric allows for flounces or a scallop ruffle across the bottom, but we'll use it for the bodice and add a new ribbon for a decoration at the floor." I pin up a length of the dress to show Mrs. Silas the effect it will make. "We'll open the dress at the bosom and move the waistline up two inches so that it slopes in an empire that will hide the waistline without emphasizing any plumping of the midriff."

I remember how my auntie Aileen imparted her wisdom as a matter of course rather than make a request or ask a question, and I summon that boldness now.

"You'll have a basket of flowers to hold just beneath your bosom," I say to Charlotte. I try to estimate how much larger she will be by July. "As long as no one takes them from you, you will be fine."

THE LIGHT IN the sewing room is high and bright, the window shuttered. I cannot see the evening pour from gray to black, but I feel the day fade as I work. I must watch each stitch to be sure that it is the same length as the ones before; I must be sure that I do not lapse into my own split stitch—which is stronger, of course, but not what was used by the original seamstress.

When Nat enters my mind, when I think of Felicity or Edward, when I wonder if I will ever be free of my secrets and fears, I push them all away. After Sunday meeting and on every subsequent night that week, I work on the pink flowers and then the yellow. If I have some magic in my needle, there will be an enchantment in the dress that will enhance the bride's delicate beauty, the shimmer of pink silk and netting, the spray of flowers.

CHARLOTTE IS READING with her head bent toward the lantern when I climb the stairs to her room the following week. Her hair falls across the page when she looks up.

Captain and Mrs. Silas have gone out and the two of us are alone for the first time. I ask what she's reading, and she shows me a cover with a floral design.

"The *Ladies' Magazine.*" She opens to a list of the contents. "It's a smart book with poems and stories."

Without her mother the girl is vibrant.

"Mrs. Sarah Hale is the only lady editor I've ever heard of." She thrusts the magazine into my hand. "You may borrow it if you like—you'll enjoy it, and I have so much to read."

Beside Charlotte's bed is a stack of four books, fresh from the bookseller. I don't see the harm in borrowing a magazine and so I thank her and tuck it into my basket.

"We can try the dress now," I offer.

Charlotte nearly hops out of bed.

"Mother insists I stay off my feet all day—I was a sickly girl and she hasn't forgotten it. But I'm not sickly anymore."

The dress is beautiful on her, the fit generous with room for her to grow, the new flowers and stitching indiscernible from the old.

"It's beautiful," she says.

"You are beautiful in it."

"But you're the one who made it so, and I'm grateful—truly. Mother gave me permission to order new petticoats and dressing gowns for the baby, too. She said if you come next week, she'll pay you generously for everything."

THE SILASES' STABLE boy has always taken me in his cart when I've traveled home from here after dark, but tonight I'm delighted to find Zeke waiting outside the kitchen door.

"Mrs. Silas told me to take you home," he says with a flourish of his cap. "Glad to be of service on such a lovely night."

I step up beside him and pull my shawl around my face. I put the basket at my feet and make sure the magazine is tucked away.

The center of Salem is dark, the storefronts and shops closed up for the evening. But on the waterfront, where the ships sit like gods or mountains against the blue-ink sea, there are lanterns and bonfires and groups of men passing bottles. Beside a ship, two ladies with long dark hair and red skirts dance for a circle of men.

"You're safe with me, so take a good look, Mrs. Gamble," Zeke says. "This is the world right here come to Salem."

It is like a dream of a circus, or what I imagine a circus might be, a tableau from every corner of the globe. At the end of the wharf, men from China squat in a line along the water and talk quietly among themselves.

"Chinamen bring silks and lanterns and take cotton, tobacco, and shoes," Zeke says. His words are like a string of orange threads stretching across my lap. "It's luxury they're after, and so they buy up linens and dresses from France and England, pottery and glass, Italian crystal."

On and on Zeke talks as he drives me the length of the wharf and then back north again. "If you don't mind another turn in the night air, I'm happy to oblige," he says. I nod, taking in the dancing, the smell of what the men are smoking in their pipes, all of it lulling me into a state of happy wooziness, as if I have taken a long drink of rum punch, and then another.

We are on our second trip along the wharf when a Colored man in a cap and soiled shirt steps up to Zeke's side of the carriage.

"Do you know where I can find Mrs. Remond's cake house?" he asks.

"You head that way, look for the large lantern sign in Higginson Square," Zeke tells him with a brisk nod.

There it is again, the feeling that something is happening at the cake house; that the lantern sign is for more than just cakes.

"The cake house will be closed," I say when the man has gone. "What would he find there now?"

Zeke keeps his eyes ahead and takes a drink from his flask.

"It's no business of mine what a man is looking for."

"I suppose not," I say. But I am almost certain now there is something Zeke and Mercy and the Remonds are doing in secret together, and I hope it is not a smuggling ring that will bring them ruin. I have seen what greed and hunger can do to a man and woman. Only a family as rich as the Silases can successfully guard against secrets that destroy.

AT HOME I bathe my feet in cool water from the well and try to put the day and the docks out of my mind. The scrimshaw buttons at my bedside call out to me, but they do not tell me what they want—only that they were once in Nat's hands, and then they were in mine, and now they are beside me.

I roll them in my palm. The rhythm is soft and cunning, and the sound of their clacking brings the cat curling around my legs.

Night sounds come through the walls and shutters—bullfrogs and wildcats and dogs in the distance. I light a candle, prop up a pillow, and find the new magazine Charlotte Silas pressed into my hands. I read a poem about faith, a sad missive about the loss of a child, and begin a long tale told by a gentleman who has returned home to Boston only to discover that his childhood friends cannot be found. The sadness of his desolation puts me in mind of my own solitude, and I am about to put aside the magazine when I see the words *witchcraft delusion.*

Nat told me that no one in Salem speaks of the witchcraft delusion anymore. Yet here are those very words in a story titled "The Manuscript, Charles Cunningham."

Now I'm wide awake and reading again from the beginning. The story is long and strange, told by a man who claims he fought in the colonial rebellion and saw trunks full of English tea dumped into Boston Harbor. The storyteller harks back to a lady in Boston who keeps a hidden manuscript, and those passages reference the Salem witchcraft delusion.

I pore over the story again, and it is just as Nat said in front of the *Gazette* office: witch trials, a manuscript, and tales of long-ago Salem. I run my hand over the printed letters. The cat's body vibrates at my feet and warms the blanket. The cottage is quiet, and I can picture Nat reading the story aloud to me, tilting his head as he does when he knows he's hit upon something clever.

Witchcraft. Solitude. Open doors that draw in a man before he has time to think twice. I can feel him with me at the precipice of something, much as I stood today at the Silas house, much as the man in his story peered through a doorway that opened like a secret and invited him inside.

Salem, 1692

Tituba is the first accused.

"You dare to make a witch cake in my house?" Parris beats his slave to the kitchen floor. "You will confess or endure torments you cannot imagine."

Goodwife Sarah Good, a beggar much despised for slinking about the village with her young daughter, is second.

Widow Osborne, accused and acquitted of witchcraft before, is third.

On the morning of their examination, John Hathorne strides into the court of Oyer and Terminer with a single intention: he will make the women confess.

Sarah Good is brought before the court in chains, and the young accusers—Betty Parris, Abigail Williams, Ann Putnam, and Betty Hubbard—cower and shriek. Hathorne quiets the room as best he can, recites aloud the Laws and Liberties of Massachusetts concerning the identification of witches, and opens A Discourse on the Damned Art of Witchcraft *to the passage from Exodus 22, verse 18:* Thou shalt not suffer a witch to live.

He is ready to begin.

"What evil spirit have you familiarity with?" Hathorne demands of Sarah Good.

"None."

"Do you dare to say you made no contract with the Devil?"

Again, Sarah Good answers in a single word.

"None."

"Why do you hurt these children?"

"I do not," Good says.

The afflicted girls shriek. Hathorne rises from his chair.

"Then what creature have you empowered to do so?"

"None."

Hathorne directs his attention to the children and orders them to "look to Goodwife Good and tell me if this is the person who has hurt you." The four girls twist in their chairs like tortured puppets and scream, though no one has lain a finger upon them.

"Then how do you explain their torment?" Hathorne demands.

Sarah Good doesn't feel well. She needs to relieve herself, to curl into a corner and retch as she did when she carried her little Dorcas to birthing.

"It's Osborne," Sarah Good cries. "Widow Osborne torments them, not I."

From the edge of the crowded meetinghouse, William Good shouts, "She is a witch or she will be one quick enough," and Hathorne calls Sarah's husband to stand beside his wife.

"What proof have you? What has your wife done to hurt you?"

"Nothing yet." Good eyes his wife, who has taken hold of a chair and is trembling. "But her bad carriage to me tells me she is an enemy to all that is good—and I have seen a wart below her right shoulder only this week and known it to be the Devil's mark."

Through a crack in the meetinghouse door, four-year-old Dorcas peers at her mother and closes her ears to her father's words. Dorcas tugs on her red braids. She has no one to speak to of her fear, only the bright welts along her arm where she sucks for comfort when there is no food or Mama at home.

— FOURTEEN —

The harbor postmaster pushes a parchment scrawled with my name across the counter.

"Came by one of Captain Derby's schooners from the South," he says. At the sight of Edward's handwriting, my heart hardens to a shield.

My Dear Wife,

It's the twenty-eighth of April and the letter is dated April first and so it's traveled from ship to ship in very good time.

I write to tell you that I have not squandered our investments, for I intend to fulfill my promise to your father and return his trust in me with manifold profit. Here in the Charleston markets I paid a very small coin for medicines to relieve pain and aging and invested in a marvel of seeds and spider eggs from an African slave trader. I'm certain you'll appreciate the wonders of these elixirs and enjoy the wealth and health they bring us. In Baltimore I discovered astonishing things that will enrich us beyond our wildest dreams. I dare not say more, only that you should keep watch over our closest neighbors and be prepared to help when I return. I pray there is a child on the way. If

you send a letter to the shipmaster in Liverpool addressed to the New
Harmony, *I will receive your good news when we arrive there. I trust*
you will use your needle to feed yourself only if it is necessary, and that
you stay safe and content keeping the garden and home for my return.

Until then *I remain your devoted husband,*
Edward

I read the note twice and shove it into the bottom of my basket. Edward is greedy and deceitful—so different from Nat, who offers practical advice and even inspiration, who speaks of enchantments and
encourages my needlework. Now Edward dares tell me to feed myself,
as if he has only now realized that his treachery left me penniless.

And what does he mean about our closest neighbors? I've grown
fond of Mercy and Zeke and the little ones. Even if they are engaged in
a secret venture with the Remonds, I would never do anything to harm
them. The very idea of it disgusts me—Ivy and Abraham are innocent
and precious. The eggs they leave at my doorstep, the potatoes I find in a
little pile, are like gifts from the faeries left for me in the night.

Edward betrayed me, but I would never betray my friends.

I'M STILL STEWING over the letter when I reach Felicity's shop and Abigail rushes to greet me.

"You'll never guess it, Isobel."

I cannot gather my tongue quick enough, and she doesn't wait for a
reply.

"Nat Hathorne came in to see about your gloves. But he didn't buy
any because—can you imagine?" The pitch of her voice rises. "Because
all three pair were sold this morning!"

With my mind on Edward's letter, I've forgotten to look in the shop
window. Now I see there's a new shawl laid out where the gloves were
last week.

"Two ladies from Philadelphia came yesterday," Abigail chatters on.
"They were wearing smart dresses made with ruffles and velvet trim, and
their traveling bonnets were the most delightful things you can imagine—"

"And?" I cut off her rattling. If there's something for my own profit in Salem, I must see to it before Edward returns. The thought of helping him with a brew or plot that he's hatched with Pap's stolen gold is more than I can bear.

"The ladies paid six dollars for all three pair without blinking." Abigail drops her voice as Felicity approaches. "Felicity told them *a recluse in the countryside* made the gloves."

Given the money my work has brought her, I expect Felicity to smile at me. But her face is the same as always, flat and unreadable.

"The gloves were sold, as Abigail has told you," Felicity says. "The buyers have a fashionable shop in Philadelphia and asked for two more pair like the first, and two others decorated with a wisteria vine—they're fond of their wisteria in Philadelphia."

So much is happening, it's difficult to hold on to my thoughts.

"Do you hear me?" Felicity demands. "I need you to make more gloves."

I look at her with a steady eye and see not only her betrayal but Edward's, too. The moment I must stake my claim has come sooner than expected.

"If you're easily getting two dollars for each pair, then I should have at least a dollar," I say. Felicity looks at me as if I'm not even speaking, and I wonder if any sound is coming from my mouth. "I've done the arithmetic, and a three-hundred-percent profit is much more than any importer makes."

I have indeed spoken aloud, for Abigail stares at me openmouthed.

"A profit of one hundred percent is still very much in your favor," I add, for now my mind is crystal clear.

"I'll give you a nickel more per glove, not a penny more." The woman does not blink or blanch.

"That's hardly fair," I say.

What crosses Felicity's face is hostility, even contempt.

"If the gloves weren't in my window, the ladies from Philadelphia never would have seen them."

"I didn't understand the gloves would fetch such a price." I cannot believe I'm still speaking, and yet I'm finding the words and the strength.

Nat is right—I have a temper now, and I am bold. "They brought you a very fine profit."

"Forty cents a pair," Felicity says. "You don't have to take it. I can find someone else to do the work."

I don't imagine she can find anyone to make the gloves as I've made them. But if they're worth so much, and the ladies are willing to buy more, then I shouldn't disrupt the exchange—not until I can meet these women and make them my own customers. I plan it all out in this moment: if I can convince the ladies to hire me directly, I won't need to wait for the banquet or depend on Nat to buy my gloves. I will be able to restore Pap's stolen gold and use it however I please.

"If you feel in all fairness that's all you can pay for now, Mrs. Adams, then I'll do the work for the ladies."

"For *me*." Her expression is pure triumph. "Four pair for the Philadelphia ladies, and two more for the shop. You will make the gloves for *me*, and you'll do it by next week. Now go home and get to work."

I'M FURIOUS. WISHING to make what neither Edward nor Felicity can steal from me, I pack a workbasket and go in the direction where Nat told me he works. The harbor is fresh, and I settle on a gray boulder that looks out to the rocky shore.

I failed at the leopard, but there's another story I heard in church on a recent Sunday morning. This is the scene I want to put on my shawl for the banquet.

With Felicity's words ringing in my ears, I put aside her gloves and use the last of my charcoal to draw Adam and Eve in the Garden of Eden. Eve picks an apple and gives it to Adam—this is the story the minister told to teach us that a woman cannot be trusted. But Eve merely offered the fruit to Adam, I wanted to shout from the back of the church. Adam could have said no. He could have tossed the apple deep into the Garden.

He ate it because he wanted its sweetness.

He wanted its sweetness.

I sketch these words into the vines around Adam and Eve and hold my drawing up against the sky.

I draw Adam's hair curled behind his ears and give Eve my own narrow torso. The sketch is modest yet hints of desire. It's biblical and decorated with fruit: the ladies of this town will love it.

I'm admiring my composition when a shadow falls over my hand.

"You found the spot."

Nat puts a leg up on a rock and peers down at me. It's the first I've seen him without his cloak, and I'm struck by the lankness of his frame, the length of leg, and the breadth of his shoulders. We're alone here. There's a wide smile on his face. What secrets he has—his ancestor presiding at the witch trials, the gallows curse and its legacy—are not so different from my own. The discovery of his story in the magazine only made me feel closer to him, as if he has invited me to follow him through a strange passageway to his place of enchantment.

And now we are here. He slings off his shoulder bag.

"I saw your gloves in the shop window," he says when I don't speak. "But by the time I stopped to inquire, they were gone."

"The price was very dear." I find my voice and say it with pride. "No one in Salem paid it. Felicity sold everything to two ladies who have a shop in Philadelphia."

I tell him I'm decorating new gloves with fruits and wisteria for those ladies.

"You should make the leopard," he says. "Something strong and striking will surely help them remember your name in Philadelphia."

"But that's the problem—they won't know my name in Philadelphia."

"This isn't the time to be modest," Nat says.

He hitches up his pants and crouches with his back against the rock. We're almost side by side. The sea stretches out in front of us, gray and green. In all my time with Edward, we never sat together like this on a spring afternoon and gazed out to sea.

"Your work fetched a high price. When the gloves are worn in Philadelphia, other fashionable ladies will want a pair for themselves."

I'd hoped that he'd advise me how to proceed in the face of Felicity's deceits, and now he has. Edward takes, and Nat gives.

"Felicity isn't telling anyone the work is mine," I say. "She invented a story about a recluse in the countryside who makes the gloves."

When I've told him everything, Nat says, "Felicity Adams should pay you a fair wage and you should insist on it."

"I don't believe she will, and so I must make my name in Salem just as you said—at the banquet, with a dress and a shawl so triumphant that she cannot stop me once it is seen."

When he asks what I have in mind, I uncover my sketchbook and let him study the design.

I've hidden Adam's and Eve's bodies behind the cluster of vines, but it's clear they're undressed in a garden. It's all I can do to stay so close to him without trembling.

"This is enchanting." He touches a finger to the leaves, but if he sees the words I've hidden there, he says nothing. He turns the sketch one way and the other. "But you've forgotten the serpent."

The minister spoke of Eve as temptation. He said little about the serpent's interlocution; he blamed not the snake but the woman.

"Temptation is the heart of the story, embodied by the snake," Nat says. "Desire never comes without some pain. The snake is the instrument of both, bringing first temptation, then the anguish of banishment."

A bold slice of heat goes through me.

"I read your story in the *Ladies' Magazine*," I say before I can stop myself.

"What story?"

I pull the magazine from my basket.

"This one—about the manuscript and the Salem witchcraft delusion. The story within a story about a Salem doctor. I assume the witchcraft delusion, the witch troubles, and the witch trials in Salem are all the same?"

He slides his back down the rock and gives a nod.

"You're a careful listener, Mrs. Gamble."

"Surely others must have guessed the writer is you."

"The editor made so many changes I cannot rightly call the story my own," he says. Until this moment he's seemed confident and self-possessed. "Anyway, the *Ladies' Magazine* isn't widely read outside of Boston," he says. "You're the first to ask me about it."

"I see."

"I'll tell you another secret." He looks up at the sky. "I wrote a novel and published it anonymously."

A novel is a remarkable thing, I want to say.

"A love story," he goes on. "It's an awful, sophomoric book and as soon as I saw it in print, I was ashamed. But it was already done and paid for, and when the *Ladies' Magazine* editor praised it in a review, I sent her four stories right away. She took two and encouraged me to send the other to a Mr. Goodrich in Boston. I sent them last month—and added that strange bit about the old married couple."

Nat makes a fist.

"Yesterday I had a letter from Goodrich saying he doesn't want them. He wants stories for ladies and children instead."

His face is open and vulnerable, etched with a pain that looks much like the desire I've seen on Edward's face.

"Mrs. Gamble, will you tell me in complete honesty: What kinds of stories do you think ladies want to read?"

"I can only speak for myself." I choose my words carefully, for I want to help him as he has helped me. His eyes are closed, but I know he's listening. "I like stories about adventure and history such as yours. But I also want to read about a man's character, as well as his penchant for romance. I want to know how to recognize a good man from a bad one." I pause and ask the question gently. "Do you have family stories you might draw upon?"

His eyes fly open and he looks at me with a fierceness that makes it impossible to look away.

"What have you heard?"

"I've heard about the judge and the witch trials," I admit.

His face pinches, and in a flash he understands.

"I thought you might, now that you're working at Felicity Adams's shop."

I have the urge to tell him about Isobel Gowdie and my own secrets, just to soothe him. But I hold my tongue.

"I feel the curse of his cruelty on me every day," Nat says. "Whatever was passed down I have to cast off—if not by blood, then by ink and words." He looks hard at me. "That's what I keep trying to write—some salvation for myself and my family."

"It was a long time ago," I say.

"Their families suffered because of mine."

"They shouldn't blame you."

"And why not?" he asks. "His ancestor's blood runs in my veins."

"Bad men can do good things, and good men can do bad things. Perhaps your grandsire was both good and bad," I offer.

He jumps to his feet, shoves his hands in his trouser pockets, and paces in front of me.

"I know man's nature better than most because I see what others refuse to," he says. "The darkness hidden in men's hearts, secrets we keep even from ourselves. What's good and bad both—that's what I'm trying to put in my stories."

Gulls caw overhead as if to warn me that his world of enchantments is dangerous. Selkies and kelpies and faeries entertain themselves on human foibles and on our impossible desires for love and safety, and yet we don't stop seeking these things.

"Ladies would rather read about love, I think," I tell him. "How to recognize a true man, how to choose well."

"Love rarely trumps the darkness in men's souls." His words are more red than gold. "Secrets inside of secrets; *that's* what I want to write. Churchgoing Devil worshippers who meet under the moon. Family shame passed down through generations. Salem ladies who walk about town as if they or their ancestors never sinned," he goes on. "Men who judge others harshly while hiding their own terrible deeds."

He squats in front of me and grips my hand. His fingers aren't gentle, but I don't pull away.

"I need to write these stories so that I can be free of the ruin my forefathers brought on our name. So that one day I can leave it all behind."

"Would you leave Salem?"

"Dear God, I hope I will."

I keep my voice steady. "Where would you go?"

"I spent my boyhood in Maine, where the water is icy and bracing." He shakes his head as if he's just come out of the cold water. "I'm free there. I can breathe the air and walk the woods without fear or judgment. I'll be going soon—Uncle William is having my first gentleman's coat made and we'll go north when it's finished."

"You're leaving?"

"Only for a short journey—but one day I'll leave for good."

He picks up the glove I put aside and uses his finger to trace a pattern of vines round and round until he's at the center of the palm.

"I saw you go into the Silas house by the kitchen door," he says.

I don't say a word. He takes my hand and places the glove on it, pulling the fabric down over one finger at a time.

"The Silas family." This is my pinky finger. "The Good family. The Martins. The Easty family." It's almost as if I'm looking at someone else's hand as he tugs the glove snug over one finger at a time. "Felicity Adams and her sister. They're all descended from the accused or the accusers. From women hanged or those who sent them to death."

The glove is on. He lets go of my hand. Every bit of me longs to snatch him back.

"Felicity Adams?" I ask.

"Her grandmother came down the Parker family line. Alice Parker was hanged, but her sister stayed and married a man from Marblehead."

My hand is tingling with both desire and apprehension.

"The Silas family?"

"Mrs. Silas's maternal great-grandmother was one of the very first hanged."

I told her my secret, and now I know why she did not send me away.

"And yet they stayed in Salem? Why would they?"

He looks pained but not bewildered. I would like to put a hand to that pain, to draw it out from him and soothe my own at the same time.

"The families were poor and broken and there wasn't anywhere to go," he says. "In a new town they would have had to present themselves to the minister and ask to be welcomed into the church. If they were refused, they couldn't stay. And you can well imagine the neighboring villages didn't want any part of what happened here."

I wonder, as I always have, who helped Isobel Gowdie and where she went after she escaped.

"It still seems hard to imagine anyone would stay after what happened."

"And yet they did." He surprises me with a laugh. "Twenty years after the witch trials, two Hathorne cousins married the granddaughters of Philip and Mary English—a couple that was accused of witchcraft."

"Were they killed?" I cannot imagine marrying the descendant of someone who accused Isobel Gowdie.

"No," he says. "Philip and Mary English escaped."

"How did they do it?" I feel suddenly light-headed, picturing Isobel Gowdie dancing on the roof of her burning cottage.

"Money." He gives me a rueful smile. "English was one of the wealthiest men in Salem, with a fleet of ships and a storehouse full of imports. They escaped from the Boston jail and later returned to Salem and raised their children here."

"If they had money and means, why did they come back?"

"Money again," he says with that same smile. He looks painfully handsome, troubled but also animated. "Most of the accused families had their property seized to pay court fees and penalties. But English was powerful and rich and had enough loyal seamen to keep his fleet going until the witch trials were dissolved and repudiated by the authorities the following year."

I'm struggling to imagine the families of the dead and the families of the accusers living side by side, going to the same church, walking the same streets.

"The governor shut down the whole proceedings, terminated the court and the trials. And when it was all over, the accusers apologized." Nat gives that dry cough of a laugh again. "Judges apologized, too. Everyone but John Hathorne, who insisted to the end that he could have done nothing differently, given the evidence that was put before him. Given the power of Satan and his minions."

Nat recounts at least a dozen village marriages and bloodlines descended from the time of the witchcraft delusion. It's difficult to follow, for the names changed when women married from one generation to the next. But the essence is clear.

"Life had to go on." He shrugs. "A hundred years later, my own mother married into the Hathorne family."

I want to tell him about my ancestress more than ever, but something stops me. The colors and the curse are bound up together, and to keep one hidden I dare not speak of the other.

And yet silence doesn't protect us from the past, as I well know. When a legacy haunts a family the echoes reverberate even if no one hears them. This is what Nat is saying and I know it's true. I feel it is true, for Isobel Gowdie's legacy haunted my mother to the end of her life, even as it haunts me now.

"And what about the curse?" I ask. "The one you said you must repair?"

"The curse of my grandsire's behavior is its own horror," he says. "But there was also a curse hurled from the gallows by little Dorcas's mother."

He says it now: "'If you kill me, God will give you blood to drink.'"

I feel my face burn as if stung with tears, although it is dry and hot in the sun.

"If you don't believe in witches, why would you believe in curses?"

His face twists, and I cannot read it.

"A dark soul can cast a long shadow over the living and the dead," he says. "Who's to say that enough hate and anger can't bring about something terrible?"

"And Dorcas Good?" I must know the fate of this child. "What happened to her?"

He shakes his head.

"I'm still searching. There's nothing in Felt's history of Salem, and I haven't found her fate in the court records. But I won't give up looking."

"If hate can bring a curse into being, then what can love do?" I ask. "Perhaps that's something you can write in one of your stories instead of so much horror."

I dared to say the word *love*; now I hold my breath and wait.

"We're very much the same, you and I," he says. "You tell stories with your needle, and I tell them with my words. I'm writing for my reasons, and you are stitching for your own."

He touches a finger to my sketchbook, where the story of Adam and Eve is spread out the length of a shawl.

"If you want courage, stitch courage," he says slowly. "If you want love, you should stitch love. You should make your leopard, Mrs. Gamble. Your leopard, and Adam and Eve, too."

His hands are still, but I almost feel him reach for me. I almost hear him whisper my name. *Isobel.* Soft red and gold.

Boston, 1692

Tituba will never forget the thorned branches that seemed to reach for them as she trudged out of Salem behind the magistrate's cart with Sarah Good and Widow Osborne. Now the widow is dead.

Tituba looks to where John and Elizabeth Proctor sleep entwined on the jailhouse floor while Rebecca Nurse, Sarah Cloyce, Sarah Good, Susannah Martin, and George Burroughs huddle alone.

"If we were witches we'd get out of here." Goodwife Martin speaks to no one and to everyone, to the darkness and to the cracks of light that pierce the stone walls.

Tituba is cold. None of the other Salem slaves spoke in her defense. Not even John Indian came to her aid. She was forced to make a pact with the devil Parris, who promised to pay her bail if she confessed. Now she can do nothing but curl her hands around her own hunger and wait for Parris to keep his word.

"Your man has been afflicted." Goodwife Martin is talking to her now. "I saw John Indian twitch and howl like one of the little girls. How long before they come for you, Black Witch? How long before we all hang because of you?"

Tituba turns away. She doesn't look around even when the jailhouse door opens and four more women are shoved into the darkness.

"Ye can kill each other, witches. No one will stop you," the warden says before he locks the door.

Tituba closes her eyes.

"I am not a witch," she hears Sarah Good whisper. "I am not a witch."

— FIFTEEN —

"The Silas family's a slaving family." Mercy's face is stubborn and hard. "I told you to sell your gloves to them, not to go in the house and make friends."

No one is supposed to know I've done work for the family. But Zeke brought me home in his carriage last week, so he knows—and so does Mercy.

"But there are no slaves here in Salem." I'm standing in a patch of sunlight beside her garden early Thursday morning. "I thought slaves are only in the South."

"Slaves built our wharves." Mercy squares off her jaw, which makes her cheekbones stand high. "Slaves were only set free in the Commonwealth about a minute ago. Just 'cause you don't hear about them doesn't mean they weren't here. It doesn't mean their ghosts aren't still walking about.

"Captain Silas's grandfather ran a slave ship," Mercy goes on. "The uncle, too. They got two nephews running a sugar plantation in Jamaica right now—it's the meanest life you've ever seen down there."

Ivy and Abraham are in the chicken coops scattering corn, the sound of their voices blue like gentle rain. The secrets of Salem don't seem to weigh on the children, and I'm glad when I hear Abraham's bright laugh.

"Mercy—" I hold out a bit of beeswax that I found at Blackwell's, but she doesn't look at it.

"Sugar, rum, cotton, cod—back and forth to the islands." Mercy spits on the ground. I recall the captain said something similar on our voyage. "Those slaves are dead, but their blood and toil is in this very dirt."

Anger and something deeper flashes in her eyes. *Keep watch over our closest neighbors,* Edward wrote.

"A slave catcher brought my grandmother from Africa in leg irons." Mercy keeps going. It's as if she wants something from me and won't stop until she gets it. "She was a strong woman with a long, strong spine. Proud, too. Would have been beat to death in the sugar fields for that pride, but a white man took a liking to her and brought her north for a comfort woman."

"A Silas man bought your grandmother and brought her here?" I want her to know I am listening, but I worry I am missing her meaning.

"Not Silas," she says. "Man by the name of Kyle Fellowship. He called my grandma Circe and kept her in a room at the back of his house in Bristol. My mama was born in that room."

"Mercy, I don't have anything to do with Captain Silas." My words are strained. "I've only taken one job with the Silas family. Did they do something awful to your grandmother?"

Mercy stares past me, just as she did the first day we met.

"A slave man is a slave man, that's what I'm trying to tell you," she says. "Fellowship sold my ma to a neighbor who used her the same way. Ma was about to birth me when the man gave her fifty dollars and sent her away."

Mercy points her finger for emphasis, lest I misunderstand the man's intentions.

"Only because he had to, mind you. New law said a man couldn't buy or sell a slave here anymore, and he'd have to vouch for Ma and for me, too, if she stayed in town. So he gave her the money and sent her away."

Mercy shakes her head.

"Ma was lucky the man gave her money so she'd get good and gone. Most weren't so lucky—most had to stay in place and work for wages too low to live on. But Ma came to Salem and bought this bit of land from Widow Higgins's husband."

She nods to the chicken coops, the yard, and the small buildings. I notice a patch of marigolds coming into bud.

"The town folks didn't like us being here instead of over on Rice and Pond or up on Roast Beef Hill with the other Black folk. But Ma knew chickens and said this was the right place, and Mr. Higgins didn't care what the others thought."

The children come running from the coop but stop when they see me. I raise a hand in greeting and wonder again what secrets Mercy and Zeke are keeping and what Edward thinks is happening here.

"What do you want, anyway?" Mercy demands.

I remember the beeswax that's softened in my hand. "I brought this for you."

"Why?"

"I'm going to use it for the ointment when I harvest the pennyroyal. I want you to try it."

She rolls it in her palm the same way I've been rolling the scrimshaw buttons, holds it to her nose, and nods her approval.

"Also, I brought back your glove form, but I still need my own."

She tells me to wait and returns with a new glove form that smells of the green forest and the branches that were cut to make it.

"Zeke's gone to see his wife in Lynn," she says. "Made this for you before he left."

I try to return her form but Mercy won't take it.

"Use both, your work will go faster and you can pay my cousin for what he made." She names a price and I tell her I'll be right back with the coins. When I return, Mercy is sitting with Ivy between her knees, rubbing the beeswax along the edge of the little girl's forehead. Ivy's eyes are closed, dreamlike, and Mercy is humming a low tune. When I put the coins into her palm, she doesn't miss a stroke.

On Sunday I take my regular seat in the last row at the East Meeting House beside a family of farmers who are dusted yellow from the fields. The wife is a small, fidgety woman who plumps her skirts when she sits. Some ladies might scorn the family with their smell of fields and manure, but I'm comfortable beside the sons. Their cheeks are covered with yellow fuzz, their wrists are red, and they follow along in the hymnal closer than any grown man.

I bow my head when it's time, sit and rise with the others, but I don't hear anything. I see the Easty family fill two long rows and remember their ancestress was hanged. I watch Captain and Mrs. Silas from the back and wonder if anything is written in the Salem history book about their slave ships.

Nat spoke of Susannah Martin who left seven children when she was hanged, and Martha and Giles Corey whose own nephews made the accusations and then took their uncle's property when they were carted away to jail. And this is what I think of now—not God or the minister or the sermon or even the colors and my needle, but the accused and the accusers living side by side after the witch trials were over. Of John Hathorne refusing to admit he'd been wrong, even after the accusers begged forgiveness for bringing false witness against their neighbors. Of little Dorcas, the red-haired girl in Nat's story—maybe she was hanged and even the record keepers were too horrified to put it in writing. If I have learned anything these months in Salem it's that history isn't what's written or told. History is hidden away in dark corners and shadows, just as Nat says.

And yet there is the lovely Easty daughter holding a babe of her own in church this morning. And there is Nat's uncle Robert Manning, who grows fruit trees in his famous orchard, praying with his eyes closed and his voice raised to God. All of us standing, sitting, praying, and living with the weight of all that came before. All of us holding secret longings and desires.

I DON'T WALK through town after church but take the path that runs along the sea. Gulls are overhead, the smell of roasting nuts and coffee beans and the flecks of yellow hay pepper the air. My heart pounds as I round the bend and see the rock where Nat and I sat last week. I know it's foolish to hope he's there now, but still I'm disappointed when the boulder is empty and there's no sign of the hour we spent here, no body or spirit waiting for me as if the days never passed.

I lean against the boulder and spy a scrap of pink and red tucked into a crook between two smaller rocks. It's not fabric, I discover, but a thorny branch of pink hawthorn flowers twined together with a single rose.

I look high and low, toward the sea and away. Starlings, crows, and sparrows sit in the hemlocks that circle the rocky outcrop. There's no May tree, no rosebush. The flowers can't have found their way here by anything but a human hand. *His* hand.

My body fills with great, buoyant joy. I find a scrap of cloth in my pocket and quickly stitch a simple letter *A* with red thread. The cloth fits in the palm of my hand. I roll it like a tallow candle and slide it into the shallow where I found the flowers. He said if I want love then I must stitch love. I trace my own fingers across my palm just as Nat did, and remember the feel of his touch.

THE FLOWERS WATCH me, and I watch the flowers. For three days and nights I labor over Felicity's gloves. The rose and hawthorn blossoms stand in a cup of water on my table, their vibrant colors and fragrance leading me into an enchantment I cannot resist. Embroidery may be women's work, but as the hours pass in a dazzle of color and cloth I imagine a shop of my own and a business far away from Felicity and Edward. Petals, stems, leaves, and fruits pour out in designs I have only imagined in my mind's eye, and when I finish a long stem of roses it is as if they are arms reaching for an embrace.

My hands ache, my eyes water, and my back and neck are needled with pain, but I do not stop working. I am racing against time.

Dawn is rising when I line up the gloves and step back to admire them. I see the words—*LOVE, COURAGE*—rise and then fall away. I did not plan them, yet there they are.

THE SIX PAIR of gloves are wrapped in plain cotton when I bring them to Felicity in the morning. She makes a show of talking while she opens the wrapping, but when the gloves are laid out on the counter she goes silent.

She reaches for a glove with a red rose sewn upon the back. This is the one Nat put on my hand as he traced out Salem's lineage of accused and accusers.

Felicity brings the gloves to her nose as if she expects to find a fragrance. I see the letters *L-O-V-E* in the white space between the green leaves, the red petals, and the tiny yellow flecks of pollen. I didn't draw them out, and yet they rise.

She folds over the edges where I've stitched my scarlet *A,* but doesn't seem to see it or the letters between the white spaces.

"I won't ask you what you have done with these gloves, and it's best that you don't tell me," she says.

"What I've done?" I can't look at Felicity without thinking of our common history, each of us descended from a woman accused of witchcraft. "I've made them rich with color, just as you asked."

She counts the coins into my palm without looking at me. Even with the extra twenty cents, it's far less than what the gloves are worth.

"There's something strange in the patterns," she says. "Almost an enchantment."

She is right and I know it—there is an enchantment in the gloves.

Am I a witch? And if I am, what am I to do with a power I do not understand? And if I do not understand it, how can I keep from revealing it to others? How can I know that it will not harm or betray me, that it will not call into being things I do not want?

And what of what I *do* want? What of that?

THAT VERY DAY I buy a new set of green and gold beads for my banquet shawl, then take a stroll through town. It is a warm afternoon and the sun stretches farther than it ever did at home at this hour. As always, I'm alert for a glimpse of Nat as I come upon a small cluster of onlookers watching the Light Infantry band practicing near Hamilton Hall. Their thumping drums mark a beat that one little boy keeps with a stick he waves like a baton, and the colors of the music are red, white, and blue like the stars and stripes of the American flag.

On the board at the Charter Ale House I look, as always, for notices of ships coming and going. I read in the *Gazette* that Darling's ship left Charleston for Bermuda the third week of April, but there's nothing about the *New Harmony* posted here. I wonder what Edward is doing and imagine a bucket of spiders weaving webs across his small cabin.

Two Colored gentlemen have come up beside me to study the ship lists, and an elderly lady elbows past me with a small handwritten note she's affixing to the board.

"Mr. Remond, Mr. Woolman," she greets the men. "You see this here?"

Free Negroes Beware:
A slave catcher has been
seen on these Salem streets

"Friends say he's looking for a mother and child who ran off a Baltimore plantation," she says. "Man named MacGreggor."

"I hear it's an eight-year-old boy they're hunting." Mr. Remond drops his voice.

"I don't think the child is here," the other gentleman says with a wary glance in my direction. "Things been quiet lately."

I read the note again. A mother and child must be running from their slave owners and seeking freedom here.

"Why would a slave catcher come here?" I blurt out.

The woman turns her bright eyes on me.

"You're not from here." It's not a question.

"No, I've come from Scotland." I am grateful when she doesn't say anything cruel.

"Slaves escape north for the freedom they deserve as one of God's own," she says, and her voice is kind. "But the law still lets plantation owners come after them and take them back in chains. It's always worse for them after that—they're beaten, some have their tongues cut out or get sold farther south where the lash is crueler and it's near impossible to escape."

Just before dawn on many days I hear Ivy and Abraham whispering at my well, and in town Zeke always stops to ask how I am faring. Mercy tried to tell me the cruelty is right here, and now I've heard it again. I've been living in Salem for two months, and all the while there have been people—children—running for their lives.

What else is slipping through the spaces that I don't see? What other dark secrets is the city hiding?

Salem, 1692

John Hathorne and the Reverend Cotton Mather enter the Goods' cottage as sunset falls. William Good brings four-year-old Dorcas to stand before them. The girl's hands are dirty, her braided red hair stuck with bits of straw and twigs.

Dorcas confessed to the court yesterday, but John Hathorne knows himself to be a good man—he will not convict a child of witchcraft without affirmation from the Lord himself.

He bends down now and wills himself to speak gently.

"You did not need to confess if you are not possessed by Satan," he tells the girl. "Do you understand?"

Dorcas nods. Her stomach is empty and sour.

"Are you a witch?"

She holds herself hand to wrist, and scratches at the marks she made sucking on her arm.

Hathorne puts a finger to the row of red marks.

"Did you do this to yourself?"

The girl recoils and shakes her head. Her father has told her it's nasty and unnatural to suck at herself this way.

"Then what did it?"

"A snake," she whispers.

"Where is the snake?"

Dorcas wants her mother.

"Mama," the little girl whispers.

"Is the snake here now?"

Dorcas shakes her head and puts a dirty thumb into her mouth.

Hathorne and Mather sigh with a heavy resolve. A snake in Sarah Good's home is surely a spirit familiar or an incarnation of the Black Man. It's all they need to go ahead with the mother's sentence.

As for the child, her sentence will come later, when they have time to pray upon it.

"We need to take the girl now," they say to the father. And William Good releases his daughter without a word.

Sarah Good keeps her eyes on the blue sky as the wardens take her by the elbows and push her up onto the gallows. She is remembering the child she birthed on the jailhouse floor, the way it took one breath and succumbed without a sound.

At least little Dorcas is still alive. It is her one consolation and the reason Sarah Good summons her voice now.

"I am not a witch," she whispers. "I am not a witch, and my daughter is not a witch." No one seems to hear. She must summon more strength.

A magistrate is standing at the foot of the gallows in a tall black hat. Is it John Hathorne or Cotton Mathers or the devil Nicholas Noyes? She cannot make out if it is one man or three. Her eyes have lost all focus; there's only the blue sky now and the chance to say one final thing to these accursed men.

"I am no more a witch than you are a warlock," Sarah shouts to the black hat and to the blue heavens. "I am not a witch, and if you kill me, God will give you blood to drink."

The floor beneath her opens. She holds out her arms to God. The sky swallows her.

— SIXTEEN —

Nat's rose and hawthorn flowers are still on my table when I am called to the Silas house to finish sprigging Charlotte's veil.

I find the back door open and slip into the empty kitchen, where embers still warm the hearth and the smell of bread fills the air. There are footsteps on the stair and Mrs. Silas appears in her white house gown and robe. I think of Mercy's hard words about the Silas family and their slave money, and remember the first time I heard Mrs. Silas's imperious voice speaking to a dressmaker. She was lying then, talking about her daughter Charlotte visiting the Great Lakes when the girl was hidden at home.

"The dress is perfect, Mrs. Gamble. You're a gifted seamstress," she says now. She hands me the veiled hat and I begin to secure the pink flowers on it. "Best of all, you've made my daughter happy. And I care very much for her happiness."

She looks tired but otherwise unbowed as she sits like a queen and watches me work.

"Do you mind living out where you do?" she asks after a while.

I bite off the edge of a pink thread and thread a needle with white.

"I have neighbors nearby," I say. "I don't feel alone there."

"Zeke and Mercy." She nods. "How do you find them?"

"Find them?"

"Are they reasonable enough? They should be happy now that they're getting their own Negro church, but you never know what any of them are thinking."

I feel Mercy's anger rise in me, and am reminded of the slave catcher and his purpose.

"They're a fine family," I say. "Zeke has a wife in Lynn, and Ivy and Abraham are good children."

"You don't know what they're truly like." I see that imperial tilt to Mrs. Silas's chin. "We gave them their freedom and they still refuse to move out of my way on the street right here in Salem."

I didn't assume that Mrs. Silas was evil just for marrying a man whose father brought slaves across the ocean. But I have a different feeling about her now. While she goes on about how Black folks should show more gratitude, I remember Mercy's gentle hands as she rubbed the beeswax into Ivy's temples. I want to tell her that Mercy loves her daughter the same way she loves Charlotte.

"Charlotte needs petticoats and other lady's items," Mrs. Silas says, one thought running right into the next. "We'd like you to make them with the same attention to detail that you've brought to everything you've done for her."

"I hate to rush my stitching," I demure. Mrs. Silas may have left behind the subject of Mercy and Zeke, but I'm still stuck on her words. "I have much to do for Mrs. Adams at the shop. You might want to take your order to someone who can put two or three girls to the task."

"Nonsense," Mrs. Silas says, and her words become visible, silver and black and shaped like an iron fence. "You have almost two months. I will pay you double."

Double is much more than I am earning at the shop or for my gloves.

"Charlotte has asked only for you," she adds.

I told Nat his ancestors' sins don't belong to him, and I believe it. Why should Charlotte and her child bear the burden of her father's sins?

"I'll need thirty yards of white muslin, linen, and cotton," I say at last.

"Then buy forty of each." Mrs. Silas hands me twenty dollars in printed bills. "And sew a set of whites for the babe as well."

∞

MY JOB IS to hold my tongue and make Charlotte's whites, and this is what I will do. Each time I think of Edward's theft and lies my determination grows: I will have what I want with my needle, and Edward be damned.

I hide the paper money in a knot in the wall and buy cotton and linen from several merchants so that no one will suspect I'm making a quantity of petticoats. I bring my steel scissors to be sharpened at the knife shop near the wharves, and buy transparent paper and blue powder chalk at the stationer's to make the patterns.

I've always wanted to be a pattern-maker; to make my own embroidery designs for my own creations. Now I will do it all, from design to transfer and on to the stitching itself. There is no reason a woman cannot do all of these jobs.

Back home, I clear off the table and close up the cottage so there is no breeze. After I've drawn out a length of irises twined with leaves and flowers, I fill the pounce bag with new blue chalk and stamp the designs on the cloth. This is exactly how I will transfer my Adam and Eve scene onto the banquet shawl, so I'm glad for the chance to practice now.

Soon Charlotte's petticoats and tiny baby gowns hang across the backs of my chairs and spread across the table like the pale wings of angels. When I leave in the morning and return at the end of the day, I study them and swear they've moved. What stories could Nat tell about souls pinned up with sleeves and collars, souls spread out across a kitchen table or hung on a clothesline from the front to the back of my cottage? I'm sure that he would speak of ghosts and dreams and thwarted desires—but maybe, if he could see the way the white cloth seems to dance across the cottage, he might tell a hopeful tale. Not all ghosts are sinister, I know, for my own mother's spirit voice has come to me from beyond and offered comfort when I needed it.

The songs and the sounds of my girlhood fill my mind as I stitch, and many nights I work until I hear Mercy's children whispering through the woods just before dawn.

"Hurry, Ivy."

"I'm not fast as you."

Their voices remind me that not all voices in the shadows are filled with terrible secrets. Their voices tell me it's time to put my needle to rest, and I'm asleep before the children leave my yard.

ONE DAY MERCY comes for water in the morning instead of the children. She's surveying the pole beans I've tied up, and when I step outside she greets me by holding up a small jar of thick amber liquid.

"Brought this for you." It seems she's softened to me. Perhaps she's sorry she was harsh when we spoke last. "Maple syrup from the sugar house. If I give it to the children, they're likely to drink it away."

"I saw marigolds in your yard," I say after I've thanked her. "It's good for skin troubles, I remember that from Edward's shop."

I offer to make her a tincture and an ointment for the scratches and bumps that are risen on her arms—she says it is poison ivy, but it looks more like a rash from some sort of wet work—and she agrees.

"The beeswax you brought is nice." She holds up the jar. "You have any bread for this syrup?"

She follows me into the cottage, where I quickly cover up Charlotte's whites with my red cape. The whites are hidden from sight, but my cape is right there for Mercy to see. While I cut a piece of bread, she runs her finger over the sea monsters I sewed while the captain stitched his own whites.

"You say your mama taught you?"

Her hand hovers over the iris, the tiny letters where I stitched *LOVE, LOVE, LOVE* to see if I could hide them beneath other shapes. Just as Nat seems to always have a notebook in hand in which to write down his thoughts as they arrive to him, I've been using my cape to record memories, to test my ideas, and to practice my tiny letters. I meant it to be a private workplace for myself, but I cannot deny that it is something more—a protective cloak that has kept me safe and warm, that has carried me across oceans and time and wishes and fears.

I'd like to fold it away from Mercy's eyes, but it's too late now. My gaze goes to the place where I stitched Nat's words—*YOU INTRIGUE ME*—but she is leaning over to examine the flying figure of Isobel Gowdie.

"Why d'you have a witch here?" she asks.

There's no sense denying what's there in plain sight.

"My ancestress was accused of being a witch in Scotland. I learned her story when I was girl."

Mercy takes the bread and dips it into the jar of syrup, holds it out to me. It's fresh and sweet in my mouth.

"They say *witch,* but what do they mean?" Mercy muses. "*Witch* is a reason to kill you; *witch* might be someone to heal you; *witch* can be the Devil, or *witch* can be a woman so beautiful she makes you lose your sense. They've got so many ways of calling you a witch, they just change it to how it suits them."

She puts a pinky in the jar of syrup and puts a bit on her tongue.

"They hang her?" she asks plainly.

"She escaped."

Mercy nods as if I've finally said something that makes sense to her, and so I go on—I tell her about Isobel Gowdie, raising my voice and pointing my hand high when I repeat her incantation.

"'And if you kill me hell will reign on earth'?" In Mercy's mouth, the words sound different. Like something in a theater. "She truly say that—'lain with the Devil's forked prick'?"

Her whole face lights up and she's almost laughing.

"Now, that is a smart lady," she says. "Man thinks you are powerful, you got to find and *use* that power."

Mercy seems to be saying the same thing my mother told me before she died.

I lean in to listen more closely.

"That's something we all have to know," Mercy goes on. "Black woman, poor white woman—and especially a woman with your red hair and the way you talk."

"My red hair and how I talk?"

She crosses her arms and looks me up and down.

"You don't know it?"

I look at her face for a hint, but see nothing.

"Know what?"

"Isobel, I'll say it straight. With your red hair and foreign tongue, they don't think you're much better than us."

"Who are you talking about?"

"I'm talking 'bout them"—she waves a hand toward the door, toward the yard, toward the sky—"all of them. Mrs. Silas and her family, men in Salem and Boston—anybody who calls himself a true American thinks they're better than everybody else. That's why I don't like to see that Silas lady use you like she does."

"I'm Scottish." I draw myself up, as if I have forgotten how the ladies in the shop cringe when they hear how I speak.

"That's right—and they think the Scots are about as low-down as us Black folk. Maybe better than Indians but not by much."

"Scots are English—" I have longed to say it to Mrs. Adams's customers. Instead, I am declaiming to a woman whose mother was a slave. Mercy cuts me off, and the color of her words changes from plum to slate gray.

"Americans aren't English; they hate the king and the crown. Right here is where their war started. You know that, right?" She doesn't wait for me to answer. "Anyway, why do you keep saying you're English? You curtsy and go to dances at the royal court?"

Now she glares. Nat's rose scents the cottage with a sweet fragrance as it begins to brown on the edges like silt at the tip of a summer lake.

"No, but—"

She folds her arms across her chest.

"You had a meeting with King George?"

"No."

"Then you aren't English and you're sure not American," she says. "Out there, to them whose families have been in Salem for two hundred years, you ain't much better than Ivy or Zeke."

I want to protest. Mercy seems to be saying that only children born to women who were born here can be truly American.

Maybe this is what I've missed all along.

"But there's another kind of strength we've got," Mercy goes on. "I'm talking about me, my folks. It comes from knowing the difference between who you are and who they think you are."

I feel the rightness in what she is saying. I'm shaken, but I listen. She seems to draw herself up the way Isobel Gowdie has always stood straight and tall in my mind.

"You learn how to move through places so folks don't see you, then you can do things folks don't want you to do. You can do it right in front of them and they don't realize. And you know why? Because if you're nobody and you got nothing, then they don't feel your threat, and they hardly see you at all."

"I'm not nobody," I say.

She's nodding, but in a different way.

"That's right," she says. "*You* know that, but *they* don't. You've got to work the space in between the two. When you're near invisible and quiet and polite and a nice sort of pretty like you are, folks don't notice all you can do. Problem is, with that red hair of yours, you're still seen everywhere. Everybody recognizes you. But that's easy to fix."

She takes one of my bonnets off a peg.

"You just put up your hair. You put on a brown cape and plain bonnet when you don't want to be seen or noticed. *That's* when you use your power. Sometimes you got to act like you are nothing—so long as you remember that it's a lie. So long as you remember you're as strong as you believe you are."

Salem, 1693

Tituba, little Dorcas Good, Sarah Carrier, and ninety-three other falsely accused women, men, and children stumble out of Salem and Boston jails when the court of Oyer and Terminer is suspended by the governor of the Commonwealth of Massachusetts.

Judge Hathorne watches them limp back into Salem—the orphaned children, the widows, the daughter who testified against her mother. He rages at the magistrates who recant their verdicts and at the accusers— Betty Parris and Ann Putnam first among them—who apologize for the terror they wrought.

"The victims believed Satan was here and I still believe it," Hathorne tells his wife. "You stay clear of them, for changelings are always among us and I would not trust the lot of them, certainly not with my soul."

At night, poor Martha Carrier's daughter lies awake and wishes John Hathorne would fall dead in the street. At her bedside is a needle Sarah found tucked into an eight-pointed flower embroidered in the center of a handkerchief.

She remembers the day her mother put away the cloth and needle. "Such adornment is forbidden," Martha had said. "But we can keep it here, Sarah—we can keep something beautiful for ourselves alone."

Terrified at what might happen to her otherwise, Sarah testified in court and said her mother was a witch. Now the courts have said the trials were all a terrible mistake—a frenzy that should never have happened. But her mother is dead, and it is Sarah's own fault. She has so many questions she can hardly sleep: Has her mother gone to heaven or to hell, and will she ever forgive her? Should Sarah burn the handkerchief with its eight-pointed flower? Should she carry it in her pocket? Or should she use it to make a poppet doll with silver-gray hair just like Judge Hathorne? Will it hurt him when she pricks the fabric? And if she leaves it outside his door with a needle stuck through it, will it blind him?

Sarah sees it in her mind. One day John Hathorne's body will lie in the cemetery beside his father's, their two grave markers like cold, pale twins beneath a gray sky.

— SEVENTEEN —

I arrive at Felicity's shop to find two ladies in fine hats waiting at the door on Monday morning. I know right away they are the Philadelphia women who've come for my gloves—but before I can say good morning Felicity bustles them inside. She makes a fuss about using the key she keeps on the chain around her waist and dusting off the counter before she sets down her bag.

"Please bring the ladies tea." Felicity speaks as if I am her kitchen girl.

Move between the spaces; know when it is your moment. Hide your strengths until it's time to use them.

I go up the street to fetch hot water from the cartwright's shop. When I return, the ladies are seated on the divan, each holding a pair of my gloves and admiring the work. The ladies' traveling clothes are made of the finest-quality silks in deep jewel colors, and I wish that I were wearing my finest dress, embroidered with my mother's irises.

"We want to order a dozen more," the fairer lady says. She speaks with the confidence of a man, and her words are bold and black to match. Certainly she is not endeavoring to walk through the world unseen. "We'll pay you half now, and the second half upon receipt. You may send them by post."

"I've never seen any embroidery work that matches hers," the second lady adds. She is handsome and her hands are pale and strong. "You have a keen eye, Mrs. Adams, and we'll pay what's required to urge your woman along—we need the gloves right after Independence Day."

"They must be her work and no one else's," the first says firmly. "And they must be made of free cotton, of course." I prick up my ears, for I have not heard the expression *free cotton* before. "Naturally we can't sell anything made with slave labor—Philadelphia women demand cotton grown in free states or in England."

"A true Christian woman will not wear anything but," adds the second woman. She calculates the sum and writes a banknote of credit.

I want to ask these women how they've come to operate a business that takes them from Philadelphia to Boston, Salem, New York, and beyond. I want to know if they're shrewd and unfair like Felicity or if they've found another way to run a ladies' shop in a world of men. But all I can do is mark their names: Miss Diane English and Miss Elizabeth Southwick at the Cherry Street Shop in Philadelphia.

ABIGAIL AND I are leaving for the day when Felicity asks me to stay behind. Abigail shoots a last look to me.

"You heard the ladies," Felicity says. "How soon can you have the gloves?"

The white-on-white work for Charlotte Silas has taken over all of my time, and I barely have time to work on my shawl for the banquet.

"I've begun a new set of petticoats for my husband's return," I say. "When Edward comes home my time in the evening will belong to him."

"Your husband isn't here yet," she says. "I'll pay you a dollar a pair to have them finished by the first week of July."

"Twelve pair will take countless hours," I protest, although in truth it can be accomplished with great effort—and a little bit of enchantment, if it can be summoned.

"The ladies paid half already," she says. "They expect a timely delivery."

"Then I'll take half my payment now, too, so that I can buy the finest threads and begin as soon as you're able to get free cotton gloves."

I've forced her hand. She doesn't like it, but she counts out my money in silence.

I'm set to walk out the door when she asks, "What word do you have from your husband? Evelyn Boyle's husband wrote that there was trouble on Captain Darling's journey."

"Trouble on the journey? What sort of trouble?"

"Only that one of the men delayed them; she didn't say the reason."

I saw the captain sail his ship through storm, gale, and sickness. I know the command he has over his men, the respect and love Ingo gives him, and how he uses that strength to keep the crew in line.

If there's a problem with one of the men, it's bound to be Edward.

I DON'T HAVE to wait long to have my answer, for two mornings hence the postmaster slides a packet across the counter. He doesn't arch an eyebrow or even look at me, but I have the feeling that the postmaster has more knowledge of the city than almost anyone. "Two letters for you."

One letter is from Pap, the other has the *New Harmony* seal but is written in an unfamiliar hand. Fearing terrible news, I break the seal and open it quickly.

Dear Mrs. Gamble,

I trust you are well. I'm writing with difficult news of your husband. I regret to inform you that when it was time to leave the port of Bermuda he did not return to my ship. My men were unable to find him and we were forced to sail on without him. I left instruction that I should be alerted if news of his whereabouts reaches any shore. I am sorry to send bad news and will keep you informed if I should learn anything more of his fate.

I remain in your debt and service always.

Yours,
Capt. William Darling

Edward isn't on the ship. Edward may not return to me.

At first it's a fact. Then it's a fear. Then it's hope, white and light as a feather.

∞

AT THE EDGE of the Common, brick houses stand like large mountains guarding the city. Schoolboys run past with their shoes in their hands. The church bells ring twelve, then one. When Nell leaves the Silas house on her afternoon errands, I call to her from afar.

My friend waves a finger at me, and we meet on the other side of the green where the road is wide and empty.

"Charlotte and Mrs. Silas are both grateful," she says. "All is well in their house thanks to you." She's so warm, her words so green and bright, I think I will burst into tears.

"And what of you, Isobel?" She looks at me more closely. "Something is wrong—what is it?"

I know Nell is my dear friend, for when I tell her the captain's news, her face crumples.

"What will you do if he doesn't come home?"

I see Nat's face, the glove that he pulled over my hand one finger at a time; the rose that stands on my table, the May tree flowers that have loosed their fading fragrance in my cottage.

"I've seen you with your beau," I blurt out. "It's never been that way with Edward."

"He's your husband," she says. "But I fear . . ." Her words trail off into the color of a dried plum.

"Go on, Nell."

"I fear he may have taken an island woman," she says finally. "A man can leave and never look back, I've seen it happen."

I tuck an arm through hers.

"I've kept your secrets," I say. "Now will you keep mine?"

"I'll keep your secrets always, Isobel."

I take a deep breath. "Women have never been my husband's weakness."

When I tell her why we left Scotland her face is smooth, as if she's heard it all before.

"My mother says a woman must hope for the best but prepare for the worst," Nell says.

We've done a turn around the pasture on the edge of town and are returning to the Common when Nell raises a hand and her face brightens.

Her beau, Stephen, is loping toward us in his white apron and cap.

She puts her face next to mine, and her words are the same fresh green they were on that first day we met.

"Charlotte will be married in that dress thanks to you. My best advice is to stay in Mrs. Silas's confidence. Opportunities will come to you. You won't even know where they've come from, and they'll be there. Mrs. Silas will look out for you."

BACK HOME, I'M ready for my father's words to soothe me. I press the envelope to my nose and smell tobacco, the comfort of my father's pipe beside the fire. I close my eyes and see the chair where Pap would have sat when he wrote the letter. I remember my hand in his and the way he pressed the gold into my palm the day I left.

His letter begins full of good cheer.

My wife has had another child. We named her Mary-Rose, he writes. He tells me of the babe's fair face and dark hair and follows with news about home and the city. It is a long page that continues on the back side.

> *Your brother has left to find work as a pastry man in London and can be reached care of the George Inn in Southwark. He will be very happy to have a letter from you.*
>
> *Finally, daughter, I must tell you I'm not well. My breath is heavy and my body weak. I sleep but am never rested. I do not tell you to worry you, daughter, but only so that you are prepared and know that I have thought of you often and loved you dearly. Remember you have a gift, and you must use it. I will smile down on you from heaven if I am lucky enough to go there, and you will feel my love when the sun shines on your face.*
>
> *Your loving father*

I don't believe it. I can't believe it.

Yet I know Pap would only write the truth.

In my mind I do not see Pap's face but his hands, the way he turned his cap in them, the way he put his two large palms on either side of my face and gave me courage. I see his hand pushing across the page writing this letter, and I feel the table beneath his palms.

I've stitched through sadness and through fear; I've stitched through joy, trepidation, and hope. And so I find comfort the only way I know how: I work. I work the doves on Charlotte's camisole, the ferns brushing the edges of her petticoat. I stay at my needle, but as the night grows darker and the cat curls against my legs, I know I'll never see my dear pap again.

It's past midnight when I put aside Charlotte's whites and find a piece of pinewood-green velvet I've carried since I salvaged it from home. It is the finest cloth I have.

In my sewing box I find the last of Captain Darling's silk threads. I use the black thread for the leopard's long body, the dark brown for the edge of its spine. I work so deeply that when the needle pricks my finger, I do not feel it. Only the drop of blood on the cloth stops me, and even then only for a moment.

For two nights and days I work the needle.

I make the leopard's eye with white pearl beads and black silk and fill the width of the velvet with whiskers that reach from one corner to the other. It's oversize and strange, almost frightening. But when I hold it up, I see it is strength and courage. I recognize the letters in the spaces between the colors, and although Pap won't see them, I believe he'll feel them there.

Dear Pap,

I have a new friend in Salem who said that if I want courage, I should stitch courage. If I want love, I should stitch love. I have stitched both for you. You made me strong and gave me love and I thank you always. Kiss the babies and tell them I love them all the way in America. I will write to Jamie in London. I will always cherish you. When I have a son, I will name him Seamus after you.

Your loving and devoted daughter always,
Isobel

At home in Scotland, the May trees will have filled the hedgerows with white blossoms, then with a sweet fragrance, and when the blossoms fade it will smell like death. I post the package and pray it reaches Pap before it's too late for him to feel my love. And when it's done, I do what I promised Mercy: I harvest the pennyroyal, boil it down to a tincture, mix it with the beeswax, and deliver it to her.

She takes it in a single motion and closes the door, and I feel more alone than I have in a long time.

My father is dying. Edward isn't coming home. It could mean freedom, but it might also mean disgrace. I saw the delight in Felicity's face when she told me there was trouble on the ship. When she asked me to fetch a bolt of fabric, I could feel the mills in Lowell reaching for me.

—— EIGHTEEN ——

I'm sorting hooks and eyes when the bell rings and a tall man in a hooded cape comes into the shop. Felicity is in the back room. From the corner of my eye, I see her stand and brush off her skirts.

The man removes his hood and shakes off the rain. It's Nat.

He opens his fist and puts a curled scrap of cloth on the table. The white cotton is smudged and soiled, but the scarlet *A* stitched by my hand is deep and true. I'm frightened of what I feel—dizzy excitement, a pulsing in my head. It's been more than a week since I last saw him, and much has changed.

"I read the notice in the *Gazette*." His words are quiet; they're made not of gold but of light. "The *New Harmony* will be seven more weeks at sea."

I want to tell him my pap is dying and that Edward isn't on the ship. I want to ask if he's done any writing about love or about the good that's sometimes hidden even in the hardest men. But Felicity has trained her eye on me, and so I speak of the weather. I prattle about the rain and how it's good for the garden. I say something inane about cabbage and green onions.

"And there is a plant I saw once in Scotland." I speak to fill the space that his face opens in me. "A Venus flytrap that eats insects right out of the air."

His mouth curls into that bemused smile just as Felicity joins us.

"Good morning, Mr. Hathorne." It's the same voice she used with the Philadelphia ladies. "I'm delighted to see you. Have you come to find something for your mother or sisters?"

He told me he's solitary, even shy, but I haven't seen it until he points to the display window and blinks as if to remind himself to speak.

"I'm curious about the new gloves."

"They're one of a kind," Felicity says. "Custom-made and quite enchanting."

She takes the pair with the red rose from the window. I wonder if he knows they are inspired by the rose he left for me. I wonder if he sees the words between the spaces.

"If you want a pair, you may order one," Felicity says. "I don't know how long the lady will need to make them, as it's a slow process."

"I imagine it must be." Again, he seems to stammer.

"I think your mother would like these gloves, Mr. Hathorne." Felicity's words curdle and I can see in her posture that she assumes she has the upper hand. But Felicity is mistaken, for he hasn't come for the gloves. He's come for me. Whatever is happening between them is secondary to the soiled scrap of white cloth with the scarlet letter I've hidden away in my pocket. "If she's going north, you must order them now so she has them before she leaves."

Nat asks the price of the gloves. When she tells him, he seems to gather up his words so they come out strong and clear.

"Mother would never want anything so costly. She prefers simplicity."

The past is here now: I see it in the way Felicity looks at him through the corner of an eye and the way he shifts his gaze away—as if she is remembering his great-great-grandfather's cruelty and the death he brought to this city.

"My needlewoman will decorate men's gloves as well," Felicity says. "Perhaps she can put your initials in a pair of calfskin."

"I've just had a new waistcoat made," he says. "A pair of calfskins would be just the thing. Or an embroidered vest rendered with a stag or a leopard. I might consider these for myself if a price might be agreed upon."

A leopard. He's said it aloud.

A leopard is a solitary hunter. But who is the hunter, and who is the prey here?

"I'll inquire," Felicity says. "Come back soon if you wish to place an order. Her work will be in high demand as we approach the Light Infantry banquet."

After he's gone, I wait for Felicity to speak to me about stitching a leopard on a vest. She must find it an unusual request. But her face is clouded, and I feel sure she's remembering the fate of her ancestress.

I hate to think of a kinship with Felicity, but it is undeniable that she and I stand on one side with the accused, while Nat stands on the other. And yet he is one of the few people I trust in this new world, and the tenderness and excitement I feel for him blots out everything else. Even the curse that Isobel Gowdie shouted from the rooftop. Even the curse— *God will give you blood to drink*—that follows Nat.

He came for me, and I want him.

THAT NIGHT I dream of my mother standing beneath a tree beside the River Clyde.

"Do I want my husband to come home?" I ask her. Even in my sleep I know I'm at the edge of life and what comes after. "What if someone else is meant for me?"

I know she has an answer, but she doesn't want to say it.

"Mam?"

I reach out a hand and catch her hair between my fingers. She begins to fade away.

"Mam—wait."

She turns and says, "Isobel, think of the faeries beneath the May trees. Remember what I told you."

"What did you tell me?" My fingers are knotted around a tangled filament of her red hair. But before she can answer, she has crossed the river and faded to white, then to light, then to pounding rain.

The rain roars like the Falls of Clyde, and the knocking on my door is like the sound of footsteps crossing rocks.

Knock, knock, knock.

"Isobel, I need help."

I sit up. It's not a dream.

Knock, knock.

"Please, Isobel. It's Nat."

I rub my eyes and strike a match to light the candle, and that is when I see the filaments of red hair still in a small tangle around my fingers.

He begins to say my name in a flat singsong. "Is-a-bell, Is-a-bell—"

I ball the hair into the pocket of my dressing gown and crack open the top of my Dutch door to find him in the pouring rain. Right away I know he's drunk.

"I'm hurt." He holds up his arm and I can see the jacket sleeve is torn away. His face is scratched, his lip bloody. "And I'm freezing; please let me in."

Now I am fully awake. I look about my cottage with the same crystal clarity I felt the day the constable came for Edward in Glasgow. My heart is pounding, and then my mind is perfectly clear. Charlotte's petticoats and layette are everywhere, pure and white, arms in one direction and skirts in another like angels frolicking on clouds. I gather the pieces into a corner, take the cover off my bed, and throw it over the white work.

I do not lie, even to myself. I know why he's come and I know that if I open the door, I will have agreed to the beginning of something. I smooth my hair and rinse my mouth with water and then let him stumble into the cottage, soaked through and shivering.

"My new waistcoat is ruined," he says. "My first and best gentleman's coat—newly made and now—"

He lifts his arm. The black coat is made of superfine wool, a tight weave that must have come from England. Half the sleeve is missing, and the liner is shredded. I pull over a chair and he slides into it, making a strange, strangled sound.

"I played cards in Marblehead." His words are garbled and muddy, the color of dirt. "I don't usually go so far—"

I stand behind him and pull at the good sleeve of his jacket. When I tug it off, the back of his head falls against me. His face is scratched. There are dark whiskers running across his chin and above his lip.

"You've been drinking," I say to his upturned face. His eyes are luminous.

"Rum—too much rum." Rum puts me in mind of Edward, but I push away the thought.

Nat tells a story in fractures and fragments: a quarter-moon, owls in the trees, oil lamps and jugs of rum, a man with a gun and another with an Indian who stood at the door without speaking.

"I won," he says, struggling with a muddy shoe, and I help him by pulling on the heel. When it slides off, paper bills and silver coins pour onto the floor. "All of this, Isobel—it was all so that I can buy your gloves."

My heart blazes.

"The bastards tried to take it from me. Just outside town I was hit from behind." He swings his fist as a man will do when telling of a tavern fight. "One was tall, the other was quick and had a knife—but I fought and got away."

When he twists, I see blood on his shirt.

"You're hurt."

He lowers his head like a child and raises his arms to let me slip the linen over his head.

The cut is small but deep in the thick of his dark chest hair. I press my finger to it.

"It has to be cleaned and stitched."

I have boiled water in the pot from this morning, a clean rag, and lye soap. I scrub at the wound, prepared for his protests, but he's too drunk to feel much pain.

"I need a new coat," he says. "Same as this one. I know you can do it—will you help me, please?"

I press the skin together and sew four, five, six stitches into his chest. Nat bites on his lip but doesn't cry out. His eyes are closed. His wrists are bony, arms ropy. With his shirt off he's more length than muscle. Hair runs in a line down his chest and belly and disappears into his trousers. I remember the captain's fever and seal the stitches with a generous coating of pennyroyal ointment.

"You have to rest." There's no place for him to lie out but on my bed. I help him to his feet. "Come."

On his bare back I see a rash of tiny wounds like the scratching of a cat's paws, small and sharp—some crusted, others fresh. It looks as if someone tried to claw something from his skin.

"Did they do this, too?" I touch a spot between his shoulder blades.

"That's nothing." He twists away before I can treat the area with the ointment.

I wonder if he's been with a woman who scratched at him in passion and am stung with a sickening jealousy. But when I bring him tea he sings my name and the green envy dissipates.

"Is-a-bell." I hold the tin cup to his lips and he takes a sip. "Is a bell to ring."

His words are a golden bell now; the gong that rings them is fire red. I am startled by the affection in his voice and even more by the desire—*Is-a-bell, IS-A-BELL*—as he says my name over and again, his words getting smaller until he's asleep, his mouth half-open, snoring gently.

All around me I see the red shadow of my own name fading in the air—as if it is a curse, or a benediction, or a witch's spell.

IS-A-BELL
IS-A-BELL

HE SLEEPS, BUT I do not. I sit in the chair by the bed and remember every moment I have spent with him—the gold and red of his voice, even the way his face grew sad and tender when he spoke of his father. I remember all of it.

I press my tongue to the roof of my mouth, flat the way it went when I saw him that very first day on the wharf. I put a hand to his bare shoulder and for an instant I put my face against his skin. My heart is pounding, but his breath, long and slow, long and slow, makes a new rhythm.

I WAKE CURLED on the floor beside my bed, and in a single breath I remember he is here.

He has to leave before the children come to the well. I allow myself a moment of vanity to comb my hair and splash sleep from my face. Then I shake him awake.

"You have to go while it's still dark."

He sits up bleary and confused, blinking until he realizes where he is.

I see many things cross his face before he decides on the most practical, the least troubling.

"Will you make me a new coat? Can you finish it for Friday? Please, Isobel. I have no money for a new coat and I can't have my uncle knowing I was gambling."

I smooth down my wrinkled dressing gown as he climbs off the bed. I do not even inspect his wound, for I am overwhelmed now that he has slept in my cottage and in my bed.

"I can't make a new coat in three days, but I'll repair this one if I can find the fabric."

He pulls his shirt over his head and again I see the scratches on his back are a puzzle of crisscrossed angles, almost a patchwork of red-and-brown plaid.

With a start, I recall the pitiful penitent who wandered outside the cathedral in Glasgow applying a thorny whip to his own back. It was whispered that men did such things to punish a guilt or even to purge a carnal desire. The thought of Nat doing the same should quake me, but instead, it draws me closer. Here is a man who is as at war within himself as I am with my colors and the fear of my own power.

And if he has a lust in him, perhaps it is for me.

Before I wed Edward, a lust like that would have frightened me. But I've seen what comes from a man who doesn't try to control his own desires.

"I'll come back tonight." Nat is putting on his boots by the door.

"Not tonight."

"Then tomorrow. Put a candle in the window if I may come."

I find the filaments of red hair in my pocket and, without thinking why, tuck them into his vest just before he shrugs into it. *Think of the faeries beneath the May trees,* Mam whispered. But in life she never wanted me to think of the faeries. She didn't want Pap frightening me with those stories.

"There's always a candle in the window—if there is no candle in the window, then do not come," I say.

We step into the yard and I look up the hill toward Mercy's place.

"Go now." I want to reach for him. I remember the smell of tobacco on his shoulder like the tobacco on my pap's letter and fold my arms around myself as he walks into the morning dusk.

It's the last moment between night and day, and as I strain to watch him fade down the hill, something moves across the hillcrest on the other side of the yard.

I hold myself perfectly still. It's not the children, for they come straight down the hill, their watery voices gently announcing their arrival.

I hear a whistle from the north.

Have the cardplayers followed Nat to Salem? Have they surrounded my cottage?

The sky is blooming pink against a dark violet night when I see two figures—a man and a woman—running in the direction of the sea. Something in the way the woman moves is familiar. As she flashes between the trees, I see the side of her face. It's Mercy in her turban, running as quiet as could be through the last moment before the morning light.

Then she disappears, as if I imagined her there.

Like everything that's happened tonight, this too fills me with the dark and light of the past and the present, the spoken and the unspoken, desire and ruin and the sweetness of Nat repeating my name. Isobel. *Is-a-bell. Is a bell ringing and ringing and ringing.*

Salem, 1701

Tituba is finally free of the howling that comes from Proctor's Ledge whenever she wakes before first light. For years she could not sleep without seeing the craven branches of the May trees that reached for her along the Witch Path, or hearing the tug of lumber beneath her friends' feet before the snap of the noose. And there was always, just before summer, the death stench of the May tree blossoms that rotted along the hedgerow.

The long, dark months in the Boston jail are the price she paid for this freedom, for John Parris never looked for her when the trials were over, and she never returned to his empty house. Instead, she has lived in a lean-to behind the thick sycamore in the north wood and eaten what she foraged off land and sea.

It took sixty moons alone in the forest to cleanse away the haunting. She did it with nettle to ward off those who wish her ill, raspberry and lavender for strength and wisdom, chamomile for healing calm, lemon verbena and calendula for courage and health, all of it grown and gathered here where rock meets the sea and the seals come at dusk to swim.

The Parris family is gone now, the Proctors' farm has passed from hand to hand. John Indian married a slave woman and lives in a clearing this side of Lynn, where he works in the master's barn for free. Tituba believes the land is like people, and neither should be owned. This is why she is leaving now—going west, where no one will ever own her again.

Before she leaves, Tituba goes to the girl-woman who lost her mind right there alongside her for eight months in the dark prison; the girl-woman who still wanders back and forth on the Witch Path calling for her mama.

"Dorcas," Tituba whispers. "Your mama sends her love. She says you are a very good girl and you will see her again soon."

Tituba sees in Dorcas's eyes that the girl will not live much longer.

Tituba will be long gone when Dorcas takes her last breath. She sees this, too, the horizon opening to her like a candlelit room. John Indian forgotten and Tituba flying along the westward road singing of freedom.

— NINETEEN —

"Are you ill?" Abigail asks.

We're pinning up a blue silk dress. There are ruffles and mutton sleeves and a neckline to accommodate the buyer's ample bosom.

"You're quiet," she adds. "More than usual."

I cannot keep my mind on my tasks, not with the night's activities roiling in me like a storm: first Nat singing my name and sleeping in my bed, then the vision of Mercy running through the dark.

"I'm tired today." I try to keep my face natural. Fortunately, it's easy to set Abigail talking.

"My neighbors are a Black family." I use the word Mercy uses when she speaks of herself. "Were there many slaves in Salem back in the day?"

"Some." Abigail holds up the selvage edge of the fabric and measures for the width of the skirt. She's a silly girl sometimes, but now her face is solemn. "Salem folks like to pretend they had nothing to do with slavery, but it's not true. Salem captains traded cotton, rum, and slaves. It made them rich—filthy rich, some say. There were more slaves here in Salem than in Newport or Boston." Abigail rattles off the names of cities that are spoken of with great pride. "The governor freed them before I was born, but I remember a family that came into my pop's butcher shop for soup bones. The children were free but the mother and father were still slaves. Born and died slaves, that's what my granny told me."

I've seen downtrodden Black men with bent backs working long days on the docks, and I've had time to think on Mercy's grandmother, kept in the back of a man's house where she was used to sate his lust.

"I heard the Silases were a slaving family," I say.

"I've heard it, too." She nods. "The ministers who preach against slavery in Lynn hate the slaving captains. They made money on misery and in Lynn we don't abide it."

"Do you think they're cruel people?"

Abigail tucks a sleeve into place and then straightens, looking at me as if I am the fool.

"Any man who owns or sells another man is cruel, Isobel. Can you imagine it otherwise?"

I think of Mr. Remond and the old woman talking about a runaway slave. Ivy with bits of colorful ribbon in her hair. Mercy running through the dawn. Mrs. Silas and her unkind words.

"Isobel." Abigail is standing now, pulling at my sleeve. I've been lost in thought. "Isobel, the hem is finished. Get up, I think you truly must be ill."

"I'm fine." I stand so quickly I feel faint. "I'll have a cup of water and I'll be fine."

IN THE AFTERNOON I show Abigail the scrap of wool I cut from Nat's coat sleeve.

"I want to make a new coat for Edward," I lie.

"Felicity will know where to find it."

"A lot of that fabric came from London last month," Felicity tells me right away. This is her skill—knowing where to find the best materials for the best price in Salem. "It's a superfine wool. Very costly. It comes in twice a year. Many merchants in Salem own a coat made of it."

"I found a scrap of it in Newell's shop. But I'll need at least one and a half yards."

She tells me where I might find another lot and seems pleased to say that even with the increase in my glove wages, I'll be able to afford only a small bit of it.

"Perhaps you shouldn't make anything now," she says. "Your husband may return to you much changed. I have seen it many times."

She's right and yet she's wrong. For Edward was changed before we ever came to Salem. And Edward isn't returning to me now.

"I'll make it up according to the measurements I have and wait to make the final adjustments when he's home."

"Don't forget about my gloves," she says.

"I promise you'll have them in time, Mrs. Adams."

I use Nat's coins to purchase a length of the superfine wool and silk to patch the torn liner. I clean the waistcoat and trim off the frayed bits, hold his coat on my lap like a shadow of him, and inhale the smell of lint, cigars, and the tavern where he played cards.

I remember the first time I saw him on the docks, how he wore the red and gold of his voice like a crown.

I've kept the scrimshaw buttons in a small bowl by my bed. Now I roll them in my palm and listen to the sound they make, like tiny chicken bones in a cup. I work until it is very late. In the morning there are four eggs in a bowl beside my door. I've slept so deeply I did not hear the children come into the yard.

It's well past dark the next evening when Nat leaves his boots at the door and slips into the cottage. I'm glad I've prepared my pencil and the length of string to take his measurements, for the cottage feels very small now that he's here.

"I'm ashamed I came to you that way. I don't blame you if you've changed your mind." He's quite sober, and there's a weight about him that wasn't there before.

"I have not," I say.

The expression on his face when I hold the black wool against his torn coat is admiration and something more.

"I found it in a tailor's shop at the end of Essex Street." I'm tense and hopeful, but for what, I dare not admit, even to myself.

"Did I give you enough money? Did he ask why you needed it? Did he want to know what you were making or for whom?"

"I had enough money," I say. "And said as little as needed."

I take up my tools and run my measure across him. His chest is forty-two inches, his shoulders are forty-four.

I've touched him and it hasn't burned me like a flame. But it might. I can feel it.

"I'll stitch the sleeve and mend the liner," I say.

He puts on his old jacket and looks around the cottage for the first time. He sees my yellow curtains, and Edward's apothecary book on the shelf, and his gaze falls upon the stack of Charlotte's unfinished petti-coats.

"They're a private order," I say.

He reaches for a bleached bit and hovers his hands over the place where I've put rosebuds at the nape of a chemise.

"May I?"

"Touch lightly." I remember his fingers counting out the names of the old Salem families and the shock of his touch on my skin. I think of the crisscrossed marks on his back and the guilt and the ghosts he carries.

"You shouldn't waste your needle on beautiful work that will never be seen," he says.

"It pays well. And what's private can also be beautiful."

He cocks his head to look at me sideways and I feel myself blush.

"There's something in your needle that evades analysis of the mind." Nat puts a finger to one of the infant gowns. "Yet it's there, I can feel it."

With his finger on the small white gown and eyes squinting into the dim light, he seems part of a story, the mirage of something that was once solid and will be solid again.

"May I ask you something?" I'm thankful I don't sound as uneasy as I feel.

"Anything."

"You told me there's a story about this cottage."

He nods. "But it's not a happy one."

"I'm not afraid of dark tales."

He settles himself on the stool.

"Widow Higgins was a midwife." He speaks slowly at first. "She was the midwife who brought my sister into the world. She wasn't a widow then, she was Mrs. Sally Higgins, a young bride."

He hesitates.

"You may as well know it, for everyone in Salem knows—my mother was with child when my parents married. Sally Higgins attended my sister's birth while my father was at sea."

I see the violet haze rise with his words, the same color I saw about him that first day in the dry goods shop.

"Sally lived here in this cottage with her husband and her sister. The man was part Indian, and so they lived out here where no one bothered them. When he choked on a chicken bone and died, her sister became strange—spoke of men and women sneaking through the woods and visiting with the Devil, and in Salem there can be no talk of the Devil without raising a suspicion."

He stands now, growing animated with the rhythm of the tale. What's on his face is like the excitement I feel when the colors I'm working and the thread-picture in my mind are the same.

"One night the sister was found on the docks in a torn and bloody shift—she said a man with a long white beard had violated her. There was terrible gossip, no one could believe the widow's sister would have such bad luck without a stain of her own. Soon the town turned on her, and not long after she was found dead."

Perhaps it wasn't Mercy I saw running through the dark—perhaps it was a ghost. Perhaps the cottage and the woods are haunted. *Beware the devil in the forest,* that's what the widow herself told me the day we landed here.

"Only the Negroes would have Widow Higgins at their births after that," Nat says. "No one else wanted anything to do with such a cursed family. Eventually she moved to live among them over on Rice Street."

It strikes me that I've spent my time with the widow noticing only what she wants me to notice, speaking only of what she speaks of. Now I know that she has secrets, too. Ones she's hidden well.

"The Higgins cottage was empty until you took it." He looks around now.

"Because they died here?"

"No," Nat corrects me. "The husband choked at a supper party in town. The sister was found near the almshouse. No one ever died here."

But still, death is near me, for my pap will be dead soon. In the darkness, with Nat so near, I feel the first real tears since I read his letter.

Men don't like it when women cry. When the creditors came the first time and I wept in front of Edward, he pushed away from the table and strode out of the room. But Nat's face is creased with sympathy when he sees my tears.

"I shouldn't have told you," he says.

"It's not the story," I hurry to explain. "It's my pap." A choke catches in my throat, and I wrap my arms around myself. "I had a letter—he's dying."

Nat comes close enough to put his hands on my shoulders, and I step into his arms. In the dark and wet muffle of my face against his sleeve, I weep.

"It's all right." I haven't had a man's arms around me in many weeks, and never so tenderly. "It's all right."

We stay this way until my sobs stop. Nat strokes my hair, and it's comforting: pleasing and forbidden at the same time. I swipe at my face, knowing that it's red and my nose is running.

"I didn't mean to do that." I pull away without looking up at him. "I've made a mess of your shirt."

I step out of his arms, and for one breath I think he will pull me back to him. But he doesn't.

"You should go now." I begin wrapping up my tools and putting them away. "Three nights from now your coat will be ready."

Just as soon as I've spoken the words, it seems he's vanished.

I FINISH THE final details on my work for Charlotte and close the tiny necklines in the baby's clothing. I work at Felicity's gloves and mend Nat's coat sleeve in tight black stitches that mimic the ones already in the lining.

The first time I lay with Edward, I didn't know what would be. I wore a white gown and knew to expect his weight on top of me, and blood—that was all. I knew the act gave Edward pleasure, but I didn't feel any for myself. Night after night I closed my eyes, until one night I kept them open. I watched him moan and puff and saw his face flood with fear, then pain, then relief.

The day Nat took my hand and put the glove on it, I saw that same pained hunger in his features. I watched, mesmerized, as he slid the glove down my fingers one by one like a lady's stocking. And I felt my tongue flatten. I felt a great thirst.

Now I drag enough water into the cottage to bathe myself head to toe. I read in Edward's book how to make a pessary with honey, beeswax, and herbs to ward against pregnancy. I have beeswax I've not yet used for the pennyroyal ointment; I mix it with honey and crushed fennel seeds until it's thick as cork, and put it as deeply inside as I can manage. I take the candle from the window and stand outside, watching stars streak across the sky. Somewhere in the distance I hear dogs. Maybe wolves.

My husband stole from me. My husband may never return to me. It's the last thing I think before Nat slips into the yard.

"There are shooting stars." I point up at the patch of blazing sky where a shower of white and yellow stars streak through the night. Do they foretell chaos or good fortune? I can't decipher what the sky is saying. "Come look."

He is seven, perhaps eight inches taller than me, but it's a fraction of a distance when we peer up together.

"I'm sorry about your pap," he says. I see the shape of church bells, the round and deep gong of his words. He leans closer and his shoulder brushes my face. "I hate to see you sad."

"I'm not sad now."

I look up and hold his gaze. It's just as it was that first day on the dock. But he's close enough to touch me now.

His first kiss is gentle. The kiss of a sea breeze.

— TWENTY —

Until Nat undresses me and runs a hand down my waist and tucks into me, I've never felt the dark rush of blood in my head that comes like music. I've never been bound and twined with a person so that I don't know where I end or where he begins, never seen waterfalls of color on my skin when someone touched me.

Now it's here.

I lead him into the cottage and lean over the table to blow out the candle. Nat steps behind me and puts his hands on my waist. I'm afraid, but I'm not afraid.

He takes the pins out of my hair one by one, gently tugs the tendrils down around my neck and shoulders.

"Are you sure?" He's mannered, almost shy.

"Yes."

He pulls down my bodice.

I close my eyes.

He lifts me onto the bed.

I'm a married Christian woman and, yes, I'm afraid of the brew he stirs in me. But sin, God, and the Devil aren't nearly as real as the throttle of his breath in my ear, his taste of salt, and the white-hot coil that goes through me like thread in the eye of a needle.

I'm a witch and he's a sorcerer. Or perhaps he's the sorcerer and I'm the cauldron. I wrap my arms around him and touch the place where his shoulder is scratched and raw. He cries out and my eyes fly open.

I want to know him down to the soul.

AFTER, I'M NOT prepared for him to see me flushed and raw. I pull on my petticoat and fill a bowl with vinegar and water, then walk into the dark yard and wash him away. I'm still collecting myself when he comes outside and puts a hand to my waist. His thick hair is combed into waves, and he is dressed. He is himself, put back together with the help of my needle and thread. But I am changed.

"The jacket is good as new," he says after a while. "As if it was never torn."

"Will you come again?" I ask.

In the silence I hear crickets and pond toads. Somewhere, a dog howls.

"If you want me." He brushes the hair from my face and kisses my cheek as a brother would kiss a sister. Chaste.

Then he's gone.

I am still standing in the yard at dawn when the children come for water. They move quietly, their words hushed, their faces soft with sleep.

"Good morning, Miss Isobel," Ivy greets me with a shy smile. She puts warm, fresh bread in my hands, then runs up the rise behind Abraham and disappears into the thicket.

Sunlight sprinkles through the trees.

I rip off a piece of bread, then another and another, cramming it into my mouth as if I'm starved. The colors Nat raked across my skin have taken on a life all their own—swirls in the sea with Poseidon churning mischief and lust. Venus born on a shell. The leopard and his mate wrapped around one another in a ring of wild roses.

I'm wide awake now and I sketch first, then practice with thread. When I'm ready, I put a new pattern on a pair of gloves for the Philadelphia ladies. All day I sit in the sun and stitch. If I were to regret what I've done with Nat it would be now. But I'm not sorry. Look what's come of it: the colors, the beauty, the living things that pour out of me in needle and thread.

I WORK AT the dress shop on Wednesday with sterling attention so that Abigail notices nothing. On the way home I stop at Chaise & Harness and buy a dozen small white pearl beads and thirty tiny turquoise beads, each the size of an eyelash.

In my yard I find a package in brown paper leaned up against my cottage door and no one in sight but the cat. She comes toward me, then mewls and turns away as if she can sense that I am changed.

I tear open the package to find a new book with a blue leather cover and gold-tipped pages: *The Fair Maid of Perth* by Walter Scott. *Printed in Scotland,* it says inside.

Perhaps my own father touched these pages, laid these letters into words. My throat aches as I run my hands over the book and begin to read.

Soon I discover that the fair maid of the title is Catherine Glover; her father is a glove maker in Scotland in the year 1400. I scan the pages: Catherine is embroidering a fine pair of hawking gloves. A suitor appears, then another, and another.

I told Nat that women want to read love stories to know if a man is good, if love is true, who and what can be trusted. Now he's put a love story in my hands. And the heroine is a glove maker.

IT HAS BEEN three nights since I took him to my bed. Three nights that I have waited and he has not come.

In Salem the church bells toll nine o'clock curfew and all good men and women lock their doors. Every night since my husband sailed away, I've closed my shutters against the moon and the wolves at the sound of the night bells.

But when the bells ring nine this evening, I don't close my shutters. I leave the candle in the window and sit with the book open in my lap. Scott's story skips along, but I can't follow the twists and turns of the plot.

At the sound of his step, I open the door before he can rap upon it.

His cheeks are red from the walk or from some strong emotion, and the color makes his eyes more luminous. I thank him for the book in a jittery rush as he hangs his jacket over a chair. In one motion he crosses the room, puts a hand to the back of my head, and runs it the length of my hair. His finger catches on a tangle and I feel a bright orange burst of pain. I cry out, and desire flashes in his face.

He takes the handful of my hair and pulls back my head.

"Show me," he whispers, his voice the rough red of a tongue. "Show me that temper of yours."

I sink my fingernails into his shoulder and smell blood. He puts a hand to my mouth, presses me into the bed. His eyes lock on mine—a dare, a dare, a dare. Pain and pleasure, quiet and wild, gentle and insistent.

MY LEGS ARE weak when I light the candle and pull on my dressing gown. I am silent, for I know there are few words between what's forbidden and what's shameful, and that silence should not be breached.

After a while Nat tugs on his white shirt and trousers and opens the book to the place where I left off.

"Shall I read to you?"

I clap, the sound like small orange stars of flesh on flesh.

Nat reads to me like a man telling a tale upon the stage. He speaks Catherine's lines in falsetto whispers and the evil suitors' lines with a booming baritone, and I feel the Scottish hills and rivers in his voice.

"I had it in mind to write my own story about a lovely Scottish needlewoman," Nat says when he's reached the end of the chapter. "But of course I can't write it now."

"You'll write something better and publish it with your own name." He frowns, but I go on. "I still don't understand why anyone would spend years writing a book and not put his name on it."

Nat's been light, even giddy. Now he grows serious.

"Ladies can scribble their poetry by the fireside and no one cares as long as they've done their chores. But writing is suspect activity for a strong and able man."

The book is in his lap, pointer finger holding the place. I still have

Catherine's suitors in my mind: the rogue who is too rough, the lover who is too timid.

"Could it be that you're too sensitive to the judgment of others?"

"No." He pushes back the hair that's fallen over his brow. "Last month I was walking out of the *Gazette* offices when a farmer strode right up to me and said, 'Nathaniel Hathorne, better men than you work on the docks while you do nothing but groom horses and lay about reading books all day.'"

Although Nat does his best to sound indignant, it's clear the public dress-down shamed him.

"What did you say?"

"I asked how he supposes I might better spend my time and he said, 'Doing an honest day's work, and then another and another.'" Nat gives a tight smile. "So I asked, 'Are you offering me a good wage, sir?' and at that he sputtered a few choice words and stalked away."

Nat curls his fingers through mine, his fist clenched.

"One day you'll be known, Nat. Your name and your work."

He raises my hand to his lips.

"I hope one day my name and writing will be known and admired. But for now I'm thankful that I'm not known. So long as you'll have me, Isobel, I'm thankful for my obscurity—and for yours."

He comes after dark, arriving and retreating in shadows as the first weeks of June slip away. I sleep little but have the energy of a dozen children—working the gloves at odd hours, transferring the Adam and Eve scene onto the shawl, using the turquoise beads for a rim of sky and tiny spots of red for the apple tree.

I return to the East India Marine Society Hall one day to study the leopard tapestry and sketch out tall orange flowers and an exotic row of spiny red coral. Later, Nat tells me he's spent his days reading through old Salem documents and records.

"Searching dusty old court records in search of stories. Battles and brutality, shipwrecks and landings, landslides and storms. Yesterday I found a book with the names of all the Salem families who were loyal to the English during the war."

He sits in Edward's chair and tells me about men who crossed the ocean in search of paradise almost two hundred years ago.

"But it wasn't a paradise here." He presses his feet on the floor and tips the chair back so that it is balancing on the rear legs. "There were hatchet battles and Indians and the Puritans with their harsh sermons, hard-backed church benches, and cat-o'-nine-tails. What were they looking for? This is what I want to know—what were they looking for here in the squalor and mud?"

He leans across the table to run a hand along my arm. "What kind of hunger drives a man into the perils of the unknown?"

I fear he is going to ask why Edward and I came to America, and I am relieved when he doesn't.

"There's no New World anywhere on earth," he says. It seems he is working out questions that have weighed upon him for years. "No matter what we tell ourselves, men are all the same everywhere. We imagine a utopia, settle a new land, and declare that we're making something new and better. But it's folly, Isobel. Man's nature is full of shadows and dark desires. In every man's heart there is a coffin and a grave, that is what I know."

As he talks, I begin to understand that Nat Hathorne is looking for more than stories and fame; he's searching for answers from dead men who cannot give them—from his father and his grandfather before him, through lost time and vanished fortunes.

I think of the expression I have heard from both Nat and Mercy: *true American*. Why do men bind themselves to a flag and a nation when women bind themselves to passion and love? Why do men fixate on the past when every woman I have ever known is trying to remedy the present while she builds hope for what is to come?

When Nat has run out of words, I stand and put my hand on his shoulders. He runs his hand along my waist and up to my bosom. He plays at pinching me, and when I don't pull back, he does it again—just hard enough for the shock of both pain and desire.

This time when he takes me, my cries match his. My body clenches, and he presses his hand against my mouth, then pulls back and stares at me. I see in his face that it is as I knew it would be. I am something new in this new world, too.

— TWENTY-ONE —

I make a new plug to keep away a child. Beeswax. Honey. Fennel seed. I read in Edward's book that pennyroyal is useful in ridding the body of what's not wanted, and so I grind torn pennyroyal leaves into the mixture with mortar and pestle until I can form a farthing-size coin thick enough to stay in place.

When I lick a bit of the mixture from the pestle it's sweet and fragrant, a small garden inside me.

He comes four nights in a row and stays until just before dawn. We follow Scott's young Catherine Glover to a hiding place where she's nearly ravaged, and I finish two new sets of gloves for Felicity while he sleeps beside me.

The gloves sit on my table where Charlotte's intimate whites lay in pieces only last week—purity and lust existing side by side just as they might in a woman's heart.

"You've surpassed yourself." Nat holds his open palm over my gloves the way he holds his hand over me in the dark—an inch away, aching to touch. "I must have a pair for the banquet. My uncle has agreed, and I can pay you directly."

"I'll sew whatever you ask, but you have to buy them from Felicity. I've given her my word." I know my bleeding is on its way for I am jittery and filled with a tense expectancy. "You know I can't risk my position at the shop until I'm sure I can secure my name," I add.

"Then make a leopard," he says. "For power and courage."

Because he has asked me, I put aside the shawl and work the new gloves in a torrent of inspiration—a noble beast surrounded by small bouquets of scarlet hawthorn. Two nights hence, when he puts them on, they're perfect.

On the right hand is a paw, an eye, an ear, the jaw. On the left hand is the other eye, the whiskers, the curl of the leopard's tail. At his wrist, just where the pulse beats, there is a small posy of hawthorn flowers and beneath it, hidden inside the inner seam, a tiny scarlet *A*.

"A tincture of hawthorn will revive a failing heart," I tell him, putting a finger on the flowers. "But too much of it will kill a man."

He looks up at me with a strange expression.

"Is that the magic you've used to enchant me?"

He smiles, but I'm startled.

"I have no magic."

"Oh, but I think you do." There's a glint in his eye and a hard edge to his words. He puts a hand to my wrist and runs it up my arm, then kisses me. He tugs lightly at my hair.

"You can't give them to Felicity," he says. "I must have them. I must have your magic."

I want nothing more than to put my mark on him and send him into the world with my breath in every thread, and this is what I tell him. But I cannot take the chance that Felicity will cut me loose. I must be wise in this.

"You cannot have them, Nat." I pull him to me and bite on the tip of his ear. "These are for Felicity, and you must buy them from her."

ABIGAIL LOOKS AT me longer than usual when I enter the shop.

"Have you changed your hair?"

"I washed it."

She squints at me, and it's all I can do not to check myself in the looking glass.

"You look very pretty."

"I used eggs whipped to a froth," I say. "I'll bring you some if you'd like to try it."

"Why the fuss? If I didn't know better, I'd think you have a secret beau."

I toss my head and give a gay little laugh that I've learned from her.

"I rather think that *you* must have a beau, Abigail."

"I do." She is animated as she tells me about a shoemaker in Lynn who has been seeking her out after Sunday meeting. "He's shy and handsome and full of compliments and small talk about the sermon or the weather—this week he admired my gloves. He asked where he might find something as fine for his sister or mother, and I told him the gloves we have at Felicity's shop are far finer."

In addition to everything else to stitch and sew, I must make my dress for the banquet. I ask Abigail what she'll be wearing, and when the shop is slow and Felicity is gone, she insists I try red and pink fabrics—although I say they will be hideous with my hair—then laughs when she sees that I am right.

"Blue will be your color." She holds up a pale blue, a navy blue, a bit of teal blue-green. "You'll need a clear blue, darker than robin's egg."

I decide on a blue that matches the hue of the sea. I don't have money for fine silk, but perhaps when Mrs. Silas has paid me for the petticoats and layette, I will.

"You'll look as fine and rich as any lady in a dress decorated with your own embroidery," Abigail says. "As long as the work doesn't give away the secret about your gloves."

Abigail has hit upon my exact plan, of course. Felicity won't like it, but the banquet night will be my coming out among Salem society. I can imagine it clearly: Nat will watch from across the room as I loop my shawl with Adam and Eve and the bit of red apple around my shoulders. The ladies will circle around me and admire my dress—so many, so quickly, that Felicity will have no time to stop them or speak against me.

I believe that Nat is right—the Infantry celebration will be the eve of my triumph. And Edward won't be there to ruin it or take it from me.

∞

I GLANCE AT Nat lying beside me in the dark, his profile noble, his lips perfectly smooth. His eyes are closed, and he's so still that I'm startled when he speaks.

"Do you know, Isobel, that there are days when I put a dishcloth or handkerchief over my face and lie alone on my bed for hours?"

I nearly laugh aloud. "Why would you do that?"

He allows a laugh at himself, but it's more strained than joyful. "I imagine myself a man imprisoned."

"Imprisoned by what?" For a moment, I think he might say he's imprisoned by me. Imprisoned by love.

"By the things I can't escape."

"What things?"

"The past. Our ghosts. My own worst darkness."

Yes, I want to say: I have watched you do this to yourself and I wish that you would stop.

He fishes for his handkerchief by the bedside. It is a plain one, the kind he uses to mop his brow. He brushes his fingers across my eyes and bids I close them, then places the cloth gently across my face.

"Now open your eyes."

I do as he says. The cloth is white, the room is dim and warm. I smell the salty essence of him on my face and in the air.

"What do you see?"

I see his words, but they're faint, fading.

"Nothing."

He puts his lips to my ear. The world beneath the blindfold is white and shadowed.

"Look past *nothing*. See what's visible beneath the mask."

The handkerchief rises and falls like a curtain that opens and closes with the wind.

"Your breath and mine, moving together," I whisper.

He trails his fingers across my bare shoulder and I shiver in the warm evening.

"Plato tells a story of shadows and caves," he says. "The shadows aren't truth, but the people in the cave believe they are. They believe what they see and they fear it."

At my waist, the brush of his fingers.

"In the cave beneath my handkerchief I look into the truth of my own soul. Into the darkness."

At my thigh, the trail of a jagged fingernail. I see a tunnel of fire, a red opening in the sky.

"What do you see?" I ask.

"What I desire," he whispers.

His leg presses against mine beneath the blanket. I lift a hand to take away the cloth, but he catches my wrist and pins it.

"And what do you desire?"

"You."

He rolls on top of me and presses his mouth on mine and I surrender everything and everyone I've ever known to the hard grip of his hands around my wrists, his weight pinning me to the bed, the taste of blood when he bites my lip.

HE TAKES THE handkerchief and blots at my lip when we're finished. His face is right above mine. It looks pure and purged, naked and vulnerable.

"Your work is magical, Isobel." He traces a finger along my collarbone. "How do you do it?"

He's told me that he looks for ghosts in shadows and that he finds me there. I am sure now that I love him and that he loves me.

"It's you," I say quietly. "When you touch me, there are"—I search for the right word—"*explosions* of color."

His whole face curls into something like envy or covetousness. I close my eyes and narrate the colors as best I can—persimmon, cinnamon, India-ink blue, lemon yellow, poppy red, tangerine.

I try to describe what I see, but it's only when I fetch my sketchbook and show him the drawings that he begins to understand.

"Has it always been this way?"

I dare not look at him, for I have always known that to speak of my colors was forbidden.

Yet everything we've done is forbidden and it's only brought him closer.

"When I was a little girl my mother's words were sapphire and emerald, my pap's were caramel taffy." I tell him about my first sampler and Mam's painful warnings. "Voices faded to gray when she died and didn't come back until I crossed the ocean. I've never spoken of it to anyone."

"I know what it is when the world goes gray from grief," he says. He reaches for his notebook, wets his finger, and turns to a blank page. "Now tell me from the beginning—slowly."

The beginning was the sound of my parents' voices, or it was the wind. Or maybe it was the sampler.

I start there.

"The letter A is red," I say.

"Red like an apple?" He scribbles something in his notebook.

"No," I say. "A is a scarlet letter."

"Like the one you left for me at the boulder."

"Yes."

He asks more. "Do you see the colors when you sleep? Do you see the colors when you speak? And what color are my words right now?"

I describe how words and letters rise in front of me like clouds in the sky—weightless and transparent—and I begin to see that voices come in colors and shapes that change, but the color of each letter in a sampler or on a sign is always the same: A is red. B is blue. C is yellow.

"Your voice is red and gold." His face lights when I say it, and yet I want to weep. "My mother warned me to beware of these things. She said the colors could be construed as a curse, or some sort of witchcraft."

"I think it's a gift," he says. "Or it's a gift and also a curse—as full of pain as it is of glory."

Can the colors be both a blessing and an affliction? Perhaps he's right and the colors are like the two of us—accuser and accused, pain and desire come together across time and oceans to heal our wounds. Perhaps this is the secret that I've been trying to see all along, that together we are whole.

As FIREBUGS IGNITE and the moon wanes, he comes to me with his handkerchiefs and his rough grip on my wrists, with stories of his uncles and snippets of tales scribbled in his notebooks. He whispers that he sees his father in the folds of cloth draped across his eyes, and I whisper that I have heard my mother speak to me in my dreams.

"I'm working on a story about a young man who looks over a garden wall and longs for a beautiful girl who's forbidden to him," he tells me one night.

I'm in my sleeping gown, curled against the wall at the top of my bed. A single candle lights his face as Nat describes succulent trees, thirsty plants that reach across the page bursting with color and longing.

"There's a plant with gnarled branches and large red blossoms," he says. "The girl loves the plant like a sister—she even sits beside it and combs the blossoms." He turns a page in his notebook. "But there's something wrong."

"What is it?" I ask.

"The plant she loves is filled with poison that can kill with a single drop."

My needle stops.

"And what will you do with that poison?"

"I haven't decided," he says. "Either the plant she loves will kill her, or she'll eat the blossoms bit by tiny bit until the poison is in her blood and she's become poisonous to the man who loves her."

"That's—horrid."

He props himself on an elbow, one bare shoulder in the air.

"You gave me this idea, Isobel. You and your colors and that gorgeous Garden of Eden—the blessing that's also a curse. The pain that's also pleasure."

"I never believed such a thing before," I cry. "It's you who taught it to me."

I cannot bring myself to look at him. But I know that desire comes with a price. I know now that pain can be pleasure, and pleasure can be pain.

"Are you not pleased with me?"

"I'm saying I don't want to read about love that kills."

"Perhaps I haven't explained it well." His tone suggests this is doubtful. "Or maybe you don't understand that literature is meant to reveal deeper truths about men. Intuition and colors are fine delights, but in pursuit of my craft I have to look beyond them."

I'm still young, and he has been to university and understands much that I do not. I don't want to quarrel, and I certainly don't want him to see my tears.

I bite my lip and slip out of bed. In the yard, toads fill the night with mud-green croaks and groans. Crickets and cicadas sound bright pink high notes. Firebugs rise from the brush at the edge of the yard.

Nat finds me under the bright half-moon and puts an arm around my waist. I wipe a wrist across my tears so that he doesn't see them.

All this time I've waited for another letter that would confirm that Edward is alive. And every week, when there's been no news, I've thought of my bonfire and the way I trampled the ashes of my husband's church coat into the dirt. And I've wondered if I could have made my own wish come to pass.

"Isobel, you're in my veins now—you know it, don't you? You're in my blood."

Now is when I should tell him about the captain's letter.

"And when Edward returns?" I ask instead. "What then?"

He brings my hand to his lips. His words come through my parted fingers.

"Isobel, when he comes back it will hurt me terribly. This is the price I'll pay, but I'll love you from afar as I always have."

He has never spoken of love before.

"Do you love me from afar? Even when you are right next to me?" I keep my voice light. I'm thankful that it's dark and he's looking up at the sky.

"From the moment I saw you on the dock with your red cape and your red hair flying, I was drawn to you. And you knew it, and you drew me closer."

He touches my face.

"Your red hair, your fierce spirit—I told you, I felt as if I'd summoned you from my own mind."

"But that's a story," I say. "And I am here, and very real."

"You are. You're very real."

He pulls me close and puts his lips to my ear.

"I looked at your cloak," he says. "Why have you stitched a red-haired witch flying through the air?"

For a moment I feel as if I've fallen through time. My mother is telling me the story of Isobel Gowdie, snow is falling outside the window of our cottage in Abington, she's warning me to never reveal my colors. But it's too late. I've already shared them with Nat.

"That's my ancestress Isobel Gowdie," I whisper. "She wasn't a witch, but the men believed she was, and they were frightened of her."

I tell him the tale and he listens raptly.

"A witch who escaped and lived. Isobel, even if I didn't conjure you, surely you were meant for me to find."

The first time he said this, I felt flattered and desired. But now I'm standing before him with a life of my own and a heart that is my own. I've told him my secrets and shown him my passion, and he's made a deep mark upon me. And still, he looks at me and sees only himself.

"I'm more than your invention. Nathaniel, I think of you—" *All the time.* I don't dare to say it. "I think of you, Nat, and what might happen if Edward didn't return—"

"If he doesn't return? He will return, Isobel." He puts his cape on the ground and pulls me to him. "The ship will be here in just a few weeks— perhaps sooner. And I'll have to say goodbye to you, although it will hurt me more than I can bear."

His words aren't red and gold but black like newsprint—not the color of his voice but the color of his stories written with pen and ink.

I should tell him about the captain's letter. What he desires is forbidden, and what's forbidden, he desires. But it needn't always be so. I should tell him now. But I'm afraid that when I say it, everything will change. And I couldn't bear it now, for my bleeding is late.

Scotland, 1710

The infant opens her mouth and mewls like a kitten.

"Mama, she's hungry."

Isobel's hair is gray now, and she wears it in a long braid curled around her head. Long ago, when she woke beside the river and her child was gone, Isobel was sure that she'd lost her true heart forever.

But she did not. The proof is in her arms now, a wee babe with red fuzz on a scalp that smells of snow and the scent of winter trees. Tomorrow she will leave a pot of pine ointment beneath the May trees to thank the faeries who came to her that night on the river so long ago, and brought her to the Wood Witch.

Isobel has never known if her first child died of the torment or if the faeries took the babe's life as payment, but either way, they kept Isobel alive long enough to see her granddaughter.

"We've named her Isobel," her daughter says. "For you, Mama."

Isobel Gowdie closes her eyes and blinks back silvery tears. She remembers her first husband and the reverend's wife, who helped her escape, and the Wood Witch who said she belonged in the world of men. Isobel does not know if the Wood Witch was right, for the world of men is filled with laws that she has never understood. But Isobel is certain that she belongs in this moment, where she is a red-haired woman in a chain of red-haired girls weaving backward and forward through time. Where she is holding a granddaughter in her arms.

— TWENTY-TWO —

It's the last Sunday in June, when all of Salem goes to church meetings. Today is the day I'll tell Nat I've missed my bleeding and that Edward isn't on the ship.

I tie up my hair with a green silk ribbon, put on a fresh petticoat and bloomers, and tuck sprigs of lavender in my chemise. In a straw hat adorned with periwinkle and pale pink tea roses, I walk out to the boulder where we left our tokens of affection. From there I go north through the forest until I reach an old, wide sycamore that divides the path in two.

You'll know it by a bull's-eye carved into the trunk, Nat wrote in a note left at my doorstep yesterday, as promised. *My uncle and I threw knives there when I was a boy.*

I go left, as he instructed, and soon Nat appears on the narrow path with his long, listing stride. I fall into step beside him and he's careful, putting out a hand for me, holding back branches as we climb through bramble and rock. Summer has come early and crickets are calling. The forest is thick with pine and the smell of sap; we haven't gone far when he puts out a hand to show me a wild turkey with two chicks in the shrub.

The path rises, and I see the blue-and-green water dancing between the trees.

At last, he stops at a thick stand of hemlock. He draws back the branches and opens a passage.

"You first," he says.

The pine needles fold around me. I'm in darkness for one moment and then I'm stepping into a cove. The foliage closes behind us and we're in a hidden inlet by the sea. A blanket is spread upon the rocks near the water, waiting. Nat has been here already and prepared for us.

He unties a sack from a low tree branch and soon we have a picnic of bread, cider, and boiled chicken. I can't remember the last time I've eaten. I've forgotten to listen for Ivy and Abraham. I've forgotten about food.

Nat uncorks the cider and hands me a chicken thigh.

"It's enough food for three—did you pack all this?"

I'm nervous. The sea and sky seem to separate from one another; my voice sounds as if it belongs to someone else.

"My sister Louise is always trying to feed me—she thinks I forget to eat."

A brigadier floats far off across the horizon, and then another. We're quiet together as we eat. After a while he takes out his notebook and writes. I'm trying to imagine how I'll tell him all that I must—I've used the herb plug and rinsed with water and vinegar every time, but it's been more than six weeks since my bloods and nearly four weeks since the night of shooting stars. It could have happened then, or it could have happened any of the nights that followed.

The sun is at the top of the trees when he looks up and reads to me about a midwife who helps deliver a child out of wedlock. As the new mother is dying, she begs the midwife to keep the child for her own "so that no one will know he was born a sin."

The midwife agrees and loves the child as her own. But what begins as a tiny birthmark on the infant grows as the boy grows, until it is the size and shape of an ugly mushroom across the back of his hand.

I feel my hands twisting one across the other.

"The boy was good and pure," Nat reads. I bite my lip and will him to look up, to see how the story is hurting me. "But the sin had to be paid for, and so it would be."

He chews on his pencil, looks at his notebook, and crosses out entire paragraphs.

"It's not a good story," he says. "Not yet."

"Couldn't they live happily?" I say after a moment.

He shakes his head before he puts aside his notebook and looks out to the horizon where sky and water meet.

"I like to swim here," he says.

"I don't know how to swim." I'm miserable, but he seems not to notice.

"Then I'll teach you—the day is warm enough."

He pops up and holds out his hands to me. His hair is in his eyes and he pushes it away with a toss of his head. He's left the darkness of the story folded inside his notebook.

"Today?"

"Yes, today. Now."

A sly look comes over his face and he pulls off his jacket, then shrugs off his suspenders and strips to his breeches.

"What if you're seen?" I cry, but his boldness lifts my spirits.

"I've been swimming here since I was a boy, and I've never seen a soul. It's the one place in Salem where I'm truly free."

He scrambles to the edge of the rock and dips his foot into the water, then jumps in. He surfaces with a howl, yelping and shaking his head like a pup. I've heard that a lady with child shouldn't step into cold water. But I'd like nothing more than to bring on my bleeding even here and now, for then the burden would be gone and everything would be easier.

"Come in," he calls. His eyes fleck green in the light, the color of the sea on a calm bright day. "Step there—onto the rock."

His happiness is seductive. I've stepped this far into sin, and it hasn't felt like sin. I've gone this far in the dark, and now I'll show myself to him in sunlight and he'll see that I love him.

I strip to my petticoat and step onto the dark, wet gray rock. "Here—" He scrambles to where the water is up to his waist and takes my hand. "Come in here."

The water is cold and it empties my mind of every sadness. I feel a tug in my abdomen and welcome it. He puts his hands on my waist and I look up into his face. We've never been this close in daylight. There's stubble on his chin, but the cheeks above his whiskers are smooth and rosy. His green-gold eyes in the bright sun are the color of a cat's, or a moonstone, or a yellow gem.

He's strong and sure of himself as he narrates each step I'm to take—bend my knees, lean forward, let my arms float and then my legs rise up behind me. It is effortless—the water holds me. He puts a hand under my belly and I am prostrate on the sea. My petticoat floats around me like a cloud, and he shows me how to float, then to blow air bubbles and move my arms in long, steady strokes.

"You've got it," he says. "Now kick."

He takes his hands from beneath my stomach and shouts again, "Kick, kick harder," and with two kicks I'm propelled ahead of him to the edge of the inlet where a circle of rocks is all that stands between me and the wide Massachusetts Bay.

"I'm swimming," I shout. A snout and then a black head bobs up in the water on the other side of the rocks. It's a seal, followed by another. I begin to call to him, to say "Look," but then my mouth is full of water and I am choking and he is behind me, his arms under mine, and then he's holding me up, breathing words of encouragement into my ear, taking me close enough to shore that I can stand on my tiptoes.

"There are seals." I sputter and snort up the salt water that's gone up my nose. "Did you see them?"

"I saw them," he says. "Sometimes one comes and looks across the water when I swim alone."

He presses himself behind me, and together we look out to the sea as my breath calms.

"There." I point to silky black heads bobbing up and down, swimming away from us now. I think to tell him about the selkies—seal-women who shed their black skin and come to the land in human form. Or the dark-haired selkie seal-man who romances a lonely woman and breaks her heart. But then Nat runs his whiskers along my neck, and all my words leave me.

"We're free here," he says.

"And cold," I say, for my wet skin in the air has turned a slight blue, and goose bumps rise on my skin.

Perhaps he feels liberated and unclaimed here, where the earth is like a bowl of blue water and blue sky. But I'm not free.

We scramble back onto the shore and he tosses the food off the blanket and wraps it around me. He crushes my face into him and kisses me and rubs the blanket along my arms and legs to warm them.

"You'll dry quickly in the sun," he says.

We stretch out on the rocks, and he twirls a bit of my hair. I look up at the sky, my cheek resting against his shoulder. Now. I must tell him now.

"Do you like it here in Salem?" he asks.

I love you. This is what I want to say—that I believe we have a shared fate, accused and accuser destined to mend our family stories one to the other. If there is a power in stories, surely there is power in ours.

"I like the sea close by. I like the sky at night," I say instead.

The light in his eyes is the color of candles.

"If you were to leave here, would you go home to Scotland? Or would you like to live somewhere else?"

Is he asking me to go away with him?

"I'd like to go to Maine." My ears buzz with my own pounding heart. "I'd like to go to Maine with you."

His finger stops curling my hair. Too many moments pass before he says evenly, "Maine is beautiful in summer."

He describes the morning air, a lake the color of sea glass. He speaks of silence cut by loons at daybreak.

"I'd like to take you to Maine." He twirls a long piece of my hair around his finger. "I'd like to show you Sebago Lake and the White Mountains."

Only a short while ago I felt the whole ocean and the whole world was open to me. I was swimming, and he was behind me making sure I didn't flail.

"It's light and clean in Maine, nothing like Salem—there are too many ghosts here, too many shadows and secrets. Too much cruelty— too much terrible history."

He's speaking of his ancestors now. I've seen him go dark in this way and then I have lost him.

"You're not like them," I say. "You're not like your grandsires, you didn't condemn women to be hanged or whipped through the streets, and your family didn't have slaves when others did."

"Slaves?" he asks.

"Yes, slaves," I say. How long has it been since I saw Mercy and her children? "I was told that the Silas family and others in Salem had slave ships."

"Old Captain Silas is dead and no one in Salem trades in slaves anymore—there are laws against it."

"But did he?"

"Maybe he did." He is irritated.

"I heard men in town talking about a slave catcher looking for a child," I say.

Nat looks up at the sky.

"A slave is a valuable bit of property." His hands are propped behind his head, his elbows poking out like wings. "A strong Black man is worth four hundred dollars or more—a child is worth half that, but it's still a good deal of money."

An uneasy feeling comes over me. My wet clothes haven't dried. The sun is past high noon, and folks will soon be freed from Sunday meeting for an afternoon stroll in the forest.

"It's best not to interfere in the property of others," he says. So casually. As if he doesn't know any children like Abraham or Ivy.

"But a child is a living person with a heart and a soul."

He sits up, shrugs off my hand. The spell between us is broken; the moment I might have told him about Edward is gone.

He brushes tiny pebbles off the backs of his bare arms.

"My family never owned slaves, Isobel." There's a catch of impatience in his voice. How can Nat hate the men who imprisoned innocent women and not the men who chained and enslaved fellow human beings? "Slavery is the South's problem, not mine—let's not talk of it on such a lovely day when we have so little time left."

IT'S WELL PAST noon when we lace up our dry clothes and our shoes and leave the clearing in the hemlocks. We're quiet on the path, for there's a sadness now that our day has come to an end.

We haven't walked very far when I hear carriage wheels and Zeke's cart clips toward us from the north. Nat is behind me and the next minute he's gone. I try to keep my eyes from dancing around in the brush as Zeke stops the carriage and tips back his hat.

"Miss Isobel, what brings you up this way?"

The horse recognizes me and nuzzles at my hand through his bridle. I'm glad I've put my cap back on so that Zeke can't see my hair is wet.

I've always felt safe with Zeke, felt the goodness of him. It was Zeke who helped me plant my garden, Zeke who escorted me home after dark, Zeke who made the glove forms that I use to make my meager living. But now his voice is strange, and there is no color—no juice in his letters, no dusk in his words. He's stripped everything out of himself so that he's as empty as the feedbags tossed beside a stack of sapling buckets and wooden barrels in the back of his cart.

"The day is too pretty to spend inside at Sunday meeting," I say. Birds caw overhead, and Zeke glances farther along the path. He is distracted, as if he's seen something amiss in the forest.

"And you?" I draw his attention back to me so that he doesn't spy Nat. "What brings you out this way?"

He scratches his head.

"Been checking on the maple trees," he says.

"I've tried your maple syrup." I shade my eyes. "The sugar house must be back that way?"

Zeke nods, and I can see that he's impatient to get on. As soon I step aside, he taps his horse and moves on. When he's out of sight, Nat comes out of the clearing, his face no longer soft as it was when we swam.

"There's nothing to do at a sugar house at the end of June," he says. "Something unnatural about him up this way."

"Yes," I agree, although I hate to acknowledge it, for Zeke is my friend and he has helped me. "I felt it, too."

Nat frowns.

"I'll watch you from the forest," he says. "You take the path and I'll stay hidden until we reach the tree that splits the road. You'll be safe after that."

There's a ferocity in his face; it turns the key that he's fit inside me and I finally speak what I feel.

"Nat." I close my eyes. What he's shown me is true and right: love is pain and pleasure at once. "I love you, Nat."

I don't wait for an answer but spin around and run—yes, I run—in the wake of Zeke's carriage and horses, all the way home.

— TWENTY-THREE —

Nell looks at me from head to foot. It's early evening, and pink heather twilight fills the sky between the trees behind my cottage. It's been a month since I first took Nat into my bed. I know I've changed, but I don't know how much until my friend is standing at my door.

"You're thin, Isobel." She takes my arm and exposes the underpart of my wrist, pale and almost translucent. "And your cheeks are flushed— have you been in the sun without a bonnet?"

She pulls me into an embrace.

"I've come for Charlotte's trousseau," she says. "Please don't worry about your husband—no matter what happens, you won't go hungry here."

Nell sits at my table, as I have always hoped that she would. I light the lamp and lay the white-on-white pieces out for her: four petticoats, two nightdresses, and six camisoles for Charlotte; tiny gowns for the babe and a baptism gown with a train embroidered with every flower that Mrs. Silas could name.

"Your work is flawless," Nell says. She runs her rough hands along the scalloped edges as if they are made of lace meringue that might crumble at her touch. "Mrs. Silas will be so pleased."

Nell puts two gold pieces on the table. It is more than half a year's wages at Felicity's shop.

"She asked me to pay you with this."

I think of what Mercy told me. But I take the money. I need it.

"Hide it well," Nell says. "My mama kept her money hidden in the garden—she dug it into the dirt."

"And what if a chipmunk digs it up like an acorn?" I ask. "And runs away with it in his mouth?"

Nell laughs.

"You put it in a tin, silly goose. My mother put her silver in a tin and buried it beneath her pumpkins."

We laugh about silver and gold pumpkins, and then Nell's face goes serious.

"I have something to tell you." Her words are shaded green, a country glen of splendor. I wonder, not for the first time, what I can learn about a person from the color of her words.

"We're eloping," she says. "By the time Charlotte is married next week, Stephen and I will be husband and wife."

"Eloping? Why?"

"His mother doesn't want us to marry, because I'm a Catholic," she says. "But he loves me." She is laughing again. "He loves me, Isobel, and I love him."

It's been days since I told Nat I love him, and I've heard nothing from him.

"Where will you go?"

"We're going to Boston tomorrow—we'll get married by a priest."

"Will you tell Mrs. Silas?" I ask. "Surely she would help you."

"I'll tell her after we're married," she says.

"He seems a wonderful fellow."

"He's kind and true, generous with his customers and gentle to his cows. He hates cruelty and injustice. If he had the money to be educated, he would make an excellent minister or lawyer."

She must see something in my face, for she puts out her arms and pulls me to her as she says, "I wish it was different for you, Isobel."

"Maybe it will be different one day," I say. And then, I dare to whisper what I have thought for many weeks. "Maybe Edward will never come home."

"If he doesn't, then you'll prosper without him."

As we stack up the petticoats and wrap them in a plain cotton sheet, I hear carriage wheels approaching.

"It's Zeke," she says. "He's come to bring me back to town."

I walk outside with her, but Zeke doesn't get out of the carriage. He says hello and tips his hat, but he's not as friendly as in the past, and I wonder if he saw Nat with me—if he knows more than he's revealed.

"Nell," I say. I want to tell her everything has changed for me. I want to tell her that I am in love with Nathaniel Hathorne and that my bleeding is almost two weeks late, but I can only hug her to me and whisper "Good luck" into her hair.

TWO DAYS PASS. I wait, but Nat doesn't come.

He said he was going to Maine with his uncle—perhaps he's already gone and had no way to tell me. I wonder at the carelessness I saw in him, the flash of something I didn't want to acknowledge. But he's in me now in every way, and I'm heartsick that he is absent.

I line up the last pairs of gloves for the Philadelphia ladies and make the marks. I make the stitches but feel no joy in it. I watch the needle push through the fabric all day long, something alien and separate from myself.

It's only work; it is not my heart. And still, my bleeding has not come.

ON THE FOURTH of July, I roam the Common licking a lemonade ice in the heat. It's America's Independence Day and the whole town is out for the celebration. The summer air smells of roasted meats, peanuts, and fire—scents that usually make me happy, but today make me queasy. A parade of men in costume marches through the center of the square singing and banging drums. Children and dogs run alongside them, making a ruckus. Girls vibrate with holiday merriment as they twirl long colorful ribbons on sticks. Boys blow wooden whistles and toss balls in the air.

Booths along the square sell gingerbread, sugarplums, and confectionary, spruce beer and lemonade. Mrs. Remond's cake shop offers red-and-blue sugar cookies, Mr. Tillerman is selling his liquorice whips, and Mrs. Spencer is doing a quick business selling her Gibraltar candies at the new price of three pennies each.

I'm looking for Nat, and at the same time I'm trying not to look for him. I want to see him, and I want to see him before he sees me. It's been six days. He's never stayed away so long without forewarning, and I'm desperate for him to find me.

At a root beer booth, three or four strange men stand with city magistrates and other officials.

"Runaway slaves make up counterfeit papers and move freely in our northern cities," one says. His words are hard green, tinged black. "But I think it's our duty to send them back south where they belong."

"Not to mention collecting the reward," says another with a foul chuckle. I turn to see what a slave catcher looks like, but he is ordinary in every way, with a curled mustache that is waxed and trim. Evil in the shape of an unexceptional man.

"A good neighbor will do that," says a third, who wears a white carnation in his lapel. "Just like you would with a runaway cow or a horse. It's the right thing to do, no matter what the Quakers have to say about it."

There's a man with a monkey in a red hat who takes peanuts from his hands, and a group of rowdy boys—perhaps the same boys who taunted the widow on the day of our arrival—who toss pebbles at the poor creature for sport.

Folks I know from church or from town greet me, and I move as if in a daze.

"The *New Harmony* is due in port soon," one says.

"You'll be a sight for your husband's sore eyes, Mrs. Gamble," says another.

Every few moments it seems I see a man who looks like Nat, and I must remind myself not to say his name aloud.

At the waterfront a line of bonfires is burning and smoldering, tended by a cadre of shirtless young Black men who blink away the sweat that pours into their eyes. I walk south along the water where I've never gone before, away from the festivities and families full of happiness. At the almshouse, I see children playing hoops with the old top of a rusted barrel and wish I had something to give them.

The lemon ice sours in my stomach—God forbid I ever have a child who plays hoops at the almshouse—and I hurry away. I pass fishermen's houses that face the open sea and the soap factory that backs up against a long field. Along the lake is a dock of rowboats, and some of them are in the water. I see a family with a child. A man and a woman. The man looks like Nat, but of course it is not.

Kites dip and soar and twirl in the air. A trio of young ladies comes skipping along the lakefront, and a boat in the water comes to shore. A man hops out and splashes. His back is to me, and his shirt is the blue of Nat's shirt. He puts out a hand and tugs the boat, and lopes to the left just as Nat lopes to the left. But it is not Nat.

I trudge home as rockets begin to whistle through the sky and find Mercy at the well in my yard.

"It's so hot I ran out of water." She looks me up and down. "You been in town?"

"Yes."

"Freedom Day they call it, but freedom for who?"

I see it now. *Freedom*, the way the word leaves her lips and flies up in a blaze of yellow tipped with orange like a flame. Mercy and freedom are linked, like the chain of something worked with a long tambour stitch. Like the rosebud and the hawthorn branches I embroidered together.

THE NEXT MORNING I heed Mercy's advice about going unseen. I tuck up my hair and walk close by the window of the Mannings' stagecoach office, but Nat's not inside. He must have gone north without telling me. Perhaps his uncle rushed him away. Perhaps he saw someone, or someone saw him, and he's afraid to come back.

Twice I walk by our gray boulder, and once I even sit and wait. But I dare not wait long, for I'm freezing even in the July heat. I'm shivering from fear and shame and something that makes me feel so ill I can only think it is love, or the child, or both.

∞

On Tuesday morning I deliver one dozen pair of gloves to Felicity, who holds each set up to the light as if she's looking for a secret hidden there.

"How have you done it?" It's as if she's angry. "These are a marvel."

The gloves are a part of me—they have my flesh and tiny bits of blood where the thimble did not stop the needle from piercing my skin. They have Nat, the colors he left on me. They have what I've seen in the Marine Society Hall, the flowers on my walks, even sprigs of hawthorn that I do not expect Felicity to recognize.

"I'm glad you're pleased." I struggle for a breath and hear my words come out as if through a long, tight reed. "I've worked very hard to please you, Mrs. Adams."

With Felicity's money in my pocket, I walk through town slowly. The wet heat drags me down, the lack of sleep has put me in a daze. I do not notice the rain clouds until I am up on High Street where the rope makers and cutters have their stores and shops. A clap of thunder shakes the sky, but I do not want to take refuge anywhere but home, where Nat can find me if he wants me. Where I can hide away if he does not.

I'm hurrying to stay ahead of the rain when the newspaper office door opens and Nat steps into the road without looking up. His face is dark gray, as if veiled. In his hand he clutches a sheaf of papers.

I freeze. I want to run to him. I want to cry out. I want to hide.

He heads east, walking away from me. He is moving as if he is treading through cold water, cold fury, something frigid and impenetrable.

It's a thick, dark day now with storm clouds gathering from the east. I keep my eyes on Nat as he rounds the corner quickly, the dusty street kicking up behind him. I am distraught with all that I see on his face—all the days and nights that he has not come to me, or sent word, or left me some sign of his affection.

He's suffering, but he's kept himself away.

I take the shortcut past the graveyard and skirt the black iron fence that borders the north of the cemetery. Wind whips and my hair rises with it as if something is tugging at me. And then I see Nat. His back is to me and he is kicking at a tombstone, ripping his papers into shreds.

His jacket is off, and I can see faint streaks of blood at his shoulder again. His name leaves my lips in less than a whisper. For the first time in my life I see the color of my own words, and in them I see the story that he told me about the girl in the garden, the poisoned plants that I drew while he read, the mother who dies in childbirth.

Who is the deathly girl in his stories? Who is the girl who dies of love?

I understand now—it is me.

Salem, 1808

Infant by her side, daughter and son sleeping in their beds, Elizabeth Manning Hathorne watches her husband prepare for his long sea journey. The city has grown fat with cod and sugar back and forth to Africa and the West Indies, and this has made the Salem sea captains rich. Their wives walk past her in dresses finer than any she's ever owned, and Elizabeth covets their silks for herself and her daughters.

"This trip will secure our future," Nathaniel says when he embraces her in the morning.

Elizabeth knows her husband hopes to earn enough to build them a true home and restore his family name to the glory it once held in Salem.

She remembers when she wanted him desperately, so that they could be joined like a river to the earth. To be earth and river and wind—this was what she wanted.

She imagined herself a poet. Now she only wants the silks and a fine home in which to entertain her brothers.

When word comes that her husband has died at sea of yellow fever, Elizabeth Hathorne looks at the four-year-old boy who sleeps with his father's cap on his pillow and she tells him to be brave.

"Your father had a great name, and now it is yours alone to carry," she says.

But she is not brave. She puts on her widow's weeds and moves back to her father's house, and she lets little Nat run along the docks chasing ghosts and shadows until he, too, imagines himself a poet.

TWENTY-FOUR

East Meeting House is surrounded by well-wishers lining up to enter on the morning of Charlotte's wedding. It's only half past nine, but the benches are already full as I squeeze into a standing space where I'm pressed against a wall. Nat enters with his sister on his arm and walks to the family pew, looking neither left nor right, and I feel a stab of utter sorrow that he has not looked my way.

At ten o'clock the church bells ring and Mrs. Silas enters on the arm of a gentleman I do not know. She stares straight ahead as she makes her way to the front and takes her seat. The groom appears beside the minister. He's tall, with a shock of red hair. His jaw is square, and instead of the nerves I expected, he's smiling.

When Charlotte enters on the captain's arm there's a great rustle of dresses and shoes and small gasps from the ladies. I've made the dress and seen Charlotte in it, adjusted the bustle and created the length of netting that falls over her shoulders to her waist—and still, the sight of her makes my eyes mist. Charlotte is a kind girl, and I am glad that she has this radiant moment.

The ceremony is long, but I don't hear it. I am watching Nat from behind, the way he keeps himself erect between his sister and his uncle Robert Manning.

I haven't forgotten what I saw and felt beside the graveyard two days ago, but now I understand that something must have happened since he last came to me; something must be terribly wrong.

As he joins the throng to leave the church his head is low, eyes lidded beneath a heavy brow. I understand why Abigail says he's strange, but I also know how sensitive and deeply expressive he is, how his quiet demeanor hides deep emotions and doubts. I feel certain that he knows I am there; I will him to look up at me but he does not raise his eyes. I feel that I will die of shame, of heartbreak, of longing sliced through me right there in the church.

THE BRIDE AND groom lead a joyful procession through the streets and through the gates of the Silas home, and I follow.

In the yard there are two long tables filled with a luncheon of poached fishes and a roasted pig Mr. Remond has prepared. The very people who were polite and silent as they filled the church now push and prod at one another to get to the food. Plates are passed, and everyone is talking at once. In the crush of people I do not spy Nat or his family, but I find Nell at the table, cutting and boxing wedding cake for the well-wishers. On her hand is a silver band.

"You've done it." I'm so consumed with my own pain that I don't know how I smile for her.

"Mrs. Silas insists we take a wedding trip to Newport," she says, her eyes bright and shining. "I'm so very happy."

The wedding cake is a lemon confection with frosting that has been put in the icehouse to harden, and there is a fruitcake with white sugar topping. From afar, I watch Charlotte and her husband smile. I watch the way she keeps her flowers in front of her and the way he puts his hand atop hers. I worry that others will see what I see, the way he seems to make a web or a wall with his fingers, the way he seems to stand in front of her to shield her whole body from the eyes of the crowd. But the shawl I have made keeps her figure disguised, the slightly larger and more fashionable bustle lifts the skirt where it might otherwise have clung to her full abdomen.

Charlotte isn't afraid. Charlotte is the cherished daughter of a captain, and every day of her life she has been loved and believed that love is her due, and it seems that this has made it so. Slaving money might have enabled this life, but does that make her love less true? Does that mean she doesn't deserve her joy?

I don't have an answer, but I cannot wish her ill. For if Charlotte can be radiant, if she can have a husband who looks at her with adoration despite what I know, then anything is possible. Anything *must* be possible. I want to believe it and I must believe it and so I believe it.

WHEN EVERYONE HAS eaten their fill and celebrated the new couple's union and the well-wishers are on their way, I see Nat walk away from the luncheon with a sister on either arm.

I leave in the opposite direction, fighting back tears.

As I pass through the main square, a rough man with a gun at his waist comes out of Mr. Crombie's woebegone tavern and spits onto the street. He takes me by surprise, for I've seen men like this only on the wharves, among the roughest sailors. When I glance around to see if anyone else is a witness, I spot Zeke at the edge of the square, almost out of sight, his face hardened in an unfamiliar way. I know in an instant that this rough man must be the slave catcher.

"Good day to you, Mrs. Gamble."

A voice at my shoulder, a hand on my elbow. I'm so on edge that I let out a shriek.

"Hush, dear, I didn't mean to startle you." It's Widow Higgins, her voice the hue and shape of shadows. I haven't spoken with her since Nat told me the story of her husband's and sister's deaths and the shunning that followed.

The widow stands close, as she always does, and I see something that might be fear in her eyes.

"Salem loves a summer wedding," the widow says now. Her eyes roll up in her head and for a moment it seems she's going to have one of her spells.

"Widow Higgins . . ." I speak her name, hoping it will snap her back to attention. "I didn't notice you at the luncheon."

"But I saw you, dear." She refocuses her eyes on me. She's still closer than I'd like, but at least her gaze is clear. "You must stay away from Nathaniel Hathorne, Mrs. Gamble."

I wonder if my own eyes might roll up into my head. I feel faint.

"Why must I do that?" It's all I can do to keep my voice steady. To say less instead of more.

"I saw you gazing at him in the church," she says. "He may be handsome, but there is cruelty in his family."

She looks at my face, at the curls carefully arranged beneath my bonnet, at the place along my jaw and neck where Nat ran his lips. She cannot know my secrets with a simple glance. She cannot see colors in my words or the traces of his fingers on my skin.

"Don't worry, your infatuation is safe with me," she says at last.

I press my fingers to my temples, feel bile rising up in me.

"Remember that your husband's ship will return soon." She pats my hand. "And when it does, you must remind him to bring the next payment for the rent."

"I won't forget," I say. But of course, Edward won't be returning on the ship.

IF I HAVE any powers at all they are in my needle and thread, in the work that I do and the things that I imagine. That evening I sew one of the scrimshaw buttons onto a bit of brown sackcloth, but it looks like a grave in the mud. I tear it out and find the scrap of fine wool that I cut from Nat's torn jacket on the night he came to me. I sew the button firm upon it. As daylight fades, I walk out to the rock where we first sat together and tuck the cloth into the space where he left the rose. I stand there for some time and imagine him finding the button, bringing it to me.

Hours later, he's at my door.

"My uncle and I are leaving for New Haven in the morning." He looks down at his feet, which he shuffles in the dirt. It's dark. Behind him I hear the night owl calling and a swallow's whistle. There's nothing in his hands. It seems he hasn't actually found the scrimshaw button but has come of his own accord. Did I summon him, or did I not?

"You've stayed away so long." There's a catch in my throat.

"I'm sorry, Isobel. I've thought of you and longed to come, but my family has been much upon me."

"I've been wretched without you."

He reaches for me, but I fade from his touch.

"I would have sent word if I could," he says.

"The rock—" I bite the inside of my mouth. I don't want him to see my tears. "You could have left a sign or a note at our rock."

He raises a hand to my cheek slowly, and I do not pull back this time.

"How long will you be gone?" I ask.

"Three weeks or more. Through the end of August if we go on to New York or Philadelphia." He pauses, and the air is heavy between us. "Your husband's ship will be here in a few days," he says into the silence. "I dread our goodbye, but it's best if I'm gone when he returns."

I pull gently out of his arms. He's called me his darling Isobel, his beauty, his red-haired flame, a woman with poetry in her needle.

"I had a letter from the captain." I'm standing with my back to the lighted cottage room. I can see his face, but I think he cannot see mine. "Edward may not be on the ship."

He looks at me with a puzzled expression.

"*May not?* What do you mean?"

I tell him what little I know.

"If the captain wrote to you in the spring, why didn't you tell me sooner?" There's an edge in his voice that wasn't there before.

"I didn't know what would happen—I thought that any day I might have a letter and there would be some certainty. Edward can be very unpredictable."

"And you've heard nothing more?"

"Nothing."

I step to one side, and the light from the lamp illuminates Nat's face. He looks tired and wary.

"What trick do you think he's up to?" Nat asks. "I heard he went about the city taking investments for something he called the elixir of life. He went to my Uncle Robert and made a proposition—as if my uncle wouldn't know that alchemy is nonsense."

"Nonsense?"

I remember the book that Edward did not want to let go. George Ripley's *Compound of Alchemy*.

"Do you pretend not to know it?"

"I pretend nothing," I say.

"The elixir of life promises everlasting youth by turning silver into gold." Nat's voice drips with sarcasm.

From the first day I met Edward, I believed that he had a deep knowledge of medicines. I doubted his self-control but never his knowledge, for he had the books to prove it.

"But it is herbs and other . . . things. Spiderwebs," I try, hating how my voice falters.

"Spiderwebs?" Nat scoffs. "Now who's lost to hopeless enchantments, Isobel?"

I remember when Edward whispered in my ear that I was fearless, and in saying so he made it almost true.

"Did your uncle give him money?" I ask. In all the time we've spent together, we've never spoken of Edward. Now I feel ashamed, as if Nat's known all along that Edward is a fraud and a thief.

"My uncle put him out at the heel," he says. "But the apothecary on the next block gave him money, and so did a few others. He speaks well, your husband, and there are always men hungry for gold."

At this moment I realize that if Edward doesn't return, everyone who invested in his venture will be my creditors, and I will be in their debt.

"Why have you never told me?"

"I assumed that you were aware of your husband's business propositions."

Silence hangs between us.

"It's possible that he won't return." I've imagined Nat would receive this news with delight. Now I understand that we have seen things differently from the beginning.

"You're fortunate that you have a great skill—and the ladies in Philadelphia have already bought your work." His gaze is impenetrable and his words are hollow.

"Yes, I've thought the same." I feel my tears coming. "I know the ladies' names and might go to them directly."

"Then you can finally do what you've urged me to do—put your name to your work."

"And what about you?" I ask. "What will you do?"

"I'll do the same. I'll make my name one day."

His face is half in shadow now. I feel him pulling away, but I have to ask.

"Would you come to Philadelphia if I went?"

He shakes his head slightly, as if there's water in his ear.

"You're another man's wife." I see these words in white and black, the colors leached from them.

"The Philadelphia ladies know nothing about me," I say. "They don't know I have a husband—they've never spoken to me. They don't even know my name."

"But I have a name." His voice is both defiant and resigned. "And it is known. It's one of Salem's first and finest. Without my name I'd be nothing."

In this moment, I see a thread begin to unravel. The black around the letters breaks apart, and his words become invisible.

"What we have is consecrated here in Salem, where I found you." He speaks slowly, as if to make his words impeccably clear. "Here we have unblemished passion, Isobel, a union that needs no notice or approval of society or community—"

I try to speak, but like a preacher in the pulpit, he keeps going.

"Isobel, you're an enchantress." He puts a hand to his heart, and for a second I am hopeful. "I found the scarlet letter you stitched inside my jacket pocket. I even found the whirled pieces of your hair in my vest that first night. You wanted me to come to you and I did. You sewed temptation and temptation arrived."

Once he said, *I invented you and you came.* Now he's saying the opposite: that I am the conjurer, and he is the conjured.

"What if there's a child?" I blurt out the question.

He stiffens.

"There is no child. I've watched you when you thought I was sleeping; you're wise in these ways."

"My bleeding is late, Nat."

He shakes his head.

"Isobel, you know that everything is upon me. It's my obligation to make the Hathorne name great again."

"I saw you in the graveyard." I can hardly breathe. "With blood on your shirt. Kicking at a tombstone with your family name etched in it. Is that the family you'd choose over me?"

"Then you've seen the Devil in me—you've seen what the curse has done to me." His eyes burn. "How it tears at my soul."

"And I don't mind it. That's what I'm telling you." I'm weeping quietly now. "I can soothe it. You've said you want to be free of your burdens, to ease the suffering and the guilt. Let me do that for you."

"I can't be soothed. I don't want to be soothed." I hear his agitation growing. "The hand must be here—" He presses his hand flat against the tip of his nose. "When I covered your face with the handkerchief I was trying to show you the truth of my darkness. I don't want to lift it—I don't want to be soothed. To take away the anguish would be to take away everything I want to put down on paper. I wouldn't know myself without it."

"That makes no sense, Nat."

"My family has educated me at great expense," he nearly shouts. "It doesn't have to make sense to you."

He is shaking, as if stunned by his own words.

"This is our child. Your child." I say it because I must. "If Edward doesn't return I'll be free after a time to marry again."

He takes a step away from me.

"You're another man's wife—you aren't a widow."

"We can go someplace where they've never heard of Edward Gamble or John Hathorne." I'm pleading now. "We'd be free of them both."

"Free?"

"Yes, free of your ancestors and of Edward—free to be your own man and a father to our child."

"I'd lose everything if I left here."

"You'd be leaving behind the people you hate and the name that crushes you."

He looks toward the trees at the edge of my yard.

"If there was no child, maybe in time . . . If it required just one single act of courage, then I would do it. But you're asking for a lifetime, year after year—the shame and weight of it would kill me."

"And what will it do to me? Will you not help me?"

I grab at his hands, but he pulls away.

"You bewitched me with your red hair and herbs and your stories of your ancestress—I can't give up my name for that."

"Bewitched you?" Now I am the one shaking. "What do you mean, bewitched you?"

"I am not a fool, Isobel. The colors you see, the things you told me. If it isn't a form of bewitched alchemy, then you must be mad."

"That isn't true, Nat. None of it is true."

He steps back into the yard.

"I told you—I found the red letter you sewed into my coat." His voice comes from the shadows, disembodied and haunted. "The same one you left for me by the boulder."

"I am not a witch, nor have I bewitched you—I only ask for your help, Nat. Will you not help me?"

I'm speaking not to his face anymore but to his ghost.

"I won't be trapped by you," he says from the dark. "I must have time to think."

Scotland, 1815

It is a cold and rainy day when Margaret MacAllister gives her daughter a needle, thread, and linen for her first sampler. The boy has gummed her breast raw, and even with the tea-and-comfrey salve, Margaret is irritable and exhausted. But five-year-old Isobel is never a burden— loving, obedient, thoughtful, and attentive, the child mimics her mother's every move, carefully marking her letters on the slate until they are neat and straight.

"You put the thread in your lips to wet it and then you pull it through like this." She smiles when Isobel's lips purse like a tiny rosebud as the child works the black thread through the eye of the needle.

Her own dear aunt taught Margaret to stitch at this same age, long before her own mother thought she was ready. Aunt Eilidh was always singing, always brightly dressed, always making up snatches of songs that no one understood.

"The wind is pink, the river sighs blue, and the sound of chickens is a purple thread pulled through," Aunt Eilidh sang. "The birds tell me when the rain is coming because their songs go from white to gray."

Margaret didn't see how or when Eilidh went from singing to scream-ing, but she remembers when her uncle tied the woman's hands behind her back and put her in the carriage kicking and shrieking. All the chil-dren were weeping, but Uncle Graeme set his face grim and promised he'd bring his wife home better than before.

"Dr. Cotton's asylum in St. Albans is the best, and we want to be sure our Eilidh comes home rested and at one with God," he said before he snapped the reins and drove the cart away.

"The village people say your aunt talks in tongues with the Devil, and I fear she has fallen into the space between this world and the faerie world," her mother told young Margaret. "Your uncle has used his every penny to take her for help. 'Tis best to let the doctor do what the priest could not."

But Aunt Eilidh never came home, and Margaret learned that it is better to lie and hide away your truth than to be taken away in a cart kicking and shrieking.

So when Margaret puts the babe Jamie in his cradle and makes her husband's tea and bread and folds the washing and finally goes to see how Isobel's work has come along, her heart stops at the sight of a red letter A *and a blue letter* B.

"What have you done?" she whispers. "What is it that you see?"

—— TWENTY-FIVE ——

I wipe my face and hack the young pennyroyal in my garden.

I'm in such a state I cannot distinguish what I fear from what he said. Did Nat say *never*, or did he say he needed time to think? Did he say he would come back for me or that he could never be with me?

You bewitched me, he said.

That, I remember. He used the colors against me, the very thing that bedeviled me in his arms.

I must have time.

If there was no child. Yes. If there was no child.

I mash the leaves and stems and set them to brew over the embers.

Women came to Edward in Glasgow for such remedies; if they were married he refused, but if they were unwed he helped them. I admired that about him, the way he'd been generous and passed no judgment on the young ones who'd gotten themselves in trouble.

For a moment I almost wish Edward were here to put the brew in my hands, the way he rubbed the ointment on my burn the day we met. But that man is long gone, and so, too, is the girl I was then.

∞

WHEN THE BIRDS wake and only the maids and the blacksmiths are out, I go to the apothecary on Washington Street to buy a small bit of black cohosh and a thimble of juniper berry. In the dim shop with a mounted ram's head above the door, I also ask for a pinch of savin powder for a pain of the lower back.

The elderly man shakes the grains into a tiny tube, but doesn't hand it over.

"You're Edward Gamble's wife," he says. Why have I not anticipated that he might recognize me? "I invested a bit of my own money in his quest. What word do you have from him?"

Everyone knows what savin is for. I have said I have pain so that he would give it to me without asking questions. But now he knows who I am.

"The ship will be here soon," I say. "I'm sure you'll know his outcome almost as soon as I know it myself."

His eyes dim, but I can see by the way he tilts his head that he has had a good look at me.

"You be sure to tell your husband that Theodore Bartholomew is eager to see him," he says.

AT HOME I bar the door shut. The cottage is tidy, my work is stacked neatly.

The bed in daylight is different from the bed where I have been with Nat in the night. I see it now—one way in the dark, another in the light. One way if I'm with child—another if I'm not.

I mix the brew according to the instructions in Edward's book.

The herbs are bitter. I bite the inside of my cheek to keep them down, but they come up. I drink again, a dark mud to shake the womb and bring on my bleeding.

Then I lie on my bed and wait. If it kills me, too, it is no matter.

THE CHAIR SLIDES sideways, and the dead rose speaks to me.

Nat bangs at the window—*without my name I'd be nothing.*

The great-aunt who lost her mind calls to me in bright red letters. *Go and dance,* she screams, *fly with the birds and sing,* and the crazy tapestry of her sampler flaps from a flagpole on a tilted tower.

Adam and Eve climb the apple tree.

Maple syrup is the color of blood.

The melon seed is a child. Abraham is calling from the forest. Ivy is at the well. Mercy's voice comes across the ocean.

"Isobel?"

It's dawn or dusk, I can't tell by the light. There's a stink of blood, dirt, and waste.

"Isobel—open the door."

The door latch rattles. I open my eyes. I cannot remember if I saw the red star in the sky or if it was in my mind. I've been curled up in this corner for hours, perhaps days. My red cape is in a heap on the other side of the cottage. My dress and bloomers are wet.

"Isobel." The voice is real. I know that voice. "Ship's come in and Captain Darling's asking for you."

My throat is afire.

"I'm here." I clear away the juniper twigs that rip at my windpipe and say it again, louder. "Mercy—I'm here."

Mercy puts her face against the window glass. Her eyes roll toward me with her mouth wide.

"Open the door," she orders.

I pull myself across the floor and push away the bar at the door. Mercy sees the vial and smells the sick and right away she knows. She takes my chin and twists my face up so she can see my eyes and I can see hers.

"When did you drink it?"

Was Nat here yesterday? Two nights ago? Have I missed work at the dress shop? Has Felicity sent someone for me? I don't know.

Mercy lifts my skirts and I'm far from my body, somewhere in the realm between life and death. I wish Mercy were a witch. I wish I were a witch. Because if we were witches, we would be stronger.

"There's no blood," she hisses. "How far are you?"

"A month and maybe some weeks," I say. "Not far."

She takes off my soiled bloomers. She is close and warm and smells like hay and gingersnaps.

"I saw a lady die this way, damn you—damn you."

She puts her hands under my arms and heaves me onto the bed.

"Mercy, please—I can't have this child."

She's stronger than I expected. I can't see her face, but I feel her fingers probe me and her hands roll across my stomach.

"Please help me, Mercy, you know what to do."

I haven't left the cottage as tidy as I thought. The mortar and pestle are on the table, the small jars of essence and tinctures beside them. Mercy lifts one, then the next.

"Savin powder, pennyroyal, and juniper berry together? Lucky *you* didn't die, much less the baby."

She turns through Edward's book, leaves me for a while, then brings back a vile-smelling brew.

"Drink," she says.

I heave until I'm turned inside out. I wail and cry and beg her to take the child, and all the while she says, "Hush now, this baby doesn't want to be shook out, and I'm not letting you die."

MERCY IS HERE when I wake. There's sun in the room and the top of the door is open to the yard. I hear birds. Mercy is humming softly. Without the turban her hair is big and loose, the round shape of a wildflower turned to seed. Her needle is flashing through fabric like a hummingbird drinking water from a flower cone. The days and nights of sickness, the heavy sadness, all of it is awake in me now.

Mercy fetches my clean bloomers from the line in the yard. She's tidied the cottage, cleared away the jars, swept up the herbs, and rinsed away my sick. Even the bed linen is washed and hanging in the sun. My red cloak hangs on a hook near the door, with the story I have told there folded away.

"Your color is better," she says. She brings me a cup of warm nettle broth and watches me drink it.

"Isobel, you listen. Folks are weak or blind or just have no sense." She takes my chin and lifts my face to hers. I blink away tears. "Folks fail you even when you love them—leave you when you need them. But you've got to be strong even with all that—you hear me?"

"I thought he loved me."

Her eyes and lips narrow.

"He called me—" *A witch.* I cannot speak the word. "He said I be-witched him."

She's nodding now.

"That's what they say when they want to get free of you or when they're afraid," she says. "Hush now, don't think about him. You need your strength—I told you, the ship's come in."

Her words are meant to soothe me but they are steely gray knives.

"And Edward's not on it; otherwise he would be here and drunk by now," I say.

"Captain didn't say anything about your husband."

I struggle to sit up, but fatigue keeps me down.

"Did the captain come here?" I don't want him to see me this way.

Mercy puts a soothing hand to my wrist.

"He sent Ingo."

"His first mate?" I slump back onto the bed. "Why?"

Deep emotion crosses her face.

"Ingo, he's my man."

Her words are brown and thick like Ingo himself.

"Ingo is your man?" I had no idea, yet it seems right and true.

"That's right." She stares at me hard as she says it.

Ingo and Mercy. Mercy and Ingo. My mind stretches around this like a long band reaching across the globe to connect two far-off cities. All of the things that have never added up seem to stand like rungs in a ladder in my mind: Ingo and Mercy are lovers. Ingo and Captain Darling have been together for a long time.

I pull myself up by the elbows until I'm sitting. The room stays steady. Mercy's dark sack of goods is set against my bed. The cat is on the window ledge licking her paws.

"Ingo's coming now to bring my wares to the docks."

I have forgotten what day it is.

"Is it market day?"

She shrugs away my question as if she hasn't heard it.

Two whistled notes, low to high, slice through the window in a bright pink sound.

"It's Ingo," she says. "You rest now."

She stays outside a long time. As their voices move away from the cottage, I open Mercy's black sack and unfold a trio of shawls.

One is stitched with flowers, one is decorated with ships, and one has a wide tree like the sycamore near the secret cove where I swam with Nat. In each of them I see a word that I could not see if it were not for my colors—*FREE*—stitched in overlaps of the same-color thread, visible to me because of the way the letters stand out against the cloth. *F* a burnt orange. *R* a purple red. *E*s a deep forest green.

When Zeke came down the path in his cart that day near the sycamore, I knew he was hiding something; when Mercy was running through the night it was as if her life depended on it. I knew something wasn't right. I have long suspected they are smuggling something, and now I wonder if that something is slaves running to freedom.

Mercy is strong-willed enough, and she has spoken to me about moving through places unseen.

Yet it would mean she is at great risk, and the children are, too. I don't believe she would risk Abraham's and Ivy's lives. Yet the word is there, undeniable to my eye. *FREE*.

I FALL IN and out of sleep and when I wake, Mercy is back in the cottage stitching a sash. Her black bag is gone. Her hands are steady and there's a warmth about the room that's been missing since Nat stopped his visits.

I must let a small sob leave my throat, for Mercy looks up as if she's heard something. Her face is flat and smooth, a polished surface.

"All right," she says. "It will be all right."

Her words are neither yellow for truth nor the elderberry I have come to trust.

"Did Ingo tell you what happened to Edward?" I ask.

She comes to sit by the bed, her hand warm on mine.

"Seems your husband bought up a good amount of poppy and other herbs and used them all on himself." She speaks as if she's telling a story about a stranger, her voice matter-of-fact. "He was wild, wouldn't get on the ship. The captain went around and repaid his investors here in Salem yesterday. Darling won't tell you, but a woman should know what she's up against."

Mercy's face was closed off to me when we met. Now she is a friend. I must know now if she and the children are in danger.

"I've seen the words in your work," I say. "And I've been to the forest and seen the wide sycamore with the faded bull's-eye in the trunk. I saw Zeke there, and I've seen the tree embroidered on your—"

"What were you doing way up by the sycamore?" Her question has a bite, as if she suspects me of something.

It takes a good deal of effort, but I get up to rummage through my basket until I find the gloves with the leopard. Nat's gloves.

"I was making these gloves, far away from everything and everyone."

I hold them out for her to see. This is as close as I can come to telling her the truth of that day, when Nat said that slavery is not his concern. When I told him I loved him and he said nothing in return.

"For a man who don't deserve them," Mercy says.

She knows.

A cramp grips me round the belly and I start to shiver.

Mercy puts an arm around my waist and helps me back to the bed. I breathe her air and she breathes mine. She smells of hard lye soap and lavender. I put my cheek on her shoulder and rest it there. Mercy may know more than I wish her to, but I have seen some things, too—I have seen things, and the full picture is almost visible to me—

Checking on the maple trees, Zeke had said when he came down the path that day.

"Something is happening beyond the sycamore," I say. "Up near the sugar house."

Mercy is still, like a cat.

"Sugar and maple syrup," she says. "Sap and kettles for brewing."

"Something else." I'm struggling for my words, spent from what's been said and from what's been held back.

Mercy's face clamps shut.

"You don't worry about that," she says. "You forget about anything that don't make sense to you round here, and I'll tell you something I know for sure—Nat Hathorne will never be a father to this child."

"But it's his," I choke out.

"No." She grips my chin and lifts it so that I'm looking into her face. "This is *your* child. Your mam's grandbaby. You hear? This child is yours." The words are clear. I hear them, but I do not want to.

And then I see them, hard yellow like a winter sun.

—— TWENTY-SIX ——

I'm not strong yet, but when the captain comes to my door wearing the jacket I embroidered with knotted rope and seashells on the sleeves, I smooth down my hair and step into the yard. It's the first I've ventured outside since Mercy found me choked on my own sickness.

"My God, it's good to have my eyes on you." Darling holds me by the shoulders and peers into my face, and I let his cloudy sky-blue words bloom over me. "Let me have a look at you—"

Captain Darling seems calm and proud in the summer light, as sure as the carved lady at the prow of his ship. I put my arms around his neck and he wraps me in his. Darling is shorter than Nat but taller than Edward. He's sturdy, and when he lifts me off my feet I feel buoyant and frail.

"Mercy says you've been sick." His eyes crease as he steps back and takes me in from head to foot. "You're thinner than ever, Mrs. Gamble. Just as pretty, but too thin."

"I'm getting stronger now."

Captain Darling looks younger than I remember, and I see that indeed he *is* younger than his ship and stature suggested to me on the crossing. His cheeks and forehead are ruddy from the sea but the skin around his mouth is fair and delicate, like a bird that has just lost its feathers.

"You've taken off your beard?"

He runs a hand across his chin and grins.

"Once in a while the sun has to shine everywhere, else my face would be smooth and pale as a babe's bottom."

In spite of everything, he makes me laugh.

Behind the captain I see the bed of pennyroyal that I hacked down, jagged like a sharp-toothed kelpie's mouth. Only a few days ago I wanted to let poison take this child—and even myself—to the grave. Now the captain is smiling and his blue words remind me that I came to America full of hope. His words were the first to have color for me during the crossing and here they are again, the color of a turquoise gemstone or the trim around the eye of a peacock feather.

I give him a turn around the yard and he admires my beans and long vines with budding cucumbers. He talks of fruits for sale on the wharves and the taste of coconut and fresh pineapple on the islands.

"I should like to taste it—just as you describe it, right from the trees," I say.

"Then you will," he says. "If I can make it happen, you will."

He leans against the well and has a drink from the ladle. When he looks into the sky, I know what is coming. For of course he has not come simply to see my garden.

"Did you get my letter?"

"I did."

"Then you know Edward isn't on the ship." Oh, how gentle his voice is, in every shade of blue.

In my state, I can't stop my voice from breaking. "I'm very sorry for it, Captain Darling."

"Please don't cry." He presses a handkerchief into my hand and I remember how safe I felt on his ship even when the seas were rough. "You've done nothing wrong, Mrs. Gamble. I'm sorry I didn't take better care to watch him."

I've done many things wrong, and it shames me to think of them in the light of day, with the captain here.

"It isn't your fault," I say. "I knew it could happen and never told you."

I tell him about the opium and why we left Scotland, and all the while his face grows redder.

"I should have had my men drag him back to the ship and lash him to a mast until his cravings were gone." He's angry. I've seen his anger only twice before, both times on our journey when wind and rain threatened to blow us off course.

"It might have worked," I say. "But not for long,"

"Poor lass. I'm sorry." He reaches into his pocket and takes out a small leather pouch. "These are your husband's fair wages. I want you to have them."

"I won't take your money, Captain. I know you've paid Edward's debts—there cannot be anything left of his wages."

"I can't have you go hungry."

I push away his hand.

"I have my work. I'm making gloves and other things, you needn't worry."

"Your work is surely worth a pretty penny, but thread and gloves cost money, too. Don't be proud, Mrs. Gamble."

"I'm getting along." I feel a stubborn pride at the doubt on his face. "The work is good—let me show you what I've done."

He waits in the garden while I consider Adam and Eve on the shawl and decide on the gloves for Felicity instead.

Captain Darling praises the flowers and wisteria, and then his eyes light on the leopard. Courage and strength, Nat asked for. I'm still waiting for him to find either in himself; I'm still hoping and still heartbroken.

Darling reaches for the gloves and I surrender them.

"I saw the leopard in the East India Marine Society Hall—you sent me there, do you remember?"

"I do," Darling says. "And I told you the custodian is a trusted friend."

He tries on the gloves—the very pair I meant for Nat. His hands are wide and strong and the leopard seems to contract and expand, to flex its muscles and open its jaws as he bends his knuckles and admires the work.

"Very handsome. Splendid!" He puts the sack of coins on the ground at my feet. "I have a small dinner to attend. I'll buy them, and it will be a fair exchange—you can't refuse me now."

I don't say yes, and I don't say no. But I have a queer feeling that I do not want to stop him: I want him to wear the gloves, and I want him to think of me when he looks at them. Nat be damned; I want to take this treasure away from him and give it to the captain.

"We sail in two days," Darling says before he goes.

"So soon?"

"A quick run with the schooner up to Nova Scotia and back. There's a shipment of whale oil waiting." Here, his blue eyes cloud. "I'll be back in August and will look in on you then. If you ever want to come closer to town rather than live here alone, I will help you do it, Mrs. Gamble."

I'M IN MY garden slowly digging up radishes when Mercy comes down at the end of the day. I'm relieved to see her, for I do not want to be alone with my despair. The captain's visit was a reprieve, but the darkness is close and the doorway between life and death that Edward once spoke of seems nearer than ever.

"The captain was here," I tell her. "He didn't tell me the truth about Edward, but he came close enough. He took my gloves—said he's going to a small dinner and—"

"A small dinner for a hundred people," Mercy says with a huff. "Hosted by old Captain White at Hamilton Hall. Every summer he invites all the Whigs, and Captain Darling goes so that . . ."

I don't hear anything else she says.

"A hundred people—you sure?"

"I helped Mrs. Remond and her daughters chop carrots and onions for the beef this very morning."

"He can't wear the gloves there." Panic burns my throat. He said it was a small dinner, and I did not ask him to keep my secret. "He can't show my gloves to a hundred people."

"Can't stop it." Mercy shakes her head. "The men are well into the wine by now, and turtle soup will be served at seven sharp."

Mercy doesn't understand what will happen if my work is revealed. Even I am afraid to find out what the penalty will be.

"Felicity Adams lies about those gloves; she doesn't tell anyone they're my work, and I've agreed—it's our arrangement."

"Already done," Mercy says again. She takes the hoe from me and eases me onto a stump. "And that's not what matters."

"I have been warned of Felicity's ire many times," I say. "It does matter—very much."

"Not as much as this child matters," Mercy says.

"But Felicity . . ."

"That's not what's important now," she says. "Because pretty soon— maybe here and now—you've got to think about this baby. And you've got to decide some things."

"Decide?" I decided to marry Edward and he ruined us. I'm not de- ciding anything else until Nat returns from the trip with his uncle. "I decided to work for Felicity so I could earn the money I need to live."

"You've got a child to think of," she says. "A child's the most precious thing you'll ever have. And right now, before it's too late, you've got to decide how you're going to keep yourself and this child."

"I don't want to decide," I whisper. Every choice I make is wrong.

"Doesn't matter what you want—don't you see? The baby needs you and is gonna need you for a long time. I've seen what comes from trying to shed a child that wants to be born. I've seen sorrow and misery and a motherless child and that's not what your child ought to be."

Her words are too close to my fears.

"Stop it." I turn away, but she follows me like a dancer, keeping her face in mine.

"You think you're the first woman to make herself a fool for a man?" she asks.

I think back to the night it began. There were shooting stars—I thought that was a sign. I was angry at Edward. Nat's colors were bright and vivid, and I thought they were my fate and my promise. My gift and my curse.

"Well, you aren't," Mercy goes on. "You're foolish, but you're brave and strong—that's what you've got to remember."

My mother told me the colors could ruin me. I was a little girl then. Maybe she wanted to say more. Maybe she wanted to explain that there were many ways a woman can be ruined and that the colors might mis- lead me exactly as they did when I was with Nat.

"You listening?" Mercy's face is filled with urgency. "You've got to make a life for you and the child."

"How?"

"Your needle is how. Trust the needle. You've got a gift for colors, you've got to use it."

I DON'T KNOW what will happen when I get to the shop, but I'm expected on Tuesdays at ten o'clock and I go. I leave early, for my nerves will not let me stay at home any longer. In the last row of hemlock and heather before I reach the wharf, birds that took up roost in spring are warbling and learning to fly. The busy work of spring has turned to the glory of deep summer just as the words my pap told me have come around again through Mercy.

Trust the needle.

In my pockets I carry the needle case I brought from Scotland. I've used all six needles in my work and am bringing them to show Felicity—from a quarter inch in length to six inches long, tucked into the pocket beside my pliers and stiletto blade. *Trust the needle, trust the needle.*

I'll explain things to Felicity. If the captain said the glove work is mine and she's found it out, then we can make an agreement—one that is mutually beneficial. I remember the captain used this term with Edward, and I am prepared to use it now.

But the moment I step through the door, I know things are different. The shop is dead quiet but for the sound of crates hissing across the floor in the small storeroom. Soon Felicity's heels tap from the back to the front of the shop. When she sees me, her face twists into a snarl.

"What are you doing here?"

"It's Tuesday."

"Tuesday?"

"I was sick last week—"

"Sick? Sick, you say?" I have never liked the torn autumn colors of Felicity's words. Now, streaked with brown and black, they are ugly. "I know what you're doing with the money I gave you—"

Abigail is against the wall behind Felicity, shaking her head and waving her hands as if to shoo me away.

"Yes, sick—"

Felicity advances toward me.

"How dare you sell gloves to the captain?" She looks as if she will slap me.

"The captain came, he put them on . . ." I try to stammer my explanation, but the force of her anger ties my tongue.

"Four ladies came into the shop asking for your gloves yesterday," she says. "'Mrs. Gamble's gloves,' they said. I told them you're a liar and a thief—that you stole the gloves from me and gave them to the captain—"

"The captain knows," I say.

"Knows what?"

"He knows my work. We came from Liverpool on his ship; I knew him before I worked for you."

"The captain has gone around Salem and paid your husband's debts." Felicity must see surprise on my face, for she shivers like an animal before it attacks. "Are you surprised that I know it? You have very few secrets here, Isobel."

"My husband works for him—that's all."

Felicity continues on as if I have said nothing.

"Adultery is a crime here. Women who succumb to the charms of another man while their husbands are at sea are disgraced and put out."

Put out. I have heard this expression before.

"Perhaps you didn't know it, Isobel—a woman can be put out of Salem for adultery."

I feel a sense of wild fear, as if Felicity is indeed a crow and I a sparrow being pecked to death by her hard, yellow beak.

"It's not as you say," I chirp, but it is a mere squeak.

"What do you think the town will say when they know your husband isn't here and the captain has staked his word and reputation for you? When they know you're a liar, a thief, and maybe an adulteress—do you think they'll look kindly on you?"

"I'm sure we can make an agreement," I manage to sputter. "I won't mind if you pay me a fair price."

"Pay you? A fair price?" Her voices rises to a shriek. My work has summoned evil, just as my mother warned. "Are you mad? You came in here like a beggar girl with that filthy brogue of yours and I took you on and trusted you and you betrayed me. Now get out." She raises her hand. "Get out, you dirty little liar—and don't you dare go near my Philadelphia ladies!"

Her words burn in my ears—*dirty little liar . . . filthy brogue of yours*—as I back out of the shop and turn into the alley, where I nearly trip over a washerwoman crouched beside a wheeled basket.

"Get on with you," the woman says, and I spin down the street, barely able to see where I am going.

—— TWENTY-SEVEN ——

All my life I've feared accusations of witchcraft. Now I see my mother was right about hiding my colors and I was foolish not to heed her. Echoes of the loud mills in Glasgow, the faces of pale children near the almshouse, even the cold-cellar memory of Master Dwyer's Tambour Shop fill me with dread. The washerwoman is singing her song and waiting for me. Felicity is eager to call me an adulteress. The May trees along the Witch Path have spent their flowers and the long-gone shadows of the women hanged here on Gallows Hill seem to mock me.

Ruin, hunger, heartbreak, death, and disgrace—I feel them coming. Before this week I thought my course was clear: I would go to the banquet, show off my dress and shawl, and find customers of my own. I would wait until the time was right and then speak to the Philadelphia ladies when they were next in Salem.

But everything has unraveled, and all that is left is a pile of silks and a shawl with Adam and Eve and a red apple in the middle—the temptation of a woman bedeviled, sewn with my own hands.

I lay the shawl across my bed and know that even with the beaded blue sea, shimmering red crystals, and flower petals covering Eve's naked bosom, I cannot wear it to the ball when accusations of *adulteress* and *temptress* are so close upon my heels. In fact, I don't know if I dare go to the ball at all.

IN GLASGOW I worked beside girls who were thin, pale, and quick with their needles. They chattered some days but on most they were silent, each in her own silo of hurt. For Anne it was the red-splattered cough. For others it was a ring of bruises on a wrist, sunken eyes, or an empty lunch sack.

I envied their whispered camaraderie; I was too young to know that each girl held her own sadness—her own auntie, stepfather, or brother who had walked her into the tambour shop as Pap had led me. Or that surely each girl folded into her bed on some nights and wept, quietly and alone.

But I understand now that there is want everywhere.

I've met ladies beloved and ladies bereft; ladies who are afraid to walk in the streets for fear that someone will mock their dress or twisted arm, purple scar or red birthmark. Watching them, I have begun to learn how a woman apportions and gathers what she needs to survive; what she sacrifices for beauty, sustenance, health, or children.

I think of Mercy telling me that I must learn to move through the city invisible, so that I might do what I must. It is not unlike what Mam said, that I must hide myself and my colors and yet prepare for the day my time would come.

And I think of the washerwoman in the alley by the shop. Why did I never see her before? Why was she there on the very day I ran from Felicity?

When the evening bells ring nine o'clock and I close my shutters, I swear I hear the *bean-nighe*'s tuneless song in the distance and the neigh of the kelpies running along the sea. Try as I might, I cannot come up with any course of action that has not already been tainted, warned against, or broken my heart. I'm not Isobel Gowdie standing on a blazing rooftop screaming at the evil men. I am alone and frightened. I have lost my job and perhaps my entire reputation here in Salem.

∞

I'VE JUST CHOKED down my first food in days—an old roasted potato found on a brick in my hearth—when there's an ugly scratching on my door.

It's evening, and the August night is thick. The woods are alive with tiny sounds that throb through the trees. It could be Nat, who heard of my troubles and rushed home to me. It could be Mercy. Or it could be Felicity, come to exact her vengeance.

"Mrs. Gamble?" It is a woman's voice I don't recognize. She must sense me there, my bare feet on the floorboards, for she calls again. "Mrs. Gamble—"

"What do you want?"

"You don't know me, but I admire your work. And I'd like to speak with you, please."

I unlatch the top of the Dutch door to find a woman only a little older than me, wearing a faded blue dress.

"My name is Ginny," she says. "I admired the gloves in Felicity Adams's shop and heard that you're talented enough to make most anything."

Ginny has narrow shoulders and a small waist, and I can tell that the skirts of her dress hide strong, wide hips. I have not combed my hair or washed my face in days, but if she notices, she gives no indication.

"Wives in town sometimes trade food for money or needlework. We're here, you know—looking out for one another." She holds out a warm loaf wrapped in paper. "I'm terrible with the needle, but my breads and apple cakes are wonderful."

She pushes the loaf into my hands. "My George is a clerk, but he wants to study law and needs an apprenticeship. He can't go to the Light Infantry banquet without a proper waistcoat. My mother used to help me, but—" Ginny's voice goes high and small. "But she's gone now."

It takes no more than her grief for me to decide.

"Do you have his measurements and money for broadcloth?" I ask.

"I brought his day coat and the measurements are near the same." She fumbles in her pocket and pulls out her coin. "And I have this."

"You take that coin to Chaise and Harness and pick the cloth you want."

I tell her how many yards and remind her that she'll need a liner, too.

∽

THE NEXT DAY, I'm making my way through the tangle in my garden when another woman startles me there.

"I need a dress," she says. "If I go to the shops, my husband's mother will think me a spendthrift. But it has to be better than anything I can manage myself, or else she'll be cruel about it."

The following morning it's a mother with her daughter. I know right away that they are poor, for the girl's face is sallow and the mother's dress is threadbare.

The girl's fingers and hands have the evidence of too much time at her needle, and her eyes are pink and strained. She steps forward and I see that she is hunchbacked.

"Please, if you can help me make a cape that will—hide this."

The mother takes in laundry, she tells me; her daughter does all the mending for her customers.

"She's not got the skill to do what she wants, but she has an idea," the mother says.

I bend down so the girl and I are eye to eye. Her voice is sweet and strong, the palest blue of distant stars. "I'm called Lily."

I promise to make her something that will help, and they leave me with a length of midnight-blue wool that surely must have cost them a great many hours of labor.

I GROW ACCUSTOMED to women coming at strange hours, and so I am awake and already at my needle when Nell knocks at my cottage early this August morning wearing a crisp white apron and blue-striped smock. Her face is flushed and rosy, and she greets me in a voice as green as a meadow.

"Charlotte's child was born." Nell beams.

I am taken aback. Could she truly have been so far along?

"So soon?"

"He's tiny but healthy." Abigail shrugs away my question. "A boy named Charles for his grandfather. Mrs. Silas is on her way to Phila-delphia now."

I imagine the house where the child was born, the fine pieces I sewed for his first cradle, and the gown for his baptism. I picture Charlotte well loved and safe, tucked into her bed as she was when I first met her. And I am jealous in a way that I do not like and cannot banish.

"You were a great help, and Charlotte hasn't forgotten," Nell adds. "She asked me to remember her to you. Also, Isobel, I heard what happened at Felicity's shop. Tell me how I can help."

The crystal clarity that I have felt only twice in my life—when the men came in Glasgow and again when Nat came to my door—comes to me now. Perhaps I don't need the Cherry Street ladies in order to go to Philadelphia. Perhaps Charlotte, who once took me into her greatest confidence and relied on my trust, will help me now.

I craft a careful note to her; I write that I'm proud she thought to share her joy with me and that I wish her and the child the greatest health. I ask what styles the ladies in Philadelphia covet for autumn and winter and what trim and decoration she favors.

I would like to gift you a dress made entirely to your desires. I am
prepared and eager to visit you before the winter comes. We can make
a splendid dress befitting your new position in Philadelphia society.

I wrap the note around a pair of gloves adorned with wisteria, send them off with Nell. And I wait.

I WAIT FOR my morning sickness to pass. I wait for the heat to break. I wait for sorrow and bitterness to let go its ugly grip on me. I wait for Charlotte's reply. And I wait for some word from Nat.

All through August the ladies knock at my door—servant girls, tired mothers and wives, poor American and Irish, Scottish, and Black women.

"My sister is to be married—"

"A sleeve to hide my twisted arm—"

"A dress to conceal my condition so that I can go to work—"

Some bring cloth, others bring coin. One brings a stepping stool made by her husband; another brings two blue glass cups. Most bring food: warm bread, boiled eggs, a ham hock cooked with pepper, cod cakes.

My cottage becomes a crowded workshop filled with cloth, half-done garments, and foodstuffs that fill my shelves.

"IF YOU CAN'T eat it all, there's plenty who will," Mercy says when she sees my shelf stuffed with food that will soon spoil. "We'll take care of it."

She returns the next day to help me pile baskets into the cart, then climbs into the seat beside Zeke.

"Where shall I sit?" I ask.

"Best you stay at home," Zeke says carefully. "We take Mr. Remond's banquet extras all the time—sometimes we call on the poor folk out past the pig yards where things are worst."

I have never told a soul about the poorhouse that began my journey here, but I have great sympathy for any who might be in need of help and protection.

"I see no reason why I should hide from the trials of poverty."

"We're going far," Mercy says. "Past the old ironworks in Marblehead and the stables in Lynn behind the shoe factories."

"If you're going to Lynn, I need to see a cobbler."

Mercy eyes my waist, where I have left the apron ties loose.

"I'm strong enough, and my boots are in terrible need of repair."

I lift my foot so she can see the broken sole and she gives a nod. It doesn't please her, but she squeezes next to Zeke and makes a place for me on the seat.

Seated beside Zeke I think of the day I saw him near the sycamore, the same day Nat taught me to swim. I don't like to think on that afternoon, for it seems it is the moment everything changed—the seals poked their heads up and I thought of the selkies. I asked Nat about slave ships in Salem and he told me slaves are no worry of his.

Is Nat a cruel man or is he a weak man?, I wonder for the hundreth time. Perhaps he is both. *Without my name I'd be nothing,* he said. Perhaps one leads to the other, although I cannot think of what might come first, cowardice or cruelty.

∽

"SICKNESS IN THERE. Disease, death," Mercy says when we reach the almshouse. "You can't go inside."

"I'm not afraid of those things."

"You should be, especially in this heat," she says. "Stay put."

While I wait in the yard, two children with bare feet and tattered clothes run up the path and stop at the almshouse door. A man with one leg comes next, wearing one shoe and using a crutch that is anchored around his opposite shoulder with a soft leather binding.

My mind goes to young Lily, whose cloak is troubling me. I'm not happy with my work, for it won't do what the girl so desperately wants, which is to hide how she is different. I am thinking of it when a woman carrying two buckets suspended from a smooth pole yoked across her back trudges up the hill, and an idea comes to me.

In Lynn we travel the twisted lanes behind the stables. Unlike Salem, where even the most crowded streets have a taste of the sea air, Lynn stinks of glue and curing leather mixed with animal and urine, and it overpowers the narrow lanes. Zeke stops the cart in front of a tall wooden building with a five-high row of windows that puts me in mind of Glasgow factories. Girls my age pour out the front and side doors, their hands stained the color of burnt leaves from the leathering. Beyond that, behind the shoe lanes, are small streets lined with shacks where children who seem to have no minders are running about, some crying, some squabbling, one with a terrible cough that makes me turn away. A lone mother, thin and forlorn, stands in a dark doorway holding a babe on her hip. The deeper we go into the squalor and despair, the more worried I become. This might be me, if I am not careful.

We reach a small cluster of brick homes and Zeke stops the cart. Mercy takes a bundle of burlap from beneath her seat and goes to the side door of one of the houses. It seems she's just climbed the step when the door opens, the package is exchanged, and Mercy is back in the cart.

"I remember the man on the wharf, you gave him a burlap sack, too," I say to Zeke.

Mercy nods.

"We help each other," she says. "Food, sometimes a little more."

At the bottom of the hill, with the brick homes behind us, Zeke stops the cart beside a cobbler's ten-footer. The shoemaker is a Black man old enough to have seen many hard seasons, perhaps to have been a slave himself; the years are evident by the ashy lines on his face and his nearly toothless mouth. I show him the cracked soles on my boots where water has begun to leak in. His work is quick, with thick black tar.

Before we settle up I ask if he can fashion a leather strap to my description. He looks at Mercy and asks, "Why would she want that?"

Mercy nods at me, says, "She can tell you best herself."

I explain it simply enough, and Zeke lets out a low whistle.

"I believe you're a lady who finds a solution to most anything," he says.

"Like you and Mercy," I say. I give them a sly, encouraging look. "I believe I know what you are doing with your embroidery and the sugar house."

Mercy shocks me by grabbing my wrist. "Get down out of this cart," she says.

She tugs me into a crumbling doorway, where she turns with a look on her face like nothing I have ever seen.

"Whatever you think you know is wrong. It is as wrong as Nat calling you a witch, and as dangerous as anything you could ever imagine. If you want to be my friend you must never speak of it. You must never see it. You must never say it. Ever."

Keep silent: I have been told this by women I love and trust and by women who care nothing for my fate. But how can I live and be silent? How can I speak and be safe?

"Do you hear me?" Mercy asks with another rough shake of my wrist.

I nod, and she says nothing more.

TWENTY-EIGHT

I'm counting out the last of my coins and worrying how I will pay for food and fuel when a sallow white man in a black hat knocks at my door. He leans on a crooked stick and spits tobacco juice into a tin. It is the undertaker in his patched black coat, and the sight of him pitches me back on my heels.

"I hear you need work."

I have a flash of my pap in his coffin, gray-faced and gaunt, and I know in my heart that my father has died. I'm not yet twenty years old, but it's already clear to me that death moves round the earth the same as the sun, illuminating one land while stealing light from the last, taking souls as it rolls across the great scape of mankind.

"That's true," I say. Perhaps Nat has sent him. Perhaps this is the sort of help he means to give me.

"A child is dead. A boy, not ten years old." The undertaker lets out another stream of brown spit that hits the tin with a sharp zing. "Folks think it's bad luck to make a child's shroud." He looks me up and down. "But maybe that don't matter to you?"

He offers a fair fee, and I agree to stitch sailboats and birds and to finish by tomorrow morning.

"See that you do a good job," the undertaker says before he goes. "The dead make steady work."

It's on this very night, while I'm sewing birds onto the boy's shroud, that I feel the infant flutter deep in me for the first time. It startles me at first and I stay perfectly still, waiting. I haven't realized how I've held wonder and fear so tightly together until I feel it again and laugh out loud in sheer joy.

A FEW DAYS later, on a sweltering afternoon, I'm heading to the notions shop for more white thread when I pass the Charter Ale House and see Captain Darling at a table in the window. He taps at the glass, waves me over, and meets me at the tavern steps beside the shipping news posts.

"I returned just yesterday." He takes off his hat, wipes the sweat from his brow, and wastes no time on niceties. "Widow Higgins tells me you were dismissed from your job by Felicity Adams, and that my gloves were the cause."

His eyes on me are discomfiting. My child is three months along. I've begun to feel the fullness in my abdomen and have let out the stays on my day dress. I'm carrying a package of lavender-checked gingham and hold it at my waist just as I told Charlotte to hold her flowers to disguise her bloom.

Adulteress, Felicity called me, even without knowing anything about Nat or the child.

"It's for the best," I say. "I'm doing my own work now."

"It must be a blow," he says. "I haven't forgotten about your dream for a dress shop."

"Please don't worry yourself." In truth, I'm pleased that he remembers. The days I sat with him working white on white were some of the sweetest I have had since I left home. Now they seem from another life, when all was still innocent. Now I must worry that my friendship with the captain puts me in danger of gossip and more. I must remember all that I have been warned.

"I don't like to think of you alone in the long winter," he adds before we say our goodbyes. "The cold is hard here, Mrs. Gamble—long and bitter."

∽

I AM TENDING my garden the next morning when the captain comes into my yard with a sack on his shoulder and drops it at my feet.

"I saw this on a boat in Nova Scotia and thought of you." He opens a drawstring to reveal a rainbow of silks—deep saffron, jewel-like magenta, a pillowy pile of deep green blue the very hue of the horizon where sea and sky met on the day the colors returned to me.

"This is beautiful." I touch the green blue.

He lifts it into the light, where it shimmers like a mirage. If I were still planning to attend the banquet, I would wear this color.

"Verdigris. True green. In France they call it *vert de Grèce*—green from Greece."

I'm reaching for the length of it when the heat hits me and I swoon.

Darling steadies me with two hands on my waist right at the thickening, and I dare not look at him.

"Sit, Mrs. Gamble."

He fetches water from the well and brings the brimming ladle to me. His hands hover around my face as I drink, and there's a strange tenderness about him. Captain Darling's attentive protection feels like a steady ship upon the sea. But I cannot forget Felicity's words or what the town will say of our friendship.

"I can't accept a gift so dear," I say, although I am already imagining the dresses I might make of these silks.

"It's enough to start up your own seamstress shop."

I will have no shop here, but I don't say this to him.

"Except everyone will know I couldn't buy such fine silks—there would be gossip."

Darling frowns.

"Then we'll make it an investment," he says. "When you sell the dresses, you can repay me with interest."

I can't deny this is a reasonable business offer, one that a clever woman wouldn't turn down. With silks like these I can make glorious dresses to bring to Philadelphia as soon as I hear from Charlotte. I can even approximate her new measurements and make one to suit her.

"How much interest would you charge?"

He doesn't smile or twist his lips into the amused grin that I have seen on Nat's face. His gaze remains fixed on mine, clear and steady.

"What do you propose is fair?" he asks.

I think back to those first weeks in Salem, when I heard the men talking about business in percentages.

"Ten percent," I say.

Darling nods.

"We must shake on it, as I have seen it done," I say.

He tips back his cap. His eyes are bright.

"We can shake on it," the captain says. "But I have not forgotten that I owe you my life, Mrs. Gamble."

I remember those words, blue as sky and white as clouds, right before we sailed into the great Massachusetts Bay.

"You don't owe me your life, Captain Darling, but I will accept your silks and your terms," I say, and we shake as two merchants might.

The captain eats both scones that I offer and passes the time telling me about the landscape in Nova Scotia, "just up past Maine," he explains. I blink away the memory of Nat teaching me to swim in the secret cove, Nat describing the cold water in the lake of his boyhood summer days. For just a few moments I let myself soak in the sea-and-sunlit landscape Darling describes.

He is still sitting in my yard when Mercy comes with a fastening hook she promised for Lily's cape. Ivy is with her.

"Where is your brother?" I ask as I realize I have not seen Abraham in many days.

Ivy tucks herself behind Mercy and grabs the edge of her mother's apron. I've noticed the little one is always more talkative when her brother is beside her.

"Abraham's gone north." Mercy's quiet words are flat and small. She's carrying two empty chicken feedbags across her shoulder. Something is wrong—the pitch of her words is slant and her throat is tight.

"Where?"

Mercy glances at the captain, her face strained in a way I have seen only once, that day in Lynn after we visited the shoemaker.

"He's got an uncle up Canada way." She does not sound convincing.

I look from Mercy to the captain.

"Will he be back?" I ask.

Mercy reaches behind her to pat Ivy's head, and I understand that she's afraid of something.

"Can't say for sure." She looks at me with the same hard expression she gave when I asked about the sugar house and her embroidery.

I think back to the slave catcher, the lady in town who warned Mr. Remond, their talk of an eight-year-old boy. About Abraham's age. Perhaps she has hidden her son away so he is not mistaken for a runaway.

"Best not to think on it too much," Mercy says.

I want to assure her that I will say nothing. "I pray he takes good care," I say instead, and try to impart meaning in my words.

Soon they leave for town together and I'm left watching their retreating figures—Mercy holding Ivy's hand, the captain leading the way. I put a protective hand across my abdomen and hope I will never have to say a sorrowful goodbye to my child, for I have grown accustomed to her—yes, I believe it is a girl—and love her already, just as Mercy loves her own.

FOR WEEKS THE heat is merciless. Two old merchants die in their beds, and the undertaker is at my door twice more. I wonder why he has come to me again, but I need the work and don't ask why.

I begin to fashion dresses from the captain's silks and imagine I will sell them when they are done. Perhaps Mrs. Silas will help me find buyers. Perhaps Charlotte will bring me to Philadelphia. All I know is how to stitch, and so this is what I do.

Even in the worst heat in the final days of summer, the ladies trickle to my clearing. I finish the cape for Lily and show her mother how to position the strap and lace up the back, tightening it a little bit more each day. The girl straightens ever so slightly and her face brightens. Her mother cries, but I do not, for I can see that Lily is a girl who doesn't want pity.

After another visit from the undertaker for a daisy-covered shroud, Widow Higgins comes to collect her rent, counts out my coins, and slides them into her pocket.

"It's only enough to keep you through December," she says.

"I know." We're outside in the clearing, where the leaves on a few trees are tipping yellow, as if trying to call autumn to come and quench the earth. I'm glad she cannot see the captain's silks spread out inside, for I still don't trust her. The truth is, I hope to be gone by December. I'm still hoping for a letter from Charlotte inviting me to Philadelphia, still thinking that Nat might return home and come to me.

"I won't put you out in winter, you needn't fear it." The widow glances at my skirt, where a generous apron covers what I don't want seen. "But you must have your story worked out."

I've never seen colors in the widow's words, and I don't see them now. I try to keep my mind on what she's saying, but I think of all the voices that have no color for me: hers, Edward's, Mrs. Silas's.

"You must have your story," the widow says again. "And you must tell it soon."

She looks at me with her watery eyes and my mouth goes dry. What have I missed by ignoring the voices with no colors?

"You know my story," I say carefully. "I came from Scotland with my husband. He sailed off with Captain Darling and didn't return."

"That's not the story I mean." I notice she has a brown mole in the middle of her eyebrow. I focus on the eyebrow so that I don't have to look at her face.

"Then what?"

"You're with child."

I'm approaching my fourth month. She's the first person to confront me with it, but she won't be the last. I'm far too slender to hide a child for long.

"I know sooner than most," she says. "But it'll be evident to everyone eventually, even with your clever needlework."

The mole winks at me through the widow's white eyebrow. I feel the child shift inside me and silently will her to be still.

"When it's clear the child isn't your husband's, you'll be asked to name the father—it will be demanded of you. Do you understand? I'm telling you as a friend, Mrs. Gamble."

I have feared the widow since that first day on the docks. I cannot stand before her and let myself be cowed.

"Then I will speak plainly also." If I cannot stand up to her now, then

I will never be able to face anyone. "I admire your strength, but I don't know whether you are friend or foe."

The widow straightens.

"I'm a friend of those in need," she says. "I know you're the same. And I'm telling you that an adulteress is unwelcome in Salem. Do you know what they did to the Puritan women who were caught in adultery? They whipped them, branded them, put them in prison. Some called them witches—and when I was alone here, they called me the same."

I haven't forgotten the terrible story Nat told me about the widow's family.

"I was told a story about your sister."

"You know nothing of my sister." The widow smells strangely sweet, as if she's been drinking molasses. "Think about yourself and your child. There are dangerous men in Salem and you should beware, for some are devils."

"Devils?" I challenge her again, for I do not want to be infected by fear. I will stand on the roof and shout if I must. "What form do they take, these devils?"

The widow stamps her foot on the dirt. The sun slices through the clouds and shines directly on her face.

"Any man can be a devil. Ship captains, magistrates . . ." Her eyes roll side to side and she falters. "Judges, slavers, bounty hunters—"

The widow's eyes close, her shoulders jerk twice. Her fingers drag across the door as she starts to slide to the floor. Perhaps an evil spirit has taken hold of her. I look around, but there are no faerie lights, no strange song in the air, no breeze at all.

"Fear them—" She swoons.

"Who?" I ask the widow. "Who should I fear?"

"All of them. The first families, their pride and lies—"

I catch her under the arms and lower her in the shaded doorway, then fetch a wet rag and put it against her cheek.

Her mouth is open, and some spittle runs from it. I stretch her out so that she's lying on the floor, her feet outside the door and her head on my wooden boards. She's an old woman with a line of white hairs along her chin. They are visible only now, this close.

Long moments pass until she breathes more steadily.

"You fainted," I say. "You should rest."

"It was the sun," she says. She uses my shoulder to drag herself to stand, pats her skirt to check her pockets, and hears the coins rattle there. "I must get on—just a little water first."

She brushes leaves and sticks from her skirt and seems to not remember what she said. But she has reminded me of the washerwoman's song and the undertaker at my door, the accusations Felicity flung at me.

When she is safely gone, I take the Adam and Eve shawl from the shelf where I folded it away and wonder what price it might bring. I consider the people in town I can trust, and finally I remember Mr. Saul, the custodian at the East India Marine Society Hall, who is well acquainted with decorative items from around the world. The captain told me that Mr. Saul is a trusted friend, and I still have the note he gave me when he sailed away with Edward.

Once I loved the shawl with its rich tapestry of the Garden. Even when Nat read his story of the poisoned plant I kept at my work, putting large orange and yellow flowers and adding a snake curled around the tree of life.

It seems a long time ago when Nat said if I want love, I should stitch love. I did, trusting it would be true. But there's no reason to keep what pains and shames me. I will sell the shawl and be done with the myths that I once foolishly believed.

I'VE PACKED THE shawl in my basket and am walking to my errands— first the postmaster and then the Marine Society Hall—when I see Nat turn the corner onto the Common. He left in early July and now it's September. I've waited and imagined this moment. Now he's here in a fresh blue coat I don't recognize, walking with one arm folded at his back and a lady on his arm.

He is well rested and strong. His good health, the jaunt in his step— they shock me. I want to rush ahead; I want to disappear. I want to hide and I want to put myself in his path.

He's looking in a shop window. The lady is still on his arm and I'm crazed with knowing who she is. I cross the street opposite them and try to see her reflection in the shop window glass. My heart hums in my ears, a whine like a horde of wasps.

Her color is Nat's, her hair is Nat's. I'm filled with relief, for I recognize her from the day I saw him with his notebook in the notions shop. It's the sister he calls Ebe, not a woman he's courting. I look up and down the line of her spine and then the length of Nat's legs. How well I know those legs. Many nights when I cannot sleep, I remember them warm against me.

Nat seems not to notice me, but Ebe is looking at me now. Her eyes are steely. She glares for one more second, then pushes her brother's arm and walks him away from me just as I turn to the postmaster's window.

"Here you are, Mrs. Gamble." The postmaster slides a white letter sealed with blue wax across the counter to me. "From Philadelphia."

I shake away the wallop of Nat's appearance and allow myself a spike of nervous hope. I can go somewhere new; my child and I can start again. I've heard Philadelphia is a beautiful city filled with industry and good people, and I have great affection for my Charlotte.

Outside, I lean against the whitewashed building and peel back the wax seal. Charlotte's letters are soft and twirled, like those of a young girl. I remember pressing my ear against her swollen belly when the child was rolling there.

Dear Mrs. Gamble,

Thank you for your note and the lovely pair of gloves. My little family and I are happy in our new home here. Much as I would like to welcome you in Philadelphia, I am afraid we do not have room for any visitors.

> *May God Bless and Protect You,*
> *Mrs. Charlotte Hillsborough*

At home that night, I close the shutters long before the bells ring nine and lie in the dark. This poor child will depend on me alone, and it will take more than a shawl to save us.

— TWENTY-NINE —

Abigail doesn't wait to be invited in but steps past me into the cottage. A large hat and a fashionable veil hide her face, and she smells of starch and burnt leaves.

"Did Felicity send you?"

"Don't be silly." She removes the hat and veil, and her hair falls in tendrils around her cheeks. "She never says your name—and I wouldn't spy on you even if she asked."

Abigail takes a seat at my table, removes her gloves, and pulls a shawl from her basket. It's partly decorated with beads and golden threads, which she shakes in my direction.

"Look at this mess I've made! I can't figure how to make pumpkins that don't look like fat stupid birds. Can you help me?"

"I may be able to. . . ." I reach for the shawl, and Abigail doesn't stop her chatter.

"I miss you so very much, Isobel. Felicity hired her cousin's daughter and the girl counts my stitches—" She opens a folded packet of threads for me to choose from a rainbow of colors. I pick the burnt orange of a pumpkin gourd, and wonder what price my own shawl will bring. "And if I forget to put a needle back she brings it to me and holds it up until I say I am sorry."

Despite her chatter Abigail is skilled, and it doesn't take her long to fill the pumpkin shape with a cross-stitch and then a long stitch so that the gourd is both fat and round. When she's mastered it, she stands and stretches. For the first time, she notices the ladies' clothing around my cottage and inspects a red-and-white-checked dress I am embroidering for a little girl whose health is poorly.

"You're keeping busy, Isobel," she exclaims. "How are you feeling? Are you resting and eating well? Are you taking in mending? What are your plans?"

I don't like her meddling.

"If you came for gossip, I have nothing for you," I say plainly.

Abigail drops the dress and takes my hands in hers.

"Isobel—I'm your friend." She tips her head to the side and looks into my full lap. "You must realize that I've known your secret for a long time."

I open my mouth to object, but she doesn't stop her prattling.

"We were on the same moon cycle, don't you remember? I knew you missed your bleeding because you rinsed your rags in the back and hung them to dry and then you didn't."

This isn't the first time that Abigail has surprised me with her cunning intelligence.

"I thought you might have lost the child when you missed your days at work. But you look wonderfully round in the middle, so I know you and the babe are healthy."

Abigail is examining a man's jacket I am repairing when it slips off a hook and reveals a dress I am making with the captain's silks. It is the verdigris green.

"This is exquisite." She lifts the edges of the dress toward the light. "You must use this to make a gown for the Light Infantry banquet. You know it's the most important event of the season, all the town's dignitaries wear their old uniforms from the days of Mr. Madison's war—"

"I'm not going to the banquet," I say.

Abigail stops her rattling and tips her head at me again.

"Nonsense," she declares. "You must."

It's been a long time since I took anyone into my confidence, and I am not trustful even now. But Abigail does not seem to notice, else it does not deter her. In a flash she has draped the green silk around my shoulders and begun to pin it in an approximation of a gown.

"What has Felicity said of me?" I ask.

Abigail narrows her eyes.

"She doesn't dare say much, Isobel. She cannot very well accuse you of anything when the captain himself said the gloves are your work. She won't put her word against his, for Captain Darling is very well liked in Salem and respected by everyone. Think about it, if she speaks against you then she'd have to explain why there are no more gloves coming into the shop now that you're not there."

Abigail props the dress on my shoulder and steps back to study the effect.

"The color is perfect with your hair and eyes." She claps her hands and brushes away the gathering where I've tucked up the empire waist. "Take off your skirts, I must make the measurements and cut the fabric now."

I comply—it is enjoyable to have her attentions, and the dress will go twice as fast with her help, no matter who it is for.

"You mustn't hide your condition," she goes on. "You must walk into the banquet and announce to everyone that you're having Edward's child."

Nat said that he needed time. Nat said *perhaps if there was no child*.

She looks at my belly, which is bulging when I sit, and I see the child is evident even now.

"I don't expect the child until February or March—a full year since Edward's ship set sail. Who will be fooled by then?"

"That doesn't matter," Abigail insists. "What matters is that you tell the story and make them believe it. There's already gossip in town, and Felicity will gladly do her part to turn others against you—you must go to the ball and say you're carrying Edward's child. And you must let me start telling others the same right now."

She tips her head.

"Unless . . ." She leans across the table. "Will the father stand beside you?"

I think of Nat in town, his sister on his arm. Healthy, upright, and untroubled. So unlike the man who insists he hates Salem society.

I wish I could love him fully or hate him fully and be done with it.

"Isobel, does he know of your condition?"

I nod.

"And has he said he will stand beside you?"

My mind is racing—do I hate him or do I love him? Do I want him or would I scorn him?

"No."

Abigail takes this in with a simple nod, all while shaping the dress with pins and tucks and small stitches. "Then you must go to the banquet with your friend Nell and do as I've said."

She sees my grimace.

"Perhaps you don't know it, Isobel, but without a family to speak on your behalf you can be put out of Salem for almost anything. Judges and ministers delight in punishing a fallen woman. You must make the dress and do as I say."

I do as she says, and make the dress in verdigris green. True green, to cover a lie.

— THIRTY —

My nerves are so racked the night of the banquet I can barely button my cloak.

There's a flush in Nell's cheeks and her eyes are bright. Her husband exclaims over the way we look together, "like two lasses from the Scottish and Irish countryside."

I've made a fashionable veil to cover my face, and before we get out of the carriage I fold up the cape and snap the veil into place using the scrimshaw buttons I bought when I was first under his spell. I'm surprised at the relief the veil brings. Seen but unseen, hiding in plain sight as Mercy advised.

There are other ladies also veiled, and when we pass one another I peer through the lace and try in vain to read their eyes. *What are they hiding?* Nat said that every heart has a grave in it, but I didn't know what he meant until now, walking masked amid a crowd with my own fear and sadness hidden in plain sight.

FROM OUR PLACE beneath a wide chestnut tree hung with lanterns, Nell, Stephen, and I stand shoulder to shoulder with at least a hundred other shopworkers and house servants who've come to watch the wealthy revelers and dignitaries arrive behind the marching band.

The black iron fence that circles the perimeter of the yard is marked by tall, flaming torches that dance in the night. The windows and interior of the hall glow with hundreds of candles. The sound of bugles, flutes, and percussion float through the open windows, each with its own thread of color—shiny yellow for the triangle, ropy lavender for the violin, dark blue footsteps for the bugles.

"There's Captain Derby now." Nell points with her chin toward an aging man dressed in a long, flowered gown and a small Chinese cap. He looks foolish, and when Stephen stifles a laugh, I can't help but smile, too.

Captain Derby is followed by the lieutenant governor, who wears an ornate red military uniform and a pompous hat adorned with feathers. Captain Silas wears a sash I decorated with his family crest, and he does not look my way. I see three ladies wearing gloves that I made, one in a long brocade gown with turquoise-blue birds that match the peacock feathers I stitched upon her gloves. I have not worn my Adam and Eve shawl, but as I look around the room, I'm more sure than ever that my work is very special. Among Salem's finest people, Felicity's threats and warnings seem small, and I wonder at the power I have given her. Perhaps Nat's idea was right all along: to reveal my handiwork at just this moment might have been my triumph.

After the captains and leading merchants come Salem's wealthiest proprietors—the chaise-and-coach maker is followed in the procession by the genteel shopkeepers Messieurs Choate and Downing, whose wives wear dresses made at Felicity's shop. I recognize the yellow gown with wide sleeves that I was working on the day Nat came looking for me. Behind them, Felicity Adams keeps step with a man I don't recognize. Abigail follows behind on her beau's arm, floating in a burgundy gown with a scooped neck and tight sleeves, the pumpkin shawl around her shoulders.

I watch for Nat, sick that he will come and sick that he will not. Still, I'm startled when at last he walks through the gate, cheeks blazing. He looks uneasy in his wool cloak and is scowling at the ground. Two uncles walk in front of him, and he has a younger sister on his arm. The uncles are laughing. Robert, who cultivates a fruit orchard, is juggling three golden apples as he walks. Louise is delicate and pretty, with a ring of dark hair and pale skin like Nat's own. She looks at Nat and speaks what can only be words of encouragement. I watch her lips and it seems that she's said, "It is a dance, only a dance."

WHEN THE SCORES of banquet goers have entered the hall, a side entrance is open to those of us who have bought a ticket only for cider and music. Stephen leads us through the door to the cider station, where sheer curtains and a long table separate our modest fare from Salem's finest. The hall is decorated with squash and pumpkins and fall colors, all aglow with candlelight as if a harvest moon is rising.

As I sip the sweet drink and settle myself, I overhear men talking on the other side of the curtain. Their faces are masked by the sheer divider, but I see enough to know they are men of fine dress and comport. They wear ruffled shirts and elegant tailcoats and stand with their champagne and Madeira in fancy glasses, their chests puffed out.

"The fool was sick with the poppy and whatever else they gave him," says a gentleman.

"Darling paid off his debts—you can be sure the man won't show his face here again," another man says.

Nell comes up and takes my hand. She moves as if to speak and I purse my lips, waving a finger toward the shadows of the men. It is a gesture so small, no one else would notice. Side by side, I know she can see that I am rounded, that my body is changing. But still she has said nothing.

". . . would think he would be sailing to the Far East again," one of the men is saying.

". . . satisfied bringing sugar and rum to and from the islands."

Nell gives me a questioning look. She is quiet tonight, somehow frail in a way I have never noticed. I wonder if she could be expecting a child, too.

". . . a dirty triangle of trade, but he doesn't seem to mind."

Their voices have woven together like stitching that is tight and purposeful.

"The British do whatever will bring the most gold, then claim to be the better men because they've outlawed slavery," another says.

Through the curtains I can make out Mercy and the other women laying out platters, going to and from the kitchen with plates piled high with roasted vegetables and colorful yams. Nat is beyond them, standing with his back against the wall. The musicians have begun to play a dancing tune.

"Darling must have a woman in a port," a deep-voiced man says.

A stab of jealousy surprises me.

". . . buying a schooner," says the other.

I've seen notice in the newspaper that Captain Darling is in want of a smaller schooner and the offer of a price. The men say something more about the captain, but Nell is at my shoulder.

"Come, Isobel." She draws me away from the curtain.

"Swift sailing, nimble . . ." The reply fades as we move away from the men. "Married to . . ."

Their words confuse me. I try to draw in a breath and find that I am full. I try to exhale and find I have no air. My heart is racing and I push my way toward the door.

"Isobel—"

I plunge into the autumn night, pull off my veil, and gulp at the cool, dark air as if I am drowning. There are torches burning along the perimeter of the yard. Children are on the brick walk tossing apples and eating doughnuts that Mr. Remond has sent out to them. They are carefree, joyful.

"Isobel—you're giving me a fright." Nell is beside me, her hand gripping my arm.

Behind the children I see some of Salem's poorest men lined up for doughnuts, too. I've gone twice now with Mercy to the almshouse and seen the worst that poverty rends here in the New World. The faces of the hungry are familiar to me, their forlorn postures, gaunt cheeks, thin arms.

"Isobel, come away from here." Nell steps in front of me and obscures my view of the men. I see fatigue and kindness in her face.

"Wait—"

I step around her. A man with a dirty vest has taken his doughnut and turned away. There's something about him. The yard is ablaze with autumn flames that dance with the light of the torches in the yard. I can see only the outline of his shape as he steps into the shadows of the nearby trees. For a moment it looks like Edward.

I FOLLOW NELL to a bench on the gray stone patio and let her bring me water. I say nothing about the man, for surely my husband wouldn't return to Salem without coming to me.

"Shall we leave now?" Nell asks. "To be honest, I don't feel well."

I know she's being kind, and so I say I only need to sit awhile.

"I'll go when you're ready," she says, and sinks beside me onto the bench.

I'm thankful for the shadows on the veranda, for the flames that catch only a part of her expression and my own. What did Nat say—that every person lives in shadow, that every person has secrets that others cannot imagine?

"I'm expecting a child. Edward's child." The sound of it is a lie, and I know that Nell knows it. But she puts her arms around me and tells me she is glad that I am blessed with it.

"Charlotte and Mrs. Silas wish you very good health," Nell whispers. I'm caught in the crook of her arm, my face pressed into her neck. "Charlotte loves you; she told me herself. But she can't go against her mother; she never has and never will."

So Nell knows, and so do the Silas women. I should have expected it. Nat always said there are no secrets in Salem.

I struggle to pull out of Nell's embrace, but she doesn't let me go.

"It's all right, Isobel," she says. "I'm your friend."

When Nell finally lets me go, her eyes are bright with tears. We go back inside, but for the rest of the night I am numb. Abigail finds me and pulls me to her, and she and Nell talk for a moment about what they call "my blessing." I barely hear their words.

All the way home, I lie beside my friend in the back of the cart and look up at the sky passing over us like a black cloak.

∞

I'M STILL IN my dress when a voice at the door startles me.

"Isobel." His voice. "I saw you at the banquet." I know his hands are on the other side of door, the flat of his palms that are so familiar. "I've had time to think—I want to help you. Let me help you."

I want to open the door. I want him to take me in his arms. I want his lips pressed against my cheek, that simple act of affection and comfort. I want to go to Maine with him, to see stars in a bowl of sky and the sun a golden torch above cool blue water.

"Do you hear?" he asks. His voice is tender. Urgent.

I slide my feet across the floor, lean my shoulder against the door. His voice is so close.

"I've got a friend in Raymond who'll keep you." I hear the sweetness and the treachery in his voice like the whisper of his pen on paper. "We'll have to travel soon. The journey to Maine is impossible in winter."

"And will you stay with me?" My own voice startles me.

He waits, and I wait. My hands are flat on the door, where I imagine his are pressed onto the other side of the wood.

"You'll have a midwife to keep you well."

"And would you be with me?"

"I can't." His voice breaks. "I'd have to give up everything and it would kill me—I mean it, I would die."

I feel the wind rise up.

"You would take me into a harsh winter and leave me there alone?"

"Please, Isobel." He is gasping now. The faded red fabric of his voice tears in two. "I want no harm to come to you or the child—I've gone to great lengths to speak to my friends and vouch for you."

I don't move, but my heart beneath my ribs is shattering, it is falling and falling.

"You can't stay here. The town will ruin you—the child will be a bastard and an outcast."

I'm on my knees, begging without words. He must feel me there, for his shoes scrape against the pebbles and then his voice comes at the bottom of the door, his face close to mine. Through the crack at the floor I feel the warmth of his breath.

"I'm telling everyone it's Edward's child," I cry out. "Go away."

He doesn't seem to hear me.

"I need some days to arrange a carriage. A week from today—on Tuesday, wait by the sycamore in the forest. Leave here just before day-light—do you hear?"

I keep my face pressed against the door, my shoulder on the floor, listening until he is gone and the night is silent. Then I tear off my gown and weep.

Scotland, 1818

Isobel Gowdie's fear and pain have been whispered through generations from mother to daughter, whispered at the last moment before death, loss, or leaving. Margaret knows that love and strength are passed from mother to daughter, too, just as the yellow-and-purple iris begets her own, multiplying beauty that is held in the bulb through the cold of winter.

She has seen the blackbird hovering at the edge of the cottage even as the snow piles up, and she has seen the scarlet blood on her bedclothes. She knows that she will die soon, and young. This is a great and terrible pain, for she wished to see many more Scottish summers, to hear the bagpipes coming over ford and field, to lie in her husband's arms, to splash in the River Clyde and run about the maypole as her children laughed and danced beside her.

But it is not to be.

Margaret cannot read and write as she wished, but she is good with pencil and paper and knows how to put hope and beauty into needle and thread.

"Here—" She pulls her daughter into her lap and opens a sketchbook full of irises and orchids. "When I was a little girl my mother took me to a field filled with irises of every size and color. We spent the whole day there, and I dreamt of them for years.

"One day you must make a dress with irises ringed around the bottom," she tells Isobel. "You must wear it when you want to be brave and wise."

That night, when the child is asleep, Margaret finds her rosary beads and prays to the Virgin Mother that what she has done is not a sin, for the irises are the color of the faerie lights, and protection from nature is not the power of the Lord.

Yet she has done what she can, and she prays that it will be enough.

—— THIRTY-ONE ——

I have a week to decide.

If I go to Maine, Nat might keep me as a mistress and in time come to love the child. He's cowardly but passionate, and the child might keep him returning to me.

If I stay, the captain might help bring business to me in Salem, even speak on my behalf to his friends, and Felicity might remain as silent and sullen as she was at the banquet—just as Abigail predicted.

But if I'm here and Edward returns, the child and I would be at his mercy. If I stay, people might still call me all the terrible things that Felicity and Nat have already said. And though I might be strong enough, my child would have to live with a shame that she didn't cause.

Perhaps I should sell the Adam and Eve shawl as I intended and make enough money to start someplace entirely new.

Just like this, round and round I go until I am worn down with indecision.

Two DAYS PASS without a single visitor, and Tuesday grows closer. I must speak to someone about my choices, for my head is spinning and I do not trust myself.

Friday morning in the sleeting cold, I pull my plain brown cloak over the red one and lurk in the alleyway entrance near Felicity's shop, but Abigail arrives under an umbrella with Felicity and I dare not speak.

I try to find Nell, but the Silas house is shuttered to the wet morning.

I take the shortcut through the graveyard on the hill and stand where I once saw Nat kicking the tombstone. On the left is the grave of William Hathorne and on the right is the gravestone of John Hathorne. The son's stone leans away from the father's. They were cruel men who punished with glee, Nat said. Men who delighted in delivering the lash and noose. Yet even as the memory of their cruelty has carved a deep scar into Nat's life, these are the men he cannot leave behind.

Is it true? Is that what keeps him from me? Or is it that I am good enough for him in the night but not in the light of day?

SATURDAY PASSES WITH thread through cloth, my ladies at the door, the exchange of work for food, the rattling of the chatelaine at my waist.

On Saturday evening the undertaker arrives holding his black cap at his heart. It is the first time I've seen his face without the cap, and the clarity of his gaze surprises me.

"I'm very sorry," he says. "It's the Irish girl."

The sky is a cold slate gray, the leaves fallen from the trees have browned on the ground. A woman steps into the yard behind him. She is wearing a threadbare blue dress and pulling a basket on two large wheels. I recognize the washerwoman and stifle a scream.

"My wife, Eveline." The undertaker gestures behind him.

"I don't understand," I say.

"The Silas maid passed." He spits out a stream of black tobacco juice. "Lovely young lady. The newlywed called Nell."

The cat curls around my legs and mewls.

"You must be wrong—" I grip the door frame. "I went to the house a few days ago—"

He shakes his head.

"Fever. It happens fast like that sometimes."

Nell's cheeks were flushed the night of the banquet and she looked frail. I remember she said she was unwell, but I thought she was being kind and selfless on my behalf.

"I could have done something." I slide against the doorway and fall to my knees. The doorway between life and death that Edward spoke of the first time we met: I am in it now.

"You couldn't do nothing to save her."

His wife comes toward me.

"Poor dear," she says. I do not have the strength to shy away from her. "Bring her water, Joseph, so I can tend to her."

Her hands are cold as she helps me into the house and gives me the water. She pulls a blanket over my shoulders and kneels in front of me. Nell is dead. Green and lovely Nell, the girl who first told me that life here had been good to her and promised it would be good to me.

"I knew you'd want to make her shroud," the washerwoman says. I look at her hands for the sharp and mud-dirty nails of the *bean-nighe* and wait for the soupy-water breath of a spirit. But this woman is only kind. She's brought plain cotton for the shroud as only the simplest folk use, and says a prayer over the cloth. But Nell deserves more.

After they're gone I spread my saffron silk on the ground. As I've done before, I lay myself atop the cloth and make a circle with my arms and legs—this is how I measure the fabric that I will need. It is as if I am making my own shroud.

I lie there for a very long time before I can pick up the scissors and begin.

When I've cut out both sides into a shape like the wings of a moth, I use the verdigris—true green, like Nell herself—of my torn ball gown to make shamrocks and Celtic stars. I want to tell the story of her life in pictures, but Nell has told me little about her history. It was always about Mrs. Silas and Charlotte, then Stephen and his cows and their milk. Her story has been about everyone else's, and now her own is over.

I find my old gray dress, the one I wore on the crossing, and rip open the stitching at the waist. There I sew in a new panel of gray-and-white calico from one of the farm ladies' dresses. This is what I will wear until the child is born.

Two days until Nat's carriage comes. And I am in mourning now.

∞

NOVEMBER IS A month of death. My garden is full of lifeless vines and beanstalks bent like broken men. The ground is iced with frost at dawn on Sunday morning as I go to the well, and I am steadying myself so that I don't slip, when a rough man steps into the yard.

I panic, thinking it's already Tuesday and that Nat has sent the coachman to find me.

But this is no coachman. It is the devil in the forest, just as the widow warned me: unkempt and dirty, gray beard down his neck and an angry red slash across his face.

"Stay back," I shout. My father never told me what to do if the faeries or the Devil came for me. "I am a Christian woman."

He comes toward me, arms raised like the pope's Christ on a cross.

"Do you not know me?" His voice and brogue are familiar but colorless, like a ghost. "Wife, it's your husband. See here, I wear the vest you made."

The filthy white vest is tattered beyond recognition, but the jeweled canister on a chain around his neck is the very one that Edward once promised he would fill with our fortune. His eyes are larger in a gaunt face, but it is him, returned as if from the dead.

I turn toward my cottage door. One foot, one spin, one lunge.

Edward is quicker. He catches my arm and puts a hand across my neck. It all happens so fast I have no chance to cry out. His eyes are close and shot with red; his calloused hands are lined with dirt. He smells of sweat and rum as he presses a thumb at my windpipe and pushes me backward into the cottage.

Inside, he thrusts me into a chair.

"Sit."

He puts the board across the door and latches the shutters, hangs his coat from a hook, and unbuckles a long, thick leather belt. The belt is hung with herb pouches. He lays it across my legs and steps his boot onto the stool beside my chair.

"Whose bastard child is it?"

I say nothing.

Without a sound, he raises a hand and slaps me. The blow is a hard, bright red. Now deep pain has the same color as Nat's voice.

"Did you think I wouldn't come back?" He pulls my hand away from my cheek and shouts, "Answer me!"

I speak to the ground at his feet.

"I had a letter from the captain. He said you refused to return to the ship."

"Lies—" Edward grabs my chin, forces me to look at him. Everything about him is clear like ice, and dark gray like a blade. His words, the air behind him, his very breath is frost and steel.

"Dirty bastard is a liar." He gestures to my lap, to the child I have felt move in me. "Is this his doing?"

Abigail told me to say the child is Edward's—to insist upon it. But Edward will know better.

"I'm sorry, Edward." I don't say it is the captain's, and I don't say it isn't. "I thought you abandoned me."

"Whore—you believed his lies? I didn't refuse anything—he locked me up and put me off the ship in Bermuda. And do you know why?" Edward's question is rhetorical. "He's catching slaves for the reward. Him and the African. I found them out."

I do not believe what he's saying, but I dare not speak.

"I thought they were bringing slaves across from Liverpool hidden in the hold." His words are slurred fast, long and ropy. "I saw blood in a barrel and chains down in the hold, heard the captain and Ingo talking about slaves in America."

Edward pulls a crumpled paper from his pack.

"I followed Darling when we got to Baltimore and saw him tear down this flyer—then I got the right idea." He thrusts the paper at me. "Go on, read it—that's right, you can see it plain and clear."

Runaway Negro Male Age 39
Suspected in BOSTON (Or thereabouts)
Slave Name Atlas // Property of J. MacGreggor
May be in company of Freckled Negro Boy Age 9
$$$$ REWARD $$$$
See J. MacGreggor at Wayland Plantation

"Small print's not here, but I got everything I needed to know off MacGreggor himself."

Abraham is a nine-year-old boy with freckles. I make a strangled sound and Edward leers at me.

"That's right, I went to see MacGreggor for myself. He's an honest Scotsman with a face full of freckles, just like it says on the notice. Those Black bastard children up the hill behind you are MacGreggor's own, that's why they got the freckles—you don't need more proof than that. Told me the woman ran off five years ago and she was with child."

"No, no . . ." I say it low, to drown out Edward's ranting.

"Yes." Edward grabs my chin and snaps it up, shoves the flyer flat against my face, blinding me like Nat's handkerchief. When the veil is lifted, will I see the hard truth about the captain? Will I see the truth even about myself—that I have misjudged Darling as I misjudged Edward and Nat? That I have trusted in yet another man who does harm instead of good?

"Mercy ran off from MacGreggor five years back. She was carrying his bastard—that's the girl Ivy; you've seen her freckles, too. The man is offering a generous reward—three hundred for the boy, five hundred for the slave named Atlas, another two for the mother, and two for the young one."

Edward keeps rambling—he talks of alleys and skulls and black magic, but I can hardly hear him because my mind is racing. What is my husband suggesting? Is the captain chasing runaway slaves for the reward? How could Ingo be helping him when he is Mercy's lover? I try to focus on Edward's words instead of on my fear or the smell of rum.

"I was keeping the flyer in my cabin, but Ingo found it—those no-good bastards came in and took it from me. 'Well, what the hell do you think I'm going to do?' I told them. 'I'm going to return that man his property and share the reward with you.'"

"Mercy's not a slave," I manage to say.

"Shut your hole."

Edward is pacing the cottage now, his dirty boots dropping sludge on the clean floor.

"That prick Darling had the African lock me up and feed me drink and poppy until I couldn't stand or see straight. Next thing I know I'm in a jailhouse in the islands."

In a flash I understand that Captain Darling is much more than simply a good sailor and a good man.

"Mercy's not a slave," I repeat. "Her mother was set free, she told me herself. Mercy was born right here in this clearing—"

He raises a hand to silence me.

"I've been watching her," he goes on. "I got a simple plan. She knows you, and you're going to help me. When I get what I want, I'll leave you to your shame—you can do what you like with your ruined life."

He sets his herb pouches on the table and begins mixing a sleeping potion.

"You get Mercy to drink this brew and I'll take her easy. Her and the little girl. Nobody will get hurt."

"Take them where?"

His face is a ragged, ugly sneer.

"Did you listen, Isobel? She's a slave; the girl and boy are MacGreggor's slave children. I'll get four hundred for the two of them, twelve hundred dollars for the lot of them—a fortune, Isobel—a fortune. And once I have the mother and daughter, she'll tell me where to find the other Negro runaways."

While the brew steeps, Edward opens the yellow wood cabinet and pushes aside the cups and plates the ladies have given me.

"How did you get back to Salem?" I ask.

"I got ways and secrets like you—I got work on a ship, how do you think?"

He paws through my things, shoves the blue glass cups onto the floor, where they shatter. With one hand he grabs my face. His thumb presses hard on my hollowed cheek.

"I know you hide money here," he says. "Where'd you hide it?"

I shake my head. He squeezes harder.

"I'm paid in food." I manage to whistle out the words through the tiny space of air, and he pushes me away.

"The hell with those scraps—I want the real reward," he growls. "I'll be damned if I'll let the captain get it from me now. Whatever lies Mercy told you, forget them. You'll go up there and get her to come to the cottage—ask her for some kind of help and tell her you'll pay—she'll come for money."

I think fast. I cannot refuse outright, not with the baby vulnerable inside me. And even if I did refuse, Edward would find another way. He escaped his jailers and made it back to Salem—it would be easy enough for him to kill Mercy and take Ivy, and I fear that Edward would do it, for his mind is taken by the drink and poppy and God knows what else. Whatever was good in him is long gone.

"I'll have to ask her for help with the needle," I tell him. "If it's not something difficult she'll put me off—she's done it before."

I pick up a strip of Nell's shroud where I've been working the green stars and shamrocks into the saffron.

Edward stands above me and watches. There are the shamrocks, the sheep, the pretty pink clover that Nell wove in her hair the day of Charlotte's wedding. With shaking hands, I take the pliers from my chatelaine to undo the work and make a tangle of the threads, green and pink together. I stitch the word *RUN* inside the shroud in floating letters the same color as the shamrocks and clover and hope that Mercy will see it as I once saw the word *SAFE* in her work.

"Hurry up," Edward says. I turn the shroud and make a few errant stitches in the seams.

When I'm finished and he's inspected the piece—"for your tricks, I know you have them"—we go up to Mercy's place. I lead the way and listen to his footsteps behind me like the devil in the forest.

Mercy is in her yard. What would he do if I cried out to her? I cannot take the risk. Mercy once spoke about the power of animals—where are they now? I wish for the birds, the chicks, something or someone in the woods to intervene. How can I not have noticed that the cat is gone, like a seal-woman selkie returned to the sea? I never told that myth to Nat, and now I see why. Because he was the seal-man who came to me and broke my heart. He was my selkie and I was the girl in his poison garden.

"Mercy, I need your help with the needle."

I feel Edward but a breath away, hidden out of sight. I've grabbed my red cape and slipped my longest needle into the small pocket beside the tambour hook. I take the cloth with the thread that I have tangled and stick it into the shroud right at the place where I have hidden the letter *R* in *RUN*.

Mercy is shrewd. Her face shows nothing, yet I know instantly she's seen it.

"Poor Isobel," she says. "Do you want to come inside? Or shall I come to you in a bit?"

I shake my head. Edward isn't far behind me. I don't know what he'd do if I stepped into the house with Mercy.

"Please come to me very soon." I speak loudly so that Edward will hear, but not too loudly so that he is suspicious. "I don't want to be delayed."

"I'll be done with my chores in half of an hour or so," Mercy says. Her words are plum and deep, with no shades of yellow. "Then I'll come down with my needle."

I have not said the word *run* aloud, yet I have spoken and she has heard me.

BACK AT THE cottage Edward talks and talks. While we wait, I pick at the tangled bits of the shroud and stitch Nell's name over and over. Nell's voice, a shamrock green. A pure spirit, generous and loving.

Every few minutes he grabs me by the arm or the chin and threatens to strike me. He has a coil of rope, ready for Mercy.

Perhaps thirty, then forty minutes go by. The sun moves toward noon. Edward becomes restless.

"Where is she? What's she up to?"

I don't look up from my work, for I don't trust myself. I'm expecting something to happen, although I don't know what. Perhaps Zeke will check on me. Perhaps Mercy will run and no one will come. It is Sunday and my ladies never come on meeting day.

"Shall I go up and ask again?" I ask.

"You wait here."

It seems Edward learned something at sea—he learned to tie knots. He ties my hands around the table leg, wraps a longer rope around my shoulder and arm, bolts the shutters, and shuts the door.

When his footsteps are gone, I wait only a moment, then struggle to get loose. The ropes tighten at my wrists. I drag myself and the table across the floor, but even when I kick up the latch the door opens only an inch. Edward will be reaching Mercy's place by now. It won't be long before he finds her or finds that she's already gone. I must get out. For if I die now, so will my child.

Once I put the scrimshaw button on a scrap of cloth and Nat came. Perhaps it's in my power to summon him again.

"Please come to me," I say into the empty room. Am I calling God? Nat? The captain? I don't know. I am again in the doorway between life and death, where I have seen my mother and waited for Nat and where I fell when I learned that Nell was dead. "Please send help," I cry.

THE GENTLE VOICE outside my cottage is amethyst and silver yellow.

"Mrs. Gamble? It's Eveline, the undertaker's wife. He sent me to you."

I listen for some false note or trap, but I know amethyst is good and that she is good, too.

"Are you alone?" I ask.

"I come only with God," she says.

So it is God who answered my plea.

"Come in, and hurry, please."

Soon she has untied me.

"My husband did this—he's dangerous," I say. "I fear he'll be back soon." I strain to hear a sound from up high, but all I hear are dogs in the wind. "We have to get away."

I turn my cloak inside out so the bright red won't be easily visible through the dull forest. Eveline is small and wiry and effortlessly keeps my pace.

"You shouldn't run in your state. I'll go ahead and get my husband's cart," she says.

She sprints up the path and out of sight, and for a moment I am lost. It's cold and everything is shadowed in the November mist. I long for any color at all, any light in the gray autumn air.

Then soft voices the color of ferns seem to come out of the forest, rising through the bare tree limbs. They call my name: "Isobel."

I clutch my cape around me. The tambour hook and long needle are in the narrow pocket hidden at the clasp.

"Isobel, run down the path," the voices tell me.

The tree branches are bare. Brown leaves are thick underfoot. I remember running through the dark toward home on summer evenings when my mother's voice was calling me through the twilight. This is the same silver sound, but the woods are not leading me home this time, they're leading me into the unknown.

The cold air is wet on my face and the voices seem to rise up in silver-yellow and amethyst—they flood the path ahead as if it is strewn with hundreds of bright irises. Their voices are clear—

"Run, Isobel."

I run around a bend and stumble, but a hand catches me before I fall, grabs my shoulder, and twists me around.

"Eveline!" I cry.

But it's Edward, his face contorted in hatred and fury.

"Where is Mercy? Where did she go? What did you tell her?"

He throws me to the ground and beats at my face. My fingers find the needle hidden in my cape.

Trust the needle.

He is the weight of all the fear I felt the night they tore apart our home in Glasgow. He is the weight of a body on top of mine, reeking of rum. He is the weight of my stolen gold and the dreams that went with it.

Trust the needle.

He is abandonment and shame. He is Nat and the icy way he turned from me; Nat and the promise that is no promise at all. The needle draws out easily.

Trust the needle.

The words are Pap's, but the voice comes from the past, from inside, from above and behind the trees. Women's voices speaking to me of women's work, women's tasks, women's friendships, women's graves, women's hope, and women's strength.

Is it Isobel Gowdie? Is it the women in the forest? Is it my mother or my grandmother? Is it God?

It's all of them—they've all come now, for this is my time. Edward is screaming and I am screaming and the voices in my head are screaming—*I have lain with the Devil's forked prick inside me, and if you kill me hell will reign on earth.* The long, sharp needle that I carried across the ocean is like a blade between us, the length of my hand.

"I'll kill you!" Edward screams.

His hand grips my wrist and he bends the needle in my direction. The point is inches from my face and he is inches from my face and then I roar with all the fury of my life. I twist up and jab the needle into his eye. It enters with the soft ease of cloth shredding.

THIRTY-TWO

I push off his weight and Edward tumbles onto the dirt. He's screaming "My eye, my eye!" when I scramble to my knees. My hands are covered in blood and the forest is ablaze with his cries and beneath them are the soft voices of my ladies in the trees.

"Hurry, Isobel." Urgent hands on my shoulders.

"Come on, Mrs. Gamble, you have to hurry."

Women's voices: two, then three of them.

"Run on, Isobel, run on."

I run with the wind and the women of the forest. I run until Zeke and the undertaker gallop up the path to meet us. The horse is breathing hard.

"Get in," the undertaker says.

He indicates his cart, the one that carries the dead. I remember the hat in front of his heart when he told me Nell was gone. I hear Edward still screaming behind me. I climb in.

A blanket covers me as we jolt to a start and ride away. It's cold and the forest is deep. Edward's screams fade beneath the clatter of the wagon wheels and pounding horse's hooves.

Hours pass and I grow colder. I smell the day slipping away, ocean air replaced by the scent of spruce, pine, and iron blood. When I have to make water, I let it seep out of me into the folds of my dress where it warms my flesh, then chills it.

I listen for my mother in the darkness, for I am in the doorway at the brink of many things—past and present, awake and asleep, hope and despair. But her voice fades before I can hear what she might say to me, and I know that I need something more. Someone alive on this side of the divide. Someone I love, who loves me.

THE CARRIAGE STOPS and I wake from my stupor. There are footsteps on gravel, the blanket lifts, and Zeke's whiskered face is framed by a blue-black sky with a silver moon. His breath is wispy in the cold air. White stars blaze above the leafless forest.

The child hasn't moved, and that's all I can think of.

"Let's get you inside," Zeke says.

It's been hours since I climbed into the carriage, or maybe it's been days. Time has tangled around me and I'm unsure of anything but the brittle silence of the November forest and the rusty smell of Edward's blood on my hands.

I crawl out from beneath the blanket, my arms and legs stiff as they unwind. The horse snorts and paws the earth as Zeke helps me over the lip of the carriage and onto the ground. I don't ask where the undertaker has gone or how Zeke became the driver, for it makes no difference. My feet and fingers are numb but I can feel the hairs in my nose, each one a crisp line.

"Where am I?"

"Sugar house."

A shape rises slowly out of the blackness before me: a low shack hidden in a grove of maples. Zeke unlocks the narrow door and stands aside. The threshold glows from an inner flame.

"Safe here," he says. "Go on in."

THE SUGAR HOUSE is long and dark, with a hearth and fire at the far end. Mercy stands before the flames.

"Come sit," she says.

Her words are the color of ripe plums turned inside out—pink on the edges, deep purple brown inside. Mercy and Zeke talk in low voices, and then he's gone.

"You did real good." Mercy's face is soft and full. "And you gave us enough time."

"Where is Ivy?" My voice is barely a whisper.

She indicates a corner of the dim room where the girl is sleeping beneath a blanket.

I feel my body waver and sag. Somehow in the warmth I'm more afraid than I was in the cold dark.

"I don't feel the baby."

Mercy makes soothing sounds as she leads me to the mattress beside the fire. She takes off my cloak and cap and washes my hands and face with warm water. I can feel the places where Edward struck me when she pats them with the rag. Her hands are holding me, tending to me.

"I haven't felt the baby move since I got in the carriage."

She puts her warm hands beneath my skirts and lays them flat upon my skin.

"Not much blood here," she says. "Hush now."

Mercy closes her eyes, puts her face to my belly, and begins to hum. The sound is a thin pastel green that deepens and fades with her simple tune. Green is Nell's color. Green is goodness, something wholesome that can be lost or taken away or kept alive in the dark winter.

"You warned us so we could run, me and Ivy." Mercy is half singing, half speaking, all of it so quiet I can barely hear her. "Didn't think her legs would do it, but she's strong. God was with us and we met one of your ladies on the road and I told her to send for Eveline. Looks like she did right, too."

I crane my neck to whisper, "Your man from Baltimore is looking for you. Edward told them he knows where you are."

"Shhhh." She presses me back onto the lump of pillow. "Nobody's going to find us here. And it's not me he's looking for."

"It *is* you." I must make her understand. "A man named MacGreggor in Baltimore. Edward said there's a very big reward."

Mercy shakes her head. The whole room seems to shrink to a place beneath her hands—a globe the size of my belly glowing, the round firmness of an iris bulb.

"He ain't looking for me." Mercy looks at Ivy's sleeping figure. "But I got to protect the child."

"I don't understand."

"You're in it now, so you should know." Mercy's voice is a singsong that turns to waves of purple. "It's Ivy's father who's looking for her. The white devil named MacGreggor. He's Abraham's father, too."

"And their mother." I say it slow, because she didn't understand me the first time. "He's looking for the children and their mother."

"Like I told you, I was born free right here in Salem." Mercy hums.

"Are you saying you're not their mother?"

She shakes her head.

"In heart I am. But not in body."

"And you were never a slave?"

"Born free," she says. "What I told you about me and my mama is true."

"Then who is their mother?"

Mercy lets her breath out slow. I think of her on the wharf the day we arrived. Zeke on the path the day Nat taught me how to swim. Abraham gone north.

"The children's mama was a slave by the name of Ida. Five years ago, MacGreggor brought her up with him to Boston. Didn't care that she was carrying his child. Brought her and their son, too—a comfort woman, she was, you know what I mean? He used her the way he wanted.

"Pretty Miss Ida and her big belly was sitting in a hotel lobby in Boston one afternoon when our own Mr. John Remond walked right up to her and said she didn't need to stay with the man who owned her. 'You're free here in the Commonwealth of Massachusetts,' he said."

Mercy's hands are warm on my skin.

"Ida was a slave in Chesapeake Bay, and she cared for nothing more than seeing her children to freedom. Ran off into the Boston market, just about right under the master's nose. When MacGreggor and his men were looking for her, she found her way here."

"Here?"

"To me. To this place, the sugar house. Ida was the first. Ivy was born right here, on this very floor."

She's rubbing my belly, humming low and steady.

"If they were free, why did they have to hide?"

"There's no justice for a slave," Mercy says. "Slave escapes to the North, she's free. Slave catcher finds her and gets a judge to sign a paper, he can put her in chains and bring her back down south. Ida was born a slave so her children were still slaves, and if the judge signed a paper, any man could've brought them back to MacGreggor."

"Like Edward planned to do for the reward," I realize. "And that rough man Zeke and I saw the day of Charlotte's wedding."

"That's right," she says. "Reward and rumor of a runaway brings every kind of low man to town."

I've seen how justice and the law work for some and not for others. Even in Scotland there was rich man's law and poor man's law.

"Ida was weak from running. Baby came early. When she started bleeding, she said, 'My children got to be free.' And so they were."

This is the story Nat read to me the day of our picnic: the promise extracted from the midwife upon the mother's deathbed. How did he know?

"Before she died, Ida begged me to get a message to her brother back in the Chesapeake. Said Atlas would come for the children one day. He would find a way free; that was always their plan. We did what we could and kept the children with us. And after five years, Atlas came—not too long after you got here, Atlas found his way to us."

I remember the sound in the woods, the sight of Mercy running before the dawn. The man who wasn't Zeke.

"But slave catchers were on his trail, and we had to get him north. We sent Abraham with Atlas like we promised—the captain took them."

"Captain Darling said he was making a run for whale oil," I remember.

"That's right." She nods. "They weren't safe here. You can't stay in Salem now either, not with what you did to Edward," Mercy says. "You know it, right?"

"Edward wanted to kill me," I say. "And he meant to, until I stabbed his eye."

"No law will blame a man for beating a wife who has a bastard child in her belly." Mercy's hands are sure and steady. "Law doesn't care why a woman does what she does, just like the law says a slave can be free here and a slave can be caught here. Don't try to make sense of it. You just got to keep moving."

Mercy ends her humming singsong and takes her hands from beneath my dress. She puts her cheek against mine and says, "Your child's gonna be fine, but you got to rest now, you been through something real hard. You did good."

She puts her hand on my forehead and I swear I hear her say the word *love*. Even with my eyes closed I can see the letters, plum and yellow as Mercy's words are. But when I open my eyes her mouth is closed, her lips are together, and the only sound in the room is the low thrum of Ivy's breath.

SOMETIME IN THE night I'm startled awake. My bladder is full and the kick is hard. I feel fear, then relief. The child is moving again.

I use the chamber pot and curl myself around my belly and hum a soft tune, as soft as the one Mercy sang.

Nell is dead. Edward wanted to kill me. Nat broke my heart and the Silas women turned their backs to me. But despite all that I have been through, I am safe and alive. I have done it all with the needle—made my friends and my life here, stood up against death and shame and the fear of my colors.

Since the day my mother told me to hide the colors, I have been afraid. When the girls in the tambour shop spoke quietly, I held myself apart. When Edward asked me to marry him, I accepted because I thought I would be safe with him—I thought that because of what was strange or unusual in him, he would forgive what was strange in me.

Some people, like Nat, spend their days fearing what's dead and gone because they grow to love the horrors and the shadows of their own mind. I don't want to be a prisoner of my secrets or of my past any longer. All that matters to me now are the children: Abraham and Ivy, my unborn baby, and all those who live in chains and fear.

I was wrong many times. But I have also done many things right. And I am safe here.

∞

IN THE MORNING Mercy brings me a cup of tea. I pull her hand onto my belly so she can feel the child stir.

"I saw the words in your work, Mercy—the very first day. You have magic in your hands."

She shakes her head, even as I describe the *S* and *F* linked together.

"Not magic," she says. "I told you before: if you think you've got power, then you got power. And if you think you don't, then you don't. That's how you made those letters in the yellow cloth that saved us."

"Aren't you afraid?" I ask.

"Of what?"

I struggle to name all the reasons I've feared my colors and letters.

"What if the wrong people see the words?"

Mercy shrugs.

"You be surprised what people don't see," she says. "There's nothing new or wrong with telling stories with needle and thread. Nothing wrong in saying there's people looking to be free, and people who've already found it. It's not a secret message of codes; it's not directions or a map. It's just hope, plain and true. And it's how Atlas found me when he come to Salem. He saw the word *SAFE* and found his way to us. He can't read, but he knew to look for the pattern of the letters and he found them."

"What if a minister or a preacher saw the words and thought they were witchcraft?"

"They aren't," she says. "You did the same as I did with the needle, and it saved all of us. What more do you need to know? The stitching stood against evil and now we're safe here."

Keep your powers hidden and use them when it's your time. Mam could not have known where my life would take me, but she understood that every woman will face peril and hardship—and that it's best if we keep our strengths and skills close and strong. That way, when we need them, they are powerful enough to carry us to a new beginning.

"What's going to happen to Ivy now?" I ask.

"We'll get her north to Canada the same way we got the others there."

"How is that?"

Mercy points to piles of burlap stacked against the wall, like the parcel I once saw her bring to a house in Lynn.

"You sew up the burlap so it looks like a shroud," she says. "And then you get inside it, and you get in the undertaker's cart, and he gets you to a ship heading north."

I remember the first time I saw the undertaker pulling his cart. He was like a shadow, walking. Another time I saw Zeke on the wharf carrying a burlap sack thrown over his shoulder. All those times, were there people hiding?

"The captain—" I begin.

Mercy smiles. "Captain Darling's been helping us all these many years, but there are others, too. They started during Madison's war with England and never stopped."

I let out a laugh, and the sound is strange here in the sugar house. When I tell Mercy what Edward believes about Captain Darling and Ingo, she laughs, too.

"Best if that's what that dog thinks—then he can't give anything away."

ALL NIGHT WE talk about the sugar house and how Mercy, Zeke, Widow Higgins, and the captain have helped those who've come north in the night.

Mercy points out the kettles and tools used to sap the maples in the fall.

"We used to come here just to tap and boil the syrup," she says. "Widow Higgins's husband took me here and taught me. It was peaceful—all those years we never saw a soul. When Mr. Remond brought Ida and Abraham, I thought right away to hide them here. That's how we started."

Mercy spoons out molasses and beans for the three of us and we eat.

Ivy asks no questions, but she must have many. Or perhaps her life has always been this way. I see now why Ivy says so little, her eyes always watching, and imagine how she must feel—waiting without knowing fully what she's waiting for. A sign? A moment? A knock upon the sugar house door?

"May I see your doll?" I ask.

Ivy brings the figure to me. It's stitched of burlap, small enough to hold in her lap. The doll has legs and arms and a face but no hair or clothes.

"Would you like for her to have a dress?"

"One like mine." She nods.

Ivy's dress is green and brown, the color of the forest. I realize now it is clothes made for hiding among the trees.

My cloak is stained with Edward's blood, and I do not want to take it where I am going—I must leave it behind. My story must be my own now. I must rely on myself and begin anew.

I trim around the bloody stains to cut strips from the cloak with all the figures and words I've sewn since I left home. By evening I've made the doll and Ivy matching dresses. The red comet flies across Ivy's small chest, and the doll's dress shows half a ship sail and a creature from the sea.

"Captain Darling says this one is good luck." I point to a fish with wings that he inspired, and the blue words that sparked my colors when he spoke them. *I owe you my life.* "You be sure to show this to him when you see him."

TOWARD EVENING THERE's a birdcall outside, then a knock. There are no windows in the sugar house, only a sliding latch in the door.

Mercy slides the latch and opens the door to Widow Higgins, bundled up against the November cold.

"Your friend was buried yesterday." She comes to sit beside me as she takes off her layers of wool. "I stitched together the pieces of the shroud I found in your cottage, and she was put in it in the Silas home. Someone remarked that the shroud could only be the work of the old woman who made the gloves for Felicity Adams."

So not everyone knows about the captain's gloves and the lies Felicity told.

"There is no old woman."

The widow smiles.

"I know," she says. "I've always known your needle and your colors, special as they are."

The widow has gone to my cottage and brought my sewing tools and warm brown cloak. With it around my shoulders I feel that I'm no longer the woman who came across the ocean in red and walked into one of Nat's stories. I'm the woman Mercy saw, and the woman who saw Mercy and the words barely visible in her work.

"The captain sent this." Widow Higgins hands me a long package wrapped in brown paper.

It is a new card of Chinese threads, the rainbow of possibility the captain gifted me on the crossing. Captain Darling was the first man who ever said it plainly; who put color in my hands and said I could be an artist.

I pull the threads from the card one by one and soon I've begun stitching a design of symbols onto one of the burlap sacks that will be used by the undertaker one day to carry an escaping slave through town.

I stitch Nell's shamrocks and the captain's wild sea animals for luck, and by morning my work is stitched across an endless ocean and sky. I have put my love and gratitude, hopes for freedom, and wishes for the world into this very shroud, and now I understand: by keeping silent I hold my gifts and my strengths close. I do not need to speak of them aloud; I can let the colors speak for me.

TUESDAY, THE DAY Nat's carriage is coming, I wake to low voices in the predawn darkness to discover Mercy and Widow Higgins folding Ivy into the shroud I decorated with sea animals and shamrocks.

"Captain Darling's ship is waiting," Mercy explains to the girl. "You will be with Auntie Higgins or Joseph the undertaker or Captain Darling. We'll never let you be alone for even one moment—they'll take you all the way to your brother and Uncle Atlas. You just have to keep yourself quiet."

Together we stitch the child safely inside the shroud, leaving a small space for her to breathe. Just before they set off, I tell the widow where to find my Adam and Eve shawl.

"Sell it for me," I say. "Give the money to the captain, to pay for what's needed."

As Ivy and the widow ride toward the dawn and the wharves, I lie abed and feel my child kick and roll in my womb.

My heart aches as I think of Nat's promises, the ones I thought he'd made, and the ones I will never get to see. I imagine his coach rolling up to the sycamore tree where I stood that afternoon with him hidden behind me and Zeke in front of me, and I think of all the lies that were hidden that day and all the truths I know now.

All along I imagined Nat would be in the carriage, but now I see in my mind what likely would have been—me, alone, handing a small bundle to the coachman. Climbing into an empty, cold cabin. Riding unaccompanied into the snow.

THIRTY-THREE

All through winter, I stay in the sugar house and sew silk dresses and sing to the unborn child. I stitch and study and sift through my colors until the understanding is firm in me: Red is passion and knowledge, but it's also a warning of pain. Blue is hope. Yellow is truth, except when it's part of fire. Orange is joy. Green is goodness and home. Mercy's voice is plum brown and yellow, like autumn preparing for winter and then a new spring. Jewel tones like my mother's voice and the amethyst of Eveline and my ladies in the forest—they are the women who help one another in ways that can be seen and also in invisible ways that aren't always known.

It's not that we are witches or faeries or that we deny God. It is that we are more beautiful and strong together than apart.

MERCY AND WIDOW Higgins deliver me of the child when it is my time. The birth is easy, and the babe is born wailing yellow, blue, and soft green like the petals of an iris. Her hair is raven, her eyes the color of stars. She's not a red-haired girl but she's beautiful and the sounds of her cries are the colors of hope, truth, and home.

I've been in Salem a little more than a year. I've spent five months in the sugar house, long enough to make four dresses plus gloves, petticoats, white on white, and more—enough to start a shop of my own.

On an early spring day, I put on a new yellow dress and a matching cap on the babe's head, and Captain Darling comes to me. We stand in a patch of sun and he puts a thumb on the babe's cheek and brushes her forehead, almost like a minister offering his blessing.

"She's named Margaret, for my mother."

"Margaret," the captain says, and the word is a pure joy. "Margaret, from the Greek for 'pearl.' She can be our pearl of the sea—yours and mine, if you wish it."

The captain's hat is in his hand, which he holds at his heart.

"Do you know what I am saying, lass? I would marry you, if you would have me."

I thought this might come, but not so soon.

"But I have a husband, and I believe he still lives."

Darling's face goes red.

"I should have taken him to Liverpool and dumped him where I found him." He doesn't hide his anger well, but he controls it the way a sail controls the wind. "It was a terrible mistake."

"I should have warned you he was prone to the poppy," I say.

"Well, you needn't fear him anymore. His eye pussed out and took his sight. He's blind now, and his mind is gone—I brought him to the almshouse in Boston where they'll keep him fed and alive. Still, I suppose it's best for you to go where he or the law can never find you."

When his eyes meet mine, they are warm and full of affection, steady and true as they have always been. And I think perhaps if my heart had not been broken, I might have turned to him.

I'M WAITING ON the rock when the blue rig comes for me. I know this cove. I know the water here is deep enough for a good-sized hull, and I know that if I fall into the sea I can swim.

Margaret is in my arms, wrapped in a blanket for traveling. Captain Darling comes down a short ramp and I turn to Mercy, who has dressed in forest greens and browns for this day.

"Are you sure you won't come with us?"

My friend's face is pained, lips pursed, her cheekbones the same wonder that they've always been.

"I got work to do here," Mercy says. "'Long as men are cruel and greedy there will be refugees from other worlds, children running to freedom. Folks who need help."

I put my arms around her and feel the strong sinew of her shoulders.

"Thank you and bless you for everything. I hope I'll see you again," I say, but I think she knows that it will never be.

"You take good care of your baby. And look in on my Ivy when you get where you're going."

I cry when we say goodbye, but the tears are so full of gratitude and joy that they feel not like weeping but like prayer.

THE CAPTAIN STEERS his rig toward the wharf where the *New Harmony* waits in port. I have learned from Mercy that the captain has already brought ten runaway slaves to safety and that he has hopes for many more.

"Where are we going?" I ask.

"The place where you and your little Pearl of the Sea will always have a home with me, if you wish it."

His eyes are the blue of his words, and his words are the blue of the sky, and I feel something I have not felt since I said goodbye to my pap: safe with a man, and full of hope.

AS WE SET sail in the *New Harmony*, I stand at the stern to take a last look at Salem. There are the busy wharves, the boats from every land, the shingled rooftops and tall brick houses that line the shore and look out to sea. There are the seamen and cottars and the sailmakers, the merchants and the girl who sells flowers. And there he is—a tall man in a too-long black cloak.

Did he know I would be leaving this morning? Has he been wandering the wharves in search of a woman with red hair?

Before I understood the strength of Mercy and the widow and Ingo and the captain—even Ivy and Abraham, mere children and yet chattel to some—I might have wept at the sight of him standing alone.

But I will not weep now.

I smell cinnamon and coffee and pepper in the air, the same sweet and bitter scents that first greeted me in this harbor.

Margaret yelps. I have held her too tightly.

I turn her around so that she can see the place where she was born. So that her father can see what he has lost.

Even from this distance, I'm sure that Nat is looking at us.

When I hold her high over my head—like a banner or a flag—he puts out a hand to steady himself. Raises his arms and reaches toward us. His mouth opens, but if he makes a sound, I do not hear it. I will never hear it.

I bite the inside of my cheek so hard that I taste my own blood. All the nights come back to me, the shock and the wonder of it all. The pleasure and the sorrow. The stories he told me, and the ones I will never know.

I loved him. I cannot deny it. I loved him with a pain that cuts me deep, even now.

IN THE CABIN where I traveled from Liverpool with Edward there's now a small drawer lined with soft blankets for baby Margaret, and a chest piled with silk cloth in every shade of blue: indigo, midnight, azure, sapphire. Beside it is a large piece of canvas and skeins of fine wool threads, just as I asked.

Outside, I hear the sailors shouting to one another. I feel the ropes pulling, the wind catching the sails. Someone cries out, "North," and another calls out, "Canada bound."

My tambour hook and sharp needle were lost on the path where Edward beat me down. But the pliers are in my pocket and the tiny scissors I carried from home tucked into my chatelaine have been sharpened for the journey. Margaret is snug in her makeshift cradle. She watches as I dry my tears, then open the canvas and spread it across the small table.

The sea rocks the boat, but I am steady. I have learned to trust my own eye and my own hand.

We leave the Massachusetts Bay and the sails catch the wind. I see the open water out the round window. I thread the needle with red yarn. I bend to the cloth.

Salem, 1849

The tallow is still burning as Nathaniel begins the final chapter of the novel that has come out of him in a torrent of memory and zeal. The attic room is warm and close, the slanted ceiling so low above his head that he cannot stand without stepping sideways out of his old oak chair.

His hands are blue with ink, his back strained with months hunched at the desk. He neatens the crooked pile of pages and slides the last of his old journals into his canvas pouch.

In the kitchen he prepares a bowl of warm chocolate and bread while Sophia puts the children into their beds, and when she settles on the couch to listen, he begins to read aloud. This has been their custom since their courtship began; no matter how long or short the piece, she listens with her eyes closed, hands folded upon her lap, and does not interrupt.

Hours pass, and husband and wife can hear the rhythm of the sentences, the beauty in his descriptions of Hester Prynne, the horror that seeps onto the page whenever the old doctor lurks around Minister Dimmesdale.

On and on he reads, dropping the pages onto the floor one by one until at last he reaches that final passage when Hester and Arthur Dimmesdale are reunited in the graveyard and the evidence of their twinned souls appears in the embroidered lettering on their tombstones.

When Nathaniel looks up, Sophia is staring back at him, blanched and wide-eyed, mouth agape, tears streaming down her face. And so he knows in an instant the story has done all that he wished it to, and more.

"It is a love story," she whispers. "You are the reverend. But who is the woman, Nat? For she is not me."

For three days Sophia lies in bed ravaged by a migraine that tears at the edges of her mind. When she rouses at last, it is to go up into his attic like a ghost, find the notebooks, and turn through the inked pages with a half-blind eye. But Sophia cannot bear to read any of it. She looks out the window at the sound of Nat coming home with the children. And in one motion she runs down the stairs and throws her husband's journals into the fire.

Halifax Bay, 1852

I left America as I'd arrived, on a ship, by the sea, looking ahead. Behind me was a shattered love, a treasured friend, the ghosts of cruel men and the women who fed them. What lay ahead I did not know, but I knew not to fear it, for fear of the unknown had never done me any good.

When we reached Halifax, I put my new dresses and embroidered fineries in the picture window of Captain Darling's sturdy white house at the head of the harbor. I made my bed in the kitchen maid's room behind the hearth and was free to tend my child.

Because the harbor freezes early, the captain and Ingo didn't stay long. They saw us onto land, brought me to see Ivy and Abraham with their uncle Atlas, and soon sailed south again. Alone with Margaret, I unfurled the work that I'd started on the journey and added to the canvas tapestry bit by bit. Spring and summer passed in a blur of baby and the strange light outside my window that changed each day. The sun this far north is scant in winter, and the days are short. There was plenty of time for sleep as snow and ice laced the world white, and fatigue and sorrow went through me like the tides.

When the frozen city thawed that spring, the seamen's wives and officers' ladies came out of their houses, blinking in the balmy light and looking for color in the gray landscape. They put fresh coats of paint on their wooden doors—red, yellow, and a clear blue that bloomed like early flowers as winter melted away.

I had been there almost a year when two ladies stood in front of the captain's window one morning and exclaimed over my dresses. It was May, and I caught the fragrance of a May tree blooming on the other side of the neighboring yard.

"The price must be very dear," one of the ladies said. She spoke the King's English, but her companion answered in a thick Scottish brogue.

"I'm sure I don't want anything so fancy," she said.

Their voices were purple and magenta like my ladies of the forest, and I rushed out the door in my work smock, holding Margaret on my hip.

"Whatever you need, I'll make it for you," I called.

Virginia and Clara became my first friends here. I told them I was a widow and the captain had saved me from starvation, which didn't feel like a lie. I gave my name as Isobel MacAllister and have been known thus ever since.

My new friends brought me broadcloth and showed me the plain and simple fashion of the city. By autumn I had as much business as I could manage. I swept clean the captain's front parlor and turned the whole room into a dress shop filled with neat stacks of cotton cloth and brocades the captain brought home from his voyages.

"Your shop needs a name," Clara said. She was wearing a deep blue walking costume I'd made and was twisting in front of the looking glass, trying to see her new self from every angle. Her hand was on her hip and her voice was as green as Nell's once was.

I knew right away the name would be Lighthouse Dress Shop—everyone agreed it was a grand name—and just as quickly as it came to me I saw a banner with a red-and-white lighthouse, yellow rays of sun, and a row of irises at the base.

EIGHTEEN YEARS PASSED happily. Margaret and I lived in an apartment above the shop in the house that Darling owned, and the town accepted that arrangement. Halifax was the new home of the British naval fleet in the Americas, and the wealthy naval officers' wives longed for fashions that mimicked those in Europe. Soon I subscribed to the *Godey's Lady's Book* and used their color plates and patterns to make new and finer dresses with hoop skirts and tightly corseted waists that I could never stand to wear.

Ladies brought me day dresses, work dresses, and collars to embroider. What I heard in their voices I put into their attire in simple ways—a pink whipstitch trim, a sliver of red piping—always in the color each lady inspired. I saved my rich threads for nights when Margaret was asleep and then added them to the tapestry I'd begun on the

New Harmony, attaching larger pieces of canvas and adding velvets, beads, and more as it grew like a map of my own life, ever larger, always changing.

MARGARET WAS A bright and sometimes fiery child: loving, stubborn, and curious about the world. I taught her to sew but the needle was a slippery thing in her fingers, and when the colors had no meaning for her, I was relieved. Although it tried my patience when my daughter was willful about what she did and did not like, I was thankful that she was not a secretive person as her father was. Within the realm of decency I let her dress as she liked, and read what she asked for. I tried always to answer her questions about the city and the people she knew as honestly as possible, with one exception: I told my daughter her father had died during the crossing from Scotland and that he had been buried at sea.

"Uncle Darling took care of us then, and has helped us ever since," I said. When she asked about her father, I told her the story of my brother Jamie's life; in this way I brought him back to me again and hoped that he was well and happy wherever he was.

Twice I wrote to Jamie in the hotel where he'd worked, but that had been so long ago, I was not surprised that no word came back to me. It is how the world is, and I tried to teach my daughter this as well: you must love what is close and true; you must look to the present and future and not to the past.

BOOKS AND READING became my daughter's passion, as I suppose is no surprise. She became a schoolteacher and at nineteen she married the schoolmaster's son, who had studied law at university. That same year she came to me with a pile of white pages covered in blue ink.

"I've been writing." She was flushed. Her dark hair fell across her face and she pushed it away with a flick of her wrist, just as her father had done.

"Stories?" I blinked back a sudden rush of tears.

"No. I'm writing about the education of girls." Her voice quivered with feeling and was so full of colors it almost blinded me. "It's for *Godey's* magazine. I remember, Mother, that you had to leave school and go to work when you were small, and that should never happen."

When she was twenty, I walked into her cottage to find Margaret bent over a book.

"It's new." She flipped the book so I could see the title. "*The Scarlet Letter* by Nathaniel Hawthorne."

It was all I could do not to grab the book from her and throw it into the fire. The sight of his name brought back all the heartache and pain that I had buried away.

But I did nothing. Perhaps Margaret saw something on my face, for she asked if I was all right, and I nodded even as I let my gaze rest on the *w* he'd added to his name. Hawthorne instead of Hathorne. Like the enchanted May tree, and the blossoms he once brought to me.

"DON'T TELL HER," Darling said. We were standing in the kitchen, having just shared a meal of mutton and bread. In all those years, we'd never spoken of Nat. "I beg of you."

Darling's face was aged by the sea but his eyes were as bright and kind as on the first day we'd met, and I saw in them all the love that he had for Margaret and me.

"You know she doesn't think you're her father," I reminded him. "She thinks her father died on the crossing."

"Let it be that way," he said. "Let it stay in the past where it belongs."

"I don't know what to do or think," I said. "I haven't even read the book myself."

"Don't."

Darling's face went red, as it does when he is angry. But I knew I would read the book in time. I knew that I had to, for everything that I had felt in Salem had come flooding back to me the moment I saw the title—all the pain and fear and hurt—and yes, the love.

But I had also come to understand that what happened between Nat and me had been the love between an unformed girl held captive by her secrets and a haunted man held captive by his ghosts.

Everything that had hurt me in Salem was behind me now. I was not that girl anymore; I had long ago stopped living in the past or fearing it. Free of it, I could see what was true—what had always been true, in a way.

"William Darling," I said, "I cannot promise you that I won't read the book. But I can tell you that I love you."

"What do you mean?" His voice faltered, but it was the same blue I had always known.

I did not love him the way I had loved Nat, and so I had not understood that love didn't require pain. That it can also be a comfort, a place of safety and happiness and home, full of hope and affection and admiration.

"I mean I love you as a woman loves a man, and I have waited too long to tell you," I said.

And when he took me into his bed that night, he was so gentle it was a whisper, and then it was a roar, and when my eyes were closed it felt as if I had never had another lover. As if time had erased everything that it could.

I bought my own copy of Nat's book, but for a long time couldn't bring myself to read it. Every old scar and wound seemed to open whenever I thought of it, and so I locked it away in a cabinet in my dress shop and hoped the questions about truth and lies and storytelling and secrets would stop haunting me.

But they did not, nor did he. And so one day when Darling was at sea and my heart was strong, I began to read.

Nat called the story *A Romance*; it began with a scarlet letter embroidered and hidden away in a scrap of cloth like the button I once slipped into our hiding place at the boulder. Hester Prynne was an outcast, just as Nat had said I would be if I'd stayed. Arthur Dimmesdale was a coward without the courage to claim the woman he loved; their daughter was a strange little sprite without a friend in the world, and I wept tears of gratitude that I'd saved Margaret from such a fate.

Pearl. He called the girl Pearl. How could he have known? Did he see us while he lay in his bed with a cloth across his eyes? Did he ask about me? Did Mercy tell him? I could not—I still cannot—decide if I felt horrified or vindicated. Frightened or liberated.

Like Nat himself, the book was a truth within a lie, and a lie within a truth.

And like everything powerful in this life, it sent me to the needle, where the story I'd been telling since I left Salem started in the blue-green darkness of the secret cove and traveled north into the wide arms of Halifax Harbor.

I'd left an empty circle at the center of the tapestry, as I'd always felt an emptiness in myself.

I knew then how I would fill it.

MARGARET GAVE BIRTH to twins the following year: a boy with red-yellow hair named Willy for the captain, and a red-haired girl named Isobel, just as we have always been Isobel, Margaret, Isobel, Margaret, going back and back through time.

When the twins were born, Ivy came across the city with her own three children. She lived with her husband among the free Colored people in the Campbell Road Settlement, a place of joy but also of hard poverty made worse by the same neglect and spiteful laws that hurt American Colored people. Still, the citizens in the settlement grew in number over the years, thanks in part to the captain and others who brought runaway slaves to freedom. And Ivy was strong; her children were loved.

She brought a toy boat her husband had carved for Willy and a bonnet for baby Isobel. She put a small package wrapped in cotton into my daughter's hands, and Margaret unfolded the tiny dress I'd made from my own cloak so many years ago in the sugar house.

"Your mama gave me this before we left Salem," Ivy said.

Margaret ran her hand along a fragment of the cape that I'd worked as I crossed the ocean from Liverpool. She turned the dress inside out to study the stitching, as the daughter of any seamstress might, and her finger worried at a knot of red thread.

"Look." Margaret's face bloomed as she turned the seam inside out. "There's a scarlet letter hidden here."

I'd long ago stopped making that mark so that no one in Salem could find me by it, and no one in Halifax could mistake it for an enchantment.

"*A* for Abington," I rushed to say. "The little village where I was born. I've told you all about it many times, the River Clyde, the waterfalls, the green of the fields."

But my daughter wasn't fooled, and when Ivy and her children were gone and the infants were abed, she called me to her.

"It's just like the letter in the book." Margaret's pale skin, her dark hair, her eyes the same pale green-gold as his. "It's more than strange, Mama—not only the scarlet *A*, the way it is hidden, but the girl in the book is named Pearl just as Uncle Darling has always called me his Pearl of the Sea. Why, Mama? What is there that I do not know?"

I wanted to tell her there are many things in this world a child must not ask. But I remembered how I'd hungered to know everything about my own mother's past so that I could understand who I was and what I should do with my colors and my fears. And I thought about my mother, who'd meant to keep me safe but instead had died before I could understand how I should live.

I'd spent half my life waiting for my time, straddling the world between the living and the dead, between God and the faerie world, between the past and the future. I did not want that for my daughter.

THAT NIGHT I got on my knees, dragged the tapestry from beneath my bed, and carried it to Margaret's cottage where I spread it before her. My needle and thread told every secret I could not speak: Isobel Gowdie, the crossing on the *New Harmony,* the cottage at the edge of Salem, Mercy's yard full of chickens, the devil in the forest, oceans of blue hope and darkness, the patterns and stitches I'd made and taught myself—a long hedgerow of pink and white hawthorn flowers, Zeke's blue cart, the tiger gloves, the purple and yellow irises my mother sketched a lifetime ago. There were the seals that came to me in the cove, the lantern sign, the cemetery where Nat kicked the tombstone, the maple trees beside the sugar house, and all of the whaling ships, the circle of friends in Halifax, the shop with my sign above the door: *Lighthouse Dress Shop and Sundries.*

In the center of the piece was the bold red *A*, half as tall as a man, as bright as when the letter first declared itself to me.

Margaret studied the banner in silence for a long time. Finally she went to her shelf and found the book with a scarlet letter ablaze on its cover.

"Is this about you?" she asked.

I remembered everything from the moment I saw him on the dock to the moment when he pulled back my hair and raised up a pained longing that no one had ever unleashed. I gave myself to him, and if I told it to my daughter then she would know my secrets. And if I told it truthfully, she would know my pain. And if I told it right, she would learn everything that I know about love and desire and the colors, about this world and the hidden world, about the man with the red-and-gold voice who was almost the ruin of me.

And she would know how I survived.

NOTES AND ACKNOWLEDGMENTS

I was in ninth grade when I first read *The Scarlet Letter*. I don't remember how I felt about the love story, but I do remember how I felt about luminous young Pearl. Hester was a mother, Dimmesdale was a minister, but Pearl was a wild child and I saw myself in her.

Much like Hawthorne, I was a desultory student and a voracious reader, preoccupied with family matters and the question of how I might fit into the world. Pearl was unpredictable; her fate hung in question until she sailed across the ocean and later came into great wealth. For my school research paper, I focused on Pearl's symbols—Pearl in the moonlight, Pearl in the forest, Pearl asking Dimmesdale if he will stand beside her and Hester on the scaffold.

Years later, when my own children were reading *The Scarlet Letter*, I recognized Hester Prynne's seminal importance as a heroic woman who defies powerful men and vengeful villagers by wearing the symbol of her shame like a badge of courage. I understood that while Hester could not escape her past or her fate, she could harness her power by summoning the strength of her creative fortitude.

I gave that creative fortitude to my character Isobel Gamble.

∞

Hester began with the question: What if Hester Prynne told her own story? I traced America's historical fiction back to the beginning—to *The Scarlet Letter,* published in 1850—and rediscovered Hester as our first historical feminist hero *and* our original badass single mother; a woman Hawthorne created to both challenge and substantiate the notion of female weakness.

Hawthorne was a secretive man who burned many of his letters, papers, and journals. He published only five novels in his lifetime; all but *The Scarlet Letter* spring from a known inspiration—*Fanshawe* is based on his college experiences, *The Blithedale Romance* on his time at the experimental utopian Brook Farm, *The House of Seven Gables* on his family's role in the Salem witch trials, and *The Marble Faun* on his years in Italy.

We can only speculate upon Hester's true origins, as there's no source evidenced in the author's life or writing, no original manuscript or notes to study. Many scholars remark on a guilt and shame that Hawthorne carried all his life. Writing in the *New Criterion* in 1985, the literary scholar James Tuttleton says, "[S]ince *The Scarlet Letter* deals with adultery, could it be that Hawthorne committed adultery and expiated it through the act of writing the novel? Is he a closet Arthur Dimmesdale or a Parson Hooper mystifying his audience in the act of performing an obscure penance? Some critics and biographers have thought so. . . ."

Writing *Hester* was a delicious journey through the possibility and plausibility of this very idea.

Every novel has many threads woven together to form a whole—many seeds are needed to plant a rainbow—and this one is no exception. I read countless books and articles about Hawthorne, most notably Brenda Wineapple's biography *Hawthorne: A Life* (2003), my dearly missed friend Louise DeSalvo's *Nathaniel Hawthorne* (1987), Nina Baym's seminal *The Scarlet Letter: A Reading* (1986), and Henry James's *Hawthorne* (1879).

Nearly every biography about Hawthorne mentions his forlorn

decade after Bowdoin College when (in his own words) he "became a hermit," took to "his chamber under his eaves," and committed himself to becoming a writer.

But a close look at Hawthorne's college years shows us a rabble-rouser who played cards and drank wine and was almost expelled for it. As Wineapple writes, "He constantly broke the rules."

I set this book in 1829, four years after Hawthorne graduated from college. Given latitude by his family to keep his own hours and wander around Salem day and night, it's easy to imagine this fatherless, handsome young man might have found a lover. She wouldn't have been a society woman, for society was strict about such things. But what of a new immigrant to Salem, married to a much older man? A woman who found herself alone, abandoned, and drawn to her confessor? A seamstress like Hester herself?

I have Susan Cheever's book *American Bloomsbury* (2006) to thank for helping me make the leap from conjecture to plausibility concerning the private lives of Hawthorne and his wider circle in Massachusetts.

Why *wouldn't* the "real" Dimmesdale have a Hester? Why *wouldn't* there be a lover?

Many things in *Hester* are based on known fact. Hawthorne's ancestor John Hathorne was an unrepentant magistrate in the infamous Salem witch trials of 1692. Isobel Gowdie was a real person who was convicted of witchcraft in 1662 Scotland. Belief in witches wasn't questioned in those times; the identification and punishment of "witches" was a matter of law. Both trial proceedings can be accessed online, and they are rich, frightening reading.

I learned much about the accusation and prosecution of alleged witches in *The Penguin Book of Witches* (2014) edited by Katherine Howe and *In the Devil's Snare* (2002) by Mary Beth Norton. For Salem history I read *When I Lived in Salem, 1822–1866* (1937) by Caroline Howard King, *The Annals of Salem: From Its First Settlement* (1827) by Joseph B. Felt, and *Death of an Empire* (2011) by Robert Booth. I visited the magnificent Salem Maritime National Historic Site developed and maintained by the U.S. National Park Service, where I learned much about the period and its shipping industry. The "Hawthorne in Salem" website offers endless visual and written material about the city and the author; especially notable is Emerson W. Baker and James Kences's article, "Maine, Land Speculation, and the Essex County Witchcraft Outbreak of 1692" (2001).

There were about two hundred African Americans living in Salem in 1829, most of them free but some only recently so. Hamilton Hall in Salem is a real establishment that was presided over by John and Nancy Remond for more than a decade. It is almost impossible to comprehend the contribution that free and enslaved Africans and Black Americans made to Salem's wealth. Rita Reynolds, chair of the History Department at Wagner College, patiently and generously answered my questions about the free Black community in early nineteenth-century America and read the novel for points of interest regarding the same. Dr. Donna Seger, history professor at Salem State University and creator of the blog *Streets of Salem,* kindly and very promptly provided endless information on historic Salem life. She generously read the manuscript for veracity of time and place. Beth Bower at the Salem Historical Society answered many questions about the city and its people. The National Museum of Scotland's digital resources, including "Mapping Slavery," provided deep insights into the history of Scottish people and the slave trade. Any errors on these topics are my own.

Thanks to Monika Elbert, scholar and editor of *The Nathaniel Hawthorne Review,* for spending time talking with me about this story. Thanks to the Peabody Essex Museum and Phillips Library. I relied on PEM'S *Painted with Thread: The Art of American Embroidery* (2000) by Paula Bradstreet Richter, along with a variety of embroidery instruction books, to bring to life the art and methods of needlecraft. Clare Hunter's *Threads of Life: A History of the World Through the Eye of a Needle* (2019) and Kassia St. Clair's *The Golden Thread: How Fabric Changed History* (2018) provided depth and texture to my understanding of textiles and needlework. Rozsika Parker's seminal second-wave feminist work, *The Subversive Stitch: Embroidery and the Making of the Feminine* (1984), informed my understanding of the duality of the needle as both a source of creative and economic strength and of female domestic submission.

Melinda Sherbring, embroiderer, banner-maker, author, and instructor, was patient and generous in answering all of my questions. I spent days burrowed in the *Ladies' Magazine, Godey's Lady's Book,* and the *Salem Gazette* archives where articles and advertisements proved a treasure trove of detailed information on period fashion, goods, and commerce. Finally, for sharing their personal experiences with synesthesia, I am ever grateful to the lovely Anna Gustavsen and Debbie Lansing.

My agent, Heather Schroder, is a true creative partner; she saw the seed of a good story in my questions and ideas and nourished it tirelessly. I can't imagine having written this book without her enthusiasm, erudition, and friendship.

Sarah Cantin, my beloved editor, is a powerful advocate with a keen ability to find and sharpen a book's depth and a character's essence. I am so grateful and lucky to have Sarah's hand in my work a second time around.

The team at St. Martin's, especially Jennifer Enderlin, Lisa Senz, and Sallie Lotz on the publishing side; Kerry Nordling in subrights; and Olga Grlic for this beautiful cover, thank you. Dori Weintraub, Erica Martirano, and Brant Janeway are a brilliant and enthusiastic publicity and marketing team, and I am so thankful for all they've done for *Hester*.

Margo LaPierre gave invaluable direction and insight as I was writing this book, as did Leslie Wells on the early draft. My novel-writing group—Benilde Little, Alice Elliot Dark, and Emily Rosenblum—were encouraging and creatively helpful. Emily is an early and deeply valued reader, as are other cherished friends Toni Martin, Martha Kolko, and Julia Martin. Melinda Rooney did an extraordinary read of a late draft. My sister Donna Lico provided early resources and happily accompanied me on Salem research excursions. Laura Morowitz and Lisa Amoroso are creative souls and artists whose friendships give me joy and sustenance. To the Pandemic Firepit Squad, thank you! Pickleball Squad, what would I do without you? My Montclair fiction-writing group—Nancy Star, Christina Baker Kline, Anne Burt, Marina Budhos, and Alice Elliot Dark—are amazing allies. I am thankful for the sister-writer friends I'm still making along the way, especially the gracious and deeply talented Sarah Penner and Fiona Davis.

Thank you to my family, near and far. I love you. My daughter, Melissa, read endless pages in draft—she is a constant ally and a treasure in my life. My son, John, never stops encouraging and believing in me and I am so proud of him. Their partners, Kirk Luo and Claudia Krasnow, also read the manuscript, for which I thank them since they *could* have said no to their mother-in-law, but instead they were excited.

Frank Albanese—husband, lover, friend, and fearless fellow adventurer—listens tirelessly to first drafts of scenes and chapters (I usually offer wine first), and his insights and enthusiasm are invaluable. We fell in love over words and books, and that has not changed. He is at the center of my heart.